FAREWELL
to FATIGUE

FAREWELL to FATIGUE

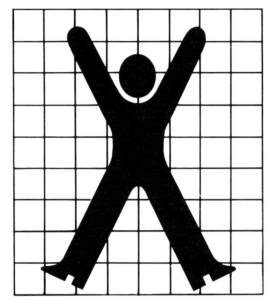

DONALD NORFOLK

MICHAEL JOSEPH   LONDON

First published in Great Britain by Michael Joseph Ltd
44 Bedford Square, London WC1
1985

British Library Cataloguing in Publication Data

Norfolk, Donald
  Farewell to fatigue.
  1.Fatigue   2.Naturopathy
  I.Title
  616.07'2   RA776.5

  ISBN 0–7181–2439–1 (cased)
  ISBN 0–7181–2624 6 (P/Back)

Phototypeset by Input Typesetting Ltd, London
Printed and bound in Great Britain by
Butler & Tanner Limited, Frome and London

To Margaret

CONTENTS

Introduction: The Modern Plague   ix
Stage One: Getting the Body in Prime Working Order   1
Step One Travelling Light   3
Step Two Limb Trim   10
Step Three The Daily Constitutional   16
Step Four Taking the Plunge   20

Stage Two: Supplying the Body with Optimum Nourishment   27
Step Five The Breath of Life   29
Step Six In the Pink   36
Step Seven Sweet Tempered   41
Step Eight Mineral Wealth   48
Step Nine Food for Thought   56

Stage Three: Providing the Ideal Working Conditions   63
Step Ten Nature's Balm   65
Step Eleven The Art of Relaxation   79
Step Twelve Natural Break   87
Step Thirteen March to the Rhythm of Time   93
Step Fourteen The Secret of Re-creation   101
Step Fifteen Time Control   109
Step Sixteen Easy Does It   117
Step Seventeen A Breath of Fresh Air   123

Stage Four: Eliminating Sources of Energy Wastage   133
Step Eighteen Poised to Win   135
Step Nineteen The Pain Drain   141
Step Twenty The Battlefield Within   148
Step Twenty-One One Man's Meat   154
Step Twenty-Two The Great Stoned Age   159
Step Twenty-Three The Bombardment of the Senses   167
Step Twenty-Four The Hormonal Power House   171
Step Twenty-Five Emotional Conflict   182

Stage Five: Releasing the Life Force   191
    Step Twenty-Six The Motivational Key   193
    Step Twenty-Seven The Hidden Power   198
    Step Twenty-Eight A Picture of Health   203

Appendices   209
Index   215

INTRODUCTION:

The Modern Plague

Have you ever wished you had more energy? Have you ever woken in the morning feeling more tired than when you went to bed? Have you envied people for their non-stop energy? Have you sometimes been too tired to make love, read a book or go out to visit friends? If so, this book has been written especially for you.

We are living in an age of great material prosperity. We are well fed. We are housed in conditions which are generally models of comfort and cleanliness. We have ample leisure time to indulge in hobbies, sports and games. We have skilled medical treatment and advice. Yet we are often less fit, and frequently less happy, than our forebears who lacked these modern amenities.

Our ancestors had to overcome typhoid, dysentery, smallpox and tuberculosis. We have to cope with a plague which is equally pervasive, but far more insidious. Chronic fatigue is the endemic disease of our age. Tiredness is now a more common crippler of people's lives than arthritis, bronchitis or chronic heart disease.

Few doctors nowadays would disagree with Dr Peter Steincrohn, a respected American physician and medical writer, who says: 'If I were to choose the one most common complaint I've heard from patients, it would be "I'm tired". People suffer from pain, cough, nervousness, headaches and innumerable other disagreeable sensations, but fatigue leads the list.'

Tiredness impairs our efficiency at work. Tiredness makes us prone to accidents in the home and on the road. Tiredness makes us irritable with our family and friends. Tiredness makes us miserable. Tiredness increases our liability to diseases such as migraine, epilepsy, backache, hypertension and heart attacks. Tiredness prevents us from achieving our full potential.

Chronic fatigue knows no barriers of social class but does appear to be more prevalent in certain occupations. When the British Heart Foundation carried out a study at the House of Commons it was found that British MPs are generally physically fit, but 'have a high incidence of minor stress symptoms'. These symptoms included irritability (39 per cent); indigestion (30 per cent); headaches (29 per cent) and insomnia (23 per cent). But the most common complaint of all was fatigue, which afflicted the lives of 44 per cent of the politicians.

Tiredness is a still greater problem for airline pilots, for while it's harmless to catnap on the back benches at Westminster, it can be catastrophic to snatch a few winks of sleep at the controls of a jumbo jet. This is an ever present hazard, according to a report published in *Feedback*, the bulletin issued regularly by the Institute of Aviation Medicine. The paper tells of a helicopter pilot who was so befuddled by fatigue that he failed to respond properly to air traffic control instructions, and turned right instead of left when approaching the runway. The pilot later admitted, 'My brain had frozen from fatigue.' It also cites the case of an airline captain who was so exhausted after two consecutive nights on duty that he fell asleep while reading the engine starting instructions. To overcome this hazard, German scientists have invented spectacles which emit a warning sound whenever a pilot's eyes close for more than a brief period.

Chronic fatigue is also a bane for many working wives and mothers of young children. No one was better qualified to talk about this than Dr Marion Hilliard, who spent her whole life counselling sick and unhappy women, and who for several years before her death was the head of Obstetrics and Gynaecology at the Women's College Hospital, Toronto. In her book *A Woman Doctor Looks at Life and Love* she talks frankly about the disabling effect of chronic fatigue. 'I believe fatigue to be the greatest enemy a woman ever faces,' she writes. 'Fatigue, carried to its extreme, can shorten her life or lead to mental illness. It will sap her strength and leave her at the mercy of transient infections . . . Most terrible of all, it robs her of the joy and vitality without which any life is gray and meaningless.'

She noted certain critical times, when fatigue is particularly prone to strike. Many honeymoons were marred, she found, because the bride was too exhausted by the pre-nuptial preparations and excitements to make love. Mothers of young children may also become too jaded to do justice to the marital bed, as can career women, who struggle to combine the roles of housewife, mother, wife and full-time employee. Women's liberation has given women increased burdens, as well as increased opportunities. Best-selling author Erica Jong said, when looking back with somewhat jaundiced eye on the results of the Women's Movement: 'We won the right to be eternally exhausted.'

Couples who are perpetually tired rarely have the most placid relationships, nor the richest sex lives. Dr Hilliard wrote: 'What detracts most from the happy bedroom? The first and most important thing is fatigue. No doubt about it, a happy married life takes energy!'

Tiredness is Tiredness is also ageing, and the quest for perpetual youth has been the *ageing* story of people's search for the well-spring of endless vitality. Some sought it by bathing in magic springs, others through taking vitamin pills, hormone injections or extracts of monkey glands. Even today we're still offered a wide range of revitalizing cures, ranging from ginseng and Royal Bee Jelly to lemon balm tea and dandelion juice.

Only recently the Soviet authorities released details of a 'Health Elixir' which they had permitted to be sold throughout the country at a 'middle ceiling price'. The drink had become a highly popular and exceedingly profitable restorative. It was made by an Estonian biochemist from a recipe which sounded more like a witch's brew than a pharmaceutical formula. The mixture contained mushrooms, beetroot, cabbage, dandelion and nettles mixed up with pigs' feet, blood and animals' entrails. Thousands of Russians took daily gulps of this bizarre potion to restore their flagging energies, until an official investigation showed it to be not only devoid of medicinal value but also toxic. Its manufacture was subsequently banned and its promoter sent to jail for a maximum fifteen-year sentence. But no doubt other herbal panaceas will arise to take its place and satisfy the seemingly insatiable public demand for bottled vitality.

These remedies flourish because too little is known about the scientific control of chronic fatigue. Hundreds of research papers have been written on the subject, but many have appeared in remote medical journals which are not available to the general public, and nearly all are couched in terms which the average layman cannot possibly understand. Yet the work is of vital importance, not just to doctors, but to everyone who wants to live a fuller, richer life. There is an urgent need for a book which co-ordinates and clarifies these exciting developments in simple, practical terms. This, I hope, and confidently believe, is that long awaited guide.

Treating the whole person I have been in practice as an osteopath for over thirty years. During this time I have realised the importance of treating people as a whole, rather than as a hotch-potch of unconnected organs. Patients may come to me complaining initially of a stiff neck or painful back. These conditions I can treat as separate entities, but I know that in many cases if I am to restore their health in full, and prevent a recurrence of their spinal complaints, I must also advise them about their general health, diet, posture, exercise and sleep. In the course of this lifelong involvement in health education and holistic medicine, I have been horrified to see how many people are content to drag themselves from day to day in a pitiful state of sub-health. Many complain of being permanently tired and dispirited, symptoms which I now recognize as the cardinal signs of the 'not-well syndrome'. These patients are not ill, they're not suffering from any recognisable disease, they're simply failing to use their bodies with peak efficiency.

At birth we are all born with the same potential for leading a long, vigorous and healthy life. If we avoid accidents, we can expect to remain lively and energetic not only in our youth but also into our eighties and nineties. (I have patients who are skiing and mountain climbing in their eighties; and others who are happily boating and going on solo, overseas holidays in their nineties.) To me, one of the great tragedies of life is that so many people fail to achieve their full potential. They squander their birthright and become tired, sick and prematurely aged. Albert Schweitzer once said: 'The tragedy of life is what dies inside a man while he lives.'

Healthy living In this book I'm giving not only a prescription against fatigue, but also a blueprint for healthy living. Our reasonable aim should be to be like Titian or Ninon de Lenclos, two historical characters who both warmed their hands by the fire of life. Titian was a man of prodigious energy and passion, who continued to work with undiminished authority and power until his life was cut short by the plague at the age of 99. Such was his sustained vitality that he was able to execute one of his greatest works, the masterly *Battle of Lepanto*, in his final year.

Ninon de Lenclos, queen of the seventeenth-century French salons, was his feminine counterpart. She was sought out for her liveliness and wit even in her ninetieth year, and was still taking lovers at an age when most of her contemporaries had either died or resigned themselves to a life of numb frigidity. Her outstanding quality, according to one of her biographers, was 'her absolutely limitless vitality, which never deserted her during the eighty-nine years of her life.'

This boundless vigour is the key to vibrant health, and the open sesame to social success and material prosperity. As Emerson said, 'The world belongs to the energetic.' In the course of preparing this book I have studied the lives of many successful figures in the worlds of politics and commerce. The one thing they appear to have in common is a seemingly endless store of vitality. This gives them their charisma and drive. President Kennedy was noted for his infectious enthusiasm and possessed these dynamic qualities in full measure. One of his aides remarked: 'The man is a calculating machine, with springs. He seems wound up and full of controlled energy.' The same could be said of the majority of self-made millionaires: Michael Korda wrote in his book *Success!*, 'The first rule of success, and the one that supersedes all others, is to have energy'.

Achieving your full potential Whether you wish for happiness, health, power, prosperity or a wide circle of admiring friends, you must first harness and release your body's stores of pent-up energy. The primary function of this book is to help you reach these goals and achieve your full potential.

Although you can dip into the chapters as and when you please, it's best to study them in the carefully ordered sequence in which they have been written. Before doing so it's essential to understand four important points:

Fatigue is largely a subjective symptom
Scientists have made valiant attempts to arrive at an objective measurement of tiredness, using such yardsticks as the accumulation of lactic acid in the blood, the decline in the ability to perform a set piece of muscular work, and the rate at which the eyelids blink. None of these tests has proved satisfactory, for they do not offer a universal measure of the amount of tiredness we actually feel. Fatigue is predominantly subjective. We *know* when we are fatigued, because our limbs feel weary and we lose our appetite for work. This crushing exhaustion is not necessarily related to the amount of work we do, and can just as easily appear in the morning after a good night's sleep as at the end of a busy day.

Fatigue is inevitable
Tiredness presents itself in two main forms. The first comes in direct response to hard physical effort, and might be described as short-term reactive fatigue (SRF). It is the inevitable depletion felt by a distance runner at the end of a marathon race, and is a perfectly natural response and a valuable defence against overexertion. It is easily understood and quickly relieved by rest, and needs neither special treatment nor detailed consideration in this book. The second form of tiredness I call chronic endogenous fatigue (CEF). This is the persistent exhaustion which is not easily relieved by rest, and does not appear to be related to any outside cause. CEF is the common contemporary curse which is the subject of this book.

Fatigue can be a symptom of illness
When a patient complains of being permanently weary the doctor's first responsibility is to discover whether the tiredness has an organic cause. This is not as easy as it might sound, for as the latest edition of a standard medical textbook states: 'There is no end to the medical disorders which may cause fatigue.'

Approximately a third of cases of chronic fatigue arriving at a doctor's surgery are found to have a recognisable medical cause. If you have any reason to believe that your tiredness stems from a particular illness, consult your doctor before proceeding further with this book. You might also find it helpful to refer to the appendix at the end of the book which gives a rough guide to self-diagnosis.

Fatigue can be either physical or psychological in origin
Fatigue more often arises from psychological causes such as boredom, stress and lack of adequate motivation than from purely physical reasons such as poor nutrition or lack of sleep. One doctor, in an analysis of 300 consecutive cases of chronic endogenous fatigue, concluded that 20 per cent were tired for chiefly physical reasons, and 80 per cent for reasons which were predominantly emotional. Most people can tell the difference between these two main types of fatigue. The chief differentiating points are shown in the chart overleaf.

Energy control Having cleared up these essential points, let's look a little more closely at the organisation of this book, which is designed to provide a comprehensive course in energy maintenance and control.

Why are some people permanently exhausted while others are brimming over with vim and vigour? The answer lies less in their genes than in the way they lead their lives. At five we may have the vitality we inherit, but at fifty we have the energy level we deserve. We create ourselves by making enlightened choices concerning the way we live, the food we eat, the exercise we take, the sleep we get, the way we organise our working day and the way we choose to pass our leisure time. We are not the products of pure chance. We are masters of our destiny. We have the

	PHYSICAL FATIGUE	MENTAL FATIGUE
CAUSES	Physical factors (lack of sleep, over-exertion) rather than mental stress	Generally triggered by mental or emotional strain
ASSOCIATED SYMPTOMS	Muscle aches	Psychosomatic ailments – tension headaches, colitis, indigestion
MOOD	Unchanged	Irritable, unable to concentrate and remember
SLEEP	Quick to establish, easy and satisfying	Restless and unsatisfying. Tendency to insomnia
MUSCLE TONE	Limp	Often tense

The complete classification of kinds of fatigue is summarised in the following diagram:

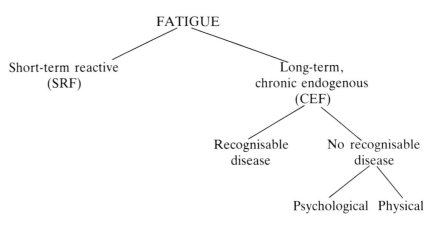

power to determine our health and shape our personalities. In the same way we can control our energy levels. We can allow ourselves to crawl dejectedly through life on hands and knees, or we can have the infectious exuberance of Titian, John F. Kennedy or Ninon de Lenclos.

Over the past three years I have made a concentrated study of the secret of energy control. During this time I have sifted through reams of medical research papers, investigated countless rejuvenating tonics and herbal pick-me-ups, studied the life histories of many exceptionally vital people, and delved into the teachings of Hatha Yoga, Zen Buddhism and Tai T'Chi. This work has led me to one essential conclusion – that chronic fatigue is primarily a disturbance of life style.

I believe that whatever your age you can rediscover the joy of 100 per cent living simply by making certain modifications in your *modus vivendi*. It's not necessary to turn your life upside down, simply to make one or two minor habit changes here and there which may be unnoticeable to your family and friends.

The only sensible time to begin this life enhancement programme is *today*. Now is the start of the rest of your life. If you want more energy it's yours for the having, and it's only 28 steps away. These steps are the essential stages in the **Vitality Programme**, your easy-to-follow blueprint for overcoming fatigue and achieving peak vitality.

The programme is divided into five basic stages. The first is designed to get your body into the best working condition, and may be likened to the servicing of a car. The second is devoted to maximising the nourishment of the body cells, which is akin to fuelling a car with premium-grade petrol. The following stage tells you how to provide your body with the ideal working conditions, which is similar to providing a car with fast, metalled roads rather than winding, pitted lanes. The fourth section advises you how to check unnecessary drains of energy, which is rather like driving a car with the hand brake on, or with poorly-inflated tyres. The final stage explains how you can release your body's stores of pent-up energy which, following the motoring analogy, is equivalent to pressing your foot hard down on the accelerator whenever a burst of energy is required.

The secret of the **Vitality Programme** is that it demands no more than a series of subtle habit changes. If you're going to breathe, you might as well discover how to breathe well. If you're going to walk, why not learn how to walk with maximum efficiency and minimum strain? If you're going to eat, why not eat a nourishing, energising diet? Once these habits have become a firm and regular part of your day's routine you have nothing further to do. Then you can say your final farewells to chronic fatigue, for from that moment onward you will be automatically programmed for health and vitality for the remainder of your days.

By following the **Vitality Programme** you'll gain not only energy, but also a slimmer figure, greater strength, better posture, sounder sleep, relief from tension, an enhanced sex life and a reduced tendency to disease. But before you turn the page and start to study the first step, take the following simple test. This will give you some idea of your present energy level. Then take the test again, six months after you've adopted the **Vitality Programme**, and see the gains you've made.

Energy Quotient Questionnaire

QUESTION	ANSWER		
	Frequently	Sometimes	Seldom or Never
1 Do you wake up feeling tired?			
2 Are you too exhausted to go out in the evening?			
3 Do you fall asleep in a chair watching TV or reading a book or paper?			
4 Do you smoke, drink coffee or eat something sweet to give you an energy boost?			
5 Do everyday activities such as shopping, housework, DIY home maintenance, gardening make your arms and legs tired?			
6 Does tiredness affect your ability to think and concentrate?			
7 Does fatigue make you irritable with your family and friends?			
8 Do you long to have more energy?			
9 Do your muscles ache at the end of a normal working day?			
10 Do you find that your contemporaries have more stamina than you for certain tasks?			

SCORING: Score 2 points for every 'Seldom or Never' answer
1 point for every 'Sometimes' answer
0 points for every 'Frequently' answer

EQ RATING: High energy 16–20
Moderate energy 12–16
Average energy 8–12
Below average energy 5–8
Exceptionally low energy 0–4

Your energy quotient represents your true age more accurately than your chronological age. When your energy levels are low, you're only half alive. Boost your EQ by adopting the **Vitality Programme** and you'll gain a totally fresh lease of life.

Special Note to Doctors

To help patients overcome the misery of chronic fatigue, a doctor must be part physician, part psychiatrist, dietician, biochemist, ergonomist, hygienist, exercise therapist and priest. The process of diagnosis in cases of functional fatigue is lengthy, as is the counselling required to bring about the necessary changes in attitude and life style. This book is designed as a handbook to guide patients through this complex process, and as an adjunct to standard clinical investigation and treatment.

It is based throughout on contemporary medical research, and is as comprehensive a coverage of the subject as is possible in a book of limited size. Certain omissions have had to be made. For example, no mention has been made of the role of folic acid in erythrocyte formation. This decision was taken because folic acid deficiency arises largely during pregnancy, and it is hoped that expectant mothers will be advised of this risk during their ante-natal check-ups.

STAGE ONE

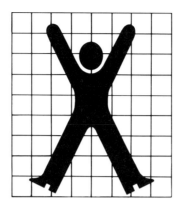

Getting the Body in Prime Working Order

STEP 1

Travelling Light

Few people realise the handicap they carry when they allow themselves to become burdened down by excess weight. You cannot be fit and fat. Racing cars are stripped of every spare ounce of unnecessary weight to improve their efficiency and performance. Athletes run in the lightest possible footwear because they know that they can make a one per cent saving in energy for every $3^1/_2$ ounces they pare from their shoes.

Yet countless sedentary adults today go through life dragging with them a millstone of useless fat. They would *expect* to feel tired and breathless if they had to climb a hill carrying a two-stone rucksack on their backs, but they can't appreciate that they can be equally fatigued by carrying the same weight around their waists as a tyre of surplus fat. They cheerfully submit to blood tests and X-rays to help solve the mystery of their aching limbs, laboured breathing and persistent fatigue, when the only diagnostic tools they require are an inch tape and a full-length mirror. They claim they are sick and tired of being fat, when what they really mean is that they are sick and tired *through* being fat.

If you're overweight at present, you are carrying with you a load of trouble. If you exceed your ideal weight by only ten per cent, you are twice as likely to have symptoms of chronic illness, such as tiredness, breathing difficulties and rheumatic aches and pains. If you're obese, your chances of contracting fatal heart disease are doubled, you are more likely to have a stroke, and you have two-and-a-half times the chance of developing diabetes. When these excess pounds accumulate they will shorten your life, shorten your breath, shorten your stores of energy and almost certainly shorten your temper!

When men of average build carry 20 lb of excess flab, they have to use about 14 per cent more energy to heave themselves from place to place. If they can summon up the will power to shed this excess baggage they immediately improve their stamina and can save enough energy in a few days to climb a mountain. Slimming also improves breathing, for when fat collects around the abdomen it impedes the lowering of the diaphragm and so reduces the amount of air that can be drawn into the lungs. Fat people are sluggish because of their faulty body mechanics and find it difficult to overcome their inbuilt inertia. This lethargy creates a vicious circle, because the quicker they tire the less exercise they want to take, and the less exercise they take the fatter they become.

Dr Jean Mayer, the eminent Harvard University nutritionalist, has examined the activity of schoolgirls of all shapes and sizes, and has demonstrated the remarkable extent to which overweight subjects conserve energy by restricting both the volume and the vigorousness of the exercise they take. He found that fat girls often ate *less* than their slim classmates, and put on weight because they led more idle lives. He found that on average they spent four times as many hours a day watching television, and took only a third as much exercise – swimming, walking, dancing and competitive sports – as the girls of normal weight. Cine films also showed that when they did indulge in sports, they did so in a much less energetic manner than their slimmer friends. As a result they burnt up fewer calories, and so perpetuated the tired, fat, sluggish syndrome.

Overweight people are plodders. They are carthorses rather than greyhounds and tend to suffer shortness of breath, muscle fatigue and general body exhaustion whenever they exert themselves climbing a slope, hurrying for a bus, or making love. Because of their physical limitations, they find it difficult to sustain long periods of physical or mental work. They are generally the quickest to wilt during protracted business meetings, and the first to sit down for a breather during country rambles. With the exception perhaps of long-distance swimming, it's true to say 'Fat folk fade fast'.

'Fat folk fade fast'

If you genuinely want to recapture your old exuberance, make a resolve now to shed your excess weight, even if it's only one or two pounds. Don't make excuses any longer. Don't blame your glands, your genes, your business lunches or the babies you have borne. The spare tyre around your waist is surplus baggage that is very definitely not wanted on your voyage through life. Don't listen to your friends who try to delude you into thinking that a little plumpness is becoming. Obesity has been socially acceptable only in cultures that prized the idle life. The Victorian businessman developed a large corporation to display his gold watch chain, and also to demonstrate that he was a member of the leisured class and so did not have to live by the sweat of his brow. Today's executives can't afford to be corpulent, because they're expected now to be tireless and dynamic workers. (A survey published a short while ago in the *New York Times* showed that only nine out of a hundred top American executives were noticeably overweight.) Among the ancient Egyptians, slimness was the foundation of feminine beauty because in that era women were required to be active and animated. Traditionally Arab sheiks are said to lust after fuller-bodied companions because they like to keep their consorts confined in indolent luxury like Strasburg geese. Not so in the West, where slimness has once more become the epitome of feminine allure, now that women are expected to share man's independence, stamina, vigour and sportiness.

Are you overweight? If you want to overcome fatigue, take the first step in the **Vitality Programme** and shed the fatty ballast that has been dragging you down and depressing your vitality. Strip off before a mirror and take a good, full-frontal look at yourself. Is there a hint of middle-aged spread, flabbiness around the thighs or perhaps the suggestion of a double chin?

If so, you are certainly overweight. Then submit yourself to the pinch test, which is the most accurate way of discovering whether or not you're overweight. Since half the body's stores of fat are deposited in the skin, it's possible to get a reasonably accurate measure of your personal level of adiposity by estimating the thickness of your skin. Pinch the skin midway between your navel and groin. You're carrying excess fat, as a man, if the fold measures more than 19 millimetres, which is approximately the thickness of a man's little finger. For women the comparable measurement is about 27 millimetres, which is the thickness of the average woman's thumb.

Once you've accepted that you're too fat for comfort, try to assess the number of unwanted pounds you're carrying. One way of doing this, if you're blessed with the gift of total recall, is to take your current weight and subtract from it the weight you were at 25. Providing you were fit and active at that age, this can safely be taken as your optimum weight. Any excess over this limit is likely to represent an accumulation of unwanted flab. These are the pounds you must aim to lose.

Another rough and ready way of estimating your ideal weight is to consult standard height and weight tables. The table shown below is the latest issued by the Metropolitan Life Insurance Company of New York, based on actuarial studies which pinpoint the weights which give people the maximum expectation of life. The allowances may be a trifle over-generous, because the survey incorporated a number of smokers who distort the figures by dying earlier than usual despite their often modest bulk.

Table 1

	MEN				WOMEN		
HEIGHT	SMALL FRAME lbs	MEDIUM FRAME lbs	LARGE FRAME lbs	HEIGHT	SMALL FRAME lbs	MEDIUM FRAME lbs	LARGE FRAME lbs
5ft. 2in.	128–134	131–141	138–150	4ft. 10in.	102–111	109–121	118–131
5ft. 3in.	130–136	133–143	140–153	4ft. 11in.	103–113	111–123	120–134
5ft. 4in.	132–138	135–145	142–156	5ft. 0in.	104–115	113–126	122–137
5ft. 5in.	134–140	137–148	144–160	5ft. 1in.	106–118	115–129	125–140
5ft. 6in.	136–142	139–151	146–164	5ft. 2in.	108–121	118–132	128–143
5ft. 7in.	138–145	142–154	149–168	5ft. 3in.	111–124	121–135	131–147
5ft. 8in.	140–148	145–157	152–172	5ft. 4in.	114–127	124–138	134–151
5ft. 9in.	142–151	148–160	155–176	5ft. 5in.	117–130	127–141	137–155
5ft. 10in.	144–154	151–163	158–180	5ft. 6in.	120–133	130–144	140–159
5ft. 11in.	146–157	154–166	161–184	5ft. 7in.	123–136	133–147	143–163
6ft. 0in.	149–160	157–170	164–188	5ft. 8in.	126–139	136–150	146–167
6ft. 1in.	152–164	160–174	168–192	5ft. 9in.	129–142	139–153	149–170
6ft. 2in.	155–168	164–178	172–197	5ft. 10in.	132–145	142–156	152–173
6ft. 3in.	158–172	167–182	176–202	5ft. 11in.	135–148	145–159	155–176
6ft. 4in.	162–176	171–187	181–207	6ft. 0in.	138–151	145–162	158–179

N.B. The weights are taken fully clad and include a five-pound clothes allowance for men and three pounds for women and should be divided by 14 to give your weight in stones. The heights are measured in shoes, assumed to have one-inch heels for both men and women.

Conventional Having discovered that you are six, ten or even 30 pounds overweight,
diets don't work how do you set about trimming off the superfluous flab to bring you into
tip-top shape? That's the question I am asked almost daily by my patients.
To help them achieve their longed-for target weights I've investigated
scores of diets, ranging from the grapefruit-only regime to the steak-three-
times-a-day-straightway-to-bankruptcy diet. I've found that they have one
thing in common – they don't work!

Conventional diets fail because they are unrealistic, tedious, dull and
anti-social. They also overlook two vital physiological facts. The first is
that people on low-calorie diets tire more rapidly than usual and compensate for this by reducing their metabolic activity. Tests show that the base
metabolic rate of fasting subjects may be cut by as much as a fifth, which
makes it that much more difficult for them to lose weight, even though
they adhere faithfully to the strictest diet. Another drawback of strict
calorie-controlled dieting is that it gets rid of vital muscle tissue almost as
readily as it dispenses with unwanted body fat. During a complete fast,
at least half the recorded weight loss comes from the muscles of the limbs,
chest and heart, which are broken down to provide a replacement source
of energy. This is another example of the cure being worse than the
disease, for if overweight makes you tired and sluggish, strict conventional
dieting will almost certainly make you yet more enervated and fatigued.

Over the years I've developed a weight-loss programme which has
helped hundreds of people slim down to their target weights. It's simple
to understand, exhilarating to follow and consistent in its results. The
method involves no laborious counting of calories or complicated dietary
control, and can be introduced with the minimum disruption of your
normal social life. What's more it will not leave you feeling weak, but will
enhance your muscle tone, improve the performance of your heart and
lungs and make you fitter and more lively than ever before.

I call the technique the W.O.W. regime, for reasons which will soon
be clear. All you have to do is to set aside one W.O.W. day for every
pound you're overweight. These days should not run consecutively and
are best arranged for the weekend when you are most likely to be free of
other responsibilities. On these days you have only three simple rules to
follow:

SLIMMING BY THE W.O.W. REGIME
W for Walking Physiological studies show that obesity is less often caused by gluttony
than by sloth. Most people who develop a middle-aged spread do so
because they've gradually reduced their level of physical activity, not
because they've greatly increased their consumption of food. Metabolic
tests at Oxford University have also revealed that some individuals have
an abnormally low rate of metabolism, and may consume only half as
much energy as others when they're lying, sitting or standing. These slow
burners put on weight with alarming ease. To help them regain their sylph-
like figures they must be encouraged to increase their metabolic rate. This

is most easily done by exercise. Vigorous aerobic activity like jogging and squash may be too strenuous for them to begin with, but they can always make a start by taking a brisk stroll, the simplest, safest and most natural of all conditioning exercises.

On a **W.O.W.** day you must walk as far and fast as you comfortably can, the minimum requirement during the day being a total of three hours walking. This will burn up energy at the rate of about 400 calories an hour. Far from being tired, you'll find you are invigorated by this healthy outdoor exercise which will strengthen your legs and improve the function of your heart and lungs, something you'll never achieve by dieting alone. This was demonstrated in convincing fashion when a sample of people who were anything from 20–40 lbs overweight were encouraged to reduce their weight by either dieting or walking. The first group were instructed to reduce their *intake* of energy by 500 calories a day, the second to step up their *output* of energy by 500 calories a day. At the end of the sixteen-week trial period there was little to choose between the total number of pounds the two groups lost, but there was a marked difference in the *distribution* of their weight loss. The dieters had lost an average of $9^{1}/_{2}$ lbs of body fat and $2^{1}/_{2}$ lbs of lean muscle tissue; whereas the walkers had shed an average of $12^{1}/_{2}$ lbs of body fat and gained about $1^{1}/_{2}$ lbs of lean muscle tissue. This left the dieters weaker than they were before the experiment began, but made the bodies of the walkers not only trimmer but also stronger and firmer.

The other reason for including walking in the **W.O.W.** programme is that it helps to burn up the fatty acids that are released into the circulation whenever the body's stores of fats are broken down. This reduces the risk of coronary disease, which is always raised when the bloodstream is loaded with animal fat, irrespective of whether the fat is derived from the diet or from the breakdown of the body's own adipose tissues.

Don't despair if you're unable at first to walk for three hours in a single day. That's why you're reading this book. Do the best you can to start with, taking care to divide the walking into short spells, followed by longer periods for recovery and rest. In this way your stamina will gradually improve. Then, as you progress with the **Vitality Programme**, you'll find that distances which previously exhausted will now barely quicken your pulse.

O for Oranges This is the second ingredient in the **W.O.W.** programme. If you want to lose weight in a hurry, you have to make an appreciable cut back in your intake of calories. This can be done – if you have a mathematical frame of mind and endless patience – by keeping count of the energy value of every particle of food you eat. Since most people find calorie counting tedious, I find it easier and more effective to put slimmers on an orange-only diet. Anyone can adhere to this diet for 24 hours, which is all I ask them to do. (Oranges do not provide a full range of nourishment, so should not be eaten exclusively for long periods.)

On a scheduled W.O.W. day you are permitted to eat an orange, but nothing else, whenever you feel peckish. A half-dozen will help to quieten your hunger pangs, since oranges are rich in vegetable fibres which absorb water in the gut and so produce a comfortable feeling of satiety. In the process you'll also get a generous intake of Vitamin C, the master vitamin which is required in larger than normal quantities when you're fasting, exercising vigorously, or undergoing any other form of metabolic stress. Eat the fruit whole and you'll extract its full goodness, for the peel of an orange supplies two to four times as much Vitamin C as the pulp. It also contains generous amounts of bioflavonoid which increases the uptake and effectiveness of Vitamin C.

By eating the occasional orange you'll also help to ward off that other bugbear of serious slimmers – tiredness. Some people suffer feelings of giddiness, faintness and fatigue when they go on a 24-hour fast. This is because their blood sugar levels fall so low that they starve their brains of nourishment. If you eat an orange whenever you feel hungry during your W.O.W. days you'll escape the tiredness and irritability that might otherwise accompany a fall in blood-sugar level, for each medium orange supplies about 50 calories in the form of readily available fruit sugars.

W for Water The success of the W.O.W. regime, like the stability of a milkmaid's stool, rests on three supports. The third leg involves the drinking of plenty of water. This is necessary to ensure the body's continuing need for fluid, and also to 'spoil' the appetite by filling the stomach at regular intervals with a calorie-free bulking compound.

Each day the body needs about four pints of fluid, a large part of which is supplied in the foods we eat, which are anything from 35 to 90 per cent water. During W.O.W. days, when you may be eating no more than half a dozen oranges, it's advisable to ensure an optimum fluid balance by stepping up your intake of water. This will also help to check your craving for food.

During prolonged fasts the body has time to adapt to the dearth of food and liquid. It can conserve fluid and lessen the normal craving for food by reducing both the volume of gastric juices secreted and also the strength of contraction of the stomach muscles. This does not happen during short, semi-fasts, such as the one-day W.O.W. regime. As a result your gastric juices flow and your stomach muscles carry on churning away as usual even though you are not consuming platefuls of bacon and eggs or spaghetti bolognaise. This can lead to tantalising hunger pangs, which can often be quelled by filling the stomach with water. Drink a glass of tap or mineral water whenever you feel hungry and you'll find it that much easier to last the day without your normal meals.

Vitality Programme – Step One   Follow this programme and you're bound to lose weight. But don't adopt the regime if you're suffering from diabetes or hypoglycaemia (abnormally low blood-sugar level). And if you have high blood pressure, coronary disease or are grossly overweight, seek medical advice first before embarking on a W.O.W. day.

If you're overweight, you've almost certainly tried dieting in the past, but don't let past failures deter you. If you want to lose weight you can do so, simply and comfortably, with the W.O.W. regime. Give the method a try and you'll quickly regain your figure and your old zest for life.

The amount of weight you'll lose during each W.O.W. day will vary according to your body size, level of activity and rate of metabolism. Follow the instructions carefully – a minimum of three hours walking during the day, nothing to eat but oranges, plus plenty of water to quench your thirst – and you're sure of losing somewhere between one and three pounds.

Take further W.O.W. days until you get down to your target weight. Ideally you should have no more than one W.O.W. day per week, to let your body get accustomed to each lighter weight.

You'll find little problem keeping slim once the Vitality Programme becomes an integral part of your lifestyle, but if you should regress at any time and put on weight, return immediately to the W.O.W. programme for however many days it takes to regain your optimum weight.

STEP 2

Limb Trim

The telltale symptoms of fatigue – pain, tiredness and aching – are more commonly experienced in the legs than anywhere else in the body. Unless you're used to distance walking, your calves will probably cry out for rest within the first few miles of a strenuous country hike. If you lead a sedentary life, your thighs will no doubt gripe the minute you start to scale a steep incline. This is the easiest form of tiredness to surmount.

The human body is a traction engine, and just like a racing car or bicycle its efficiency depends to a large extent on its power/weight ratio. A 50cc engine may be excellent to drive a moped, but totally inadequate to power a 20-ton truck. In the same way a battery hen may get by with the spindliest of limbs, which would be useless to support a six-foot man. Athletes, with their sparse bodies and well-muscled legs, have high power/weight ratios. Not so the average sedentary worker. They suffer premature fatigue because the twin vices of twentieth-century living have reduced their power/weight ratio: gluttony has made them rotund, and sloth has made their legs wasted and weak.

Few people realise the strain our legs carry. At each step we take the feet are subjected to a sledge-hammer jolt which is equivalent to about 120 per cent of the total body weight. (During running this figure rises to as much as 600 per cent, which is one good reason why the unfit should not take up jogging without considerable thought.) This means that during the course of an hour's walking the feet of an average man will receive a pounding of about 100 tons. No wonder the out-of-condition so often opt to use their cars rather than their feet to take them to the neighbourhood shops. For the overweight, the temptation to spare the limbs is greater still.

You'll find walking far less tiring once you've shed your excess pounds. If you lose 10 lbs of superfluous fat by following the W.O.W. programme you'll immediately improve your power/weight ratio, and ease the burden on your feet by the equivalent of nearly six tons for every mile you walk. To improve your mechanical efficiency still further it's necessary to take the next step in the **Vitality Programme**, which will increase the propulsive power of your legs.

'That which is not used wastes away'

Some years ago one or two 'doomsday' scientists predicted that man would soon lose the use of his lower limbs. Increased dependence on motorised transport, they warned, was making our legs an endangered species. In the totally automated world of the future legs would be obsolete and would gradually disappear, just as tadpoles shed their tails when they quit the water and find they no longer need them. Although these fears are never likely to be realised, there is ample evidence that our legs have been subject to a process of steady atrophy through disuse. Over two thousand years ago Hippocrates propounded the Law of Use which states: 'That which is used develops. That which is not used wastes away.' The more we rule our lives from a cushioned throne, the more our muscles waste. The greater our dependence on cars, the less reliance we can place on our own motive power. At one time children would walk several miles to school. Today they're taken in the family car. Mothers who would not dream of keeping their children short of food now starve them of equally vital exercise.

A generation ago adults would footslog their way to work, now they commute by underground, bus or train. Such is the modern city dweller's dependence on motorised transport that a recent Greater London transportation study revealed that Londoners now travel less than a mile a day on foot. Rather than use their legs, they'll choose to wait in rain and howling gales for a passing bus. Just over half the bus journeys taken by Londoners are for trips of less than a mile, a distance that can generally be covered more quickly on foot. At one time only the rich had the use of carriages, and they used them with far greater discretion than we use our family cars today. Queen Elizabeth I of England was a woman of formidable mental and physical powers. She had all the comforts and amenities that the country could provide, and yet she was not averse to hitching up her skirts and tramping long distances on foot. On one occasion she spent the day at Hampton Court visiting a sick friend, the Marchioness of Northampton who was dying of breast cancer. She stayed chatting with her until it was night and then prepared to return to Westminster. But she dismissed the carriage that was waiting for her, preferring to walk through the royal parks to St James's Palace, a journey of at least ten miles. Today we marvel at this feat, because to us it is incomprehensible that someone of substance should spurn the offer of a lift and choose to walk ten miles *for pleasure.*

Stamina comes from using muscles We have come to believe that one of the perks of affluence is the privilege of using hired cars, taxis and chauffeur-driven limousines. But vital people like Good Queen Bess realise that human stamina comes from using muscle power rather than horse power. You can't beat the problem of fatigue by buying a Rolls-Royce, that only allows you to be exhausted in greater comfort. Nor will you conserve your energy by motorising your leisure time activities. It's amazing the steps the wealthy will take these days to avoid using their legs. Prosperous golfers will travel around the fairways on electric golf carts, to avoid the few miles walk, and wealthy Japanese dog owners even make use of automated pet walkers, placing their dogs on a conveyor belt so that the animals get their exercise while they snooze in their chairs.

If they're not used, the muscles of the legs waste at an alarming rate. Immobilise a leg in a plaster cast and within a week its strength will have decreased by almost a third. Dr Walter M. Bortz of the Palo Alto Medical

Clinic had an unfortunate accident which gave him the chance to witness at first hand the rapidity of this wasting process. He related his experience in an article in the *Journal of the American Medical Association* entitled 'Disuse and Ageing'. 'Some years ago,' he wrote, 'my 35-year-old right leg was placed in a cast as the result of an Achilles tendon tear. Removal of the plaster six weeks later disclosed a leg that had all the appearances of one belonging to a person 40 years older. It was withered, stiff and painful. This association of disuse and accelerated ageing was striking.' This chance observation stimulated him to study many other similarities between disuse atrophy and what we generally accept as the ageing process.

Doctors specialising in problems of the elderly have observed that our maximum lung capacity declines in later life at a rate of about one per cent a year, a deterioration which also occurs in people who either are bedridden or confined to their chairs. But this is not an inevitable part of the ageing process. Give 70-year-olds a course of rehabilitation exercise and they can have the lung capacity of people 40 years their junior. The same applies to blood pressure, which commonly increases as people age. (It also mounts when astronauts are immobilised in their space capsules.) This too can be reversed by a programme of appropriate physical activity. Tests show that exercise can bring about a 20 point fall in average blood pressure readings of people aged 55 to 75 years. The same is true of bone strength. When patients are confined to bed for nine months, the density of their heel bones drops by 25 to 40 per cent. Get them on their feet and encourage them to walk about, and the bone mass will be restored as quickly as it was lost. Elderly people also suffer a gradual loss of bone strength which makes them prone to fractures when they fall, but this can be minimised if they step up their level of exercise.

Lack of exercise ages The evidence which Dr Bortz marshalled shows that we can become prematurely aged – tired, weak and feeble – not through a surfeit of years but through lack of exercise. No one can hope to enjoy a vigorous old age if they've led an excessively sedentary life. Many people who are confined to a wheelchair in their later years have sealed their fate by leading a wheel-and-chair existence in their preceding decades. By embarking *now* on a programme of conditioning exercise you'll make immediate improvements in your well-being, strength and vitality, and also lay the foundations for a healthy and ebullient old age. Strengthen your legs and you'll rediscover the joy of running up a flight of stairs. Improve your power/weight ratio by building up your calves and thighs and you'll laugh at hills that previously had you gasping for breath.

The limbs of a burly weightlifter contain no more muscle fibres than those of a puny child, they're merely developed by regular use. Carry out the Limb Trim exercises which follow and you'll soon push back the limits of fatigue. Research shows that if you contract a muscle to about two-thirds of its maximum power, and hold the contraction for six seconds once a day you'll secure the maximum possible growth of muscle power.

When students at the University of Illinois were given weight training exercises five times a week to strengthen their leg muscles they made rapid gains in both power and endurance. When they were examined at the end of ten weeks it was found that their muscles were 38 to 50 per cent stronger, and they took 47 per cent longer to reach the point of fatigue when tested on a static cycle. If improvements like this can be made with fit young men, just think what can be achieved with middle-aged clerks who for several years have indulged in nothing more strenuous than switching on the ignition keys of their cars!

Nobody is too old to benefit Nobody is too old nor too decrepit to derive benefit from a programme of sensible rehabilitation exercise. A short while ago an attempt was made to improve the health of a group of patients suffering from chronic back pain. As a result of their long-standing disability they were stiff of limb, short of breath and slow of gait. It would not have been surprising if they had considered themselves beyond redemption. Yet after a short course of conditioning exercises they all reported gains in physical well-being. What's more they found themselves walking with greater ease and economy of effort. When tested at the end of the programme it was discovered that they were using nearly a fifth less energy when they walked, an improvement which was coupled with an increased stride length, and a pace which was quickened by an average of 19 metres per minute. You too can bring the spring back into your stride if you restore the strength of your leg muscles. As a bonus you'll also develop more shapely hips and limbs. Many middle-aged men and women can still claim to have hour-glass figures, only all the sand has slipped to the bottom. Spend a few minutes a day performing the Limb Trim exercises, and you'll have legs which both look and function better.

Heel raise
Stand straight with hands on hips, raise both heels and stretch upwards as high as possible. Hold this position for two or three seconds, then return to the starting position. Repeat twenty times. If you find this too fatiguing to begin with, start with five or ten lifts and slowly increase the number of repetitions until you are performing the complete set. This exercise will strengthen your calves.

Parallel squats
Stand straight with hands on hips, then slowly bend the knees until the thighs are parallel with the ground. Hold this position for two or three seconds then slowly return to the starting position. Repeat twelve times. If this proves too exhausting start with fewer repetitions and slowly build up to the full set. Do not bend the knees to a full right-angle if the joints are affected with arthritis or other mechanical problems. This exercise will strengthen the quadriceps muscle at the front of the thigh, which is one of the major anti-gravity muscles.

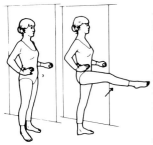

High kicks

Stand with one hand on hip and the other holding the knob of a door to give you firm support. Now swing the right leg forward raising the toes as high as possible. Repeat six times without pausing, then change and perform with the opposite leg. This movement will stretch the hamstring muscles running down the back of your thighs, and also strengthens the ilio-psoas muscle, which plays an important part in balance during walking.

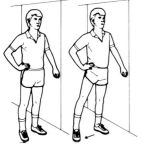

Side raises

Still clutching the door to give you support, raise your free leg as far as possible away from the door. Hold for two or three seconds, then return to starting position. Repeat four times if possible, then turn to face the opposite direction and repeat with the other leg. This exercise will strengthen the abductor muscles of the hip, which provide stability for the leg during walking, especially when negotiating flights of steps or steep slopes.

Step ups

Stand with hands on hips in front of any convenient flight of stairs. Then climb twenty times up and down the first step at whatever speed you can comfortably maintain. Each step should consist of four distinct stages – left foot on to first tread, right leg up to join it, left leg down to floor, right leg down to floor. As your level of fitness improves increase the speed of your movement. This exercise will strengthen a wide range of leg muscles, but is designed primarily to improve the circulation to your legs.

If you're unfit, you're likely to suffer muscle aches and cramps if you attempt to run a marathon, or even set out to 'find your feet' on a modest country ramble. These discomforts are mainly due to an insufficient circulation to your hard-pressed leg muscles, which may need a twenty-fold increase in blood flow during brisk walking. This augmented flow is easily accomplished in trained athletes, but not so readily achieved in the under-trained. Such aches and pains arise when the muscle fibres are not receiving an adequate supply of oxygen and when the blood flow is insufficient to remove the waste products of muscle metabolism. To surmount this pain barrier, and increase your fatigue threshold, it's necessary to improve the circulation to your calves and thighs. The only effective way of doing this is by taking regular exercise, which will expand the existing blood pathways and also provide the stimulus to open up numerous new capilliary channels.

Vitality Programme – Step Two Perform the complete set of Limb Trim Exercises at least three times a week and you'll improve your endurance and power/weight ratio. It's better still if you carry them out every morning, for you're much less likely to forget them if you make them an integral part of your daily routine like brushing your hair or cleaning your teeth. And regularity *is* vital, for muscles can be rapidly strengthened, but will equally quickly waste away if they're underused.

STEP 3

The Daily Constitutional

Winston Churchill was an astute politician, but an exceedingly poor physician. In matters of health he accepted without question the folklore of his age. This is nowhere more obvious than in his life long concern to husband his strength. In keeping with his contemporaries he believed that the pool of human energy was fixed and limited and so should be spent with a miser's care. When he wanted his wife's support in a coming election campaign he urged her to avoid becoming overtired. 'Dearest Clemmie,' he wrote, 'do try to gather your strength. Don't spend it as it comes. Let it accumulate. Remember my two rules – No walk of more than half a mile; no risk of catching cold.' His concern was admirable; his counsel misplaced. People who take life easily to avoid becoming tired, become more easily tired. Energy is like love, the more you spend it the more it accumulates.

When Rudolf Nureyev celebrated his forty-fifth birthday he was interviewed by a journalist who was curious to discover the secret of the star's immense vitality. Were there any ways, he asked, in which he conserved energy for the big occasions? 'No,' replied Nureyev, 'not when you're on stage. I give everything. If you try to conserve anything your next performance will have less go in it. Deliver goods, stretch yourself to utmost. That way, I ensure longevity.' It's only by being vital that athletes like Nureyev retain their vitality.

Inactivity causes lethargy There is an exceedingly close connection between lethargy and inactivity. At the close of a day pouring over papers at an office desk, an executive may feel totally exhausted. Yet he's not at the end of his tether. His limbs are not tired, his body is not crying out for rest. His brain is merely addled by physical inertia. To recover his vitality he needs activity, not repose; a game of tennis or squash rather than his customary evening doze in front of the electronic goldfish bowl. When actor Tom Conti played the part of the quadraplegic young man in Brian Clark's play *Whose Life Is It Anyway?*, he had to master the unnatural art of keeping his trunk and limbs totally inert throughout the entire play. He also had to overcome an overwhelming desire to fall asleep which the idleness provoked. Once his brain was so numbed by the enforced immobility that he even nodded off to sleep in mid-sentence!

To remain alive and alert we need to keep the blood coursing round our bodies. This is achieved with maximum effect only when we're on the move. While we're sitting in a chair the blood tends to pool in our legs, making us prone to swollen ankles and varicose veins. The moment we get up and take a stride or two around the room the blood is immediately driven onwards round the body by the contraction of the leg muscles. Doctors emphasise the importance of this muscular pumping action by referring to it as 'The Second Heart'. If you're anxious to avoid coronary disease, you should be equally careful to maintain the efficiency of this auxiliary circulatory pump. Go for a brisk walk or gentle jog and you'll blow the cobwebs from your mind by increasing the circulation to your brain by as much as 20 per cent. This will quickly freshen you up. After all, you may have seen joggers cough, wheeze, pant or puff, but when have you ever seen them yawn?

Walking helps you think clearly A vigorous walk will help you think more clearly and also more creatively. Aristotle was so accustomed to developing his thoughts while on the march that he became known as the 'Peripatetic Philosopher'. Socrates, Kierkegaard, Thoreau and Nietzsche were examples of other philosophers who worked out their theories while on the move, and Kant was so regular and punctual a walker that his neighbours could set their clocks by his passage through the town.

Some of the major scientific discoveries of the age have been made when scientists have escaped from their desks or laboratory benches and gone for a recreational stroll. Godfrey Hounsfield, Nobel prize-winning co-inventor of the EMI Scanner used by hospitals throughout the world, admits that he gets many of his brightest ideas while rambling idly through the countryside. In the same way James Watt had the sudden flash of inspiration which led to the development of an improved steam engine, not when he was working at his drawing board, but when he was taking a pleasant Sunday afternoon stroll early in the year 1765. 'I had not walked farther than the golf house,' he recalled, 'when the whole thing was arranged in my mind.' Activity can provide the ideal stimulus if you're stuck in a mental rut. You'll find that liveliness of body leads to liveliness of mind.

At present we live in a culture which esteems passivity and makes the conservation of physical energy one of its prime goals. We envy the person who has a home furnished with a multitude of labour-saving gadgets, and give status to those who work with their brains rather than their brawn. No wonder chronic tiredness has become the pervading sickness of the age. The Greeks were a more vital people because they realised that a healthy, vigorous mind would only be found in a healthy, vigorous body. *Mens sana in corpore sano* was the principle by which they lived. Their delight in activity is clearly shown in their art. Compare the vigour of their sculptures and paintings of wrestlers and discus throwers, with the heavy passivity of modern statues such as Rodin's 'The Thinker' or one of Henry Moore's reclining nudes.

Just as we've stripped our diet of natural vegetable fibre, and are trying to replace it by eating handfuls of bran from the health-food store, so we've stripped our lives of natural physical activity and are now struggling to replace it by buying packaged exercise. We spend a fortune equipping our homes with electric dishwashers, battery-powered tooth brushes and automatically-opening garage doors, then pay out more money to join a lavishly-equipped gymnasium so we can replace the exercise we've lost. We allot a large slice of our budget to running a car, so we don't have to use our legs, and are then forced to find additional cash to buy a cycle trainer so we can put our limbs to active use.

Jogging is unnecessary   Through our idleness we suffer a wide range of hypokinetic diseases – a term doctors use to describe conditions associated with lack of exercise – obesity, heart disease, rheumatism and chronic fatigue – which are all linked in part at least with our sedentary way of life. To compensate for this deficiency many people have taken up jogging, a strange, solitary, sweaty pursuit with strong masochistic overtones which carries what many doctors consider an unacceptably high risk of injury. (In any one year more than a third of joggers who run for six or more miles a week will develop an injury severe enough to curtail their training programme, according to a survey carried out by the National Center for Disease Control in Atlanta, Georgia.) Though jogging has much to commend it as a conditioner of the heart and lungs, it has few advantages over brisk walking, which is for most people a much more comfortable way of getting from place to place. Cardiologist Dr George Sheehan, author of the best-selling book *Running and Being*, clearly states: 'I think jogging is completely unnecessary for a fitness programme. A good brisk walk is equivalent to a jog anytime.'

If you feel worn out at the end of a mentally tiring day, don't sink exhausted in a chair, but go outside in the fresh air and take an energetic stroll. This will revive you better than a dozen cups of black coffee, by improving the oxygenation of your lungs and increasing the speed at which the blood travels round your body. A vigorous evening stroll will also help you wind down, for walking is nature's oldest, safest and most effective tranquilliser. It is the finest way of overcoming anxieties and frustrations and the ideal preparation for a sound, relaxed night's sleep.

Charles Dickens was a typical workaholic, highly excitable and chronically tense. He used walking to help him relax at the end of the day, finding that he could best clear his mind by exhausting his body. When he was working on *A Christmas Carol* he became so overstimulated that at night he often had to pace the streets of London for fifteen or twenty miles before he could get to sleep.

Walking banishes tiredness, clears the mind and improves the disposition. The octogenarian poet William Wordsworth is estimated to have walked 185,000 miles during his lifetime, a habit which had a most beneficial influence, according to his friend Thomas de Quincey. 'To walking,' he said, 'Wordsworth was indebted for a life of unclouded happiness, and we for much of what is excellent in his writings.' The philosopher Bertrand Russell, another dedicated walker who lived to be 98, was equally convinced of the psychological benefits of purposeful walking. 'Unhappy businessmen,' he wrote, 'would increase their happiness more by walking six miles a day than by any conceivable change of philosophy.'

Get tired more often The best way to combat fatigue is not to conserve energy as Churchill recommended, but to get tired more often. You can encourage this healthy fatigue by swimming, riding, rowing, cycling, jogging or playing tennis and squash. But the most convenient conditioning activity of all is undoubtedly walking. This is the ideal, all-purpose exercise which requires no expensive sports equipment and can be done at any age and in virtually any place. There are no special skills to learn and no irksome rules to follow.

Get your daily constitutional, at least half an hour long, and you'll push back the limits of fatigue and at the same time improve your cardiovascular efficiency. Recent physiological tests reveal that brisk walking helps to prevent narrowing of the arteries by increasing the blood levels of high density lipoproteins, the 'good' fats which combine with the cholesterol in the circulation and blood vessel walls and take it to the liver where it is broken down and eliminated in the bile.

Some while ago Dr George Mann of the Vanderbilt University, Tennessee, studied the hearts of a group of Masai warriors aged between 15 and 50, who rarely if ever suffer coronary disease. Every day of their lives the Masai tribesmen walk distances of about 12 miles tending their herds of goats, sheep and cattle. As a result of this constant activity they keep their hearts strong and free of arterial disease. In the West it's normal for the coronary arteries to become progressively narrowed by fatty deposits but in the Masai they were found to *increase* in size with each passing decade. Such is the stimulus of regular exercise.

Vitality Programme – Step Three Take a regular daily walk of not less than 30 minutes. Do this as a definite form of invigorating exercise, just as you might go for a jog or play a game of squash, and *not* while you're carrying a briefcase or a loaded shopping basket. Take a dog as companion on these daily circuits if you like, but not if it's a lap dog interested only in a slow inspection of the neighbourhood lamp posts.

What simpler way to keep trim, slim and energetic than by taking a daily constitutional? What better recipe than this for dispelling tensions, stimulating the circulation and safeguarding the heart? All these benefits – and they're all within walking distance.

STEP 4

Taking the Plunge

Most books on physical fitness place great emphasis on improving the function of the heart and lungs, but few pay any attention whatsoever to the equally important task of maintaining the condition of the skin – easily the largest, and certainly one of the most vital, of all the organs of the human body. Covering an area of approximately 18 square feet, the skin is intimately involved in regulating the temperature of the body, maintaining blood pressure, and preventing excess fluid loss. Its many sweat glands also act as accessory organs of excretion, ridding the body of waste salts and earning for the skin the title 'the second kidney'. Its deeper layers provide factories for the manufacture of Vitamin D, whenever they are exposed to the sun's rays.

In recent years doctors have somewhat belittled the benefits of sunbathing. Now they seem to be rediscovering its value. Recent research, published in the *Lancet* medical journal, reveals that sunbathing is the single most important factor in determining the blood levels of Vitamin D, the vitamin responsible for the formation of strong, healthy bones.

Some earlier investigations showed that sunlight stimulates metabolism and increases the number of white blood cells circulating in the blood. It has a general tonic effect, producing a delightful feeling of euphoria which one doctor described as an 'I-don't-know-what's-the-matter-with-me-I-feel-so-grand' sensation. To enjoy this stimulus it's not necessary to make a fetish of sunbathing. The possession of a Riviera tan doesn't mean you're healthy, merely that your skin has been bombarded by so much ultraviolet light that it needs to shield itself from further exposure. You can get all the benefits of sunbathing by occasional gentle exposure to the sun's rays without the need to burn, peel or dye the skin mahogany brown. Even on a cloudy day it's useful to expose the skin to the elements, for the body needs light just as much as it needs food and water. One enlightened British manufacturer – Travisglen Ltd of Swindon – has made it possible to do this in complete comfort even in the depth of winter by devising a novel range of solar conservatories. These are glazed with special panels which do not filter off the ultra-violet light like normal window glass. In these 'consolartries' it's possible to develop a tan by exposing the body to the full spectrum of sunlight even when the ground around is thick with snow.

The extent of the body's craving for sunlight has been convincingly demonstrated by numerous laboratory experiments. The sexual activity of both male and female mammals seems to flourish in the light. If female rats are kept in permanently lit quarters they remain on heat indefinitely

Conversely, if male hamsters are deprived of light, they lose some of their natural amorousness. When kept in total darkness their testicles shrink to a quarter of their normal size and they become significantly less fertile.

Natural light Recent studies suggest that animals need to be subjected to 'full-spectrum' light – natural sunlight – to achieve their full vitality and sexual vigour. Those that are kept indoors may be functioning below par because the artificial light they receive lacks certain essential wavelengths. This is the conviction of David Ball, Keeper of the Reptile House at London Zoo, who noticed that some of the animals in his care were becoming excessively sluggish when they were behind glass which cut off the sun's ultraviolet rays. 'We've now installed two kinds of light which emit a fuller spectrum, including UV,' he reports, 'and we've noticed that the desert iguanas and desert lizards, for example, are far more perky and active, have a much better colour, are feeding better, are more territorial, and more interested in sex.'

The Eskimos are equally influenced by the light, according to French anthropologist Jean Malaurie who spent some time with them in north-west Greenland. They show an interest in love – or *kujappoq* – only during the three daylit months. During this brief sunny spell, according to Malaurie, the men think of little else but hunting and sex, a preoccupation which since records were begun in the eighteenth century has led to a dramatic leap in the birth rate in March, exactly nine months after the longest summer days. As they enter the darkness of winter the Esquimos become morose, sometimes sinking into a mental malaise known as *perlerorneq*. In Europe, the inhabitants of the Arctic north suffer a similar depression and lack of energy during the three dark months of winter which is generally called 'Lapp sickness'.

Even in temperate climates sexual activity seems to mount during the sunny, summer months. In the northern hemisphere a disproportionate number of children each year are conceived during the summer months. This may be because light acts as stimulus to the hormonal glands. Some while ago two doctors from Vanderbilt University took hourly blood samples from human volunteers who were placed in a light-proof hospital ward and subjected to varying periods of artificial illumination. The researchers found that the peak blood levels of adrenal hormones always coincided with the switching-on of the lights.

Sunlight and Researchers from London's Institute of Child Health have discovered a
children's similar relationship between exposure to sunlight and the rate of growth
growth of children. They carried out regular measurements of over 400 children living in the Orkney Islands, off the tip of Scotland, which because of their northerly latitude have exceptionally long days during the midsummer months. They found that the youngsters put on significantly more height in the spring and summer than in the autumn and winter, a seasonal swing which was not observed in blind children. Sometimes the

gains in height were seven times more in June than in December, a marked variation which must be associated in some way with a light-linked alteration in the output of growth hormone from the pituitary gland.

Humans blossom in the light. If you're wilting after a long spell cooped up in an office, you're more likely to find the pick-me-up you need in the great outdoors than in a chemist's shop. The radiant energy of the sun is a vital human nutrient which many city dwellers crave. If you feel joyless, tired and jaded you may find rest at a price at a luxurious health farm, but you're more likely to recapture your lost joie-de-vivre by spending a few days strolling lightly clad and fancy free along the seashore or over country footpaths. When they're bathed in light, every back garden, every city park and every yard of rural lane affords its own natural spa. Only the artificialities of our sophisticated life-style prevent us enjoying this priceless solar therapy.

Pampering is bad for us Human beings are ill-adapted to cope with a pampered existence. Civilisation has brought us many creature comforts, from electric carving knives to aerosol packs of dairy cream, but not all these developments have been conducive to health. To shield our bodies from draughts and chills we've created for ourselves a hothouse environment. We centrally heat our offices and double glaze and hermetically seal our homes. We surround our bodies with a protective cocoon of windproof outer garments and chillproof underclothes. Ducted hot air warms our cars and electric blankets pre-heat our beds. But this perpetual heat is tiring; it dulls our mind and enervates our bodies.

Humans grow sluggish in overheated rooms. In these conditions they instinctively cut back their level of physical activity to reduce the amount of internal heat they generate. Like natives resting in the heat of the noonday sun, they keep their cool by becoming increasingly sleepy.

Stuffy, overheated rooms will favour neither your health nor your working efficiency. If you want to fall asleep in front of the television, close the windows, draw the curtains, turn up the fires and settle down in a soporific fug. If you want your evenings to be energetic, wear the minimum of clothing and keep the room temperature as low as you comfortably can. This will stimulate your body's rate of metabolism and make you brisk, bright and breezy.

Problems arose on the production line of a Philippine sweets factory when the heat rose and melted the sticks of chewing gum before they had been wrapped and put into cold storage. To overcome this difficulty the manager installed cooling equipment which kept the temperature down to an even 65°. He expected to receive a barrage of complaints from his Filipino staff, who are exceptionally sensitive to chilling. Instead they greeted the change with enthusiasm. According to Clarence Mills, an international authority on climatology, the cooler working conditions benefited both the firm and its employees. When he visited the plant in the course of his researches the refrigeration equipment had been in use for four months and had been an unqualified success. 'Instead of the expected objections from the workers, there was keen competition for jobs in the cooled quarters,' he reported. 'Women claimed they felt more energetic and were enjoying better health than ever before. There had been a distinct reduction in sick-leaves. Most pleasing to the manager, however, was the fact that he was getting a 30 per cent greater work output from the women at no increase in daily wage.'

Heat addicts Many people today have become heat addicts. At the start of the winter they set their room thermostats at 68°, which is a comfortable temperature for sedentary work. Then they step out of doors and meet a current of colder air. Some folk might greet this as a stimulating breeze and set off for the shops at a brisk, warming pace. Not so the hothouse flowers. They recoil from the chilly blast and wrap themselves round with an extra layer of clothes. This means that they're overdressed for the stores, which are invariably heated like a bakery. After an hour's shopping they're damp with perspiration, which means that their clothes provide poorer insulation. When they eventually step out into the winter wind they find it yet more chilling. So they hurry home and switch on an electric fire to warm themselves up. Once they've done this on several occasions they decide that they ought to raise the heating of their home to 70° or maybe 72°. Next year the chances are that they'll set the thermostat higher still. And the more they resort to artificial heating, the more idle their own temperature-regulating mechanisms become, and the more prone their bodies are to chilling.

The skin contains a vast network of blood vessels, which play a major role in controlling the internal temperature of the body. When the body gets too hot the smallest vessels in the skin dilate, bringing an increased flow of blood to the surface of the body for cooling. When the inside temperature drops, they contract and thereby prevent the loss of body heat. This delicate heat-controlling mechanism is essential for the optimum working of the thousands of chemical processes on which human life depends. Its efficiency is impaired by excessive heating and overclothing.

Overheating carries another risk. The human system contains only a limited supply of blood, which amounts to about twelve pints in the average adult. This is nowhere near enough to fill the body's entire arterial tree, the branches of which extend for an estimated 60,000 miles. To ensure survival we've got to husband this scarce resource. This task is carried out for us with great efficiency by a complex mass of nerve cells in the brain called the vasomotor centre. The centre exercises close control over the circulation to the skin, which acts as the body's major reservoir for stored blood. When accident victims are in a state of shock, suffering perhaps from an internal haemorrhage, the vasomotor centre immediately shunts blood inwards from the surface of the body to maintain the oxygen supply to the brain, heart and other vital organs. This closes the superficial blood vessels, and gives the skin of the shocked person its characteristic cold, clammy appearance.

The reverse occasionally happens in states of mental stress, producing what is known medically as a vago-vasal attack. In this catastrophe the vasomotor centre is inhibited by a sudden release of emotional stimuli. This leads to a rapid fall in blood pressure as the blood vessels of the skin dilate, in what might be likened to a monumental blush. With so much blood flooding the skin, too little is left to feed the brain, and the subject falls into a faint. British guardsmen performing ceremonial duties in hot weather are prone to faint for similar reasons. Dressed in heavy tunics and bearskin helmets they become overheated. The internal sluice gates operate under the direction of the vasomotor centre to shunt blood to the surface of their bodies for cooling. If too little remains to nourish their brains the men faint. This occurs not because they're ill or out of condition, but because they're failing to make proper use of their limited amount of blood. If this can happen to young, trained athletes, imagine how much more likely it is to occur among middle-aged sedentary workers.

If you overheat your body, you'll feel lethargic because blood is drawn to the skin which could be more advantageously used to nourish your muscles, heart and brain. The fuller the reservoirs of blood in the skin, the less easily oxygen can be carried to the remainder of the body.

Cold baths Early in my career I noticed that a number of my most energetic elderly patients were in the habit of taking a cold bath or shower every day. One, a famous ex-Gaiety girl, took a dip in the sea whatever the weather and time of year, and she continued her dancing training well into her eighties! Another, an eminent writer, ran a cold bath and lay in it to read *The Times* every morning. He was in his late seventies when I met him, and outstandingly lively in both body and mind. Was this coincidence, or did the regular cold dousing have an exhilarating effect?

Many of the biographies I have studied have revealed a similar link. Benjamin Disraeli was a man of prodigious energy. One of Britain's outstanding Prime Ministers, he was the leading reformer of his day, one of the cornerstones of the British Empire and the undoubted founder of the modern Conservative Party. Yet he also found time to write a biography and seven first-rate novels. Did his vitality derive in any way from his habit of taking a daily cold shower, I wonder? (His wife once described him as a man of great moral courage but little physical courage, in that when he was standing naked under the shower he could never summon up strength to turn it on, but had to call her to do the deed for him!)

Sir Henry Wood, the eminent British conductor, was noted for his enthusiasm, wit and superabundant energy. He too had a penchant for cold baths which he took at six every morning. Thus enlivened he put in an hour's study before breakfast, and then embarked on his day's work, the length and rigorousness of which would have exhausted many men half his age. The Duke of Wellington was another inveterate cold-bath taker. In fact, some historians have hinted that this practice may have helped him win the Battle of Waterloo against Napoleon, a first-class general who preferred hot baths, and suffered piles which were so painful that he was loath to mount his horse when the battle loomed.

Throughout time men have extolled the rejuvenating powers of cold bathing. In 1724 Sir John Floyer wrote the very first book on geriatric medicine, in which he praised the benefits of the cold bath. The Muscovites, Tartars, Irish and Scots had made themselves tough by cold immersions, he said, while contemporary eighteenth-century Englishmen were making themselves effete by eating hot, spicy food and wallowing in hot, enervating baths. 'Every man is a fool or becomes a physician when he arrives at 40 or 50 years of age,' he wrote. His recipe for a long and vigorous life was a judicious blend of fresh air, sensible eating, regular exercise and cold baths. It seems he was an excellent advertisement for this regimen, for towards the end of his life one of his friends, the Bishop of Worcester, wrote: 'Sir John Floyer has been with me some weeks, and all my neighbours are surprised to see a man of eighty-five who has all his memory, understanding and all his senses good, and seems to labour under no infirmity.'

A century later the cold-bath cure flourished throughout Europe. Britons flocked to the coast for a dip in the icy sea, urged on by doctors who advocated sea bathing as a sure cure for languor, lassitude, melancholia, constipation, gout and sexual debauchery. Europeans trekked to Wörishofen in Bavaria, where Father Sebastian Kneipp ran a flourishing spa which was as much healing shrine as centre of orthodox hydrotherapy. Here the local peasants jostled with Austrian grand dukes and French noblemen, all anxious to regain their youthful vitality by taking cold showers, cold baths and early-morning barefoot walks over the dewy grass. In Russia the pilgrimage was to the Khalune springs in Siberia which doctors believed had remarkable curative powers particularly over disorders of the nervous and hormonal systems. Here cripples were able to discard their crutches which the local peasants used as firewood in the winter! Here the weary regained their strength, by bathing in pools which were claimed to produce a dramatic improvement in their general metabolic action. No doubt the greatest stimulus came from immersion in the 'sacred' heart of the main pool – the Tzynkar – which even in the height of summer was kept at near freezing point by the inrush of water from an underground spring.

Stimulating the body Is cold bathing efficacious, or is it pure folklore? For once medical research comes down on the side of ancient mythology. Tests show that a cold bath can increase metabolism by 80 per cent. Taken first thing in the morning, a cold bath or shower stimulates respiration, rids the lungs of stale air and speeds the circulation. Immersion in cold water can also aid the formation of male sperm and raise the potency of infertile men. There is even evidence that cold can slow the ageing process in man as well as in cold-blooded animals, where it's well established that a reduction in environmental temperature brings about an increase in life expectancy. This suggestion comes from tissue culture studies carried out at London's National Institute for Medical Research. These tests show that isolated connective tissue cells live and multiply longer in the cool than in the heat, surviving for an average of 57 divisions at normal blood heat, but lasting for as few as 19 divisions when the temperature is raised above 104°F. It may be no coincidence, therefore, that when a group of geriatric specialists visited the Caucasian mountains they found that many of the virile centenarians in the region were in the habit of bathing regularly in cold mountain streams.

But the main reason for recommending a cold bath or shower is that it tones the muscles in the blood vessels' walls. When the surface of the body is kept at a constantly raised temperature, the cutaneous blood vessels remain permanently dilated, so they grow sluggish and weak through lack of use. But when the skin is subjected to a cold shower the muscles embedded in the blood vessel walls suddenly spring into life, as they contract to reduce the amount of blood brought to the surface for cooling. This valuable exercise has been referred to as 'gymnastics for the arteries'. Take a daily cold bath or shower and you'll maintain the agility of your superficial blood vessels, and help the brain's vasomotor centre in its vital task of controlling the distribution of blood throughout the body.

And don't harbour any fears that cold bathing will predispose you to coughs and colds and other respiratory infections. Tests at the Common Cold Research Unit at Salisbury confirm that you're just as likely to catch a cold in the warmth as in the cold, or when sitting in damp clothes or exposed to draughts. Providing you're in reasonable health you'll derive nothing but benefit from a cold dip, particularly if you finish it with a brisk rub down which leaves you glowing from head to toe.

Vitality Programme – Step Four Keep your cool. Expose your skin to sun, light and air whenever possible, wear the minimum of clothing, keep room temperatures as low as you comfortably can and take a brief cold bath or shower every day.

STAGE TWO

Supplying the Body with Optimum Nourishment

STEP 5

The Breath of Life

Science has brought us immense gains in physical well-being, but has often made us neglect the wisdom of the past. When we're tired and dispirited we turn automatically today to drugs, seeking perhaps a stimulant to counteract our fatigue or an antidepressant to raise our mood. In doing so, we overlook a natural pick-me-up which our forebears used with great success to overcome these below-par ills.

The ancients realised that proper breathing is one of the keys to vitality and health. Long before the discovery of oxygen, the Greeks appreciated that the air around them contained an energising life force. They called this force *pneuma*, a word which meant breath, energy and life as well. The Romans chose the word *spiritus* to describe this same elemental power. This was the mysterious life force which entered a man at birth when he took his faltering gasp, and which left him on his death bed, when he finally 'expired'. This was the power which filled him when he was 'inspired', and which drained from him when he was in 'low spirits' or 'dispirited'.

Eastern religions place great emphasis on gaining control over this elemental force. This has been the basis of esoteric healing for nearly two thousand years. Taoists use the term *ch'i* to describe the breath's vital essence, and practise techniques designed to direct the *ch'i* to the brain, heart and other vital organs. Tibetan men have attempted to enhance their virility by directing their breath inwards towards their testicles, a practice known as *tummo*; while generations of yogis have sought to revitalise themselves by controlling the flow of *prana* through their bodies.

The ancients knew nothing about respiratory physiology, and yet they quickly learnt that by paying attention to their breathing they could improve their health and increase their resistance to disease. We today have a detailed understanding of the anatomy of the lungs and the principles of gaseous exchange, and yet we do little to harness the life force that enters our bodies with every breath we take.

It is exceedingly difficult to excuse this oversight, for the importance of breathing must be apparent even to the most unenlightened individuals. We know that humans can go for weeks without food and days without water, but can survive for only minutes without air. Every day we need to absorb about 35 lb of air, which is six times our consumption of food and drink. Each cell in our bodies needs its daily drink of oxygen and this it can only get from the air we breathe.

Exercise helps If you've adopted the third step in the **Vitality Programme** you'll already
breathing be experiencing the energising effect of better breathing, for walking is
one of the finest respiratory stimulants.

Even if you're long past fifty and suffering chronic lung disease, your
breathing will improve if you take a daily walk. This was proved by trials
carried out at the University of New South Wales, Sydney, in which ten
elderly men, suffering from chronic chest complaints such as asthma,
emphysema and chronic bronchitis, were given a course of rehabilitation
exercise. To begin with they had difficulty walking up slopes and climbing
stairs. Most could walk no more than half a mile without stopping for rest.
Then they embarked on their conditioning programme, which consisted of
twenty minutes calisthenics a day, plus a daily walk of half to one mile.
But 'the emphasis throughout the programme,' according to researcher
Dr David Christie, 'was less on specific exercises than on an attempt to
impress each patient with the desirability of integrating physical activity
into his daily life by, for example, walking instead of driving, climbing the
stairs instead of taking the lift.' Despite their age and physical limitations
the men benefited greatly by this increased level of activity and after two
months training all but one showed 'considerable improvement in well-
being and exercise tolerance, and demonstrable increase in physical
working capacity.'

Take a brisk daily walk and you'll increase your level of vitality by
augmenting your uptake of oxygen. You'll also feel more energetic if
you've shed your excess weight, as suggested in the first step of the **Vitality
Programme**, for fatness is a major hindrance to deep breathing. When we
breathe in, about 60 per cent of the expansion of our lungs comes from
the action of the diaphragm, which divides the lungs from the abdomen.
When this muscle contracts it flattens its outline, thereby increasing the
capacity of the chest. To achieve this downward movement, the diaphragm
must be free to displace the digestive organs – the stomach and intestines
– which it pushes downwards and outwards against the abdominal wall.
This piston-like action is hampered when the belly is loaded with fat. Win
the battle of the bulge, and you'll breathe easier and feel livelier.

Lungs grow lazy Many people become shallow breathers because of the tension and
physical inactivity of modern life. At rest we use only a fraction of our
total lung capacity. As you're reading this book you probably need no
more than a cupful of oxygen a minute, whereas when you're chasing
after a runaway dog your oxygen requirement may soar to $6^{1}/_{2}$ gallons per
minute. If you lead a constantly sedentary way of life your lungs will grow
lazy through lack of use and their capacity will fall. Prolonged mental
tension can have a similar effect. Most emotional states are accompanied
by changes in our pattern of breathing. We gasp with alarm, catch our
breath when we're afraid, yawn when we're bored, groan when we're
upset and sigh like a furnace when we're suffering from unrequited love.
All our outward shows of emotion – laughing, crying, bellowing and

screaming – are but modified forms of breathing. It follows that if we want to hide our true feelings, as we so often do in our tight-lipped society, we must first keep close control of our breathing.

Shallow breathing can be responsible for much of the fatigue experienced by workers with tense, sedentary jobs. If they are to overcome this occupational hazard they must make a conscious effort to improve their breathing. In particular they should make it deeper, slower and more relaxed.

The businessman, who at his desk uses no more than one-tenth of his total lung capacity, must take some form of brisk exercise during the day to stave off fatigue and encourage deeper breathing. This will ventilate the little-used areas at the apex and base of each lung, and improve the lung's vital capacity. Similarly, the teacher who grows tired while correcting a pile of test papers must find whatever excuse she can to fill her lungs with air, for her lethargy may be due to no more than an insufficient supply of oxygen to the brain. We sometimes forget that nerve cells are just as avid for oxygen as actively contracting muscles. When mountain climbers enter thin atmospheres without special breathing equipment the shortage of oxygen produces mental fatigue which is every bit as crippling as the accompanying muscle tiredness. The brain comprises only two per cent of the body's weight, and yet it consumes nearly a quarter of our total oxygen intake. Brain fag occurs if it fails to get its necessary quota of this vital fuel and this can happen as readily in the office, factory and home as on a Himalayan mountain slope.

Deep breathing   A good time to encourage deep breathing is when you're taking your daily walk. Make a point occasionally of breathing in during five consecutive strides to fill your lungs to the full, and then out again during the following six strides. After a week increase the number of steps taken with each breath, always allowing one more step for the phase of expiration to ensure that every possible particle of air has been driven from your lungs.

Another valuable exercise is to read out loud as much as possible of a newspaper item on a single breath. The first time you try this you may manage no more than sixty or seventy seconds, but with practice you'll gradually increase your lung capacity.

The tensions of modern life encourage breathing which is not only shallow, but also often unnaturally rapid. When we're anxious, our breath tends to come in short, sharp pants. If the anxiety state persists we may fall into the habit of chronic overbreathing. This removes carbon dioxide from the blood and leads to changes in the chemistry of the blood which produce a bizarre variety of symptoms, generally referred to as the Hyperventilation Syndrome. Many of these classical symptoms are common complaints of the chronically tired patient, notably muscle weakness, ready fatigue, increased irritability, disturbed sleep, faintness, poor memory, tension pains and shortness of breath. When hyperventilation reduces the carbon dioxide saturation of the blood it provokes a marked constriction of the cerebral blood vessels which can reduce the circulation to the brain by 35 per cent. This no doubt explains the feelings of faintness, impaired memory and inability to concentrate.

To avoid the risk of overbreathing, make a point of slowing down your rate of breathing, particularly when you're conscious of being under stress. We normally breathe at a rate of about 16–18 times a minute, but when we're under pressure the rate of ventilation can easily creep up to 22 or more times per minute. This is justifiable – potentially life saving – when the stress is short lived, but can lead to chronic physiological problems when the crisis is prolonged. So consciously monitor your breathing when your life is fraught with problems, for it's when you have least time to spare that you most need to find the time for spells of deep, slow, relaxed breathing. These moments of revitalisation are never wasted for they will ease your tensions and give you a surge of added energy. Continue your pattern of rapid shallow breathing and you'll become increasingly irritable, tired and inefficient, for as an old Sanskrit saying puts it: 'He who only half breathes, only half lives.'

Good breathing is rejuvenating Cultivate the art of deep, relaxed breathing and you'll add life to your years, and may conceivably add years to your life. This at least was the firm belief of Dr Guéniat, who in 1931 wrote a book entitled *How to Live to be 100*. The publication of this book might have occasioned little stir, had it not coincided with the author's ninety-ninth birthday! Three years later Dr Guéniat was still alive and well, and eager to present the third edition of the book *in person* to the Academy of Medicine in Paris. He told his colleagues that a sound constitution was partly inherited; nevertheless he himself placed great importance on the rejuvenating effects of breathing exercises which he performed every day. As he wrote in his book:

> 'C'est que, pour rester fort et reculer sa fin,
> Il faut un vrai souci de respirer sans gêne,
> Avec ampleur, un air bien nourri d'oxygène.'

> (Therefore to stay strong and lengthen your life,
> One must have a genuine concern to breathe without restraint,
> Deeply, air rich in oxygen.)

Whatever the merits of Dr Guéniat's claims, there can be little doubt that suitably chosen breathing exercises can help to push back the limits of fatigue. Early this century William Knowles, a young British merchant seaman, developed tuberculosis of the lung and went to Montreal to convalesce. Here he came under the influence of Dr Oz Ha-nish, a physician who combined the traditions of Eastern and Western medicine. The doctor noticed that his young patient breathed badly, and so gave him some remedial exercises rather than the more conventional drug therapy. With their aid he regained his health and recaptured his old vitality. The experience also revolutionised his life. When war broke out some years later William Knowles was drafted into the British army, and as an infantry officer found himself in charge of a platoon of soldiers during the bloody battle of the Somme. In his autobiography, *New Life Through Breathing*, he recalls a moment during the battle when his men had reached the point of collapse. They were bogged down in a defensive position and he knew it was useless to urge them on since they were far too. exhausted to respond. Then, in a moment of sudden inspiration, he remembered the advice of Dr Ha-nish. 'Breathe deeply,' he called to his troops. 'In . . . out. In . . . out.' Gradually the men recovered. Slowly their tired muscle fibres and exhausted brain cells responded to the surcharge of oxygen, and gradually their energy returned. Within a few minutes, as if by a miracle, they found the stamina to continue their advance.

Breath control When the war was over Captain Knowles decided to devote the remainder of his life to proclaiming the science of breath control. To his surprise a crowd of over a thousand people attended his first public meeting. Many more joined the Institute of Breathing he formed in 1935. From him they learned that the way to better health is through better breathing. He had expected to help his students master their specific breathing problems, and many indeed reported that with his help they had overcome their bronchitis or catarrh. But many more discovered that they had gained added energy by performing breathing exercises. As one reported: 'Gradually the tired, listless feeling began to go, and now I feel full of energy and vitality.' 'I am quite astonished to find such an improvement in myself,' said another, 'I am so much more energetic, and not so lethargic mentally.' 'I find your exercises are marvellous in throwing off the fatigue incidental to a hard day's work,' explained a third.

Captain Knowles' remedies were effective, but hardly new. Sixteen hundred years ago the great Tao alchemist Ko Hung advocated similar breathing techniques. To strengthen the breath, he said, Tao novitiates should exhale the maximum amount of stale air from their lungs, then fill their lungs with the maximum amount of fresh air. Today when my patients complain of chronic fatigue I often follow Ko Hung's lead and encourage them to indulge in spells of EPIC breathing. This remedy can be applied whenever appropriate. When carried out first thing in the morning it helps to banish the drowsiness of the night; when used in the evening it helps to counteract the tiredness of the day's work. When employed during moments of mental exhaustion it assists in clearing the head and overcoming tension and fatigue.

EPIC breathing The exercise is performed in four simple stages: Exhalation – Pause – Inspiration – Containment. Each of these phases has its own particular significance.

1 *Exhalation*
When people set out to improve their breathing their initial thought is invariably to suck in the maximum possible draught of air. But you can't

pour wine into a full bottle. In the same way you can't fill the lungs with fresh air unless you've first drained them of every drop of stale air. Even at the best of times only a sixth of the air in the lungs gets changed with each fresh breath we take. If we breathe shallowly, or fail to clear the lungs of devitalised air, this poor rate of turnover declines still further. So always start your deep breathing exercises by collapsing the lungs as fully as possible. While you breathe out, imagine that you're a hot air balloon collapsing slowly to the ground. This has a relaxing effect, particularly if you quietly intone the word *relax . . . relax . . . relax* as you exhale.

2 *Pause*
When you reach the end point of expiration, hold the position for a few seconds while you emphasise the feeling of complete bodily relaxation. Then, when the body prompts you, start to inhale.

3 *Inspiration*
The object of this phase is to fill every crevice of the lungs with the maximum possible volume of air. This serves two functions. In the first place it improves the vital capacity of the lungs. Secondly it enhances the process of gaseous exchange, for tests reveal that filling the lungs with air increases what physiologists refer to as the 'transfer factor', the ease with which oxygen passes across the walls of the air cells in the lungs and enters the blood stream.

It is this phase of EPIC breathing which charges the body with *prana* or *ch'i*. So as you breathe in, repeat to yourself the word *life . . . life . . . life*, to remind you that you are imbibing the universal life force.

4 *Containment*
Breath-holding – known to the yogis as *kumbhaka* – forms an essential part of all forms of esoteric breath control. At first the practice was advocated on purely empirical grounds, but now it can be scientifically justified.

The lungs consist of a mass of approximately 300 million air sacs or alveoli, joined together like an enormous bunch of grapes. Each of these sacs is surrounded by a network of slender capillaries, which are just wide enough to allow the red blood cells to pass by in single file. During normal breathing, the blood corpuscles remain in contact with the alveolar walls for no more than three-quarters of a minute. In this brief time they have to discharge their store of carbon dioxide waste and take on fresh supplies of oxygen. If the breath is contained in the lungs a little longer, more time is allowed for the vital process of gaseous exchange.

'Healing breath' This is a feature of the yogic 'healing breath' which consists of a cycle of inspiration, breath-holding and expiration, performed to a count which is always in the ratio 1 : 4 : 2. According to the *Shiva Sanhita*, a classical Sanskrit text, the person who regularly practises this healing breath will be rewarded with 'good appetite and digestion, cheerfulness, a good figure,

courage and enthusiasm and strength'. The tonic effect of breath containment is supported by research work carried out in America by K. T. Behanan, which revealed that yogic breathing can increase the oxygenation of the blood as much as 25 per cent.

Many Eastern breathing systems recommend that the breath should be held for two or more minutes. This produces unnecessary tension and is potentially harmful. During EPIC breathing the breath should be held for no longer than three seconds, just long enough for you to conjure up a mental picture of red blood cells coursing through your body, bearing their precious cargo of oxygen to refresh and invigorate every one of your body cells.

Vitality Programme – Step Five The complete cycle of EPIC breathing consists of a phase of expiration carried out while you quietly intone four times the word 'relax'; a brief pause of little more than two or three seconds while you hold the state of total relaxation; a phase of brisk inspiration while you mentally utter three times the word 'life', followed by a two- or three-second period of containment while you hold the air in contact with the lungs and increase the oxygenation of the blood.

This exercise should be performed for seven complete cycles every morning and whenever else you are in need of a quick energy boost. After all, you'd snatch at the chance of buying a premium-grade petrol which increased the performance of your car by 25 per cent, so why not take advantage of a simple breathing technique which can so easily make a similar improvement in your personal performance?

STEP 6

In the Pink

Long before the discovery of red blood cells, it was realised tha there was a close relationship between the colour of a person's skin and their health. People whose skin was pale were often found to be 'weak and wan'. Those with a rosy complexion were recognised as being in the 'pink of good health'. Red, the colour of fresh, oxygenated blood, came to be associated with vitality. Newspapers were filled with red hot news. Young men expressed their high spirits by going out and painting the town red. Days of excitement were referred to as red-letter days; and adventurous, virile males were classified as red-blooded men. Conversely blue, the colour of deoxygenated blood, was linked with enervation and loss of spirits. So we suffered the blues, listened to mournful blue music and struggled through endless, tedious blue Mondays.

We now know why red came to be linked with energy, health and passion, for red is the colour of haemoglobin, the oxygen-carrying pigment in our red blood corpuscles. To function at peak efficiency every cell in our body needs to receive a regular supply of life-giving oxygen. Without this vital nourishment we can't think, laugh, sing, run, make love, dance or jump for joy. Haemoglobin is the substance which makes these joyful human activities possible, for it is this miracle pigment which facilitates the transport of oxygen throughout the body. Without this chemical parcel post, man's life would be as dull and stagnant as that of an amoeba. If there were no red blood cells, and oxygen had to be carried in solution in the plasma instead of in combination with haemoglobin, the volume of the blood would have to be increased some 70-fold. This means that an average man weighing 11 stone (70 kilos) would be burdened down with an extra 900 lbs of blood.

Red blood cells We owe our life to our red blood cells, which in the average human being number about 30,000,000,000,000. If they were placed end to end they would stretch three times around the equator, according to biologist Sir Julian Huxley. Formed mainly in the bone marrow, these red blood cells have a life of only a month or two. During this time they probably travel round the body 100,000 times or more and come in for considerable wear and tear. They are destroyed at the incredible rate of 72,000,000 a minute. Fortunately the liver is involved in the breakdown of the worn-out cells, and recovers about 85 per cent of their iron content. Without this vital salvage work we would all suffer from iron deficiency anaemia.

Anything which increases the number of red blood cells in our circulation makes us feel increasingly lively and energetic. Anything which depletes the haemoglobin content of our blood makes us feel listless and tired. Athletes sometimes go up into the mountains to train, because at these altitudes the rarity of oxygen acts as a stimulus to the formation of red blood cells. They may feel lethargic to begin with, and suffer symptoms of oxygen lack or mild mountain sickness, but when they return to sea level they enjoy the fillip which comes from having a blood stream supercharged with extra red blood cells.

If you've followed the first five steps of the **Vitality Programme**, you too should be beginning to feel the benefit of a haemoglobin-enriched circulation, for it's not necessary to go up in the Rocky Mountains, or winter in the Alps, to stimulate the formation of red blood cells. Every time you indulge in a spell of brisk aerobic exercise your tissues suffer a mild degree of oxygen lack. This encourages the body to create more red corpuscles. To begin with you may feel exhausted after taking your daily constitutional. But gradually your stamina will increase as your muscles strengthen, your lung capacity increases and the oxygen-carrying capacity of your blood grows.

This is a process which shouldn't be rushed. Tests show that sedentary individuals can destroy 12–30 per cent of their red blood cells by indulging suddenly in unaccustomed violent activity. If all you've exercised in the last five years is caution, don't be surprised if you feel exhausted for some days if you abruptly end the exercise famine by climbing a mountain, going skiing or playing ice hockey. Ease yourself in gradually and you'll avoid those off-putting side effects, for the gentle exercise will stimulate the formation of new blood cells, which will more than replace those tired, elderly corpuscles which break down under the strain of having to hurry a little faster than usual round the body. These extra cells will improve your work performance and help you push back the limits of fatigue.

'I was boiling over with energy'

Early in the 1970s Dr Björn Ekblom carried out experiments at Stockholm's Institute of Gymnastics and Sport which electrified the athletic world. He tested the endurance of a group of physical education students on a treadmill and then removed a quart of their blood in three separate stages. Not surprisingly the bleedings reduced their endurance by about 30 per cent, but within a fortnight their bodies had replaced the lost blood cells and they were once more performing as well as ever. Two weeks later Dr Ekblom reinfused the students with their own red cells. This naturally produced an immediate increase in the oxygen-carrying capacity of their blood, which was paralleled by a 20 per cent increase in their endurance on the treadmill. As one delighted student reported: 'I was able to run at top speed on the treadmill two minutes longer. I felt almost as though I was boiling over with energy.' But Dr Ekblom saw the significance of his work and admitted to being scared. 'Perhaps someone will make use of the results, say in the Olympics. What will become of sport then?' he mused. His fears were justified. Soon after the results of his work were published, many long-distance runners were using 'blood doping' to improve their performance, and Finland's Kaarlo Maakinka admitted that at the 1980 Moscow Olympic Games, it had enabled him to win a silver medal in the 10,000 metres and a bronze in the 5,000 metres.

Blood doping is a misguided attempt of sports scientists to improve on the handiwork of nature. It is a risky procedure, which is effective only for a very limited period. It has no place in *your* **Vitality Programme**, nor should it in that of the most ambitious, trophy-hunting international athlete. Given a sensible diet and a regular routine of aerobic exercise, you can maximise the oxygen-carrying capacity of your blood without blood doping, vitamin injections, or oxygen inhalations. Here's how you too can be 'boiling over with energy' – without artificial aids.

Anaemia   Countless people in the West, and many more in the Third World countries, suffer from anaemia, a disease characterised by tiredness, breathlessness, palpitations and pallor of the skin, which is particularly noticeable in the lips, fingernails and inner surfaces of the eyelids. It's been estimated that in the United States alone, 20,000,000 people suffer from iron-deficiency anaemia.

Anaemic conditions can arise in several ways, but basically they're provoked by a drop in the haemoglobin content of the blood. In some anaemias they result from an excessive breakdown of red blood cells, as happens in rhesus babies, for instance (haemolytic anaemias). In others they stem from an inadequate rate of formation of the red blood cells in the bone marrow, a condition which can be caused by cancerous growths, sensitivity to chemicals and drugs, or over-exposure to radiation (aplastic anaemias). But in the vast majority of cases the deficiency of haemoglobin arises from either excessive bleeding (haemorrhagic anaemia) or from a lack of iron in the diet (iron deficiency anaemia).

The adult human body contains about three to four grams of iron, which is just about enough to make a two-inch nail. Practically two-thirds of this sum is held in the form of haemoglobin, the rest being widely distributed throughout the rest of the body. Each day we lose about a milligram of iron, mainly in the dead skin cells which are constantly being shed from the surface of our bodies. To keep the haemoglobin in our blood at optimum levels we need to replenish this regular drain, which owing to the poor rate of absorption in the intestine probably means a daily dietary intake of about ten milligrams of iron. Surveys show that most adults just about satisfy this minimum daily requirement. What happens if they suffer a loss of blood from peptic ulcers, piles or persistent nosebleeds? These conditions may be trivial in themselves, but if prolonged can lead to the tiredness and debility of chronic anaemia. Each half-teaspoonful of shed blood represents a loss of one milligram of iron. To replace this drain we need to *double* our normal daily intake of iron, which many victims fail to do. People who regularly take aspirin may also become anaemic through chronic blood loss. Surveys suggest that two-thirds of the people who take three to four aspirin tablets a day suffer loss of blood from the stomach, and one doctor has estimated that the one million aspirin addicts in Britain lose enough blood among them to fill a domestic swimming pool every three days.

But the category most at risk of developing anaemia – growing children and pregnant mothers apart – are women during their reproductive years. Women vary enormously in the amount of blood they lose during their menstrual periods. Some lose as little as 10 ccs a month, others as much as 300 ccs. The average menstrual loss is 50 ccs, a modest enough drain maybe but nevertheless one which robs the body of 25 mg of precious iron. To make up for this monthly depletion women need to make sure that they eat at least 18 mg of iron a day, or even five times this quantity if their periods are really heavy.

Eating iron The sixth plank in the **Vitality Programme** is to step up your daily intake of iron. There's a lot of truth in the old saying 'Pale foods cannot make red blood', for the best dietary sources of iron are dark foods such as red meats, dark whole grains, prunes, raisins, egg yolk, molasses and all the green, leafy vegetables.

Many of the old folk cures for tiredness, anaemia and general debility involved the taking of generous helpings of iron. In *Primitive Physic*, John Wesley offers as a cure for lethargy a twice-daily dose of a concoction made from watercress, an iron-rich herb. In like manner the traditional Greek remedy for lassitude is to eat nettle leaves, either raw in a salad, boiled like spinach, or made into a tea-like infusion. Another ancient recipe for anaemia is to push a rusty nail into a sour apple overnight, and then eat the apple in the morning. All these Old Wives' Cures represented endeavours to increase the body's iron intake.

If you want to maximise the oxygen-carrying capacity of your blood I urge you to eat at least 15–20 mg of iron a day. This means a weekly helping of liver, occasional helpings of dried fruits and nuts, three or four slices of wholewheat bread a day and generous helpings of beans and green, leafy vegetables. The table below will show you how you can get your daily ration of iron:

FOOD	AVERAGE SERVING	CONTENT OF IRON (IN MGS)
Pigs' liver	2 oz	14.8
Oysters	1 dozen	12.8
Prune juice	½ pint	9.8
Kidneys	3 oz	9.0
Dried apricots	6 oz	8.2
Almonds	8 oz	6.7
Dates	6 oz	5.7
Dried raisins	5 oz	5.6
Dandelion leaves	2 oz	5.6
Ox heart	3 oz	5.3
Kidney beans	8 oz	4.6

FOOD	AVERAGE SERVING	CONTENT OF IRON (IN MGS)
Dry, baker's yeast	1 oz	4.6
Roasted peanuts	8 oz	4.2
Wholemeal flour	5 oz	4.0
Spinach	2 oz	3.6
Green peas	6 oz	3.0
Lean meat	3 oz	3.0
Bitter chocolate	1 oz	1.2
Egg yolk	1	0.9
Wholemeal bread	1 slice	0.5
Brown sugar	1 tablespoon	0.4
White sugar	1 tablespoon	Nil

Five other practical points should be borne in mind:

★ Iron is more easily absorbed in the presence of Vitamin C, so much so that a glass of orange juice can produce a threefold increase in the iron absorbed from a continental breakfast.

★ Cooking acid foods in iron pots and skillets can quadruple the iron content of the finished dish.

★ Drinking coffee and tea after meals can reduce iron absorption by 30 per cent in the case of a single cup of coffee, and by 64 per cent in the case of a single cup of tea. (Drinking these beverages an hour before mealtimes has no such effect.)

★ Investigations at Johns Hopkins School of Medicine have also revealed that heavy drinking can inhibit the formation of red blood cells within the bone marrow. According to Dr Jerry L. Spivak, one of the researchers: 'It is significant that these bone marrow changes occur at levels of alcohol use well within "legal limits". This doesn't mean that a drink or two a day is harmful to most people,' he adds, 'but it does raise another caution flag about continued heavy use of alcohol.'

★ Iron is more easily absorbed in an acid medium, so don't take antacids to cure your indigestion unless they're absolutely essential. Some people secrete too little acid in their stomach and are prone to develop iron deficiency anaemia as a result. They can be helped by eating yoghurt, sour fruits and citrus fruit juices.

Vitality Programme – Step Six There's no excuse for being short of iron. Eat 15–20mgs a day and you'll keep your blood packed with haemoglobin, the life-giving pigment. This will help to keep you 'in the pink' and full of vibrant energy.

STEP 7

Sweet Tempered

What is the similarity between a supersonic plane, a Formula One racing car and a forty-year-old teacher? The answer: all three derive their energy from burning carbon containing fuels. The jet plane carves its way through the stratosphere powered by high-grade aviation fuel, the racing car burns high-octane petrol, and humans derive the energy to climb mountains and run marathon races by burning glucose, a fuel which, like petrol and aviation spirit, consists of a complex mixture of carbon, hydrogen and oxygen atoms.

If our bodies and minds are to function efficiently they must receive a regular supply of both glucose and oxygen. Starve them of either of these vital ingredients and the fires of life die out, just as surely as a motor-car engine splutters to a halt when the petrol tank runs dry, or the air supply to the carburettor becomes choked. Mercifully we need precious little glucose to keep going at peak efficiency. Muscles, heart, kidneys, lungs and brain cells will work tirelessly and well providing there are just two teaspoonsful of glucose in the circulation. If the concentration falls below this level we become faint and show signs of fatigue, weakness and mental malaise. One of the prime functions of the digestive system is to ensure that the bloodstream always carries an adequate supply of glucose. It does this by supervising the uptake of glucose from the intestine and more especially by regulating its storage in depot sites throughout the body.

Glucose from food The body obtains glucose by breaking down the carbohydrates which are present in all animal and vegetable foodstuffs. Starches such as bread, potatoes and rice are staple parts of our diet because they are particularly rich in carbohydrate and so make excellent sources of glucose, the sole supplier of cellular energy. Carbohydrates are also to be found in milk in the form of lactose, and in fruits in a chemical combination known as fructose. In each of these cases the carbohydrate must first be converted into glucose before it becomes available to the body. This conversion is achieved with the aid of a number of digestive enzymes. When we slowly chew a piece of bread it begins to feel sweet because saliva contains the enzyme ptyalin which begins the digestion of starch. Further breakdown of starch takes place in the small intestines under the catalytic action of amylase, one of the enzymes secreted by the pancreas. The intestinal juices also contain the enzymes maltase and lactase which break down malt sugars and the lactose of milk into glucose. Even the energy stored in a spoonful of sugar cannot be tapped until its component molecules of sucrose have been broken down.

Fortunately we can safely leave our bodies to carry out this essential fuel conversion work. This is a marvel of chemical engineering which requires neither our conscious thought nor active intervention. Providing we feed in the right raw materials at one end of the conveyor belt we can be sure that the digestive factory will process it properly and keep us supplied with adequate glucose to power our muscles and fuel our brain cells. The body fails us in only one respect, that it contains no enzymes capable of breaking down cellulose, the carbohydrate which forms the bulk of plant matter. But for this unfortunate oversight we would be able to eradicate the problem of world hunger overnight by giving the starving masses grass and leaves to eat. As it is we're forced to rely on cultivated vegetables and grain harvests which are more at the mercy of droughts and crop diseases.

Different energy sources   Each race has its favourite source of energy. Generations of Chinese peasants have survived on rice. Indians have derived their calories from flat, wheaten pancakes known as *chapatis*. The Aztecs obtained their carbohydrate from maize porridge sweetened with honey, supplemented by a bean dish called *tortillas*. The early Egyptians were nicknamed the *artophagoi*, the bread-eaters, because they subsisted largely on a diet of onions, beer and bread, each Egyptian soldier getting a ration of four pounds of coarse wheat and barley bread a day when they were on active service. And the Irish became so dependent on potatoes that more than 1,250,000 of them died in 1845–6 when their staple crop was wiped out by potato blight.

Each of these foods provides a rich source of carbohydrate which the body can readily convert into energy. Nobody should run short of glucose who receives an adequate and regular supply of one or more of these basic foodstuffs. It's easy to understand why the inhabitants of Bangladesh feel languid and apathetic when their crops fail, for a handful of rice a day is not enough to keep their minds and bodies going in anything but bottom gear. But why do these symptoms afflict so many people in the affluent Western world? Why should there be so much chronic fatigue in lands flowing with calorie-rich doughnuts, sweets, chocolate biscuits, ice cream, lemonade and French fried potatoes? To answer this question it's necessary first to consider the way in which surplus glucose is handled by the body. The human machine is an object lesson in energy conservation. Just as it recovers most of the iron released from broken-down red blood cells, so it does its best to store every ounce of surplus glucose.

The kidneys have permanent instructions to rid the blood of excess sugar, and so prevent a condition known as hyperglycaemia. This is not as wasteful as it might sound, for it's unhealthy to have a bloodstream overloaded with sugar. When hyperglycaemia occurs in diabetes, for instance, there is an increased risk of infection and arterial disease. To avoid this risk, any marked excess of sugar is quickly voided in the urine.

Storing extra sugar as glycogen After a meal the blood sugar level steadily rises as glucose is absorbed into the system. Normally before it reaches the point at which it overflows into the urine, the body sets in motion an ingenious recovery system by which glucose is removed from the circulation and converted into a substance called glycogen, in which form it is stored throughout the body. The system works in the following way: immediately blood sugar levels rise, messages are sent to the pancreas gland ordering it to secrete more insulin. The prime function of this hormone is to increase the rate of glycogen formation and storage. In total the body can store no more than 500 g of glycogen. A fifth of this is held in the liver, most of the remainder in the muscles. Once the glycogen stores are replete, a second system of energy conservation is brought into play in which glucose is converted into fat. This is stored in depots which although widely distributed around the body are most noticeable in roly-poly wedges around the waist, buttocks and thighs. This complex regulatory system enables us to cope equally well in times of famine and of feast. With this mechanism to safeguard us we should suffer no problems of energy conservation or release. In practice, our affluent and artificial life-style makes us prone to two serious disorders of carbohydrate metabolism. The first is obesity, brought about because we consistently eat more calories than we require, and so are constantly adding to our fat stores. The second is hypoglycaemia, a condition in which we falter and faint from time to time because our blood sugar level falls too low to support our energy needs.

Hypoglycaemia Some authorities refuse to recognise hypoglycaemia as a major cause of chronic fatigue. In 1973 the American Medical Association published a report which stated unequivocally that 'hypoglycaemia is quite rare and does not constitute an important health problem'. Other medical authorities are equally sure that hypoglycaemia is rife and a common cause of human misery and malaise.

Dr Robert C. Atkins, author of the immensely successful book *Dr Atkins' Diet Revolution*, has carried out 12,000 routine glucose tolerance tests and found that 20 per cent of the subjects tested had unarguable evidence of hypoglycaemia. When the same test was carried out on 177 pilots of United Airlines it was discovered that one in four were prone to bouts of hypoglycaemia. Among a group of obese patients attending the Hahnemann Hospital in Philadelphia the incidence was higher still, at 42 per cent. As Dr Sam E. Roberts concluded in his book *Exhaustion: Causes and Treatment*: 'Hypoglycaemia is probably the most common disease in the United States.'

When the blood sugar level falls too low the first organ to suffer is the brain. This is not surprising, for when we're doing sedentary work the brain consumes about two-thirds of the body's total supply of glucose. The symptoms most commonly experienced are fatigue, anxiety, increased irritability, inability to concentrate and forgetfulness. Headaches, palpitations, hunger, light-headedness and weakness are other frequent presenting symptoms.

Diabetics can suffer from hypoglycaemia if they give themselves too much insulin. So too can patients suffering from disorders of the liver or pituitary and adrenal glands. But what is the explanation of the hypogly-caemia which exhausts so many people who are otherwise in perfect health? Why do their bodies temporarily fail to maintain the necessary level of glucose in their blood? Doctors call this common form of low blood sugar *reactive* or *alimentary* hypoglycaemia. This gives a clue to its cause.

Carbohydrates versus refined sugar

When our forebears ate a carbohydrate-rich snack of bread, potatoes or rice they enjoyed a slow, steady release of glucose into their blood stream. This triggered off a modest increase in insulin secretion, which took the excess glucose out of circulation and tucked it away in the body's glycogen stores. The modern Western diet – in our Coke, cake and chocolate culture – often contains a high proportion of refined sugar, which is more readily absorbed into the body. As a result when we tuck into a snack of jam doughnuts, ice cream and chocolate biscuits, we experience a sudden and marked rise in our blood sugar level. This triggers off a correspond-ingly high increase in insulin secretion. Twenty minutes later the blood sugar level may have fallen to normal, and yet glucose is still being taken out of circulation and transferred to the body's glycogen stores. At this point we feel tired, faint and hungry. So we perk ourselves up by eating a chocolate bar or drinking a cup of heavily-sweetened coffee. This boosts our blood sugar level for a short while, but may provoke another bout of reactive hypoglycaemia. So we proceed in a succession of pits and peaks, periods of lassitude following hard on the heels of spells of temporary liveliness.

Emotional stress

The same sequence of events can follow episodes of emotional stress. We may be full of energy when we're battling with an emergency but can suffer a let-down feeling immediately the crisis is over. This sudden reversal of well-being and drive is partly chemically induced. One of the body's immediate responses to stress is to increase its output of adrenalin. This hormone prepares the body for 'fight or flight' by quickening the pulse, increasing the depth and rate of breathing, and improving the circulation to the muscles and heart. It also raises blood glucose levels, by releasing some of the energy held in the liver's glycogen stores. Tests show that blood sugar levels usually reach a peak thirty to forty minutes after an emotional shock. Once the crisis is over they drop back to their normal limits, or may rebound to lower than usual levels, just as so often happens after eating a sugary snack. It is these spells of reactive hypoglycaemia which leaves surgeons so profoundly exhausted after a near-death crisis in the operating theatre, and which make actors and concert pianists so ravenously hungry once their performance is over.

Emotional stress and injudicious eating can provoke bouts of hypoglyc-aemia, but it would be wrong to make this the excuse for *all* forms of chronic fatigue. If you're constantly tired throughout the day, irrespective of what you eat, you're almost certainly *not* suffering from hypoglycaemia. If you feel tired and irritable when you go without food for more than four or five hours you *may* be prone to spells of low blood sugar. Other suggestive evidence of hypoglycaemia is if you feel dizzy, faint and weary one to two hours after eating a sugar-rich snack. To confirm the diagnosis you need to have a glucose tolerance test taken under medical supervision. This involves testing the sugar content of samples of blood taken at half-hourly intervals after eating a test meal of glucose. This will bring to light any abnormal swings in blood sugar levels and alone enables an authoritative diagnosis of hypoglycaemia to be made.

But why wait until medical intervention is required? If you want to be at your energetic best throughout the day you must maintain an optimum level of glucose in your blood. In most cases this can be achieved by making three slight modifications in your life style. These together form the seventh step in the **Vitality Progamme**.

★ To avoid sudden surges in blood glucose levels, which can provoke a trigger-happy response from the pancreas, avoid all forms of sugar and sugar containing confectioneries such as sweets, jam, biscuits, cakes, chocolates and heavily-sweetened sauces and drinks. Eat instead carbohydrates in their natural form – like rice, potatoes, and bread – which ensure a slower and more even release of energy.

This will improve your general nutrition, protect you from bouts of exhausting hypoglycaemia, and make you far less prone to put on weight. The average Briton gets nearly a fifth of his total calorie intake from sugar and can shed weight at a rate of about a pound a week simply by giving up sugar and sugar-containing foods. Tests carried out at America's Brookhaven National Laboratory reveal that the percentage of carbohydrate converted to fat is two to five times greater when subjects are on a high sugar diet than when they eat foods rich in starch. This suggests that, calorie for calorie, sugar is more fattening than bread, potatoes or rice. What's more, bread supplies us with 14 per cent of our daily protein intake and a fifth of our iron, while potatoes supply us with a third or more of our Vitamin C. White sugar, on the other hand, provides us with nothing but calories. It is the one food we can safely eliminate from our regular menu.

★ Studies show that people who eat a substantial breakfast are healthier than those who get by with no more than a cup of coffee, augmented perhaps by a slice of toast or bowl of 'refined', sweetened cereals. In 1970 a Consumer Subcommittee of the US Senate conducted an enquiry into the flourishing breakfast-food industry and found that by tempting people to buy convenience foods it was diverting consumer dollars away from more nutritious foods. Without their added vitamins, many packaged cereals were hardly more nutritious than the cartons they were packed in. 'Puffed rice,' reported one expert, 'is five times as expensive as ordinary rice and yet provides smaller amounts of most nutrients.' Analysis at that time showed that the most popular brands of breakfast cereals were the least nutritious. They 'fatten but do little to prevent malnutrition', the report stated. Their health claims, in fact, were just so much pap, cackle and puff.

To maintain energy levels during the morning, it's essential that the first meal of the day should be a true break-fast. Schoolteachers find that many pupils experience lethargy and an inability to concentrate during the final classes of the morning. This is probably due to a drop in their blood sugar levels. Surveys show that half the school children in Britain have an inadequate evening meal, while a quarter leave home in the morning without a proper breakfast. As a result many youngsters go without food for 18 hours which means they must exhaust their bodies' energy stores, which contain enough glycogen to last for only 13 hours. Unless they can quickly find an alternative source of glucose, by breaking down body protein or depot fat, they're bound to suffer a drop in blood sugar levels. This makes them tired, inefficient, irritable and unable to concentrate, particularly during the pre-lunch period. The same applies to many house-wives and office workers.

If you want to avoid the mid-morning 'blues', make sure you start the day with a sustaining meal rich in protein and unrefined carbohydrates. Babe Ruth, the legendary American baseball player, fortified himself with a breakfast of porterhouse steak, four fried eggs and a large portion of chips. Sir Winston Churchill opted for a somewhat lighter menu of grouse and caviar. I'm happier with a large glass of orange juice, a bowl of home-made muesli, a slice or two of wholemeal bread or toast, and a glass of milk, supplemented when time permits by some additional form of protein such as eggs, fish or ham.

When my patients complain of mid-morning tiredness I advise them to follow the old South American adage: 'Eat breakfast like a king, lunch like a princess, and dinner like a pauper.' On this more balanced intake of calories I find they can invariably get through the day with little dimin-ution in their energy levels or work performance.

★ Even if you're not prone to bouts of hypoglycaemia, you'll probably find it invigorating to spread your calorie intake more evenly throughout the day. I find that many people are more energetic if in addition to their customary three main meals they take low-calorie snacks in the middle of the morning, mid-afternoon and just before retiring to bed.

Cuddly Dudley Kim Dudley is a 43-year-old accountant whose work is mentally exacting but physically undemanding. For years he kept himself going by taking numerous cups of coffee liberally laced with sugar. Each drink gave him a temporary energy boost which lasted about half an hour, after which he felt as jaded as before. So he took another cup of his caffeinated syrup sucked a mint or ate one of his favourite chocolate biscuits. By the end of the day he usually felt so drained that he needed a Mars bar to boost his blood sugar level. This pepped him up until he got to the end of his homeward train journey, when he normally popped into the Railway Arm for a reviving gin and tonic and bag of crisps. By the time he finally got home his blood sugar level was once again falling, so he was happy to do justice to his wife's Cordon Bleu cuisine. And before he retired to bed he liked to have a malted milk drink and biscuits to avoid the ravages of night starvation.

Not surprisingly with this high-calorie diet Kim quickly earned the nickname of 'Cuddly Dudley'. He tried a number of weight-reducing diets and made several visits to health farms, but every attempt to slim was foiled by the fact that he thoroughly enjoyed eating and felt miserable and faint whenever he stopped. So he cheerfully followed my advice to go on a Nibbler's diet, taking six meals a day to ensure a greater regularity of energy intake, and avoid abrupt rises and falls in insulin output and blood sugar levels. The regimen worked like a charm. Not only did he feel less tired, he also started to lose weight. Within ten weeks he shed just over a stone. Soon he hopes his colleagues will stop calling him Cuddly Dudley and perhaps even start to think of him as Slim Kim!

You too would probably benefit by switching to the Nibbler's diet. Don't step up your overall intake of calories, merely spread them out more evenly throughout the day. This you can achieve by eating a smaller lunch and dinner, and adding snacks at approximately 11 am, 4 pm and 9.30 pm. These mini-meals can consist of such titbits as a small cheese sandwich, a glass of milk, a handful of nuts and crisps, a cupful of muesli, a helping of yoghurt, a bowl of thick vegetable soup or a large banana topped off with a sprinkling of cream – each of which supplies about 150 calories.

You'll feel fresher if you reduce the size of your main meals, because you won't then suffer the post-prandial torpor which comes when blood is drawn from the general circulation to supply the needs of a heavily-laden intestinal tract. By taking regular snacks you'll also reduce your risk of suffering fatiguing bouts of hypoglycaemia and at the same time lessen your chance of putting on weight, for the mere fact of eating steps up the body's metabolic rate. As a result a person who eats a number of snacks experiences several food-induced peaks of metabolism during the day instead of the customary one or two. This will keep the body's internal furnaces burning brightly throughout the entire day, and can consume an additional 200 calories a day – the equivalent of over 20 lbs of fat per year.

Vitality Programme – Step Seven Cut out sugar and sugar-containing food from your diet, and in their place eat unrefined carbohydrates, such as bread, potatoes and rice. Make your meals small and regular, and always start your day with a proper breakfast.

STEP 8

Mineral Wealth

Within an average person there is enough water to fill a ten-gallon barrel, enough fat to make seven bars of soap, sufficient phosphorus to top 2,200 match heads, carbon to fill 9,000 lead pencils, iron to forge a medium-sized nail and lime to whitewash a chicken coop. Reduced to these basic ingredients the human organism seems little more than a sorcerer's stockpot, a haphazard witch's brew of organic scraps and sludge. But the recipe is exceedingly complex and incredibly finely balanced, with each component playing a vital role in the overall master plan.

'We are what we eat'

Even primitive man realised that there was a link between his diet and his destiny. 'We are what we eat,' has been a universally accepted truism. At first the relationship was thought to be metaphysical rather than physiological. Man indulged in sympathetic magic and ate the testicles of a bull to enhance his virility and the flesh of a gazelle to make him fleet of foot. Cannibals dined on the brains of elderly sages to increase their store of wisdom, and swallowed the hearts of brave warriors to increase their store of courage.

With the advent of the age of reason we left behind these esoteric practices, and took a more scientific attitude toward the subject of human nutrition. At first the approach was over-simplistic. Man was considered to be adequately fed if he consumed enough proteins, carbohydrates and fats. Then it was discovered that certain accessory food factors – inaccurately known at first as vital amines and later labelled vitamins – were essential for human survival. Even a few grains of these wonder-working catalysts can make the difference between health and disease. Just over one-thousandth of an ounce of Vitamin C a day can prevent scurvy; much less than a millionth of an ounce of Vitamin B12 a day is sufficient to prevent pernicious anaemia.

Most health-conscious individuals are now well aware of the need to maintain an optimum intake of vitamins, and many food faddists go to great expense to supplement their diet with vitamins which either don't exist (Vitamin P) or are rarely ever in short supply (Vitamin K and E). Far fewer people take equal care to ensure a proper intake of essential minerals, accessory food factors which are just as important as vitamins but far less widely publicised.

Minerals are vital

At least twenty minerals are known to be necessary for the maintenance of human health. They are vital for the whole range of body processes, but in particular for nerve function, muscle contraction, skeletal development and hormone secretion. Fortunately most of these essential chemicals are freely available in an ordinary, varied diet. Were it not so the human race could hardly have survived for nearly a million years. But it would be wrong to be too complacent. Modern living has produced some notable changes in the mineral content of our diet. The refining of food has greatly reduced our intake of certain vital nutrients. During the milling of white flour we lose approximately 60 per cent of the calcium content of the grain, 71 per cent of the phosphorus, 90 per cent of the chromium, 85 per cent of the manganese and 88 per cent of the cobalt. A number of the drugs prescribed today also interfere with the body's normal mineral balance. Antacids taken for indigestion are liable to reduce the absorption of iron and calcium; laxatives and diuretic pills tend to cause an excessive loss of potassium; contraceptive pills lower the amount of magnesium in the circulation; antibiotics can result in low blood levels of magnesium. The chemical treatment of our domestic water supplies may also depress mineral intake, tap water sometimes having two hundred times less iodine than water from deep mineral springs. Still more disturbance is caused by the chemical treatment of our agricultural land. When the soil is saturated with concentrated fertilisers such as potash, ammonium sulphate or super-phosphate it cannot hold the less easily dissolved minerals such as iron, copper, magnesium and zinc. And if the land is not treated from time to time with traditional organic fertilisers, such as manure and ploughed-in clover, its content of humus falls. This reduces the population of soil bacteria and fungi, which in turn makes the minerals in the soil less readily available to the crops.

But what does this mean in practical terms? If the soil is lacking in minerals, it follows that the plants grown on that soil will be correspond-ingly deficient, similarly the animals that feed on the plants, and likewise the humans who are at the end of the feeding chain. At one time we could be assured of an adequate intake of minerals if we ate a reasonably varied meat and vegetable diet. Now – partly through living on refined foods grown on demineralised soils – we run the risk of being deficient in certain of these vital micronutrients.

Five anti-fatigue minerals The substances which are most likely to be lacking from our modern diet are iron, calcium, potassium, iodine and magnesium. By a remarkable quirk of fate, chronic fatigue has been identified as a possible symptom of a deficiency of each and every one of these minerals. It is no coincidence that many of the old folk cures for tiredness involve remedies rich in the Fabulous Five anti-fatigue minerals. One country remedy is a drink made by soaking scraps of iron mould in vinegar-water, a remedy which is tailor-made to counteract a dietary deficiency of iron. The elixir favoured by the hill farmers of Vermont is a daily dose of cider vinegar. This cure was studied by Dr D. C. Jarvis, a fifth-generation native of Vermont, who gives the following advice in his bestselling book *Folk Medicine*: 'To cope with chronic fatigue folk medicine knows no better treatment than this: add three teaspoonfuls of apple-cider vinegar to a cup of honey. . . .

Take two teaspoonful of the mixture when preparing for bed.' Dr Jarvis attributes the effectiveness of this time-honoured remedy to its high content of potassium, a mineral which he believes is often deficient in the modern diet, a shortage which he says leads to tension, mental and muscular fatigue, loss of memory and inability to concentrate.

Another favoured country cure for exhaustion is to eat powdered seaweed, better known to health food addicts as kelp. Peruvians living in the Andes mountains enhanced their stamina in this way, and to ensure a ready supply of their favoured pick-me-up often carried around their necks little bags filled with kelp. In the same way generations of Welsh miners fortified themselves before they left for work by eating a generous helping of seaweed, which they cooked and ate like spinach. This peculiarly Welsh delicacy is known as laverbread. The efficacy of kelp stems no doubt from its high content of minerals such as potassium, calcium, iron, magnesium and particularly iodine, the ingredient which is essential for the proper function of the thyroid gland.

How can the intake of these five minerals be ensured? If you've adopted the sixth step in the **Vitality Programme** you will have safeguarded your supply of iron. If you observe the simple instructions which follow you'll be equally sure of your intake of calcium, potassium, magnesium and iodine.

Calcium   Calcium plays a vital role in the formation of the bones and teeth and in the clotting of the blood. Calcium ions are also necessary for muscular contraction and the relay of nerve impulses. When the level of calcium in the blood falls for long periods the bones grow weak, a condition known as osteoporosis in adults, and rickets when it occurs in children. There is also a tendency for the muscles to twitch and go into cramp-like spasms. Less well recognised are the effects of calcium deficiency on the nervous system. People so afflicted frequently suffer a level of fatigue which is out of all proportion to the amount of work they do. This is aggravated by increased irritability and tension which causes a constant depletion of their reserves of nervous energy. Since insomnia frequently compounds their problem, it is little wonder that these mineral-depleted individuals often find their days dogged by tetchiness and exhaustion. These symptoms can generally be relieved by a small increase in their daily allowance of calcium.

An 11-stone man has 2–3 lb of calcium in his body, 99 per cent of which is held in his bones and teeth. To all outward appearances our skeleton seems solid and static, but it is in fact in a state of constant flux. Every day somewhere in the region of 700 mg of calcium leaves the skeleton, hopefully to be replaced by a similar quantity of calcium from the diet. To maintain an optimum calcium balance we need a ration of about 800–1000 mgs of calcium per day. Some doctors acknowledge the existence of calcium deficiency only in those rare cases when it gives rise to gross disease, and yet surveys carried out by the US Department of Agriculture reveal that three out of every ten families are getting less than the recommended daily dose of calcium.

The risk of deficiency is particularly great in people on low cholesterol diets (since dairy products are our major source of calcium); who drink to excess (because alcohol retards the absorption of calcium from the intestine); and in slimmers who stop eating bread to lose weight (since bread is another rich source of calcium).

If you want to make sure of your intake of calcium, follow the advice I give my patients:

★ Consume normal quantities of dairy products, which traditionally supply over 60 per cent of our total calcium intake. It's likely that only 4 per cent of the population has a cholesterol level high enough to warrant major dietary change. As a result there's no need for you to make any drastic alteration in your intake of butter, milk and cheese – unless your doctor orders otherwise. If you need to reduce your calorie intake to lose weight, don't give up dairy foods but switch instead to drinking skimmed milk (85 calories to the glass instead of 165 for whole milk) and eating cottage cheese (30 calories to the ounce instead of 120 per ounce for hard, Cheddar cheese.) These are less fattening, but still excellent sources of calcium.

★ Eat three or four slices of wholewheat bread a day. Wholewheat flour is another important source of calcium. White flour loses most of its content of calcium during the milling process. This is later replaced when the bread is enriched with powdered chalk, but despite this a slice of enriched white bread still contains only 19 mgs of calcium, compared with the 23 mgs in a slice of wholewheat bread.

★ Eat plenty of green vegetables, the third major source of calcium. Since the mineral content of the leaves can only be as rich as the soil on which they are raised, grow your own produce whenever possible in a vegetable garden enriched with composted leaves and kitchen waste. Failing that try to buy organically grown vegetables in preference to those raised on artificially fertilised soil which can be low in mineral content. Subject vegetables to a minimum of cooking, and recycle the cooking water in gravies, stocks and soups to make full use of their vitamin and mineral content.

★ Drink hard water in preference to soft. If your home is equipped with a water softener make sure you take your drinking water direct from the mains supply. Reports from Sweden, America and eleven county boroughs in Britain show that people who live in soft water districts have a higher than average risk of coronary disease. Subsequent analysis of the water supplies revealed that of the 13 trace elements known to contribute to the 'hardness' of the water, only a decline in calcium content was found to be linked with an increased incidence of heart disease.

★ Chew the soft bones of small fish. The Eskimos traditionally do not drink milk, but keep themselves in healthy calcium balance by eating the skeletons of small fish. If you eat 3 ozs of filleted sardines you'll get a meagre ration of 25 mgs of calcium; swallow the bones as well and your calcium intake will soar to 370 mgs.

With a glass of milk a day (570 mgs), an ounce of Cheddar cheese (225 mgs), three slices of wholemeal bread (69 mgs) and two helpings of green, leafy vegetables (280 mgs) you'll easily achieve your recommended day's ration of 1000 mgs of calcium. But it's obvious from these figures that if you adopt the currently popular anti-cholesterol diet, and restrict your intake of dairy food, you'll almost certainly end up in a state of calcium deficit. This will increase your predisposition to fatigue, and possibly enhance rather than diminish your risk of developing coronary disease.

Potassium   Potassium and sodium are two other minerals which play a vital role in the control of nerve and muscle function. There is generally a surfeit of sodium in the average Western diet, but there may on occasions be a dearth of potassium. When this happens and the body's store of potassium falls, weakness and mental confusion sets in. Some families are afflicted by a rare hereditary disease known as familial periodic paralysis, characterised by intermittent falls in the level of potassium in the blood. During these attacks the victims are unable to move their muscles, even when they are subjected to direct electrical stimulation. If left untreated death occurs from respiratory paralysis; but an amazingly rapid recovery can be produced within ten minutes by giving a stiff dose of potassium salts. This dramatic response serves to emphasise the importance of potassium.

If states of potassium deficiency are artificially induced, people become tired and listless. The average adult contains about 5 ozs of potassium, and needs in the region of half to one gram a day to replace the amount excreted in the urine. Since most foods – with the exception of fats, sugar and alcohol – contain a certain amount of potassium, it might be thought that dietary deficiencies are rare. But shortages can occur when people are under stress; on diets over rich in alcohol, salt and sugar; are suffering from diarrhoea, or are taking diuretic pills or certain anti-cancer drugs.

You'll safeguard your intake of potassium if you observe the following rules:

★ Eat a wholesome diet rich in vegetables, nuts, dried fruits and wholemeal bread, which are all excellent sources of potassium. Vegetables should be eaten raw or lightly cooked and use made of the cooking water in soups and gravies to preserve the minerals that would otherwise be discarded down the sink. A breakfast time bowl of muesli will also provide a generous helping of potassium, particularly if it's a homemade mixture rich in raisins, nuts and rolled oats.

★ Cut down your intake of salt, which can interfere with the body's normal balance between sodium and potassium ions and predispose to excessive water retention and high blood pressure. The body's entire content of salt is only three ounces, and most of us get sufficient in the food we eat without needing to add more in the process of cooking or at the table. In the West we probably eat 20–30 times as much salt a day as we need.

In its report *Dietary Goals for the United States*, the US Senate's Select Committee on Nutrition and Human Needs recommends that salt consumption should be cut by half to two-thirds, so that the daily intake falls to approximately three grams a day. This reduction can be achieved by avoiding the use of table salt and eating fewer processed foods, especially heavily salted items such as bacon, ham, sausages, hamburgers, tinned meat, salted smoked fish, pickles, sauces, Bovril, Oxo, Marmite, potato crisps and salted peanuts. Analysis, for example, shows that a Big Mac hamburger supplies nearly eight times the daily requirement of salt, and a helping of tinned green beans more than a hundred times more salt than a similar quantity of fresh beans.

By cutting down your intake of salt you'll also lessen your risk of suffering low blood sugar – hypoglycaemia – for tests show that when people prone to low blood sugar eat salty foods they suffer a drop in the blood levels of both potassium and glucose. Conversely it has been found that they can lessen their hypoglycaemic attacks by taking supplements of potassium salts. This is because potassium is needed by the body for the metabolism of glucose.

★ Reduce your consumption of sugar, and sugar-containing confectionery. Tests carried out on patients suffering from familial periodic paralysis reveal that eating concentrated doses of sugar can produce lassitude, muscular weakness and even paralysis by provoking a rapid fall in the level of potassium in the bloodstream.

★ Do not take diuretics to lose weight unless they are medically prescribed, since they increase the rate of potassium excretion from the kidneys, leading to fatigue, muscle weakness, constipation and loss of appetite. Some diuretic tablets incorporate an allowance of potassium to compensate for this drain, but there is no evidence that this is sufficient to counteract deficiency.

★ Avoid taking large doses of laxatives or indigestion mixtures or tablets based on magnesium salts – magnesium hydroxide, magnesium oxide, magnesium carbonate, magnesium trisilicate and magnesium sulphate (Epsom Salts). These cause the body to lose both water and potassium, which may lead to weakness and mental confusion, particularly in the elderly.

Iodine

Iodine is the next of the Fabulous Five anti-fatigue minerals. It is essential for the function of the thyroid gland and the production of thyroxine, the hormone which controls the rate of bodily metabolism. About three-quarters of the body's reserves of iodine are held in the thyroid gland which sits at the base of the neck. The remainder is locked in the thyroxine molecules circulating around the body. When iodine is deficient in the diet the thyroid gland enlarges in a vain attempt to increase its output of thyroxine. This often produces a tell-tale swelling at the base of the neck, known as a goitre. At one time many people living in areas with iodine-deficient soils developed goitres. The best documented of these goitrous districts were certain of the Swiss Alpine valleys, the Peak District of Derbyshire and inland American States such as Oregon, Idaho, Utah, Wyoming, Wisconsin, Michigan and Montana.

In addition to the lump in the front of their necks these iodine-deficient individuals also showed symptoms of myxoedema, a disease characterised by constant fatigue, lethargy, coldness and a tendency to put on weight. With insufficient thyroxine to speed the chemical activity of their bodies, metabolism sometimes fell to half its normal rate. All these symptoms can be avoided by ensuring an intake of no more than 100–150 microgrammes of iodine per day. To make sure you get this protective daily dose, adopt the following measures:

★ Eat plenty of fish and sea foods. The oceans contain a rich harvest of iodine, as do all sea products. Iodine-deficiency goitres occurred among the North American Indians living in the inland plains, but were never found in the Pomo Indians of the California coast who ate a diet rich in fish, octopus, lobsters, crabs and sea urchins.

★ Use iodised salt rather than plain salt to season cooked foods. This measure alone is sufficient to prevent the development of iodine deficiency, and carries no risk of overdosage since any excess iodine is immediately excreted in the urine.

If despite these measures you have reason to believe that you are running short of iodine, take a daily teaspoonful of powdered kelp, disguising the flavour if necessary by sprinkling it over vegetables or taking it in a glass of tomato juice.

Magnesium Magnesium is the last of the five anti-fatigue minerals. Nutritionalists claim a diet high in refined and processed foods is often deficient in magnesium. Since magnesium is involved in energy storage, nerve and muscle function, and the metabolism of certain members of the Vitamin B group, its lack can cause muscular weakness, irritability and mental disturbance.

Although the body contains less than an ounce of magnesium, it is excreted regularly in the urine, and needs to be replaced at the rate of about 400–800 mg per day. People living in soft-water areas may have an added risk of running short of magnesium, as do alcoholics, women taking the contraceptive pill and patients on diuretic medication.

You'll ensure an optimum intake of magnesium if you observe the following recommendations:

★ Eat magnesium rich foods, such as nuts, whole grains, fish, green vegetables, figs, meat and kelp.

★ Avoid an excessive intake of alcohol. Research reveals that moderate drinkers who take two ounces of spirits a day excrete three to five times as much magnesium in their urine as they do during periods of total abstinence.

★ Eat wholewheat bread in preference to white, since 85 per cent of the magnesium content of wheat is removed in the milling of white flour.

★ Cut down your intake of sugar, sweets, biscuits and cakes, since a high sugar diet predisposes to magnesium depletion.

Vitality Programme – Step Eight   Ensure that you eat sufficient of the five important anti-fatigue minerals: calcium, potassium, sodium, magnesium and iodine. Incorporate in your diet generous helpings of milk, cheese, wholemeal bread and green vegetables. Do not sprinkle salt on your food at the table, and where a seasoning is required during cooking try using iodised salt. Avoid an excessive intake of alcohol and do not overindulge in laxatives and indigestion remedies high in magnesium.

STEP 9

Food for Thought

Every year thousands of articles are written about the role of vitamins in human nutrition. Some make the subject as abstruse as Einstein's Theory of Relativity; others make it as terrifying as a revivalist preacher's sermon on satanism. Where lies the truth? Are we suffering on a massive scale from multiple vitamin deficiencies, as the health food magazines claim? Or are vitamin shortages rare and of trivial consequence, as many family doctors uphold?

It would take several volumes to debate these questions in depth, but only a few pages to answer the queries relevant to the subject of this book. Will vitamin supplements help to improve your level of energy? Can vitamins overcome chronic tiredness? What steps should you take to see that you are getting an adequate supply of these energy-releasing catalysts?

One of the most lauded panaceas of recent years has been Vitamin E. This multi-purpose rejuvenant is said to increase stamina, improve sexual performance, protect the heart, delay the ageing of the skin and prolong life. These claims are based on experiments which show that when female rats are completely starved of Vitamin E they miscarry and become a trifle seedy. But there's no evidence to suggest that similar problems occur in man, and since Vitamin E is widely distributed in the range of foods we normally eat, there is virtually no risk of dietary deficiency. So far I've *never* found it necessary to recommend a patient to take doses of Vitamin E. Mind you, if you're a pregnant rat, existing on a diet artificially deprived of Vitamin E, you may find it worthwhile to swallow capsules of wheat-germ oil, which is the vitamin's richest natural source. Under any other circumstances you'd do better to spend your money on something more invigorating, like a good detective novel or a day trip to the sea.

It can't be said too often, or emphasised too firmly, that while an optimum intake of vitamins is essential for the maintenance of health, a surfeit is valueless and sometimes potentially harmful. You wouldn't expect to get a better TV picture by connecting your set to a 1,000-volt power supply, nor can you expect to improve your personal performance by taking megadoses of any particular vitamin. Self therapy of this nature is generally no more than an expensive way of increasing the vitamin content of your urine.

Royal Jelly – Royal Jelly is another nostrum that finds a place on the shelves of health-
'bee nonsense'? food stockists. It enjoyed a vogue some years ago when it was suggested

that any substance which can transform an undistinguished larva into an impressive queen bee must be ideal for human consumption. The theory was given added credence when it was demonstrated that Royal Jelly, the product of the salivary glands of worker bees, was rich in members of the Vitamin B group, notably pantothenic acid and biotin. But the quantities are so small that anyone in serious search of youthful vitality would have to consume the jelly given to fifty thousand larvae before they got a physiological dose of Vitamin B. It's just 'bee nonsense', said one nutritionalist. 'I don't really believe that there is any miraculous substance in Royal Jelly which will do for me what good, straight fish and chips can't do,' said another.

The same applies to honey, the rejuvenating aphrodisiac recommended by romantic novelist Barbara Cartland. John Yudkin, Professor of Nutrition and Dietetics at Queen Elizabeth College, London University, has calculated that it would be necessary to eat ten pounds of honey a day to get an adequate daily dose of riboflavin, Vitamin B_2, and 48 lbs to get the recommended daily ration of thiamine, B_1.

But there is an *element* of truth in the adman's claims. Royal Jelly is undoubtedly good for queen bees, and there's no disputing the fact that the vitamins it contains are equally beneficial for humans, *providing* they are supplied in adequate quantities.

Vitamin B Surveys suggest that of all the nutrients known to be essential for the maintenance of human health, none are more likely to be lacking in the diet than certain members of the Vitamin B complex. Unfortunately the two most frequent absentees both play a vital role in energy transport and release. The first is thiamine, Vitamin B_1, which is necessary for nervous metabolism, the transport of oxygen in the body and the regulation of digestion. The second is riboflavin, or Vitamin B_2, which is vital for the metabolism of sugar and starch and the exchange of oxygen in the tissue cells. Gross deficiencies of these vitamins are certainly rare, but minor shortages are far more common than is generally realised. A gross lack of thiamine, for example, causes the easily recognised disease beriberi, whereas minor shortages give rise to less obvious symptoms such as fatigue, increased irritability and insomnia.

During the Second World War the Harvard University Fatigue Laboratory ran a series of treadmill experiments on human volunteers artificially deprived of Vitamin B. They found that the muscular efficiency of these vitamin-starved individuals declined dramatically during exercise tests, they tired more rapidly and were slower to recover from their exhausted state. When their diet was supplemented with either yeast or thiamine they recovered rapidly, most of the subjects regaining their previous level of physical fitness within three days.

In this instance the lack of Vitamin B was artificially induced – but what of the many people who are living on inadequate diets? How many individuals are, without knowing it, reducing their vitality by eating too little Vitamin B? An analysis of over two dozen dietary studies in America suggests that half the US population may be deficient in thiamine and 40 per cent lacking in riboflavin. Shortages are most likely to occur among the elderly and poor, but they can also arise in wealthy executives, particularly if they're under stress or trying to drown their sorrows in drink. The recommended daily allowance of thiamine is about 1.5 mgs, but nutritionalists recommend that this should be increased to ten milligrams during periods of intense stress. Heavy drinkers, and people with an exceptionally sweet tooth, are prone to run short of riboflavin, since large quantities of this vitamin are required to metabolise carbohydrates such as sugar and alcohol. Deficiencies of Vitamin B can also arise when absorption is hampered by inflammatory intestinal diseases such as colitis; in vegetarians; in women on the contraceptive pill; and in patients taking prolonged courses of antacids, sleeping pills, barbiturates and anti-seasickness pills.

In any case you'll need to step up your intake of Vitamin B when you start to follow the **Vitality Programme**, for the more energetic you are the more thiamine you'll need. Vigorous exercise such as long-distance running can make the body consume 15 times more thiamine than usual. Some of this is necessary for the conversion of sugar into energy, and some is used to help the body get rid of the waste products of carbohydrate metabolism.

If you've followed the advice I've given so far, and made sure that you're eating a well-balanced diet rich in whole grain cereals, meat, milk, nuts, green vegetables and eggs, you're unlikely to be short of Vitamin B. But there are one or two further practical points to bear in mind:

★ All members of the Vitamin B complex are soluble in water, and most are easily destroyed by cooking. So cook foods lightly, and make use of the water in which meat and vegetables are cooked in either soups, stocks or gravies.

★ Riboflavin is readily destroyed by light, to the extent that a bottle of milk loses half its rich supply of riboflavin when it's exposed to sunlight for two hours. So keep milk shielded from the sun's rays and store it in the fridge.

★ Alkaline substances such as bicarbonate of soda should not be used in the cooking of green vegetables since they destroy both thiamine and riboflavin.

★ Wholemeal bread is preferable to white bread, since the wheat germ is a rich source of thiamine and riboflavin. These essential nutrients are removed during the milling of white flour, and while white flour is enriched by replacing some of the thiamine and niacin, this does not restore the full range of B vitamins, nor offer them in their natural balance.

★ Liver is the richest natural source of Vitamin B. Two small slices of liver will provide nearly double your daily requirement of riboflavin and 20 per cent of your ration of thiamine. Pigs' liver may not be the gourmet's delight, yet it is just as nutritious as the more expensive calves' liver, and in fact outstrips it in its content of iron and Vitamin A. Aim to eat at least one helping of liver per week.

★ Yoghurt is another excellent source of Vitamin B. Early this century Professor Elie Metchnikoff, one of Pasteur's earliest co-workers, wrote a book called *The Prolongation of Life*. In it he extolled the virtues of yoghurt, which he had often eaten as a youth in Russia. He noted that villagers in Bulgaria, who ate large quantities of sour milk, often lived to a vigorous and ripe old age. Thinking there might be a connection between the two observations, he subjected a sample of yoghurt to microscopic examination at the Pasteur Institute in Paris and found it to be teeming with bacteria which he called the *lactobacillus bulgaricus*, from its country of origin. He noted that these genial organisms lived quite amicably in the human bowel, where they tended to crowd out other, more harmful germs. It was this protective action, he decided, which helped to give the Bulgarian centenarians their remarkable vitality and freedom from disease.

Soured milk creates Vitamin B Subsequent research has revealed another attribute of yoghurt and other sour milk products, such as the Russian kumyss (fermented mare's milk) which enjoyed an enormous vogue as an elixir of life in Europe before the Tsars were overthrown and the kumyss curative stations in the Southern Steppes closed. Soured milk, whether it's made from cow, buffalo, goat, camel or sheep milk, contains millions of lactic acid bacilli, the milk-loving bacteria which are the agents mainly responsible for the manufacture of Vitamin B in the human intestine. Kill off these useful allies with antibiotic drugs and vitamin deficiency syndromes can arise. Populate the gut with *lactobacilli* by taking regular doses of yoghurt and you'll lessen your risk of digestive diseases and at the same time greatly increase your intake of Vitamin B.

And you don't have to spend vast sums of money on commercially made yoghurt, which may be tasty but is often far too rich in added sugar and has been pasteurised to kill the important bacteria. Yoghurt can be easily made at home given a pint of milk, a glass mixing bowl sterilised in boiling water, and a heaped teaspoon of plain, live yoghurt to start the culture working. Heat the milk to a little more than body temperature (110° to 120°F) and then pour it over the starting yoghurt, stirring gently as you go. Wrap the bowl in a folded towel, place it in a warm place and then leave the culture to ferment undisturbed for six to eight hours. (Overnight is ideal since the mixture is less likely to be disturbed.) In the morning pour off the layer of water which will have formed on the top of the yoghurt, then put it in the fridge to chill. If you want a thicker, creamier yoghurt make as before but use a pint of UHT Long-Life milk, and add to it two tablespoons of dried skimmed milk powder once it has been warmed.

Vitamin C When planning your energy-diet you must also ensure a generous intake of Vitamin C. Three hundred years ago doctors commented that one of the cardinal symptoms of scurvy (Vitamin C deficiency) was listlessness and fatigue. Recent tests confirm that subjects on a Vitamin C deficient diet develop symptoms of fatigue six to eight weeks before they exhibit clinical signs of scurvy.

The probable reason for this premature tiredness is that Vitamin C is essential for the synthesis of butyric acid (carnitine), an important fuel for muscular contraction. British nutritionalist R. Elwyn Hughes has observed: 'It is conceivable that substantial sections of the population, although ingesting officially acceptable amounts of ascorbic acid in terms of protection against "clinical scurvy", are nevertheless in a state of chronic fatigue because of sub-optimal biosynthesis of carnitine.' This risk is likely to be especially high for vegetarians who eschew meat and fish, the major dietary sources of carnitine.

Recent research has revealed another protective role of Vitamin C, which is related to the avoidance of fatigue and possibly also to the prevention of bowel cancer. Each day we absorb a certain amount of nitrates, chemicals which are added to bacon, pressed meats, corned beef and frankfurter sausages to improve their keeping qualities. More nitrates are poured onto the land as artificial fertilisers and find their way into our bodies in the vegetables we eat and the water we drink. Most of these nitrates are excreted unchanged. But a certain proportion is converted by the bacteria in our stomach and mouth into potentially carcinogenic breakdown products known as nitrosamines. More is transformed by the nitrate-reducing bacteria into nitrites, which combine with the haemo-globin in the blood to form methaemoglobin, so reducing its oxygen-carrying capacity and predisposing us to mental and physical fatigue. About one per cent of the haemoglobin in the blood of even the healthiest individuals is in the form of methaemoglobin. This proportion is generally higher in the elderly, in people with a high intake of nitrates and especially in those who suffer from low gastric acidity. Tests show that Vitamin C helps to inhibit the breakdown of nitrates, and so preserve the oxygen-carrying capacity of the red blood cells.

No wonder Vitamin C is often referred to as the 'master' vitamin. In Britain the recommended daily dosage is set at 30 mgs per day, whereas medical authorities in America advise a daily ration of at least 60 mgs. I advise a considerably higher intake of 100–200 mgs per day, which I believe is necessary to ensure that the body is functioning at full efficiency. An intake of 30 mgs of Vitamin C a day may be enough to prevent scurvy but I'm convinced it's not enough to maintain optimum health, especially if you smoke, are under stress, are recovering from an illness, or taking drugs which depress the level of Vitamin C in the blood, such as aspirin, tetracycline, antibiotics or hormone pills containing oestrogen.

As it is, about 16 per cent of families in Britain are believed to be getting less than the minimum suggested ration of 30 mgs a day, a figure which rises to 50 per cent in February and March.

To ensure an adequate intake of Vitamin C, modify your diet to meet the following requirements:

★ Eat some fresh citrus fruit every day. A medium-sized orange contains 50 mgs of Vitamin C, which is ten times as much as an apple of comparable size. As an alternative, drink a daily glassful of orange juice (93 mgs), grapefruit juice (61 mgs) or tomato juice (40 mgs).

★ Take frequent salads, either as a main or side dish, and make them as varied as possible. The curled-up lettuce leaf, the mainstay of the railway buffet salad, is not a particularly rich source of Vitamin C. You'll fare better if you augment the standard four small lettuce leaves (4 mgs of Vitamin C) with six slices of cucumber (7 mgs), a tablespoon of chopped parsely (7 mgs), four radishes (10 mgs), a medium-sized tomato (35 mgs) and 4 ozs of coleslaw (50 mgs). This tasty plateful alone will give you a generous daily ration of 100 mgs of Vitamin C.

Your quota will also be assured if you eat a single red pepper (122 mgs) which is one of the richest natural sources of Vitamin C.

★ Eat plenty of lightly cooked green vegetables. Most people recognise the nutritional value of citrus fruits, but few realise that, weight for weight, vegetables such as broccoli, parsley and kale contain twice as much Vitamin C as oranges.

To extract the maximum benefit from green vegetables they should be subjected to the minimum preparation and eaten when they are really fresh. Vitamin C is easily destroyed by cooking, shredding, dicing, frying or boiling. Greens kept warm on a hotplate, for instance, can lose up to three-quarters of their Vitamin C content. Ideally they should be boiled in a minimum of water in a closed saucepan and cooked and served as rapidly as possible. Even then some of their vitamin and mineral content escapes into the cooking water, which is far too valuable to be thrown away and should – as I've suggested previously – be saved and used in gravies, stocks and soups.

And don't despise the humble potato, which supplies the British public with a third of its total Vitamin C intake in the summer, and practically half in the winter.

Follow these three simple rules and you won't go short of Vitamin C, nor will you need to waste money on vitamin tablets. Dr Charles Glen King, co-discoverer of Vitamin C, has never taken Vitamin C supplements, but reckons to get 100–200 mgs a day by drinking tomato juice and eating oranges and lightly cooked broccoli sprinkled with lemon juice and paprika, which is another rich source of Vitamin C.

Vitality Programme – Step Nine Ensure an adequate intake of Vitamins B and C by consuming plenty of wholemeal flour, liver, yoghurt, citrus fruits, fruit juices, mixed salads and fresh vegetables. Always cook vegetables lightly and use their cooking water in gravies, stocks and soups.

STAGE THREE

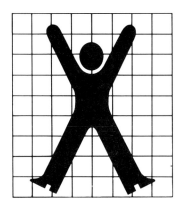

Providing the Ideal Working Conditions

STEP 10

Nature's Balm

Sleep is a natural restorative for tired minds and weary bodies. It is a universal panacea, available to all but neglected by many. More than a third of Americans report sleep problems. The main complaint of the young is difficulty getting to sleep. The chief grouse of the middle-aged is inability to get *sufficient* sleep, and the major gripe of the elderly is that their sleep is plagued by periods of fretful wakefulness. All age groups agree that sleep disturbance impairs their efficiency and makes them tired and irritable.

When an American doctor questioned a group of over five hundred men of distinction in art, science and government, six out of ten said that even a single night's impoverished sleep impaired their performance. The commonest symptoms were tiredness, mental lethargy, reduced creativity and lack of vim and vigour.

Why is sleep so vital to our health? No one as yet knows the mysterious force which compels us to doze, but scientists have built up a detailed inventory of the physiological changes which take place when we slip into oblivion. During sleep muscles relax, body temperature falls, oxygen consumption drops, metabolic rate declines and our level of consciousness sinks. The cerebral cortex, centre of feeling, imagination and conscious activity, becomes quiescent, like a gigantic telephone switchboard closing down for the night. The brain waves, which during the day are normally emitted in rapid peaks of ten a second, become diminished in both amplitude and frequency. Under the sway of Morpheus they become lazy ripples, rarely more than two or three a second. In this blissful state of relaxed torpor we have a chance to recharge our neuromuscular batteries.

'The balm of hurt minds'

The more stressful our lives, the more we crave the benison of sleep. The more emotional traumas we suffer, the more we require our night's repose, which Shakespeare described as 'the balm of hurt minds'. Many harassed housewives and overworked executives deny their need for sleep. With pints of coffee to stimulate them and quarts of determination to sustain them, they press themselves to work harder. This is like whipping a tired horse. It keeps the body moving, but only at the cost of mental and physical decline. Laboratory tests show that working through the fatigue barrier places a considerable strain on our energy stores, even though it has little initial effect on our mental performance or physical ability.

In one experiment students were asked to do complicated multiplication problems after eight hours sleep. Later they did the same sums after only six hours sleep. The results showed that the shortage of rest made little difference to the speed or accuracy of their work. But metabolic tests revealed that when they were deprived of sleep they had to work much harder to maintain the standard of their output, so much so that they consumed *three* times more energy then than they did when properly rested.

Tests also prove that the *quality* of a night's sleep is as important as its length. At the University of Florida Sleep Laboratory a team of psychologists and psychiatrists subjected sleeping volunteers to gentle electric shocks that were regulated in intensity so that the level of their sleep was lightened without their being woken up. Even with this mild level of sleep disturbance the subjects began to suffer depression, apathy and general malaise within a few days.

Sleep as a medicine The recuperative powers of a good night's sleep are widespread and profound. Sleep therapy has been employed by doctors as a non-specific medicine for over three thousand years. Asklepios, the legendary physician of ancient Greece, gained such a reputation for his cures that he was raised to the status of a god when he died, and worshipped in hundreds of temples throughout the Hellenic world. An integral part of the cult of Asklepios was the practice of incubation, or temple sleep. Patients suffering from a wide range of disorders would visit the temples, take a ritual bath to purify their bodies, and then lie down to sleep in long, open-air corridors. The healing they received was believed to result from divine visitation. The custom of temple sleep is still practised in certain Mediterranean areas, and each year many miracles are reported from the sacred island of Tenos, where the sick are permitted to sleep in the temple during the island's two special religious festivals.

In recent times sleep cures of a different kind have been practised in many medical centres throughout the world, generally in the treatment of nervous disorders. At Montreal's Allan Memorial Hospital mentally sick patients who have failed to respond to other forms of therapy have been put to sleep with sedatives for several days, being wakened only for food, drink and essential toilet requirements. The hospital reported that 57 per cent of these chronically sick patients have shown either marked or moderate improvement.

Sleep deprivation is harmful It seems that sleep deprivation is a common cause of today's irritability, tension and chronic fatigue. One Ohio psychiatrist blames the invention of inexpensive electric lighting which has turned night into day. Our mental health was better, he argues, when we went to sleep when it grew dusk, and woke up refreshed at daybreak.

This view is shared by Dr Mangalore Pai, president of the Society for Sleep Research. People are healthier during power cuts, he claims, because they are then forced to retire to bed when darkness falls. For more than thirty years he has proclaimed 'that candlelight at night helps people to relax fully and promotes dreamless sleep.' This belief is now encapsulated in his Third Law of Sleep: 'The brighter the illumination, the fewer the hours spent in sleep.' Others incriminate the development of late night entertainment – discos, night clubs, television and all-night movies – which keep us out of our beds until the early hours of the morning. Urbanisation must also take its share of the blame. For many city dwellers it's impossible to get a refreshing night's rest with the constant cacophony of sleep-shattering traffic noise, wailing children, blaring radios and slamming lift gates. People go 'moonlighting', taking a second, evening job in order to make ends meet. Working mothers stay up late after their children have gone to bed in order to get a few moments time to themselves. Commuters find that if they retire early their lives become a ceaseless round of travel and work, with no leisure time between. So they make inroads into their night's repose, and provide less time for the essential process of recharging their body's inner batteries.

These 'sleep cheats' become irritable, tired and inefficient. By building up a chronic sleep debt they risk their health, happiness, marriages and jobs. Even their lives are at stake if they nod off to sleep while driving a car.

How much sleep do we need? But how much sleep do we actually need to keep at peak fitness? A cynical, but often accurate, reply to this question is ten minutes more. In fact people vary enormously in their sleep requirements. The majority need seven to eight hours repose, but a fortunate few, like Thomas Edison and Napoleon, can get by with only a few hours sleep a night. As the table below shows, nearly a quarter of the population are satisfied with less than six hours' sleep a night. So if you regularly wake refreshed after only five hours' sleep, don't label yourself an insomniac, that's probably all the sleep you need.

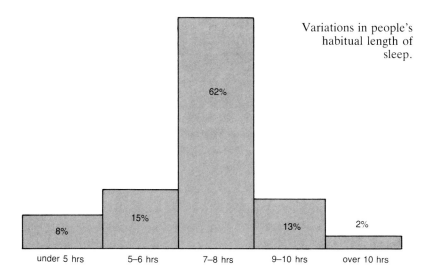

Variations in people's habitual length of sleep.

62%

15%

8%

13%

2%

under 5 hrs   5–6 hrs   7–8 hrs   9–10 hrs   over 10 hrs

If you're by nature a 'short sleeper' you can count yourself lucky. By saving two hours sleep a night you will have carved out 857 additional weeks between the time you attain your majority until the day you reach retirement age. As a short sleeper you're also more likely to be active and alert during the day. Personality tests carried out at the Sleep and Dream Laboratory of Boston State Hospital reveal that long sleepers tend to be worriers, who have to spend extra hours in bed to make up for the troubled nature of their sleep. If they can be helped to overcome their anxieties, by taking a course of psychoanalysis or transcendental meditation, they relax more and can often function effectively with an hour or two less sleep a night. Their problem was accurately analysed by Edison who said: 'The person who sleeps eight or ten hours a night is never fully asleep and never fully awake.'

According to the Boston researchers, the short sleepers they studied, who got an average of $5^1/_2$ hours sleep a night, were typically relaxed, active extroverts. As they reported in the *American Journal of Psychiatry*: 'The short sleepers as a group were efficient, energetic, ambitious persons who tended to work hard and to keep busy. They were relatively sure of themselves, socially adept, decisive and were satisfied with themselves and their lives.'

Only experience can tell you how much sleep you need. You've had enough rest if you wake *up* rather than *down*, feeling physically refreshed and mentally alert. Try and dispense with an alarm clock occasionally, and rely on nature to tell you when it's time to stir. Take an extra half-hour's sleep and see what difference it makes to your general demeanour. If you're tired at present, you'll almost certainly benefit from the extra rest.

A study of a group of Canadians over the age of sixty showed that subjects who got less than seven hours' sleep a night were more prone to suffer anxiety, tension and fatigue than those who normally slept longer. For a month these sleep cheats were encouraged to sleep an extra two hours a night. At the end of this time they all felt better, their complaints of tension, fatigue and anxiety lessened, and they discovered that with more sleep to sustain them, they were better able to cope with periods of abnormal stress and strain.

MAXIMISE THE BENEFIT OF A NIGHT'S REST
The following hints are designed to enable you to extract the maximum benefit from your night's rest. Follow this advice and you'll be able to spend less time in bed and yet still wake fresh and eager to start the day's activities.

★ *Don't take* Large-scale surveys in Britain and America reveal that between one-
sleeping pills quarter and a fifth of the population is regularly taking pills to induce sleep. This practice is fraught with danger. Tests show that the sedative effect of sleeping pills can last for up to eighteen hours. After a drugged sleep you're bound to wake up with a jaded, morning-after-the-night-

before feeling, which will last well into the following day. During this time your reaction times will be slowed and you're more likely to have an accident or a quarrel with your friends. In a nine-month trial, conducted by leading sleep researcher Professor Ian Oswald of Edinburgh University, seven out of twelve patients suffered a personal crisis while they were taking sleeping pills. One threatened to kill a relative, a second smashed her car and a third suffered fits of weeping and became unusually quarrel-some with her boss. No similar problems arose when they were switched to dummy pills.

Scientists have also found that people taking sleeping pills do not get their normal quota of dreams. This may contribute to their emotional distress by denying them the opportunity to solve their problems in their sleep and give vent to their pent-up feelings. If they stop taking the pills they often suffer several restless nights, broken by terrifying nightmares, as the body tries to catch up with its backlog of vital dream work. It is this withdrawal symptom more than anything else which drives people to ask for repeat prescriptions. So they become dependent on drugs which, although designed to buy them a measure of rest and chemical oblivion, are in fact destroying the quality of their sleep and making their days heavy with an artificially-induced lethargy.

Lively, energetic people never take sleeping pills. In fact it's difficult to see what use they have, for even patients in psychiatric hospitals can dispense with them, without ill effect, as was shown when a total embargo was placed on the use of sleeping pills at a newly-built psychiatric unit in Britain. Not one patient suffered from the removal of their sleep-inducing crutches.

★ *Avoid stimulants* Try to avoid caffeine-containing drinks for two hours before you retire to bed. These include tea, coffee and cola.

Smoking can also help to keep you awake despite the belief that a bedtime cigarette can be relaxing. This is because nicotine is a powerful stimulant, which increases the pulse rate and raises the level of cerebral arousal. When scientists at the Sleep Research and Treatment Center, Pennsylvania State University, compared the sleep patterns of 50 smokers and 50 non-smokers, they found that the smokers woke more frequently during the night and took an average of 14 minutes longer to fall asleep. When the nicotine addicts were persuaded to give up their cigarettes (they smoked an average of 25 a day) they immediately slept more soundly. Within the first three days they gained 34 minutes extra sleep a night, and experienced less trouble falling asleep.

★ *Take outdoor exercise* Most people know the difference between the healthy tiredness that comes after a day's ramble in the countryside, and the unhealthy fatigue that follows a mentally stressful day. The one leads to rapid, deep, refreshing sleep; the other to tense, fretful sleep. Although mental struggles are as tiring as strenuous physical activity, they affect us in a different way, making us too tired to sleep at night, and too exhausted to wake up in the morning.

If you've adopted the third step in the **Vitality Programme**, and begun to take a brisk walk every day, you will already be enjoying the reward of a sounder night's sleep. But don't make the mistake of exercising too late in the evening. Vigorous, competitive sports like tennis and squash are stimulants and can hamper sleep if they're taken at the end of the day.

Researchers at Downstate Medical Center in Brooklyn proved this when they tested ten college athletes. On some days these young sportsmen – swimmers, basketball players and track athletes – were told to take no exercise at all. On other days they were instructed to pursue their vigorous training schedules either in the afternoon or in the evening. When they took the exercise in the afternoons they recorded their longest periods of deep sleep. Their sleep was less sound when they worked-out in the evenings, and lightest of all when they took no exercise at all.

★ *Obey the body* Listen to the wisdom of the body. Our bodies serve us best when we listen to their inner promptings. When we're thirsty we should drink. When we're hungry we should eat. Equally well when we're tired we should rest. We are the only animal that tries to crowd all its sleep requirements into one brief period at the end of the day. Children and animals in their natural state know better. They will rush around at a hectic pace for a brief while, and then pause for either rest or sleep. We organise our rest according to the clock rather than by our inner needs. If it's 10.30 it's time for bed. When it's 7.30 it's time to wake up. But life cannot be programmed in this rigid fashion. Sometimes we may have had an exceptionally stressful day. Maybe we've had a domestic quarrel or are battling with a heavy cold. On these occasions we may need to heed the body's call to go to bed an hour or two early. At other times we may have had sufficient sleep by daybreak. Then we should listen to the body's own reveille calls, rather than waste time lingering in bed until the alarm rings.

It's significant that many of the world's most prolific workers have followed this principle and allowed their bodies to determine when they took their rest. Edison would work long irregular hours in his laboratory, then rest on his couch for three or four hours whenever he felt a wave of tiredness. When he was refreshed, he woke spontaneously, and promptly resumed his researches, irrespective of the time of day or night. Aristotle Onassis followed a similar pattern. His associates noted his immense vitality and his remarkable ability to harness and conserve his store of energy. His secret was that he would lie down fully dressed on the floor and take an hour or two of sleep whenever he felt tired. During this time it was impossible to rouse him. Then he would wake relaxed, refreshed and ready to resume the fray. As one of his biographers deduced: 'If he never kept regular hours, it was because his body had developed a personal clock that enabled him to ignore them.'

There is evidence that if we followed the example of the animal kingdom and rested whenever we felt the urge, we would lessen fatigue, enhance the efficiency of our work, and save an enormous amount of time that would otherwise be spent on unnecessary sleep, for the body recovers fairly quickly from mild fatigue, but takes a disproportionately long time to overcome the effects of profound fatigue. Sleep laboratory tests suggest that two three-hour periods of sleep can prove more refreshing than a single eight-hour spell.

Many may argue that owing to the nature of their work and family responsibilities, they haven't the freedom to sleep whenever the fancy takes them. Nevertheless we all have a certain degree of flexibility, and can benefit by paying closer heed to the body's warning signals to ease up and take a well-earned break whenever we feel the first signs of pending fatigue.

★ *Take catnaps* Many of the world's most prolific workers have used this technique to sustain their vitality. The Duke of Wellington, during the clamour of the Battle of Waterloo, could be found dozing behind a copy of the London *Sun*. President Kennedy would order five-minute breaks whenever staff conferences at the White House became deadlocked, and while others smoked or drank coffee he would rest his head on his desk and snooze.

You'll stave off fatigue if you cultivate the art of shutting your eyes and taking a brief doze whenever the mood takes you. This you should do, without thought to what onlookers may think, when you're travelling in a train, sitting in a theatre or watching TV. Every moment's sleep you record in this way will be deposited in your energy bank and will pay rich dividends.

Even the briefest of rest pauses can be invigorating. When we're tired the body automatically switches off and takes brief naps, or microsleeps, which last for anything from one to three seconds. During these lapses the eyelids droop, attention fades and the pulse rate drops, just as they do in real sleep. These spells of microsleep are the body's instinctive method of combating fatigue. They may not be noticed by bystanders, but can cause fatal accidents when they occur in airline pilots or motorway drivers.

The artist Salvador Dali made a fine art of microsleeping. When he felt tired he sat on a chair with a tin plate between his feet and a spoon in his hand. In this way he made sure he could take a second or two's microsleep without the risk of falling into a deep slumber, because the moment he dozed off he would be woken up by the clatter of the spoon slipping from his fingers onto the plate below. He claimed that he was completely refreshed by the sleep snatched in this way.

Another useful practice is to take a regular snooze after lunch. I do this every day, generally for no more than ten minutes, and feel completely reinvigorated as a result. Winston Churchill was another advocate of the afternoon siesta. As he once wrote, when explaining the secret of his war-time vitality:

'I have had daily recourse to a method of life which greatly extended my daily capacity for work. I always went to bed for at least one hour as early as possible in the afternoon . . . By this means I was able to press a day and a half's work into one.'

As you get older, and your nightly rest is more frequently punctuated by periods of wakefulness, you'll maintain your stamina more easily if you take greater avail of these daytime breaks. In one eight-week trial it was found that 40 per cent of twenty-year-olds took one or more daytime naps, compared with 80 per cent of people over seventy. If you want to keep working at peak efficiency, follow the example of Winston Churchill and take a post-prandial siesta, topped up from time to time with intermittent naps and Salvador Dali's microsleeps.

★ *Have a warm* Slowly sip a warm milk drink before retiring to bed. For generations the
milk drink natives of Kurdistan have followed a set routine before going to sleep. They have poured a cupful of curdled milk from a goatskin bag, drunk the milk, then laid down with their heads nestling on the soft, fur-lined bag and their faces pointing towards Mecca. They believe that this ritual ensures a sound night's sleep.

A similar pattern is followed by many Westerners, who succumb to the adman's pleas to end the day with a drink of malted milk. Psychologists suggest that milk appeals as a bedtime drink because it reminds us of the comfort and warmth we once enjoyed at our mother's breast. To support this theory they recall that during the war soldiers based overseas and in war zones consumed significantly more milk in their canteens than those enjoying the security of a posting closer to their homes.

But recent research shows that a milk nightcap, in addition to its emotional connotations, also helps to facilitate sleep physiologically. For some years it's been appreciated that it's unwise to eat a heavy meal last thing at night, since this leads to restless sleep. The old idea that eating cheese provokes nightmares can probably be explained along these lines, for after tucking into a rich and generous dinner topped off with a hunk of cheese you're more prone to wake up, and therefore more likely to remember any vivid dreams you might be having. So rich and heavy meals should not be taken late in the evening. Far better to observe the South American adage, mentioned earlier: 'Eat breakfast like a king; dinner like a princess and supper like a pauper.'

Equally it's a mistake to go to bed in a state of semi-starvation, for tests show that when the blood sugar level falls, sleep becomes increasingly disturbed. Just as a heavy meal increases the number of tosses and turns a sleeper makes, so a light meal of cornflakes and milk has been shown to produce more restful sleep. Perhaps the 300 calories in a half-pint of Horlicks is just enough nourishment to keep hunger pangs at bay and justify the manufacturer's slogan 'Horlicks guards against night starvation'. But there's more than this to malted milk drinks. In sleep laboratory trials at Edinburgh University a comparison was made between the effectiveness of three bedtime drinks. The first nightcap was a half-pint of Horlicks, the second a half-pint of plain, warm milk, and the third a half-pint of a drink which contained no dairy or cereal products but which exactly matched the Horlicks in calorie, protein and carbohydrate content. After volunteers took these beverages their sleep patterns were recorded. Results showed that Horlicks was a more effective sedative than either of the other drinks, from which the researchers concluded 'that not just calories are important for the beneficial effect of bedtime nutrition'. After taking Horlicks youngsters slept more restfully, and the sleep of the older adults was longer and less broken.

The mysterious X-factor which makes malted milk drinks such effective bedtime sedatives has now been identified. Trials at the University of Oklahoma Medical School suggest that their soporific effects can be attributed to their content of the essential amino acid (a building block of protein) tryptophan. For periods of days and weeks the Oklahoma researchers observed the brain wave patterns of sleeping subjects, both when they did, and when they did not, take a bedtime supplement of tryptophan. They found that after taking the tryptophan they fell asleep more rapidly, awoke less often during the night, and spent more time in deep sleep.

Obviously it was not just suggestion, or the face turned to Mecca, which gave the Kurds their restful nights. Milk really does have soothing properties, based partly on its amino acid content. You'll have a more refreshing night's sleep if half an hour before retiring to bed you take a malted milk nightcap, rich in tranquillising tryptophan.

★ *Follow a* We are all creatures of habit, and like Pavlov's dogs we can be trained to
ritual respond promptly and automatically to a frequently repeated conditioning stimulus. Pavlov taught his dogs to salivate whenever a bell was rung; we can similarly programme ourselves to fall asleep whenever an appropriate signal is given. The wise mother adheres to a regular routine when putting her children to bed: a warm bath, a milk drink, a bedtime story, a cuddly toy for comfort, the reassuring tucking in of the blankets and sheets, a brief prayer, then the final kiss on the forehead. Each step of this reassuring routine signals the switch from wakefulness to sleep. Just as a hypnotist trains his subjects to fall into a trance the moment the countdown from ten to one has been completed, so the child slips into a deeper and deeper state of relaxation with each passing phase of the bedtime ritual. When the countdown is over, oblivion descends with the snap of the hypnotist's fingers or the touch of the mother's lips.

Adults sometimes experience difficulty in dropping off to sleep, because they do not follow a set sleeping routine. They may take work or worries to bed with them from time to time. In their subconscious mind the bedroom then becomes a hive of activity rather than a haven of repose. One evening they have a late dinner and no bath, the next they'll have no meal and a scalding tub. In this way the body is given no consistent clues to indicate when sleep is due.

If you want to fall asleep quickly and easily, establish a regular bedtime routine, and train your body to accept it as an automatic call to sleep. If you're already grooved into a sure-fire sleeping ritual – sex, a book at bedtime, or ten minutes' standing on your head – stick with it. If not, start at once to create a routine which incorporates some at least of the following ingredients:

1 Take a milk nightcap half an hour before retiring to bed.
2 Soak away your accumulated tensions of the day in a warm bath.
3 After the bath take a brisk rub down. Ape the actions of a cat and have a good stretch.

★ *Switch off* For years scientists have tried to unearth the mystery of what makes us sleep. For some while they were convinced that the brain must become numbed by an accumulation of sleep-producing 'toxins'. But however hard they searched, they were unable to discover anything to support the existence of these fatiguing waste products. A far more plausible theory, accepted by many sleep researchers today, is that sleep is an animal's natural state. We become aroused from our slumbers only when we are driven by some urgent need to eat, mate or protect ourselves from outside threats. Without these external stimulants animals conserve energy by falling back into a resting state of somnolence. If this theory has even an element of truth in it, one aid to sleep is the reduction of sensory stimuli reaching the brain's 'wakefulness centre'. This means darkness, peace, quiet, a comfortable temperature, uncluttered clothing, an undistended bladder and a digestive system not overloaded with undigested food. The conditions within a bedroom should be as near as possible to those within a mother's womb – soft, soothing, warm, dark and quiet.

★ *Soothing* Abrupt, harsh, irregular stimuli cause increased arousal, whereas gentle, *stimuli* rhythmical stimuli have a sedative effect. The sudden blast of a whistle will wake you up; gentle music will lull you to sleep. A rough shake of the arm in the morning will rouse you from your slumbers; a gentle caressing of the forehead at night will soothe you to sleep. Mothers instinctively make use of these soothing stimuli to coax their infants to sleep, when they stroke their bodies, rock them in their arms and sing a gentle lullaby. Adults can use the same technique to woo the muse of sleep.

When you lie down in bed, adopt a comfortable position, and try and stay in it until you fall asleep. The more you toss and turn the more you'll keep yourself awake; for every movement you make causes a stream of messages to be sent to the brain to keep it informed of your position in space. Some of these messages will be routed to the 'wakefulness centre', where they will be interpreted as a call to action. Since the arms and legs are stirring the brain will assume that it's time to get the show on the road, rather than time to lower the curtains and douse the house lights.

If you still feel in an excited state and unprepared for sleep, indulge in a few moments' Lobe Stroking, an old technique for inducing sleep which recent laboratory tests have shown to have a definite physiological effect. When youngsters want to coax themselves to sleep they often put one thumb in their mouth and use their opposite hand to twiddle the lobe of their ear. It's not difficult to understand the psychological comfort they get from sucking their thumb; but have you ever wondered why they tickle their ear? The answer to that question is really quite intriguing. The skin around the external ear is supplied by the Alderman's nerve. This is a branch of the vastly important vagus nerve, which is a major component in the body's visceral nerve network. It is the vagus nerve which regulates the rate at which the heart beats and the force of its contraction. It also controls the secretion of gastric juices and the contraction of the muscles in the upper part of the digestive tract. Now in times past the aldermen of the City of London used to sit down to meals of gargantuan size in the dining rooms of their livery companies. If their appetites got jaded after the fourth or fifth courses and they couldn't face the roast duck which followed, they discovered that they could often tickle their palates and stimulate the flow of digestive juices by putting a finger in their ear and gently vibrating it from side to side. This is how the Alderman's nerve got its unusual name.

Indian Brahmins have a somewhat similar custom of even greater antiquity. Before they go to the lavatory to defecate they wind a sacred thread round their ear. This probably sets up a reflex which favours evacuation by stimulating the contraction of the bowels. Learning of this strange rite a team of London doctors, led by Dr S. R. Saxena of the Queen Elizabeth Hospital for Children, studied the physiological changes which take place when the Alderman's nerve is stimulated. They squeezed the ear lobes of volunteers ranging in age from nonogenarians to babes in arms, and found that this simple manoeuvre slowed the pulse rate and produced a profound drop in the force of the heart's beat.

The instructions for Lobe Stroking are simple: grasp the lobe of the ear firmly and slowly roll the opposing surfaces between your thumb and forefinger. Do this for two or three minutes, or until you fall asleep.

★ *Auto-suggestion* It's a mistake to think that people who fall asleep are necessarily relaxed. Many remain very tense during the night and as a result wake in the morning feeling fragile, frayed and fretful. Some grind their teeth while they sleep; others kick and thrash their arms and legs as if they were escapologists freeing themselves from a tightly-bound strait jacket.

To ensure a sound, refreshing night's sleep, make sure that your last waking thoughts are restful. Hypnotists know the power of the imagination. They induce a deep, trance-like state by conjuring up pictures of heaviness and warmth. You can achieve the same state of total surrender by employing the powers of auto-suggestion. As the last stage in your bedtime ritual whisper suitable messages to your subconscious mind.

Silently repeat to yourself, while breathing in a low and rhythmic fashion, phrases such as:

My eyelids are growing as heavy as lead
Nothing disturbs me – I am at peace with the world
My arms and legs are heavy and relaxed
I am completely at rest – completely relaxed
A feeling of gentle warmth is flowing through my entire body
I am falling into a deep, relaxed, refreshing sleep

If this method doesn't work, try taking a fantasy trip. It's impossible to make your mind a blank. So if you find yourself lying awake wondering how you're going to raise enough money to finance a house extension don't try and force your brain into neutral. It won't work. Endeavour instead to focus your attention on something relaxing. Take a trip down memory lane and try to retrace a favourite walk or an enjoyable seaside holiday. Imagine you're a baby in a pram being gently rocked to sleep. Try and engage all your senses on this soothing activity. If you're recapturing the tranquillity of a country picnic, listen to the trilling of the skylarks, feel the touch of the sun on your cheek and the wind in your hair, smell the scent of the flowers and revel in the colours of the pastoral scene. You'll enjoy the time you spend in this way and after a few moments' quiet reflection you'll probably find you will drop off into a deep, refreshing sleep.

★ *Accept* **Fear of the effects of sleeplessness is one of the major causes of insomnia**
wakefulness As people age they're bound to have the occasional periods of wakefulness during the night. Surveys reveal that periods of nocturnal wakefulness become more common as people grow older. One study showed that 45 year-olds wake on average three times during the night. This is because they have fewer periods of deep sleep than they did in their youth. These bouts of sleeplessness are natural and harmless. When the body needs sleep it will take it, if not during the night then at least during the day, as catnaps or brief snatches of microsleep. Canadian student Cindy Nicholas failed in her attempt to swim three ways non-stop across the English Channel, and was pulled out of the water on her final leg because she kept falling asleep. Now if the body can switch off while thrashing through the icy waters off the coast of Dover, there's no need to fear that it will not take whatever sleep it needs while sitting in the comfort of a fireside chair or lying in the warmth of a cosy bed!

Some people suffer from pseudo-insomnia. Perhaps they're natural short sleepers. Maybe they need no more than six hours sleep to restore their flagging energies. Yet if they do not sleep for the regulation eight hours they'll imagine themselves to be chronic insomniacs. Old stagers will nod off in their chairs during the day, and go to bed early out of boredom rather than need. When they wake in the wee hours of the morning they've probably had their sleep out, yet they trail along to their doctors to get a prescription for their sleeplessness. Going to bed too early, and expecting to sleep too long, are common causes of pseudo-insomnia.

Other people suffer from phobic insomnia. They wake in the night and immediately start to panic. If they don't fall asleep quickly they're sure they won't be fit to cope with the pressures of the day ahead. So they worry. And the more anxious they feel the wider awake they become. On these occasions sleep is like an unruly puppy, the harder you chase it the more it eludes you. The worrying also tends to spread. Once you've established an anxious frame of mind, you'll find problems all around you. To begin with you may worry about lying awake, the next you'll be fretting about your digestion, the parlous state of your bank account, the threat of nuclear war, the problems at the office or the way you're going to tell your visiting mother-in-law that this time she really has overstayed her welcome. Worrying at night is rarely productive. As Lord Wilson once said when he was Prime Minister: 'If the problem that is keeping you awake is not soluble at 9 am, it is certainly not soluble at 3 am, when you are feverish, neurotic, half asleep and just plain daft.'

★ *Brain Games* Another popular way of wooing sleep is to embark on any activity which requires prolonged mental concentration. Some try to find a place name or flower for every letter of the alphabet; others set out to count the number of 'a's and then 'b's and 'c's in the Lord's Prayer.

If you fancy this method you could try James Thurber's remedy. He spent the 'White watches of the woeful night' spelling words backwards, like 'gnip-gnop' for 'ping-pong'. If your mind runs along visual rather than literary lines, you'll probably have more success with the Jack Benny cure. He overcame spells of wakefulness by imagining that he was painting an enormous figure '3' on a large barn door, using only a tiny brush so that he had to make hundreds of tiny strokes to complete the figure.

★ *Contrary thought* Such is the nature of human cussedness that it's often easier to overcome bouts of insomnia by trying to stay awake than by struggling to fall asleep. In Germany, patients with sleep problems have been advised to lie in bed and try to keep their eyes open as long as possible. Tests show that this practice tires the eyes and evokes the lid-closing reflex, which is the normal precursor of sleep.

One insomniac, when sleep eludes him, tells himself frankly, 'I am not allowed to sleep for another hour. I *must* stay awake.' This contrary suggestion has him quickly nodding off to sleep. Another problem sleeper lies in the most uncomfortable position he can find and holds it as long as possible. 'When you can't sleep in a comfortable position, try getting into an uncomfortable position, lying flat on your face,' he recommends. 'After a few moments of misery, turn over and enjoy the relief of being comfortable again.'

If these tips fail to coax the muse of sleep, lie back and relax in the sure knowledge that if you give your body the opportunity it will snatch the rest it needs, if not tonight then at least tomorrow.

Vitality Programme – Step Ten Sleep as and when your body dictates – take catnaps or have an afternoon siesta. Follow a relaxing routine before you go to bed and if you still can't sleep stay relaxed and don't worry.

STEP 11

The Art of Relaxation

Tension is a symptom of our age. From the moment we are born we are under pressure. In order to meet the goals which society sets for us we are urged to compete, often in conflict with our family and friends. Schoolchildren are given the target of examination success and in their end-of-term reports are goaded to 'try harder'. Young executives are encouraged to dedicate their bodies to the work ethic, and sell their souls to their companies in exchange for the trappings of corporate power and an annual hike in salary. Newly-weds are set the goal of creating a magpie's love nest filled with technological baubles – deep freeze, stereo, home computer, power tools, video recorder and double garage. With one eye on their status in the community aspiring adults join the best clubs and patronise the right friends in a never-ending game of social snakes and ladders.

But the constant struggle for status, success and material prosperity is tiring, and often counter-productive. Many people try *too* hard to achieve their chosen goals. The moment tension and fatigue sets in, efficiency falters. Henry Ford drove his workers relentlessly to get his beloved Tin Lizzie into production, but afterwards he was forced to admit: 'We would have had our Model A car in production six months sooner if I had forbidden my engineers to work on Sunday. It took us all week to straighten out the mistakes they made on the day they should have rested.'

Sometimes we would do well to adopt the oriental philosophy of non-striving. Often our use of excessive effort is self defeating. The over-eager golfer slices his drive or misses his putt. The over-zealous tennis player serves a double fault. The out-of-work actor, desperate for a part, dries up during his audition or stumbles ineptly through his lines. The examination candidate, fighting for a first-class grading, suffers a paralysing attack of nerves the moment she glances at the examination paper.

To try *too* hard in these situations is often as damaging as to try too little. Professor Jerome Bruner of Harvard University proved this in an ingenious laboratory experiment. He gave two groups of rats a complicated maze puzzle to solve in order to reach a supply of food, and found that whereas mildly hungry rats solved the puzzle in about six tries, those who hadn't eaten for thirty-six hours, in their over-eagerness to satisfy their hunger, took more than twenty tries.

'Don't push the river, let it flow'

Occasionally we should check the endless struggle for self-betterment, and adopt the counsel of the Taoist philosopher Lao Tze: 'Don't push the river, let it flow.' Even the simplest of everyday activities should be performed with minimum effort and strain. Why do we furrow our brows when we try to think, since tension of the facial muscles cannot improve our concentration one iota? Why do we poke out our tongues when we try to thread a needle, screw up our eyes when we look at a picture or silently mouth the words we read in a book? These nervous grimaces are all symptoms of the over-exertion syndrome. If continued throughout the day these muscular irrelevancies cause needless tension and fatigue, they make our movements clumsy, and they hamper the speed and accuracy of our performance. If you analyse the movements of a skilled craftsman or top-class athlete you will find that they observe the law of minimum effort. Even when they are exerting themselves to the full they move smoothly and effortlessly. They waste no energy on superfluous movements, and keep their bodies totally relaxed until there is a call for purposeful activity.

Muscle control and relaxation Relaxation is the secret of efficient movement. Every muscle in the body is paired with an opposite number which serves the reverse function: the biceps muscle bends the elbow, the triceps straightens it; the quadriceps muscles flex the knee, the hamstrings extend it. Always there are prime movers which instigate a movement, and antagonists which must be relaxed to permit the movement to take place. Even the burliest weightlifter would be as ineffectual as a teenage stripling if he contracted both his biceps and triceps muscles while trying to hoist a barbell overhead, for in doing so he would be setting up a state of civil war in which one muscle group was counteracting the force of another. In the same way a sprinter would be literally hamstrung if he tried to straighten his knee while he was at the same time forcefully contracting his knee flexors.

Many people go through life like hamstrung runners or muscle-bound weightlifters, goading themselves with one foot on the accelerator and the other on the brake. To work with economy, grace and minimum risk of strain it's vital to relax every muscle in the body except those which are essential to the task in hand. As there are about 650 muscles in the body it would be impossible to carry out a thorough check list to ensure that every one was properly relaxed each time you move, or when you turn the next page of this book. Fortunately this is not necessary. There are certain key areas which are symptomatic of the over-exertion syndrome. Relax these regions and you can be fairly sure that the rest of your body will follow suit.

Relaxing key sites The tension control centres are the forehead and eyes, the jaw and the hands. If you're aware of being under tension, concentrate on relaxing the muscles in these key sites. Smooth your brow, unclench your eyes, uncurl your hands and slightly part your teeth and let your tongue rest limply against the lower jaw. Ease the strain from these tension control zones and the rest of your body will unwind in unison. Use the same technique when you're performing a strenuous job, or trying to complete a difficult intellectual task. Sprinters are trained to relax their hands and jaws whenever they feel themselves seizing up towards the finish of a race. You'll be less tired at the end of the daily rat race and less prone to backache and tension headaches, if you practise the same trick whenever you feel yourself tensing up.

We are a success-oriented society. But it's not only excessive striving which keeps us tense. We're also trained in childhood to keep a tight rein on our emotions. Inscrutable countenances and impassive postures can only be achieved by sustained muscular tension. We're taught to keep poker faces and stiff upper lips to hide any show of our true emotional feelings. We hold ourselves in muscular straitjackets, which prevent us experiencing or expressing strong emotions. We tense our abdominal muscles to choke back tears, freeze the muscles of our thighs to stop our legs from breaking into panic-stricken flight, and clench our jaws to keep our teeth from chattering.

Freud realised that one of our major driving forces was the relief of tension and the achievement of a blissful state of contented relaxation. When babies are hungry they become fretful and agitated. Once they are fed they snuggle contentedly against their mothers' breasts. Lovers may writhe and struggle in their urge to satisfy their sexual longings, but in the moment of orgasm they find both relief of tension and emotional fulfilment.

Relaxation brings its own reward. Its benefits are increased happiness, enhanced stamina and greater freedom from tension ailments. When we're tense we tend to overreact to irritating stimuli. We jump when the telephone rings, shout at the children when they accidentally overturn a cup of water, and blow our top when the telephone number we're dialling is constantly engaged. Learning to relax helps to check these exhausting outbursts and gives us better control over our emotions.

Teaching *relaxation* In 1954 a group of Iowa doctors and business leaders set up the Foundation for Scientific Relaxation to teach the scientific control of nervous and muscular tension. One of their first targets was local college students many of whom, under the pressures of their academic careers, were showing the telltale signs of stress – anxiety, fatigue, irritability, insomnia and inability to concentrate. With the aid of a neurovoltmeter, capable of registering muscular contractions in millionths of a volt, they measured the students' resting tension levels. They then gave them a course of eight weekly lessons in relaxation. During these sessions the youngsters sat in chairs and were systematically taught how to relax the various regions of their body – head, neck, shoulders, arms, hands, trunk, legs and feet. At the end of the two months' training they were re-tested when it was found that their average resting level of tension had dropped by 30 per cent. They discovered that by learning to relax they could conserve energy and avoid subjecting their bodies to needless wear and tear. Many reported that they slept better, had more energy and were better able to maintain their hectic work schedules. Athletes noticed improved endurance or speed in track events. A teacher of secretarial studies discovered that students who learnt to relax mastered the typewriter more quickly. A voice coach who took the training observed with delight that her throat was more relaxed than ever before. An experienced drummer found that he could drum faster after the relaxation lessons, which helped him to spot and eliminate unnecessary tensions in his arm. The benefits were many and varied. As Arthur Steinhaus, then professor of physiology at the State University of Iowa, said when reviewing the results of the study: 'From our experience with students at the college level and other young people we can report the following kinds of benefits: ability to fall asleep much more quickly, ability to do more work with less sleep, less nail biting, reduction in smoking, loss in body weight where there had been frequent "snacking" due to tension, greater power of concentration, and a happier outlook on life.'

Many other attempts have been made to help people overcome the tensions inherent in contemporary Western society. The Maharishi Mahesh Yogi encouraged thousands to take up Transcendental Meditation, a method of stilling the mind and relaxing the body which carries widespread physiological benefits. Dr Herbert Benson, Associate Professor of Medicine at Harvard University Medical School, popularised a method of relaxation which combines the sedative effects of controlled breathing and the repeated intonation of the word 'one'.

The Norfolk relaxation method I have been teaching people to relax for 30 years. During this time my understanding of the techniques of relaxation have been slowly expanding, and step by step my training techniques have been gradually refined. The method which I favour today, and which I am now going to describe in full for the first time, is easy to follow, quick to perform, and admirably suited for use by people caught up in the Western whirl. It incorporates four separate relaxation principles: postural repose, controlled respiration, imagery, and mental focus. Other relaxation techniques have incorporated one or more of these basic principles; but none before has embraced all four.

The control of breathing is fundamental to the relief of tension states. When we're anxious and overwrought our breathing becomes increasingly rapid and shallow. This can produce changes in the chemistry of the blood, as was explained earlier, and cause palpitations, muscle tensions, and feelings of heightened anxiety or even panic. These are the recognised symptoms of the Hyperventilation Syndrome and serve to accentuate the tension state. Fatigue sets in because of the inadequate oxygenation of the blood and the increased level of muscular activity. On the other hand when we relax, we breathe more slowly and deeply, and this has a sedative effect. By consciously switching to a relaxed pattern of breathing our entire body heaves a sigh of relief, muscles relax, the pulse rate drops, and oxygen consumption falls.

For centuries students of yoga have been trained to overcome tension by breathing slowly, deeply and gently. The object, according to the *Yoga Sutras*, is to make the breathing 'become lengthy and fine'. This induces a calm state of body and a tranquil frame of mind. When we're emotionally roused our cadence of breathing alters. The fearful hold their breath, the agitated pant and the amorous start to sigh like furnaces. These changes, as psychologist William James pointed out, are both the symptoms and the substance of the emotions we experience. When we're under stress we pant, and it's the panting (in company with the palpitations and churning stomach) which makes us aware that we are in fact in an agitated state. If we can control the breathing we deprive the brain of the panic signals which it interprets as anxiety. *Pranayama* (breath control) is the secret of the yogis' remarkable ability to master their moods, and to remain calm and composed when all around them is in a state of turmoil. It may be pure coincidence, but it does seem remarkable that slow breathing animals are generally less excitable than fast breathing ones, and also tend to live longer. For instance the short-lived, flappable hen breathes about 30 times a minute. The longer lived, less perturbable dog about 28 times, and the ponderous tortoise, a veritable Methuselah among animals, about three.

Tests reveal that tension can be controlled by merely focusing on breathing sounds. In one experiment 95 nursing students were given a psychological test to determine their general level of anxiety. They were then trained to lie back limply on a bed and relax while listening to their amplified breathing sounds. As they did so their muscular tensions eased and their breathing became smoother and more rhythmical without conscious effort on their part. Later they re-took the psychological test, which revealed a significant reduction in their level of anxiety. These discoveries have led me now to use a simplified form of breath control when teaching relaxation.

I also find it valuable to make full use of the imagination when coaxing subjects to relax. It was Emil Coué, the father of auto-suggestion, who first demonstrated the enormous power of the subconscious mind. Whenever there is a battle between the imagination and the will, he said, the imagination always wins. Depending on the way we control our subconscious minds, we can think ourselves sick or think ourselves well. With our imagination we can make ourselves strong or weak, successes or failures, tense or relaxed. In this way we are the architects of our moods and the sculptors of our destinies.

At the beginning of the 1920s a German physician, Dr J. H. Schultz, developed a technique of relaxation known as Autogenic Training. This made full use of imagery to control the level of bodily tension. He noted that hypnotists coaxed their subjects to enter a state of profound relaxation by giving them suggestions which triggered off a conditioned response. As we relax or fall asleep our eyelids droop, our breathing becomes slower, our superficial blood vessels relax giving a feeling of pervasive warmth, and our muscle tone falls which makes our limbs feel heavy and limp. These bodily sensations are associated so closely with the process of relaxation that they can be used to trigger off a conditioned response, just as circus elephants can be trained to stand on their hind legs at the crack of the ringmaster's whip. Schultz found that relaxation could be induced by auto-suggestion, by reciting key phrases and words which elicit the relaxation response: 'My eyelids feel heavy as lead . . . my breathing is becoming slower and calmer . . . my arms and legs are heavy and limp . . . a feeling of delicious warmth is spreading throughout my entire body.'

Similar phrases can be used to encourage a state of mental repose or cosmic consciousness. Religious mystics have chanted sentences which help to create a feeling of 'oneness', a glorious merging of the self with the infinite. Hindus when they meditate recite mantra, words which generally refer to some aspect of the godhead. The commonest of these mantra is the single syllable 'Om', which represents God in all his fullness and power.

Words are symbols, and whether used as curses, prayers or oaths can undoubtedly influence our moods for good or ill. Students of Transcendental Meditation are trained to relax by repeating a personal mantra, which is normally polysyllabic and invariably meaningless. The repetition of these nonsense syllables may be soothing, but makes no use of the emotive power of words to condition our mood or regulate our bodily state.

With ample justification Swiss psychiatrist Paul Dubois speaks of the 'therapy of words'. When people are anxious or tense, he says, they should sedate themselves by repeating potent words like *tranquillity*, *serenity* or *peace*. Others have found relaxation by reciting poetry or reading the Twenty-Third psalm. John Stuart Mill, the great nineteenth-century reformer, found relief from tension by reading the Nature poets. He claimed that Wordsworth's poems in particular were 'a medicine for my state of mind . . . and I felt myself at once better and happier as I came under their influence.'

When meditating it's also important to establish a focus of mental concentration. We can never make our minds a blank, and unless we concentrate our attention on something suitably restful we can be sure that our brains will resume their normal worrying activities. Teachers of purely physical methods of relaxation frequently come up against this snag. They coax their students to forego the tensions in their muscles, but although their bodies are switched off their minds remain free to wrestle with the normal range of day to day vexations and despairs. Some gurus get round this problem by meditating while gazing at a flower or candle flame. Muslims during their devotions focus their attention on the worry beads in their *mispa*, each one of which stands for one of the 99 Koranic names of God. Catholics tell a rosary. In other religious practices, the attention is focused on a geometric pattern or symbolic shape. Christian mystics concentrate their thoughts on the cross, while yogis of Tantric Hinduism or Tantric Buddhism limit their field of attention by gazing fixedly at an intricate geometric pattern known as a *mandala*. This is the method of concentration which, when suitably modified, is most apt for

Westerners. It forms the basis and unifying core of my four-part approach to relaxation training.

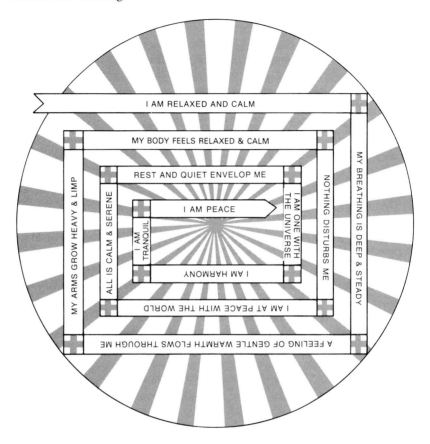

The Norfolk Mandala Relaxation is simplicity itself with the Norfolk Mandala. The instructions are these:

★ Postural repose. Choose a quiet room where you are unlikely to be disturbed. Sit in a relaxed position in a chair with the mandala resting on a table in front of you.

★ Controlled breathing. Breathe slowly and deeply. Every time you arrive at a star, while tracing the course of the mandala, focus your attention on your breathing. Take a single, deep, easy inspiration until your lungs are full; then breathe out slowly and steadily until you have expelled the last possible drop of air from your lungs.

★ Mental imagery and focus. Imagine that with each expiration you are dissipating a little more tension from your body, like a hot air balloon slowly collapsing to the ground. To increase your concentration, and focus your attention on the respiratory rhythm, note the flaring of the nostrils as you breathe in, and the slight increase in temperature of the air as you breathe out.

As you slowly recite each phrase of the mandala, either silently or as a quiet, soothing incantation, make sure that you exert the maximum influence over your subconscious mind by employing the full powers of your imagination. Really feel the warmth flowing through your body and genuinely experience the heaviness of your limbs as they sink against the chair. And as you draw to the close of the sequence of phrases, try to feel your body merging into the universe around you, and truly enjoy the feeling of tranquillity and peace which those words signify in your mind.

To rush these exercises is as futile as to hurry unthinkingly through the Lord's Prayer. Make each phrase tell. Focus your attention on it until it evokes the desired conditioned response. Only then should you rotate the mandala and progress to the next phrase, after performing a deep, relaxing breath.

Carry out these exercises for fifteen minutes a day or whenever you feel the need to relax. Some people will prefer to do them in the morning when they are fresh, others will find them more effective at night, to help them relax at the end of the day. Some will find they need to go through the cycle of the mandala only once at a time, others will derive more benefit by repeating the complete cycle three or more times at a sitting. All will discover that the more they perform the exercises, the more effective they become. Eventually even the sight of the mandala will be enough to trigger off a conditioned relaxation response.

Vitality Programme – Step Eleven Fatigue can be caused by excessive tension. Overcome this by learning to relax muscles not actively in use, by breathing properly and by using the Norfolk Mandala to help you to establish a conditioned relaxation response.

STEP 12

Natural Break

One of the most remarkable properties of the human body is its amazing ability to maintain a constant internal state despite widespread variations in its external environment. We can move from the tropics to the Arctic Circle with no change in our body temperature. We can feast or fast and generally suffer no dramatic fluctuation in the level of sugar in our blood. We can lie in bed or chase for a bus with no alarming alteration in our blood pressure.

The body's facility to maintain a constant internal state is known as homeostasis, a term which is derived from two Greek words, *homoios* meaning 'like', and *stasis* meaning 'state'. Homeostatic mechanisms regulate all the major activities of the body, and serve an essential protective function. We cannot damage our lungs by overinflation because there is a built-in mechanism which checks inspiration once a certain degree of lung distension has been reached. We don't rupture a blood vessel when we run up a hill because an early warning system detects the initial rise in blood pressure and opens up more of the blood system so that the pressure within the arteries does not exceed the danger level. Other homeostatic systems control the acidity of the blood, the calcium content of the bones and the blood flow to the brain. Why is there no similar mechanism to protect the neuromuscular system from the effect of excessive stress, strain and overuse?

The answer to that conundrum is quite simple. The body does, in fact, have a defence against overexertion. It's called rest. Unfortunately we also have the ability to override the body's call for rest and ignore the warning symptoms of fatigue which should encourage us to ease up. We can keep alert when we should be sleeping; or maintain a high level of physical activity when we should be putting our feet up and resting. In this way we can push ourselves to the point of complete exhaustion if we choose.

But we can't easily abuse our hearts, which are object lessons in the art of working with efficiency and ease. From the moment we're born to the moment we die our hearts are in constant action, beating 2,500,000,000 times during an average lifetime. Each day this tiny muscular pump, no larger than a fist and weighing less than a pound, pumps 2,000 gallons of blood. It does so incessantly and tirelessly. How? Because it observes a strict work-rest cycle. After each contraction the heart takes an enforced period of rest. The contractions do the dramatic work of driving blood around the vast arterial tree, but the rest pauses perform the hidden, but life-saving task of enabling the heart muscle to recover from its exertions.

Without the rests the heart muscle would quickly become exhausted, and heart failure, and eventually death, would follow.

Patterns of relaxation

Similar cycles can be observed in operation elsewhere in the body. When we stand, the powerful muscles of the back contract to balance the weight of the trunk over the legs. Fatigue would soon set in unless the muscle fibres had an occasional chance to rest. If all relaxed at once we would collapse in a heap on the floor. So the body organises things in such a way that groups of fibres work in alternating shifts, some resting while the others contract. Just like a team of navvies digging a hole in the road, some swinging their picks while others relax, they maintain a steady work output with minimum risk of fatigue.

Babies do the same thing when they suck at their mothers' breasts. Studies reveal that breast feeding is organised according to a regular burst-pause pattern; the baby drawing on the nipple for bursts of five to 20 sucks after which it takes a rest break of four to 15 seconds. In this way it can suckle for minutes at a time with little sign of tiredness.

This activity-rest cycle represents the biological rhythm of work, which animals observe quite naturally. A dog will chase a ball vigorously for several minutes and then lie panting on the floor to rest and recover. The same happens with children. One minute they may be chasing a puppy under and over the furniture, the next they're curled up on the sofa fast asleep.

'Four-fifths of all our troubles in this life would disappear if we would only sit down and keep still.'

But Western adults, brought up under the influence of the Protestant work ethic, have been trained to believe that idleness is a crime. Satan will find work for idle hands to do, they were warned as children. As a result in their maturity they'll often engage in any form of activity rather than give in to the urge to rest, which they regard at best as laziness, and at worst as downright sinful. How much better the example of President Calvin Coolidge, the Vermont farmer's son, who instead of boasting of his prodigious work output admitted that his favourite occupation was doing nothing. He always went to bed early, took several naps a day during his stay at the White House, and once told an agitated senator 'Four-fifths of all our troubles in this life would disappear if we would only sit down and keep still.' Coolidge knew the art of relaxation and the secret of re-creational repose. His calmness and composure enhanced his leadership qualities, and in 1924 he was comfortably re-elected under the slogan 'Keep Cool with Coolidge'.

Lesser men than Coolidge often overfill their day with work in their struggle for success. When they do so, their efficiency declines, and with it their happiness and health. Throughout time, sages and prophets have extolled the virtues of rest. As Henry Thoreau observed: 'A really efficient labourer will be found not to crowd his day with work.' This principle was observed by Jesus Christ, who during his brief but arduous ministry set aside regular periods for meditation, rest and prayer. And when he found his disciples showing signs of fatigue he immediately advised them to ease up. 'Come ye apart yourselves into a desert place,' he said, 'and rest awhile.'

The exhortations of the wise men of the past have recently been confirmed by clinical observation. Scouts have found that the quickest and most economical way to cover long distances is by alternately running a mile and then walking a mile. Athletes now pursue 'interval training', a method of conditioning which involves alternate spells of all-out running interspersed with short recovery spells of relaxed jogging, since they find that this is the most effective way of building up their stamina and strength.

Laboratory experiments corroborate the results of this practical experience. In Sweden a group of fit men were given an hour in which to perform thirty minutes set work on a cycle trainer. Some worked flat out for thirty minutes, then rested for the remainder of the hour. Others worked for shorter intervals and took more frequent breaks. When the results were analysed, it was found that the most economical way of performing the task was to divide the hour into half-minute intervals; thirty seconds to be spent cycling, the following thirty seconds to be spent in rest. This produced the smallest consumption of oxygen, the lowest elevation of pulse rate, and the least accumulation of the fatigue-producing waste products of muscle metabolism, such as lactic acid. The levels of lactic acid in the blood proved to be seven-and-a-half times higher when working flat out, than when resting every minute, yet no more work was performed! The heart also had an easier time when more frequent rest breaks were taken. When the half-hour stint of cycling was performed non-stop, the pulse rate soared to 204 beats a minute. When the pedalling was done in half-minute bursts the rate rose to only 150.

Organising rest periods When left to their own devices most manual workers instinctively organise their day's activities so that they have regular periods for rest. The old-style family gardener is accustomed to leaning on his shovel from time to time to mop his brow or admire his work. Factory workers also know the value of a 'breather', even if it's merely a short pause to unwrap a sweet, light a cigarette or take a frivolous trip to the lavatory. When a team of physiologists studied the work patterns of a group of factory workers in Dortmund, West Germany they found that the men took rest pauses whenever they were needed but concealed them from their foremen by indulging in some form of masking activity, such as idly polishing their machines. In one factory it was found that these unauthorised breaks took up 11 per cent of the working day. Since there was no way in which they could be curbed, the firm decided to accept them as inevitable and made the bold experiment of introducing official rest pauses of five minutes at the end of every hour's work. Once this scheme was instigated the hidden breaks disappeared, fatigue was lessened, and production rose by 13 per cent. Many companies now recognise the physiological importance of the work-rest cycle, and schedule rest breaks for their production line workers at set intervals during the day. The more frequent these breaks, the more effective they are. One Japanese transistor manufacturer has instigated 30-second yawn breaks, to help their employees relax and stretch their tense muscles. Several times each shift a signal is given and the women assemblers step back from the production line, raise their arms above their heads and yawn in unison. According to the manufacturer, these brief moments of respite have led to an appreciable increase in production.

If your day's work is making you tired – whether you're a housewife, shop assistant, factory worker or business executive – try to find more time for rest. Pace yourself. Take a break before you tire. Many people who have adopted aerobic exercise programmes have been disappointed to find that instead of feeling fresher for their strenuous work-outs, they seem more exhausted than ever before. The reason is that they are often pushing themselves *too* hard. Executives who jog for six mornings a week sometimes tell me that they still feel jaded and out of sorts. 'You're overdoing it,' I tell them, 'You're giving your body no time to recover. Run only on alternate days, and have a rest day in between.' When they follow this work-rest regime they save themselves time, effort and disappointment and feel infinitely better.

What's the point of wasting energy getting fit, if you never arrive at the point when you actually *feel* fit?

Exercising too hard will make you tired Many athletes struggle so hard to achieve world-class status that they keep themselves in a state of permanent exhaustion. As Olympic athlete Brendan Foster confessed: 'The trouble with distance running is that you're always tired, and the higher you aim the more tired you are.' This exhausting drive to the top can play havoc with their personal relationships by making them irritable, lethargic and dull. Duncan Goodhew, Britain's gold-medal Olympic swimmer, experienced this problem. 'Swimmers live such a horrible one-track life, and they're so bloody bad-tempered all the time that the only people who will put up with them are other swimmers,' he admitted. 'I had a girl friend once who wasn't a swimmer and who, at the time, I was very serious about. You know, she had so much energy and enthusiasm, but I felt so exhausted all the time I just wanted to go to bed and sleep.'

To make such sacrifices may be justifiable if you're seeking the ultimate in sporting success, but it's pointless to exercise to the point of exhaustion if all you want is happiness, health and youthful vitality. The **Vitality Programme** is designed to give you these rewards, with none of the privations and pains of overzealous exercise routines. Why punish yourself with aching limbs, blistered feet and bursting lungs if it's not absolutely necessary? The religious ascetics believed that salvation could only be achieved through suffering, but why perpetuate the myth? Life is too short for needless fasting and self-mortification. Treat your body gently, and it will deal more kindly with you.

Occasional
idleness is
necessary

Occasional periods of idleness are a physiological necessity, not an indolent luxury. Rest is essential for the wellbeing of both body and mind. This becomes increasingly so with the passage of time. I don't like my elderly patients to use their age as an excuse for giving up their interest in the game of life. They must play on until the final whistle; but I do urge them to pace themselves and avoid becoming overtired. At eighteen we can go out to a series of late-night parties, grow tired and recover with a single good night's sleep. At eighty it may well take several days to recover from the same weariness. Many of the symptoms attributed to age – weakness, fatigue, forgetfulness and lack of concentration – are in fact the side effects of chronic exhaustion.

Psychologists find that elderly people do not perform as well as youngsters on batteries of mental tests. Set them down for a morning of word fluency quizzes, reasoning tests and multiplication sums and they will generally score less well than their juniors. This has been attributed in the past to a natural decline in their mental faculties, but recent experiments suggest that their inferior performance may be closely linked to the onset of fatigue. When their minds are fresh they can function as nimbly as ever. In Florida, a group of 80 members of the American Association of Retired Persons – ranging in ages from 57 to 91 years – were given a series of mental tests which sometimes lasted for two-and-a-half hours. If they grew tired their performance faltered, but if they were given a ten-minute break between the tests they showed little or no decline in their mental acuity.

Short escapes

Short rests can also help us recover from periods of unrelenting stress. Just as soldiers need to be taken away from the front line occasionally to avoid the build up of battle fatigue, so we need to escape from time to time from the incessant hurly-burly of contemporary life.

Two psychologists from Cornell University carried out experiments with a flock of sheep. They subjected some of the sheep to stress, which took the form of an electric shock administered after the ringing of a warning bell. If they repeated this stimulus often enough the sheep showed signs of nervous fatigue, they stopped eating and following the rest of the flock, lay down apathetically and eventually showed signs of distressed breathing. At this point the experiment had to be brought to an end or the sheep would have died. But the experimenters made one important discovery. They found that if the sheep were given a minimum of two hours' respite from stress per day they would not show signs of mental breakdown. This brief rest was just long enough to enable their nervous systems to recover from the pounding they had received.

Although it's always unwise to extrapolate from results derived from experiments on guinea pigs, rats or sheep, there is ample clinical evidence to suggest that we react to stress in a very similar way to the Cornell sheep. If the stress we experience is unremitting and prolonged we will eventually show signs of nervous exhaustion or collapse. But if we can

snatch a few moments relaxation away from the firing line, we can no
only cope with stress but actually find it exhilarating and positively life
enhancing.

To take a ten-minute break for quiet reflection is not a symptom o
weakness or sloth, but a sign of wise energy conservation. Those moment
of precious idleness can be the most productive part of your working day
Don't worry what the neighbours think, or what your business associate
infer. You'll work more productively, and with far less fatigue, if yo
punctuate your day with regular periods of rest. Close your eyes in a chai
for a few moments, rest your head on your desk, lie down on the floo
or take to your bed for a snooze. Don't wait for your boss to instigate a
official rest pause or yawning break. Don't deny your need for rest unt
your health declines and your doctor orders you to bed.

Vitality Programme – Step Twelve Take regular rest pauses throughout the day whenever you feel the need.

STEP 13

March to the Rhythm of Time

Rhythms are as much part of our human make-up as our bones and muscles. Most people are aware, if only dimly, of the periodicity of their internal functions. They know that at times they experience fluctuations in their energy levels, mood, well-being and bodily performance.

Many women feel tired and irritable before their periods. Some are so badly affected by premenstrual tension that they cannot work for the overwhelming lethargy. Others, driven by the increased tetchiness, row with their husbands, get involved in accidents or commit violent crimes. Once menstruation starts the mood lifts and the drive returns. The change is sometimes so dramatic that the ancients believed that menstruation provided a vital purification service, ridding the body of its collected store of toxin-laden blood. That's how the myth grew up that menstrual blood was poisonous, and would sour wines, blight crops, rust iron, putrefy food and abort cattle.

The Circadian cycle Less obvious than the menstrual cycle, but equally well documented, is the 24-hour or circadian cycle. All living organisms, from cabbages to kings, are geared to this circadian rhythm. The daily revolution of the earth around its central axis patterns every aspect of our lives. It divides night from day, and provides a framework by which we organise our eating, sleeping, rest, work and play. In recent years research conducted at chronobiological laboratories throughout the world reveals that these circadian rhythms modify our mood, hormonal output, memory, body temperature, sleep, pulse rate, blood-sugar levels, powers of concentration and energy levels.

Tests at the University of Minnesota show that many mice will die if they are fed at a time of the day when they should be sleeping. Another study revealed that mice are more prone to suffer adverse drug reactions at the start of the nocturnal activity cycles than at dawn when they are preparing for sleep. There is ample evidence to show that man's dependence on the circadian rhythm is equally great.

When the Medical Research Council's Applied Psychology unit at Cambridge University studied the effect of the circadian rhythm on the working efficiency of 300 navy personnel, they found that the lowest point of efficiency came, as might be expected, during the small hours of the morning, at about 4 am. This is why Red Indians used to attack at dawn, and why the interrogation of prisoners is often carried out in the small hours of the morning, when resistance is at its lowest ebb. It also explains why more people die during this hour than at any other time of the day. It was also discovered that the majority of people are capable of peak performance in the evenings between 8 and 9 pm. This is a time when most workers have quit their jobs and are relaxing cosily in front of their TV sets.

When psychologists attached to Sussex University's Perceptual and Cognitive Performance Unit studied the memory of schoolchildren, they found that their ability to recall their lessons was greater in the afternoon than in the morning. This suggests another area in which we should alter our traditional working schedules, for in schools it is generally the morning that is devoted to memory work, while the afternoon is given over to activities which are mentally less demanding, such as domestic science and sport.

Just as our working efficiency and memory improves during the course of the day, so too more often than not does our mood. Tests on three dozen healthy male students at the University of California revealed that they were normally most depressed in the early morning, and least depressed in the late afternoon. But these cyclical changes are open to considerable individual variation. Some people peak earlier in the day than others. Some of us are 'owls', others are 'larks'. The owls are slow to get going in the morning, but function well at night. The larks wake easily, do their best work in the morning, but tire soon after lunch and need to retire early to bed. These patterns appear to be inherited and cannot be easily changed.

But the circadian rhythms are not altogether immutable. When people are deprived of light in sensory deprivation experiments their biological clocks go haywire. Similar changes may perhaps occur when we live and work in indoor environments bathed in constant artificial light. The body's internal clocks are also thrown out of synchronisation when workers switch from day to night shifts. The metabolic adjustment to this change normally takes about five days, during which time the subjects involved are likely to feel abnormally irritable and tired.

Stress and our inner rhythms

Stress is another factor which can disrupt our inner clocks. A study conducted at the University of Nebraska College of Nursing showed that post-operative fatigue can be caused by a disturbance of the normal biological cycles as well as by the exhaustion of the surgery itself. Tests on a small group of women who underwent hysterectomies or other abdominal operations revealed that their circadian rhythms were thrown out of balance for days, and sometimes weeks, after the operation.

Executives who make regular long-distance flights around the world are also liable to disturb their internal clocks. After a journey across the Atlantic they arrive at their destination suffering fatigue, insomnia, irrita bility, digestive disorders, delayed reaction times and impaired judgement. This malaise is popularly known as jet lag, but is more properly called 'time-zone fatigue', since it's caused by crossing a series of time zones which disrupts the synchronisation of the body's metabolic metronomes. The kidneys, for instance, are conveniently scheduled to produce the maximum flow of urine during the day, and considerably less by night. As a result, travellers who turn night into day by making rapid inter time-zone flights suffer the inconvenience of having to get up several times during the night to empty bladders which are still working to the old timetable. And that's only a small part of the havoc they wreak.

Extensive tests made on a group of travellers flying on a round trip from London to San Francisco showed that they suffered a 20 per cent drop in alertness and a 15–25 per cent reduction in concentration after their flights. Studies have also revealed a 5–7 per cent reduction in muscular strength at the end of rapid time-zone travel. This decline may be of little importance if the traveller's only exertion at the end of the trip is to sign a hotel register, but the change could be critical for sufferers from heart disease forced to carry a pair of heavy suitcases up a flight of stairs.

If your internal clocks are thrown out of step by stress, by spells of night work or by long air flights you're bound to feel below par for a while. Only time will overcome the lethargy you feel.

Follow your rhythms You'll function better if you follow the lead of your innate body rhythms, rather than try to fight against them. Some people have attempted to convert this principle into an exact science. At the end of the nineteenth century Herman Swoboa proposed a theory, unsupported by evidence of any kind, that the human body responded to three independent cycles. The first lasted 23 days and controlled vitality. The second waxed and waned over a period of 28 days and governed emotional vitality and sensitivity. The third covered a 33-day span and regulated intellectual activity. Each of these cycles followed an even, wave-like course with regular peaks and troughs. Individuals were expected to have unusually vigorous, creative days when two of these cycles reached a simultaneous peak. When the waves plumetted downwards together they were expected to be depressed, lethargic and especially prone to accident. So the myth of biorhythms began; and so they entered folk lore. Today countless believers have their biorhythm charts cast by professional counsellors. Others follow the rise and fall of their three cycles on specially constructed watches or hand-held biorhythm calculators. In Japan, the Ohmi railway company have issued their bus drivers with special warning cards whenever the biorhythm charts suggest that they're likely to have an 'off' day. They claim that this simple precaution has reduced road accidents by half. The Yokohama Telegraph and Telephone Company are equally enthusiastic about their road safety policy, of fixing a yellow warning pennant to the bikes of their dispatch riders whenever they're embarking on a 'critical' day. Any measure that reduces traffic accidents is welcome, and no doubt people will take extra care if they're faced from time to time with a warning card or pennant which tells them that this is the day they're likely to have a nasty crash. But the warnings have no scientific validity. Some days we may be full of vitality, at other times we may be unusually depressed, irritable, tired and clumsy, but these fluctuations do not show up on a biorhythmic chart, and cannot be predicted in advance.

Evidence for biorhythms To test the accuracy of biorhythmic predictions, a team of scientists from the Johns Hopkins School of Medicine, Baltimore studied a series of fatal road accidents in which there was clear legal evidence that the driver had been responsible for the crash. They excluded women drivers from their survey, to eliminate the vagaries of the menstrual cycle. Once this was done they fed the birth dates of the drivers into a computer and obtained a print-out of their biorhythms, complete with 'highs' and 'lows'. But they found no evidence that the accidents had occurred on the drivers' critical days. As the authors concluded; the results 'provide no support whatsoever for any aspect of biorhythm theory'.

Another trial, conducted at the Veterans Administration Medical Center in New Orleans, set out to establish whether there was any link between Herman Swoboa's cycles and mental illness. In this case psychiatrists calculated the biorhythms of over two hundred patients who were admitted to the hospital's emergency psychiatric ward. Once again they could find no link between the onset of acute mental illness and any conjunction of Swoboa's physical, emotional and intellectual cycles.

Yet scientists have no doubt that metabolic cycles exist which are tied to neither the hormonal changes of menstruation, nor to the daily, circadian rhythm. These are generally referred to as infradian rhythms, since they last for longer than a day. They affect moods, hormonal balance, and almost certainly energy levels.

The earliest evidence for this was provided in 1931 by Rex Hersey, an industrial psychologist. He interviewed a group of male workers four times a day, and assessed their mood according to their own evaluation, the judgement of their colleagues and his own observations. At the end of a year he analysed the fluctuations in their mood, which he plotted on a graph. He noted that nearly all the men showed a regular periodicity in their mood swings, but he could find no uniformity in the length of these emotional cycles. For some men the cycle lasted three-and-a-half weeks for others nine weeks.

The same applies to fluctuations in the production of the male hormone testosterone. Studies show that somewhere between a half and two-thirds of men exhibit a definite rise and fall in their output of testosterone. But there is no fixed length for this cycle. When researchers at Stanford University took regular blood samples from 20 men and measured their testosterone levels, they found that 60 per cent showed a regular rise and fall of hormone output. But the cycles varied enormously in length ranging from three to 30 days. We are all individuals, and respond to our own internal clocks which beat at totally different rates. Some of us are tortoises, others are greyhounds. Some work best at night, others are freshest in the morning. As philosopher Henry David Thoreau observed: 'If a man does not keep pace with his companions, perhaps it is because he hears a different drummer. Let him step to the music which he hears.'

Lunar cycles Individuals may also respond to cosmic changes. Just as we react to the transition from night to day, so we may respond to the waxing and waning of the moon, or the changing of the seasons. For centuries folklore has supported a link between lunacy and the full moon. This is not as unreasonable as it might seem, for our bodies are 80 per cent water, and if the varying gravitational pull of the moon can create the tides and cause major shifts in the oceans, is it not possible that it could have a similar effect on the fluid in our body? One doctor at least has no doubt that this is so. Dr Arnold Lieber, a Miami psychiatrist, has marshalled evidence to support his view that there is a close relationship between human aggression and the lunar cycle, particularly among the mentally unstable and criminally inclined. In his book *The Lunar Effect* he reports that when the moon approached abnormally close to the earth at the beginning of 1974 it caused not only exceptionally high tides, but also a steep increase in violent crime. In Miami during the opening three weeks of January 1974, the murder rate was double that of the first *four* weeks of the previous year. Likewise, the Phoenix, Arizona, fire department claim that on nights when the moon is full they get an additional 25 to 30 emergency calls. As Lieber concludes: 'Life has, I believe, biological high tides and low tides governed by the moon. At new and full moon, these tides are at their highest – and the moon's effect on our behaviour is strongest.'

Seasonal cycles Others have charted the effect of the changing seasons on our behaviour, moods and energy states. Many people feel abnormally listless when the first warm days of spring arrive. The condition, known to the layman as spring fever, is a genuine entity even though it finds no place in textbooks of orthodox medicine. It can be simply explained. When the outside temperature soars, the body has to work harder to keep cool. It does so by dilating the vast network of blood vessels in the skin, so that more blood is brought to the surface for cooling. Suddenly the body has to find about an additional quart of blood to fill these extra channels. Initially the extra volume can only be found by drawing fluid from elsewhere in the system. Later extra red blood cells are formed to restore the normal cellular balance. Since these cells are responsible for transporting oxygen round the body, there is some reason to believe that spring fever is caused by a relative dilution in the oxygen-carrying capacity of the blood; or as Grandma would say, due to 'thinning of the blood'.

Working in excessively hot rooms can have a similarly soporific effect. This was proved some years ago when a group of professors and their colleagues from the University of Chicago acted as guinea pigs, and provoked in themselves severe attacks of spring fever in the depth of winter. They achieved this by confining themselves to rooms which were heated to a steaming 90°F. This caused an immediate dilation of their peripheral blood vessels, and ushered in all the typical symptoms of springtime lassitude. For the first few days of the experiment the men were so exhausted that they could scarcely continue with their work. They found it difficult to concentrate, and experienced frequent lapses of memory and judgement.

Spring, the season when nature is bursting into life, is in many ways a low point of human activity. It is a peak time for suicides. It also marks a trough of sexual activity, despite the traditional belief that 'In the spring a young man's fancy lightly turns to thoughts of love'. When public health authorities in New York made a seven-year study of over 1,250,000 births, they discovered that most babies are conceived in the autumn, with the spring the slackest time of the year for productive sexual activity. This is paralleled by fluctuations in the output of testosterone, the male hormone, which is at a low ebb in the spring, but rises slowly throughout the summer to reach an autumn peak.

Since we are creatures of the earth, we are governed by the same forces which shape the destiny of the world around us; which divide night from day, and which create the tides, stimulate foxes to mate and birds to nest. We cannot escape these influences however much we seek to control the environment with the sophisticated tools of modern technology. We live in a regularly changing world, a cosmos which is inexorably governed by daily rhythms and seasonal tides. We are linked as by an invisible cord to the moon and stars and every other living organism.

Solar activity and its effect The sun may be 93,000,000 miles away, and yet it casts an indelible pattern on our lives. Though we may not see the occasional flares of solar activity, our cells unfailingly respond to the unleashed energy. In 1920 a French physician Dr Faure observed that sudden deaths in the South of France were twice as common during periods of sun-spot activity as at normal times. At about the same time a Russian historian, Professor A. L. Tchijevsky, discovered that the world's great epidemics of smallpox, diphtheria and cholera had tended to occur during years of maximum solar activity, and had abated in years when the sun was quiet.

Subsequent research has revealed further evidence of the remarkably close links between man's behaviour and disturbances taking place many light years away on the surface of the sun. A German scientist, Dr Reiter, studied a series of 130,000 Bavarian traffic accidents, and found that crashes increased by 10 per cent after solar eruptions. A Soviet haematologist, Nicholas Schulz, performed blood counts on thousands of volunteers and found that the rise and fall in their white blood cell count closely followed the fluctuations in the sun's activity. A few years later three New York researchers recorded the admissions to eight large psychiatric hospitals and found that acute nervous breakdown was most likely to occur when the magnetic activity of the sun was at its height. As they concluded: 'Subtle changes in the intensity of the geomagnetic field may affect the nervous system by altering the body's own electromagnetic field.'

Recognise outside forces What is the practical relevance of these discoveries? It means that whatever our age and level of physical fitness we are all subjected to mood swings and rises and falls in energy level which are imposed upon us from without. If we are wise we will recognise these extraneous forces and work in harmony with them rather than in opposition. Just as a cross-channel swimmer understands the futility of swimming against a strong current, and alters course to take advantage of a following tide, so we should organise our lives to minimise the disadvantages of our 'off' times, and make maximum use of the assistance available to us during our 'peak' periods. When you're feeling low, rest, or allow your body to freewheel. When you're feeling brimful of energy set your engines at full steam ahead, and run with the tide. Save your energy spurts for the times when they count most.

You'll make optimum use of your resources if you bear in mind two practical points:

★ The human animal is a creature of habit, and doesn't take kindly to drastic changes in diet, or hours of work. Shift workers are particularly prone to psychosomatic illness, because their internal rhythms are being continually disturbed. For instance, air traffic controllers, who often rotate shifts every few days, have a high incidence of ulcers, hypertension and divorce.

To maintain the constancy of your internal clocks try to live your life within a reasonably fixed framework. Once you've found the conditions which suit you best, adhere to them. If you're a lark by nature make a point of rising early every morning. If you feel faint when you go without food, make sure you take your meals at frequent intervals. If you find it difficult to digest a late-night dinner, try to eat earlier in the evening. Aim to be as regular as possible in your habits of eating, sleeping and exercise.

★ Although there is a measure of uniformity in the way human beings are affected by the diurnal and menstrual cycles, there is a marked variance in the way we respond to the infradian cycles. So never force yourself to work at someone else's pace. Study your own bodily rhythms and march to your own internal drum beat, not that imposed by someone else. This is particularly important for married couples, whose inner clocks will not always be set in close synchronisation. Sometimes your partner will be lively and full of energy while you feel jaded and in need of a rest. At other times the positions will be reversed. Your joint interests will be best served if you both honour your inner promptings. Don't feel guilty if you are idling while others are working their fingers to the bone. Your turn will come, when your energy levels will soar and you can take over the baton and surge ahead of your colleagues.

As Shakespeare said: 'There is a tide in the affairs of men which, taken at the flood, leads on to fortune.'

Vitality Programme – Step Thirteen Try to recognise the natural rhythms of your body and work with them.

STEP 14

The Secret of Re-creation

In the last chapter I mentioned the value of conformity and adherence to a regular routine; in this I wish to emphasise the benefits of change. Too much excitement and variety leads to anxiety and exhaustion; too little to lethargy and boredom.

Industrial health officers recognise that workers are most prone to suffer tiredness when they switch jobs. A similar fatigue strikes householders when they move home. A short while ago Dr Michael Hargreaves, a Yorkshire family doctor, published a study of new-town neurosis, the condition which afflicts people who are forced to make an abrupt adaptation to a totally new environment. The commonest symptom of the malady is tiredness or lack of energy. Sufferers are irritable, and tense and ask their doctors for a 'pick-me-up', or 'something to keep me going'. The cause of the breakdown seems clear. The move itself is exciting but as Dr Hargreaves said: 'Undoubtedly the stress of change, the urge to decorate a new home, to set out the garden and generally to cope with a new situation is very demanding, especially when this is coupled with having to look after small children or holding down a job.' The cure is simple. Dr Hargreaves found that most patients overcame their malaise within three weeks on a regimen of extra bed rest (at least twelve hours a day), plus mild doses of sedatives where necessary to ease their tension and foster sleep.

To work at peak efficiency we need to steer a narrow course between the boredom of too little change, and the exhaustion of too much.

The importance of routines Some people have a very low tolerance for upheaval, variety, and ambiguity. To maintain their emotional equilibrium they like everything tidy and ordered. A few find mental repose in monastic life, with its never varying discipline of hours, behaviour, dress and schedule of work. Others resort to comforting rituals. The Mongolians have a set layout in their tents which has barely changed in seven centuries. This invests their lives with social conformity, stability and order. The young Mongol today will furnish his mobile home as did his great-great-grandfather, with cooking pots to the right of the doorway and riding gear, saddle and harness to the left. Enter a Mongolian tent anywhere on the steppes and the interior will be the same, a central stove with metal box for dried dung fuel before it on the left (the wife's side of the tent), and dining table and Buddhist shrine with trunk for valuables to the rear.

Charles Darwin was a typical example of an individual with an exceedingly low threshold for change. Even the slightest variation in his day-to-day routine – a visit from a friend or a small dinner party – drained his energy and made him physically ill. As he wrote in his *Life and Letters*: 'I find most unfortunately for myself, that the excitement of breaking out of my most quiet routine so generally knocks me up, that I am unable to do scarcely anything while in London.'

People saddled with this predisposition should take especial care to maintain the pattern and regularity of their lives. Nature is kind in this respect. She never strains our powers of adaptation by making changes which are too revolutionary or abrupt. Day slowly fades into night. Winter sets in gently and gradually gives way to the blossoming of spring. Women are given a transitional period of several years to accommodate to the hormonal changes of the menopause, as are youngsters to adapt to the physiological upheavals of puberty.

Tiredness from under-stimulation　Fatigue can come from *over*stimulation, but equally well it can stem from the monotony of repeated stimulation or the soporific effect of *inadequate* stimulation. Even Charles Darwin found he could perk himself up by making a switch in activities. He was so burdened by the problem of excessive fatigue that he could normally work for only a few hours in the morning. After this time he had to rest on a couch. Later in his life he discovered that he didn't have to retire to bed, but could revive himself by putting his writing to one side and turning his mind to other, less demanding tasks. A brief stroll might exhaust him, but a game of cards could give him a new lease of life. As he wrote in a letter to his wife: 'This walk was rather too much for me, and I was dull till whist, which I enjoyed beyond measure.' When he was working on his theory of the origin of the species he went one stage further and installed a billiard table in his home to provide added distraction. 'I find it does me a deal of good, and drives the horrid species out of my head,' he said in a letter to a friend.

Tiredness, as Darwin found, is often job specific. We may be too exhausted to carry on assessing our annual tax returns, but not too tired to play a game of chess. We may be whacked out by an evening's ironing but still have plenty of energy to play a game of squash. In these situation a change can be as good as a rest.

Regular job rotation　William James was the founder of modern experimental psychology. His teaching was passionate yet practical, being based in many respects on his personal experience. He was an ardent believer in the principles of self determination and creative character building, largely because he himself had managed to overcome numerous childhood handicaps. As a youngster he was always frail and sickly; as an adult he was a bundle of creativ energy. In his early days the exertion of writing a letter could sometimes exhaust him so completely that he had to retire to bed for the remainder of the day. In his maturity he had mastered the secret of energy control so effectively that he could fill his days and nights with ceaseless lecturing, and writing. As a boy he suffered long spells of deep despair; as an adult he was noted for his sparkling wit and irrepressible good humour. The transformation he achieved by the conscious reshaping of his personality and life style. He overcame tiredness by a technique of mind control which will be discussed in a later chapter of this book. He also pushed back the limits of fatigue by employing a policy of regular job rotation. If he became weary of writing, he switched immediately to another task.

In this way he overcame boredom and injected himself with the stimulus of change. He always maintained a variety of interests, and knew that if he changed to a different topic he could tap a new source of energy. At one time he noted in his diary that he was simultaneously studying Sanskrit, geology, the French Revolution, electrodynamics, acoustics and the philosophy of Charles Peirce. This was a ploy he advocated to his friends when they complained of being tired of their work. Try something new, he would suggest. Change jobs, write a book, paint, take up a fresh hobby, or go on a sea trip across the Atlantic.

Recent research has confirmed the soundness of this advice. Monotonous repetition is the laudanum of the soul. The human brain is programmed to reject monotony, and will seek out novelty to keep it alert. This was proved in an amusing, and totally unexpected way during the early days of the British Ergonomics Society. The Society had been asked to collaborate in the production of a TV documentary about the effects of sleep deprivation. A number of tests were devised to measure minute changes in mental and psychomotor performance of a volunteer. He was then kept awake for two days and nights, after which it was confidently anticipated that he would show a marked deterioration in performance when subjected to the battery of tests. But, contrary to expectations, his test scores didn't falter. Although he was noticeably fatigued, and clumsy and slow in his routine activities, he came to life the moment his abilities were tested. As the researchers discovered, the mere fact of tackling a novel test was enough to banish fatigue and mobilise the subject's reserves.

Physical fatigue is often highly localised. It's possible for the eyelids to droop from eye strain, or the hands to become paralysed with writer's cramp, while the muscles of the remainder of the body are fit for a ten-mile run. The same applies to brain fag. On those occasions when the body is totally and uniformly exhausted the remedy is rest; when one part of the body or mind is selectively fatigued the recipe is a switch of activities. Professor Hans Selye, the pioneer of modern stress research, recommended variety as a means of combating fatigue and avoiding stress-related disease. He observed that the human body – like the tyres of a car, or the rug on the floor – wore longest when it wore evenly. He was convinced that by living in closer harmony with natural laws, we could lengthen the average human life span enormously. During his career he had performed numerous autopsies, yet he had never encountered a person who had died of old age. In fact he doubted that *anyone* had ever died of old age, for this to him would mean that all their organs had worn out at the same time. This never happens. Always there is one vital organ which fails before the others and precipitates death. Life could be prolonged, Selye believed, if we could ensure a more even use of our bodies.

Variety is essential for well-being People are livelier and happier when they make fuller use of their faculties and latent talents. The enervating boredom of a routine job is admirably captured by the civil servant who said that he felt like a date stamp at a post office, hour after hour he performed the same perfunctory task and the only novelty was that each morning someone changed the date. Workers in this predicament should make a conscious attempt to sprinkle their lives with variety and change. They should take a new route to work, read a different paper, switch their working hours, change their hair style, grow a beard, change their customary mode of dress, or fill their lunch hours with novel activities. Anything to lift the needle out of its groove and get it to play a different tune.

Doctors have long appreciated the tonic effects of change. Thomas Sydenham, justifiably dubbed 'the English Hippocrates', was with little doubt the finest clinical physician of the seventeenth century. He had a flourishing practice in Pall Mall, London, where he treated a steady stream of rich and famous patients. Although he had few effective remedies in his therapeutic arsenal – apart from iron to treat anaemia, quinine to conquer malaria, opium as a sedative and mercurial injunctions as a remedy for syphilis – he had a sympathetic bedside manner and a shrewd understanding of the psychosomatic mechanism of disease. On one occasion he was faced with a wealthy gentleman who had failed to respond to treatment. Despite repeated consultations and counselling he was still below par, tired and dispirited. So Sydenham hit on a devious ruse. He apologised to the patient for his inability to effect a cure, and recommended that he should travel to Scotland to visit Dr Robinson, a colleague who practised in Inverness. Dr Robinson, he said, had effected many cures for his particular complaint, and he felt sure that if he made the pilgrimage to Scotland he would come back restored to perfect health. So the patient set out on the long trek north, taking with him a letter of introduction to the Scottish specialist. But when he arrived he found that there was no physician practising under the name of Robinson in Inverness, nor had there been in the living memory of any of the local residents. The man was furious, and returned hot foot to London to vent his rage on Sydenham for having encouraged him to make the fruitless trip. But the physician was not disturbed by his verbal onslaught. 'Are you better in health?' he asked when the irate patient finally paused for breath. 'Yes; I am now perfectly well, but no thanks to you,' was the grudging reply. Then Sydenham confessed: 'You may thank Dr Robinson for curing you. I wished to send you on a journey with some object of interest in view: I knew it would be of service to you: in going, you had Dr Robinson and his wonderful cures in contemplation, and in returning you were equally engaged in thinking of scolding me.'

'A holiday is probably the most valuable insurance policy of all against stress, disease and fatigue.'

Sometimes sufferers from chronic exhaustion need not rest, but the stimulus of excitement and change. Variety can be the spice they need to invigorate their lives. Holidays can be excellent antidotes to monotony providing they're wisely used. As Dr Beric Wright, medical adviser to Britain's Institute of Directors, has said: 'A holiday is probably the most valuable insurance policy of all against stress, disease and fatigue.' But what makes the ideal vacation?

Surprisingly little medical research has been done on the subject. The studies that have been carried out suggest that thousands of people today are choosing holidays that are not wholly appropriate to their needs. Professor Pierre Delbarre, dean of the faculty of medicine at the Cochin Port Royal Hospital in Paris, has studied the subject in depth. He recommends that when we plan a holiday we should pay more attention to correcting the 'biological disequilibria' of our lives and less to acquiring a tan or rushing off to visit faraway places. He believes that most people would benefit by taking more short breaks rather than one long annual holiday. Biological imperatives, he suggests, demand that we should take two or three periods of eight to ten days' holiday a year, since this helps prevent the build up of tension and fatigue. He also recommends that holidays should be taken in the spring and autumn when we are most likely to feel fatigued. In July and August our metabolism and ability to work are at a peak, which makes summer, in his opinion, the least appropriate time of the year to take a holiday.

Holidays can help correct the 'biological disequilibria' of our lives only if they are chosen with care. On holiday we more often need to find ourselves than lose ourselves. The middle-aged executive conscious of his declining youth and virility would give his ego a bigger boost by going mountain-climbing than by taking a lazy beach holiday. The middle-aged woman whose children have fled the nest and who feels sadly surplus to requirements would probably gain more satisfaction taking a party of Girl Guides on a camping expedition than trailing round as supernumerary on one of her husband's Far Eastern business trips, for above all else she needs recognition of her value as an individual. Planned in this way, holidays can replace the missing elements in our lives and provide opportunities for self-discovery and growth. They can inject excitement and novelty into dull, routine lives; provide an opportunity for town dwellers to rediscover their grass roots, for the lonely to find company, and the repressed to let off steam.

Unfortunately most of the standard holidays offered by the travel trade today provide little opportunity for real excitement or genuine change.

People are shipped to the coast because this is thought to be the way the masses want to spend their annual vacation. But what do they get for their hard-earned cash? Is it the sun they buy, or the opportunity for a daily dip in the sea? A recent American survey showed that only one in eight people who take a seaside holiday wants to swim, and only seven per cent of the men want to sunbathe. Why then are they there?

The word *travel* comes from the same French root as *travail*, meaning to work or labour. No doubt travel in the early days *was* laborious. Voyagers in the nineteenth century were rare and had to make their own arrangements for transport, sight seeing and hotel accommodation. Trips were therefore inevitably exciting and stimulating. Less so today, when travellers have given way to tourists, a word derived from the Latin *tornus*, meaning 'a person carried around in a circle'. The early travellers came into direct contact with the native population, ate their food, observed their customs, shopped in the local bazaars, and often adopted their dress. Modern tourists travel by jet plane rather than by ox cart, and eat steak and chips in an international hotel of standard design rather than dine on bouillabaisse in a French bistro. They shop in supermarkets that could as easily be in Ipswich as Istanbul, and wear not the native costume but the standard tourist uniform of slacks and open-neck shirt, adorned not with a string of beads but a strap festooned with Leica camera, lenses and exposure meter. If they travel to Morocco they are encapsulated in a carefully protective cocoon, and are often less likely to experience excitement or novelty than if they stayed at home, donned a caftan, sat on cushions, listened to Arabic music and enjoyed a candlelit supper of barbecued *shish kebab*.

Travel in the past led to the Great Enlightenment; tourism today often ends up with the great disillusionment.

Holidays can provide refreshment without being either expensive or long. The English peasants realised this during the Middle Ages. They had no annual holiday entitlement, and normally worked hard from dawn to dusk, but recovered from their labours during the 56 holy-days, the days of the calendar set aside for the celebration of religious rites. These were essentially carefree days when entire communities forgot their routine work and gave themselves over completely to pleasure and play. Dancing in the streets and on the village greens played an important part in these festivities, in fact the Old Testament word for holiday carries the secondary meaning 'dancing in a circle', a link so well established that in 1577 the English poet Barnabe Googe said, 'Do you not know that it is a holiday, a day to dance in?' On these days the villagers held fairs, played hockey and football, wrestled, and indulged in sports like bull-baiting and cock-fighting.

Take advantage of your holidays   Our lot today is in most respects infinitely easier than that of the medieval peasant. We have an annual holiday entitlement of four to six weeks, numerous additional bank holidays plus a two-day break every weekend.

But in many ways we are poorer than our forebears, for we have lost the art of making restorative use of our leisure time. Often we return from our annual vacations more tired and tense than the day we left. And our weekends are frequently so full of rush and bustle, shopping and gardening and DIY chores that by Sunday night we're at the end of our tether, instead of being fortified and refreshed. The person who knows how to take full advantage of their leisure time has little need for artificial pick-me-ups. Given this secret, every day can be a holiday.

Here's how you can make maximum use of your off-duty hours:

★ Take regular short breaks. Both experience and experiment confirm the value of regular rest pauses. All too often patients with responsible executive jobs tell me that they're forced to take a month's holiday at a time, since they need at least a week or two to unwind and begin to enjoy the benefit of the rest. If this is true, it's a sure indication that they have struggled on too long without a break. For weeks they must have been tired and tense, working well below peak performance. Far better to take a break before you feel you need one, rather than wait until one is forced upon you by illness or exhaustion.

★ Enjoy a change of pace. If you normally work by the clock, with a tight schedule of activities which have to be completed by a set deadline, try to escape from the tyranny of time during your leisure hours. If possible ignore the relentless march of time altogether. Ban all chronometers and obey only your inner clock. Rise when you're fresh and ready, eat when you're hungry, busy yourself when you're eager to work, and rest or sleep the moment you start to feel tired.

★ Do something different. Try to introduce an element of novelty into your leisure time. Leave behind you the routine daily chores which exhaust you by their monotonous repetition, and substitute activities which bring the stimulus of change. Make a list of the goals you've strived to reach, but which have previously been denied you through lack of time or pressure of other commitments. If you've always wanted to learn to paint, take yourself off into the garden with art paper and crayons and start to sketch the bushes and flowers. If you normally tour the countryside by car, put on a pair of stout walking shoes and sample it on foot. Take up a new hobby, learn a new skill, cook different food, visit unexplored territory, make fresh friends. In this way you'll find re-employment of mind and refreshment of body.

★ Adopt a playful spirit. Try to allot part of your leisure time to jollity, fun and care-free games. We recognise that children have a need to play; so too do adults. All work and no play makes Jack a dull boy; it also makes him tired and tense. Try to let your hair down occasionally and let off steam. If you're too inhibited to do so on your own, do it in the company of your children or grandchildren.

If you capture the playfulness of a child, you'll quickly lose the world-weariness of an adult. A light-hearted frolic with your family or friends can be the perfect antidote to anxiety and fatigue.

Vitality Programme – Step Fourteen Bring change into your life when you are feeling tired or jaded. Take regular short breaks, change the pattern of your routines, try new hobbies, recapture the playfulness of a child.

STEP 15

Time Control

Each of us has the same allotment of 24 hours a day, and our happiness, health and material prosperity depend to a very large extent on the way we choose to spend these fleeting moments. Even if we are crippled by infirmity, worn down by age or sickness, we still have the power to determine how we use our limited pool of time and energy. We can fritter our day away in purposeless activities, or we can concentrate our resources on vital, purposeful tasks. We can exhaust ourselves bickering with the children and fretting over newspaper reports of crimes and violence, or we can spend our vitality building a part-time business, raising funds for handicapped children or growing vegetables in the garden. Whether we are young or old, healthy or sick, fit or decrepit, we can be either prudent or profligate with our priceless energy reserves.

The history of human progress is the chronicle of men and women who have mastered the art of filling 'the unforgiving moment with sixty seconds worth of distance run'. John Wesley was a tireless worker. During his lifetime he is reckoned to have preached 42,000 sermons and written or edited 450 books. In a time when roads were rough and journeys slow he averaged 4,500 miles of travel per year. He achieved this remarkable output by careful time control. He knew that unless he became time's master, he would quickly become time's slave. Many people nowadays regret that they have too little opportunity for reading. They wish there were more hours in the day so they could read the latest novels, browse through the travel magazines or study philosophy or social history. John Wesley didn't make this excuse, busy though he was. He got through voluminous amounts of reading while travelling from place to place on horseback. The same technique can be employed today. Wherever I go I take with me a supply of reading, a notebook and pen. Then if I'm sitting in the dentist's reception lounge or waiting for a friend to join me in a restaurant I can fill the passing moments by making notes or reading a book or newspaper cutting. It's amazing how much can be achieved in these salvaged spells which would otherwise pass unnoticed.

Specialists who are aghast at their backlog of technical reading can easily bring themselves up to date if only they would flick through the journals, tear out or mark the articles they need to read, and then study them one at a time during their idle moments. Magazine articles rarely carry more than 2,500 words, which means they can be read within ten minutes even at a comparatively slow reading speed of 250 words per minute. The average book runs for about 80,000 words, and so can be comfortably read in ten days by anyone who has a half-hour journey to and from work each day.

Use your time wisely Whatever you wish to achieve, whether it's fame, fortune, or simply success as a dressmaker or cactus grower, the goal is within your grasp providing you husband your resources wisely. Schedule your days correctly and you'll make the most of your limited stores of time and energy.

A short while ago a 43-year-old investment analyst sought my help. His main complaint was of chronic pain in his shoulders, neck and lower back, but as we chatted it became clear that this was not the full extent of his trouble. He was finding life a drag. He was tired, mildly depressed and sadly lacking in purpose. He had the feeling that life was passing him by.

'At my age I should have achieved more,' he told me. 'Some of the friends I made at university have left me way behind, and they're not particularly gifted. It niggles me, particularly as I seem to have reached a plateau in my career.'

'What do you want to achieve?' I asked, trying to get a clearer insight into his problem.

'I don't quite know,' he replied. 'I sometimes wonder if I'm in the right job. I've got a yen to run a business of my own and I think that I could make it if only I had a little bit of luck.'

Therein lay the root of his trouble, and probably the major cause of his tiredness and dissatisfaction. It wasn't luck he needed, but a clearer sense of purpose. People who don't know where they're going, can hardly know what bandwagon to jump on, or which lucky break to seize. As the old adage puts it: 'To him that knoweth not the port to which he is bound no wind can be favourable.'

★ *Plan your day* Management by objectives is now a well-established business technique and it's remarkable that so many men who see the value of laying down clear goals and targets at work should be so slow to apply the same principles in the organisation of their personal lives. Inability to do this is one of the commonest causes of frustration and failure.

Choose your goal, and then focus your time and energy on its attainment. Don't aim too high, nor attempt too little. And don't be content with vague dreams and aspirations. Pin yourself down by fixing not only your long-term ambitions, but also your short-term goals, each with a set time for their completion. It's all too easy to procrastinate if you say in a nebulous way: 'I must catch up with my backlog of correspondence.' You need to be more specific than that, and stipulate exactly which letters have to be answered and when. Set a timetable with the letters listed in order of priority. 'Thank-you letter to Aunt Margaret to be written after lunch; letters to the travel agent and local paper before dinner.'

★ *Goal setting* If you're a business executive set yourself at least one major goal per day and make a point of completing this whatever else you have to forgo. Schedule other times during the day when you'll read your correspondence, make telephone calls and hold meetings with your colleagues, and endeavour as far as possible to keep within these prescribed limits. If you're a housewife plan your day with equal care, allotting specific times for a set stint of housework, a particular batch of cooking and a controlled buying excursion rather than a vague, window-shopping spree. This will concentrate your energies, and ensure that your major tasks are completed with maximum efficiency and speed. And don't forget to leave time in your daily programme for periods of relaxation, rest and quiet reflection. These regular breathing spaces will prevent you getting overstressed, and can also provide invaluable expansion time if you get behind with your scheduled work, or are faced with an unexpected crisis.

These breaks can also be used as rewards for work well done. Publisher Michael Korda admits that he is by nature inherently lazy. He has turned this liability into an asset by employing a technique he calls 'controlled laziness'. 'If you have a big report to write that will take four hours,' he tells readers of his book *Success!*, 'tell yourself that when it's done you can be lazy again, that the only thing that's *preventing* you from enjoying your laziness is the report. Then attack it as if it were the enemy, get it out of the way, and give yourself a spell of real, pleasurable *earned* laziness.'

Try and treat each day as a distinct unit of time, and judge yourself not on what you did last week, or what you plan to do in the future, but on what you achieved today. If you find it difficult to maintain this sense of immediacy, place a suitable reminder in front of you, like writer John Ruskin who always displayed a small marble block on his desk inscribed with the single word TODAY.

Providing you exercise strict control over the way you spend each moment of the day and each ounce of energy, you can work toward any goal you choose, whatever your age or fitness level. At social gatherings strangers often tell me that they too would love to write a book if only they had the time. If I think they're serious I sometimes put before them the sterling example of Anthony Trollope. During his lifetime Trollope wrote 47 novels, five travel books and countless newspaper and magazine articles – despite working full-time as a Post Office manager. He accomplished this impressive body of work only by strict time control. Each morning he was at his desk by 5.30. During the next half-hour he would read and correct what he'd written the day before, then from 6 to 9.30 he would write, glancing occasionally at his watch to make sure that he was keeping to his scheduled output of a thousand words per hour. Undreamed of goals such as this can be attained providing you husband your powers and make the most efficient possible use of your two most vital natural resources – energy and time.

★ *Strategic* Fix your eyes firmly on your intended destination, and then find the
planning simplest way of getting there. One of the twelve labours of Hercules was
to clean out the Augean stables which hadn't been swept for decades. If
he'd set to with a shovel he might still be tackling the task. Instead he
took stock of the situation and used his brains rather than his renowned
brawn. By diverting the river Alpheus he cleaned the stables in a trice
and saved himself endless effort and time.

More economies can be made by sensible delegation. At the start of
each day sort out the work which must be done from the tasks which are
irrelevant or which can be better performed by someone else. Get the
butcher to bone the meat, the cleaner to empty the waste bins, and the
children to make their own beds. Don't spend hours typing a copy of a
report if you can get the manuscript photocopied in a fraction of the time.
And don't make a journey to see if your local library has a copy of
Brewer's *Dictionary of Phrase and Fable* if you can get the information
just as easily with a sixty-second phone call. Use your head to save your
legs. Remember that time is money, and like money it has an unhappy
knack of dribbling away from us, a little here and a little there, unless we
keep a tight control on its expenditure. Unless we husband our resources
we will find that as Seneca said: 'There are some hours which are taken
from us, some which are stolen from us, and some which slip from us.'

★ *Delegation* Learn to delegate whenever possible, and never entertain fantasies of
omnipotence or indispensability, imagining that you alone can carry out
certain tasks. It's often only when an 'indispensable' executive, or 'irre-
placeable' teacher, suffers a heart attack or nervous breakdown that they
realise just how easily they can be substituted. People who insist on doing
everything themselves also limit their opportunities for growth. This was
the experience of F. W. Woolworth, according to B. A. Forbes. 'Wool
worth once told me that his was essentially a one-man business for years,
wrote Forbes. 'Then he ruined his health, and it was while he lay week
after week in the hospital that he awakened to the fact that if his business
was to expand as he hoped, he would have to share the managerial
responsibilities.'

Don't be proud that you work a long, fatiguing day, for this is often a
sign of inefficiency rather than extreme dedication. It's only by forward
planning, delegation and astute corner cutting that you can budget your
day to leave a few precious hours for your personal use. It's the creation
of this 'discretionary time' which gives you freedom of manoeuvre and an
opportunity for much needed rest, play and creative recreation.

★ *Get started* Procrastination is the proverbial thief of time, and one of the commonest
causes of wasted energy and frittered opportunities. If you're faced with
a difficult task or daunting pile of work it's easy to find an excuse for
delay. Rather than buckle down to the chore of preparing the accounts
for the Women's Guild you can always brew another cup of coffee, rea

a few more pages of the daily paper or make one or two frivolous phone calls to your friends. Instead of settling down at once to write a tricky office report you can idle away the first few hours of the day doodling on a sheet of paper, tidying your desk, chatting to your colleagues or writing a few superfluous inter-office memos.

Freelance workers – writers, artists, designers, and composers – can find it particularly difficult to develop a strict work discipline. Paralysis can easily set in when a novelist sits down facing a blank sheet of paper headed 'Chapter One'. The only way to overcome the impasse is to make a start, however imperfect. Even if the first six pages have to be thrown into the wastepaper basket, the mental block has been overcome. From that point onward inspiration flows more freely and thoughts can be refined and shaped into more coherent form. Many would-be writers are so overwhelmed by the enormity of the task they face that they never surpass this initial hurdle. They should pay heed to the advice of Mark Twain, who when asked for the secret of successful writing replied: 'Apply the seat of the pants to the seat of the chair.'

Contrary to popular belief, procrastination is less frequently due to idleness than to deep-seated psychological causes. A short while ago the staff at the University of California grew concerned at the number of students who were getting disappointingly low grades, not because they lacked ability but because they constantly found excuses for postponing their work. So they set up 'procrastination workshops' at which the undergraduates were taught to draw up detailed work schedules with set times to complete each segment of their work. When these tasks were satisfactorily accomplished they were encouraged to reward themselves with a special meal or trip to the cinema. Once the students acquired this discipline their work improved, and the percentage receiving 'incomplete' grades fell by 900 per cent. Often it was found that the basic cause of their procrastination was not idleness but excessive perfectionism or fear of failure. As the course tutors reported: 'Procrastination maintains the illusion of brilliance, but the illusion is never tested.' If you delay action because you're afraid of making a mistake, you'll end up making nothing, and exhaust yourself in the process!

When Winston Churchill took up painting at 40 he found it difficult to overcome his timidity and dread of making an awful and obvious botch of the job. 'Very gingerly,' he recalled, 'I mixed a little paint with a very small brush, and then with infinite precaution made a mark about as big as a small bean upon the affronted snow-white shield.' At that point a painter friend entered the room and asked him why he was hesitating. Grabbing a brush she showed him how it should be done, making a few, bold strokes across the canvas. 'The spell was broken,' Churchill reported. 'I have never felt any awe of a canvas since. This beginning with audacity is a great part of the art of painting.' The same principle applies to most other fearsome tasks, which become less daunting if they are started quickly in a bold and energetic fashion.

Indecision is another cause of energy-sapping dither and delay. Primitive man had far fewer problems in this respect. He was rarely faced with more than one or two options. If some of his cattle were stolen by warriors from a neighbouring tribe he had the choice of either accepting the loss with whatever equanimity he could muster, or attempt to seek redress by going to war. Nowadays every aspect of our lives is hedged around by multiple choice. Since we don't automatically adopt the occupations of our parents, we have to decide the career we wish to pursue. We have to make up our mind where to live, what life style to follow, how many children, if any, to have, how to educate them, and the moral laws they should be taught. Our forebears invariably took their vacations at home, we are offered tens of thousands of alternative holiday plans each year. Which should we choose? How should we invest our surplus cash? Which of the rival brands of washing powder should we select at the supermarket? Everywhere we are faced with an embarrassment of choice, and the closer the specification of competing brands of cars, washing machines or toothpastes, the more difficult it becomes to make a rational selection. When faced with this complexity, it's not surprising that we sometimes give up in despair, or postpone a decision until the last possible moment. But unresolved conflict is tiring, and deferred decisions block progress.

British infantry officers are trained to overcome indecisive dilly-dallying by taking courageous action, even at the risk of making the occasional mistake. 'To do the right thing is commendable,' they are told, 'to do the wrong thing is regrettable; to do nothing is unforgivable.' This is the policy to follow if you cannot make up your mind which way to turn. If you come to a fork in the road, and are unaware that the right-hand path is the one which leads you to your goal, you have three possible options. You can play a hunch and veer to the right, in which case you reach your destination in the shortest possible time. Alternatively you can strike out along the left-hand path, and be forced to backtrack when you discover that you've gone in the wrong direction. This will take a little longer, but will get you to the same spot in the end. Or you can stay at the junction until you're sure which route to take. This is the worst possible solution, for the longer you stay at the crossroads, the longer you'll fret and fume and the less likely you'll be to find a satisfactory answer to your dilemma.

In conflict situations like these it's better to make up your mind by the toss of a coin than waste time and energy on fruitless prevarication.

★ *Concentrate your effort* Just as the sun's burning rays are more powerful when focused through a magnifying glass, so are our energies more potent when they're applied to a single task. Ralph Waldo Emerson said concentration is 'the secret of success in politics, in war, in trade – in short, in all the management of human affairs.' Scientific advance is invariably made by men and women who devote their lives to the investigation of a single phenomenon. If we brand them as absentminded professors, it's not because they are inherently scatter-brained, but because their powers of concentration make them oblivious of the humdrum things of everyday life. Businessmen get to the top because they concentrate their resources on a limited field, and refuse to be sidetracked by irrelevant issues.

Many people who complain of lack of vitality tire themselves out by dissipating their energy on fruitless activities and unnecessary interruptions. The simplest way to preserve your store of energy is to prevent other people wasting it. Learn to say 'no' to irrelevant calls on your time and energy reserves.

Research at Cambridge University has shown that senior executives often spend only one-fifth of their time on productive work, the remainder being dissipated on needless diversions and interruptions. If they filtered out these irrelevances their work would be more creative and considerably less tiring. They could avoid some of the interruptions by hanging an 'engaged' sign on the door, taking the phone off the hook, or giving their secretary instructions that they're not to be disturbed. Subordinates should be given set times for consultations, and colleagues dissuaded from dropping in for an idle chat, or gossip, which should be done over lunch rather than during office hours. As meetings are the biggest of all time wasters for businessmen they should be kept to an absolute minimum. The guillotine should also be exercised on inter-office memos and reports. William B. Clarke first showed his skill in reducing needless paper work when he worked for Ronald Reagan during his days as Governor of California. He invented the 'mini-memo' giving strict instructions that all data requiring the Governor's attention should be condensed into four paragraphs contained on a single sheet of paper. In this way he made sure that Reagan completed his work quickly and efficiently, and was back at his ranch by 5.30 every afternoon.

Effective workers know the art of concentration. William Gladstone, judged by many to be Britain's most successful politician, knew this secret well. He once said: 'There is a limit to the work that can be got out of a human body or a human brain, and he is a wise man who wastes no energy on pursuits for which he is not fitted; and he is still wiser who, from among the things that he can do well, chooses and resolutely follows the best.'

★ *Persevere* Once you've set your targets, and concentrated your efforts on getting the ball rolling, the next most important task is to maintain the momentum. Folk wisdom is replete with maxims extolling the virtues of steady, persistent endeavour. Great oaks, we're told, are only felled by a repetition of little strokes; and a steadily dripping tap, we're reminded, will wear away the hardest stone. Yet all too often we abandon a project at the very moment it is about to bear fruit.

Success attends the person who sets a goal and moves towards it little by little and step by step with single-minded dedication and concentration of effort. John Constable, surely the greatest of British landscape painters, showed little talent as a young man. Yet he worked indefatigably at his craft and at 24 was eventually admitted as a student to the Royal Academy.

Two years later he succeeded in having a landscape hung in the Academy, but no one bought it. In fact twelve years elapsed before he sold a single one of his Academy paintings, and he reached 53 before he was accepted as a full member of the Royal Academy.

John Creasey, the novelist who went on to sell 60,000,000 copies of his books, received a total of 743 rejection slips before he had a single word published. Research chemists at May and Baker tested 692 sulphonamide compounds before they discovered M & B 693, the world's first effective drug in the treatment of pneumonia. More often than not major achievements like these result from dogged determination rather than from flashes of sudden insight.

If you observe these three rules you will make maximum use of your resources, for the secret of time management lies in making full use of every passing moment. The only opportunity you have of attaining your goals lies in the 'here and now'. It's no good wasting energy dwelling on past triumphs or dreaming of future glories. The only time for effective action is now. As Edwin Bliss, author of *Getting Things Done: The ABCs of Time Management*, puts it: 'Good time management involves an awareness that today is all we ever have to work with.'

Vitality Programme – Step Fifteen Careful time management is one of the secrets of energy control. Plan your day. Use spare minutes for small tasks, don't waste them. Don't procrastinate – give yourself specific goals to attain and don't be discouraged by lack of immediate results.

STEP 16

Easy Does It

Productivity in industry is increasing every year, thanks to the introduction of machinery which creates more goods with less expenditure of labour and energy. Cars now run faster with a lower consumption of fuel and less wear on their bearings. Computers perform calculations in seconds which previously would have occupied trained accountants for days or even weeks. Aeroplanes are streamlined to reduce drag, vacuum cleaners built of plastic to make them lighter to carry, and quartz clocks constructed with so few moving parts that they can be fuelled by minute changes in room temperature. Suppose a similar quantum leap could be made in human performance? Maybe then we could increase our metabolic efficiency to the point when we could run for a whole year with only a wheatmeal biscuit to sustain us. Or perhaps we could increase the speed of flexion of our limbs to such an extent that we could run a mile in less than a minute. These advances are beyond the bounds of possibility, but lesser gains can undoubtedly be achieved in human efficiency. If we give a thought to the way we move and walk and work we can increase our efficiency and decrease our liability to fatigue.

Ergonomics During the Second World War groups of scientists got together to make the first concerted study of the way in which people work. They called the new discipline which evolved ergonomics, from the Greek word *ergon* meaning work. The researchers' original aim was to support the Allied war effort by improving the comfort of troops stationed in the tropics, and increasing the productivity of munition workers. People were somewhat suspicious of their efforts at first, because they thought that the time and motions studies they introduced were merely devices to make them work harder. Later they saw the value of their efforts, particularly in the alleviation of tiredness, which formed a large part of the ergonomist's work.

By analysing the way we work, and the use we make of machinery, chairs and work surfaces, we can improve our performance and push back the limits of fatigue. Consider the time we spend each day moving our bodies from place to place. This simple act can be performed with economy and ease, with the grace of a trained athlete or ballet dancer, or with the clumsy, cumbersome movements of an arthritic armadillo.

★ *Effortless* Very few people walk well. Sit on a park bench and watch the world and
walking his wife walk by and you'll see how very badly they do it. You'll see hobblers, waddlers, mincers and strutters, but very few people who walk

with elegance and ease. The ungainly movers damage their feet, tire their limbs and consume an unnecessary amount of energy hauling their torsos from spot to spot.

Even a brief walk to the shops can prove exhausting for people with arthritic hips. Once they have their freedom of movement restored by a hip replacement operation their energy consumption falls. Oxygen utilisation studies reveal that they are nearly twice as efficient with their artificial joints. Lesser, but nevertheless significant, energy savings can be made by people whose walking is impeded by misuse rather than mischance.

Human gait is basically an unstable affair. Every time we take a step forward we have to perform the delicate task of balancing a gangling body of five to six feet on a shifting base which at times is no larger than a bottle top. This feat is every bit as difficult as the juggler's trick of balancing a pole on his nose. Both acts take time to learn. It takes a child months to learn to walk erect: some never master the art properly even as adults, and as a result suffer needless tiredness and pain.

In recent years ergonomists have made the mechanics of walking the focus of considerable scientific research, largely in their endeavour to develop a more nearly perfect artificial leg for amputees. These studies have made it possible to lay down certain basic principles about the art of walking with economy and ease. Whatever your age, you're likely to benefit by improving the efficiency of your gait. You wouldn't hesitate to take lessons to improve your golf swing, or serving action at tennis, so why be reluctant to take instruction which can improve the way you walk? Devote a few minutes a day to the acquisition of this skill and you'll look younger, move more elegantly, suffer fewer foot, leg and back pains, and tire less readily.

Comfortable, resilient footwear also helps to limit fatigue. The body is jolted every time our foot strikes the ground. The magnitude of this force is much greater than most people imagine. If strain gauges are attached to the legs it's found that a shock wave of five times body weight quivers through the shin whenever the heel strikes hard ground. (During running the forces generated at the moment of heel strike are much higher.) The amplitude of these shock waves can be lessened by cultivating a smooth jolt-free gait, by maintaining the flexibility of the feet, and by wearing energy-absorbing footwear.

Recent chemical research has led to the development of polymers which are particularly useful to cushion the feet since they combine the shock absorbing properties of a fluid with the non-deforming resilience of a polymer. When used as insoles in running shoes, they have been found to absorb up to 95 per cent of the impact energy transmitted during the moment of heel strike. The use of these new materials in ordinary walking shoes can be expected to lessen fatigue and reduce foot pain. This was demonstrated in preliminary trials carried out recently by Christopher Dyer, a member of the faculty of the British School of Osteopathy. He took a small group of recreational walkers, ranging in age from 26 to 6. years, and asked them to report their level of comfort at the end of long distance country walks both when normally shod and when wearing special energy-absorbing insoles. The results showed that they tired far less rapidly when their feet were cushioned by a thin sheet of visco-elastic material. Irrespective of the length of their hikes, the use of the insoles reduced their experience of general tiredness by half, and cut their complaints of specific foot fatigue to a quarter of its previous level.

★ *Lifting* *without strain*   In the West we use the most inefficient way ever devised for carrying weights. This is a common cause of tiredness and muscular strain. Housewives exhaust themselves by struggling out of the supermarket bearing overladen shopping baskets; schoolchildren stagger home carrying bags bursting with hefty textbooks; executives add to the inevitable fatigue of daily commuting by transporting backwards and forwards to their offices briefcases crammed with files and managerial gadgetry. How much of this load bearing is really essential? If an athlete can make an energy saving of 1 per cent for every 100 grams they pare from their shoes, think how much effort women can save by emptying their handbags of all but the basic essentials. And do youngsters really need to cart the school library back with them every night to assist them with their homework? Professor Karl Chiari, head of the Vienna University Orthopaedic clinic, grew concerned at the high incidence of spinal deformities in youngsters. Thinking that this might be related to the carrying of heavy textbooks, he instigated a study which revealed that the average student briefcase weighs 11 kg. This means that during the course of a single school year an Austrian schoolboy may carry as much as six railway wagons in one arm. Is this effort truly justified, particularly if it is a cause of spinal distortion as Professor Chiari fears?

Carrying weights in the hand produces muscular pain and fatigue, because it involves sustained contraction of the shoulder girdle muscles. Even the bulging muscles of Mr Universe tire when they are forced to carry a heavy suitcase, because they are held tense to support the load and so are starved of fresh supplies of oxygen-carrying blood. Carrying weights in one hand also presents the body with a major balance problem which can only be solved by a disproportionate expenditure of energy. Just suppose you're carrying a suitcase in your right hand weighing 50 lbs. This load can be borne quite easily when you're standing still and your weight is borne on both feet, but what happens when you're walking and your weight is balanced only on the left foot? The weight of the suitcase is then some distance from your supporting foot, and would topple the body sidewards but for the pull and balancing action of the abductor muscles spanning the outside of the hip. It's a matter of simple mathematics to show that in this instance the abductor muscles have to exert a pull of 450 pounds to keep the body from falling sidewards. Balance is much more easily maintained if the weight is distributed evenly in the two hands. In fact, if the load is shared out 25 pounds in either hand, the abductor muscles have to provide a pull of only 160 pounds to keep the body balanced on one or other foot.

As a general principle, the more evenly a weight is balanced around the body's centre of gravity, the more easily it can be carried. This lessens fatigue and also reduces the strain on the heart as was shown when a team of researchers at the University of Alabama Medical Centre subjected 13 young men to treadmill tests. They asked the men to carry a weight of 40 lbs first in their right hand, then on their back and finally split into 20 lb loads in each hand. The difference was marked, the strain on the cardiovascular system as shown by the rise in pulse rate and blood pressure being much less when the weight was carried on the back or shared in both hands, than when it was borne in the right hand alone. Two Indian ergonomists carried out similar trials which revealed a yet more effective way of carrying heavy weights. They asked seven volunteers to use a variety of methods of carrying a 70 lb load of granite chips while their cardio-respiratory response was monitored. They found that the most exhausting way of performing the task was to carry the weight in the hand, the way we invariably use in the West. Only slightly more efficient was to carry the weight at either end of a pole balanced across the shoulders. The least tiring methods were to balance the load on the head, to carry it in a rucksack on the back and, best of all, to carry it in two packs, one strapped to the front of the chest and the other to the back. Some years ago I was the proud possessor of a Commando hiking jacket which was fashioned along these lines. It was made with pouches and pockets lining the inside, outside, back, front and sides, enabling the weight of equipment and clothes to be shared out evenly and comfortably around the entire body. With its aid I could hike for miles with heavy loads without feeling fatigue, or suffering the niggling backaches that are customary with conventional rucksacks. This sensibly engineered piece of equipment has now been relegated to the Great Trail in the sky, and I'd dearly love to purchase a replacement, but the only load carriers I can find are practical but less inspired backpacks, and fiendish assortments of duffle bags and holdalls which are designed for carrying in the hand and so are totally unsuitable for easy weight bearing. Maybe a manufacturer will hear my plea and construct an ergonomically-designed body pack. Or perhaps an enterprising supermarket chain will produce a bag which will enable shoppers to balance the weight of their groceries on their heads, like Eastern water carriers. Until that happens the best energy-saving compromise is perhaps to use suitcases and shopping baskets on wheels, or to carry loads evenly shared between the two hands.

★ *Pushing and pulling* Ergonomists can also teach us how to lift, push and pull with maximum efficiency and minimum risk of strain. One vital secret is to make maximum use of body weight. Compare two teams taking part in a tug-of-war competition. The novice group stands erect, and tries to pull the rope towards them with a puny action of their arms. The expert team crouches down so that their centres of gravity are as close as possible to the rope, then they lean back in unison and let their combined body weights do the majority of the work. Look at two men lifting a load with the aid of a block and tackle. The inexperienced worker stands back from the job and tries to pull the rope down with an effort of his arms alone. The skilled worker gets the rope as close as possible to his centre of gravity, then hauls the rope by bending his knees and applying his full body weight.

Wrong   Right

The same principles apply to other manual handling techniques. If a car breaks down don't try to push it forwards with your hands. Turn round and push it with your back and shoulders. This considerably reduces the strain on the back muscles, and minimises the risk of spinal injury. And when you're sitting in a deep arm chair, don't push yourself up with your hands. Instead draw your feet back and shift your pelvis forward in the chair until your centre of gravity lies as near as possible over your feet. Then you can stand up with minimal effort simply by inclining your trunk forward and letting the weight of your body ease you onto your feet.

★ *Labour saving in the home* Effort can also be saved by the proper deployment of equipment. Housewives could save themselves an enormous amount of effort if they made their homes and kitchens more truly labour saving. The most frequently used cooking equipment, for example, should be put on open display where it can be easily reached, rather than tucked away in barely accessible cupboards. One time and motion study carried out by the Consumers' Association revealed that a typical housewife bends 300 times during her working day. How much of this stooping is really necessary? Tests show that it takes practically three times as much energy to bend down and open the bottom drawer of a five-drawer filing cabinet as it does to open the top drawer. So considerable energy can be saved by keeping saucepans, spatulas, whisks and kitchen knives at shoulder height, where they can be reached without bending.

Food preparation becomes easier if the kitchen layout is ergonomically designed, with cooker, sink, fridge and work surface all within easy reach. Mrs Beeton was well aware of this and claimed that by re-designing her kitchen she saved a mile's walking for every nine cakes she baked! Having working surfaces and ironing boards at the optimum height to minimise bending will help to reduce postural fatigue, the bane of many housewives. A larger kitchen waste bin will cut down the frequency of emptying. An extra vacuum cleaner on the second floor will avoid the back-breaking chore of carrying this heavy piece of equipment up and down stairs. Given a little thought, numerous other labour saving economies can be made. These will help to overcome 'housewives' fatigue', one of the commonest forms of occupational disease. When Wayne University, with the backing of the Michigan Heart Association, carried out time and motion studies of a number of housewives they found that a lot of the effort expended in the home was unnecessary. Women were working twice as hard as they should, the researchers concluded, squandering their energy on wasteful movements and needless journeys to and fro.

The same applies no doubt to workers in other fields. Whether you're butcher, baker or candlestick maker, there are labour saving economies to be made.

Vitality Programme – Step Sixteen   Examine your daily activities with the critical eye of a time and motion expert and see how you can streamline and simplify your labours; even your walking can be made more energy efficient. Energy should be husbanded, enjoyed and put to fruitful use – but never wasted.

STEP 17

A Breath of Fresh Air

Fatigue can be *intrinsic*, as we have seen in the last seven chapters. It can stem from the way we use our bodies, the sleep we get, the rest pauses and holidays we take, our ability to relax, and the skill with which we plan our days and manage our limited allotment of energy and time. At other times it is *extrinsic*, being related not to circumstances within our direct control, but to the environment in which we live and work.

An obvious example is that of a person who may feel vigorous and lively at the top of a mountain, but grows weary and depressed the moment they transfer to a stuffy office. They may be lethargic and morose before an impending storm; then become energetic and cheerful as soon as the thunderclouds disperse. This close link between human behaviour and climate is recognised in some of our everyday figures of speech. On bright days our disposition is said to be 'sunny'. On dull, turbulent days we feel 'under a cloud'. On humid days we become sluggish and irritable and all too aware that we're 'under the weather'.

Doctors are now making a close study of the way the weather affects our mood and physical performance, a science known as biometeorology. This is so well advanced that in West Germany doctors can dial a specific telephone number and get a 'bioprognosis' report, which indicates how the day's weather is likely to modify the pattern of sickness in the area. One day the doctors may be alerted to expect a high incidence of hay fever, the next to anticipate a rise in the number of road accidents due to fatigue and poor concentration.

Climate affects Professor Clarence Mills was one of the pioneer workers in the field of
our bodies biometeorology. He made a detailed study of the effect of climatic change on human temperament and performance. He concluded: 'Climatic factors in life play a startling and dominating role in all we do. . . They affect man's rate of growth, speed of development, resistance to infection, fertility of mind and body, and the amount of energy available for thought or action.' He conducted animal experiments which revealed that rats brought up in a cool environment fared much better than those reared in tropical heat. They were more active, matured quicker, began their sexual cycles earlier, were more resistant to infection and quicker to solve maze puzzles. He attributed these marked differences to the enervating effect of excess heat.

Professor Mills's findings have since been confirmed on numerous occasions. Leonard Williams maintains a sanctuary for a colony of South

American woolly monkeys on the Cornish coast which mimics as nearly as possible the conditions of their native jungle. He finds that the energy levels of the monkeys are closely related to the environmental temperature. When the temperature rises to 75°F he writes, in *Man and Monkey*, 'they become lazy and sluggish. Lower the temperature to 60° and they become exceedingly active.' Our response to temperature variation is equally profound, a fact we may not always recognise.

In 1756 a large number of people died when they were incarcerated in a small airless room in Calcutta, the notorious incident of the Black Hole of Calcutta. At the time their deaths were attributed to suffocation due to lack of oxygen. In fact they succumbed to heatstroke, caused by the excessive heat and high humidity. People feel stuffy and lethargic in hot, ill-ventilated rooms for a variety of reasons, but rarely from lack of oxygen. This can easily be proved by introducing a fan into the room, which often relieves the heaviness without recharging the atmosphere with a single molecule of oxygen. The content of oxygen in the atmosphere is normally 21 per cent, a proportion which rarely falls by more than one per cent, even in crowded, poorly-ventilated rooms. A drop of this magnitude is impossible to detect, except by careful chemical analysis. In fact the body suffers symptoms of oxygen lack – tiredness, dizziness and lethargy – only when the oxygen content of the air falls below 14 per cent, a saturation which is so scant that it won't support a burning candle or match.

The body is far more responsive to other factors in the environment. When the science of biometeorology was in its infancy, a Ventilation Commission was set up in New York City to investigate the effect of climate on working efficiency. During its enquiries an experiment was carried out in which a group of men were given a monetary reward, the size of which depended on the number of times they were able to lift a five-pound dumb-bell through a given distance. The results showed that the men's powers of endurance were closely related to the climate in which they worked. When they were tested in fresh air their performance was more than eight per cent better than when they worked in stagnant air. When they worked in the heat (75°F) their performance was nearly 15 per cent poorer than when they operated in cooler conditions (68°).

Subsequent research has thrown further light on the complex relationship between the weather and human performance. It is now known that there are six climatic factors which closely affect working efficiency, energy levels and liability to fatigue. These are:

★ *Atmospheric pressure* Human beings, in keeping with all other living organisms, are remarkably sensitive to changes in atmospheric pressure. Professor Frank Brown of Northwestern University, Evanston, Illinois, has reared a number of creatures under carefully controlled conditions. His studies reveal that all organisms are sensitive to impending changes in barometric pressure. As he says: 'Every living thing in our laboratory during the past three years – from carrots to seaweed and from crabs and oysters to rats – has shown this capacity to predict very safely beyond chance the barometric changes usually two days in advance.' This is not surprising.

The earth is surrounded by a dense layer of air which weighs 5×10^{24} tons, and exerts a pressure of nearly 15 lb per square inch at sea level. This means that an average-sized person with a surface area of 20 square feet has to withstand a continual pressure of nearly 19 tons of air! Even a minute fall in atmospheric pressure, of no more than 0.01 lb per square inch, will decrease the overall pressure on the body by some 28 lb. This is quite enough to be felt, especially by tissues which have been rendered especially sensitive by inflammatory change. When atmospheric pressure falls the body tissues swell, which explains why so many people can foretell approaching storms by the onset of headaches, lethargy and rheumatic aches and pains.

Strangely enough a rapid increase in barometric pressure also causes feelings of heaviness and slowed reaction times. This makes us clumsy and prone to accident. Studies reveal that on high-pressure days traffic accidents soar by 40 – 70 per cent. This makes high barometric pressure a more important cause of road accidents than better known weather hazards such as fog and ice. The United Nations' World Meteorological Organisation points out: 'It is most noteworthy that all researchers have been able to show that the so-called trivial weather dangers to traffic – fog, slippery roads, glazed frost, etc. – played an appreciably smaller part in causing the accidents than the simultaneous disturbance to the human body caused by the direct onset of the weather stimulus.'

Unfortunately – short of living in hermetically sealed chambers – there is little we can do to modify the impact of sudden changes in atmospheric pressure. Nevertheless we should recognise their arrival, and realise that on days when they occur we may be particularly prone to feel off colour. The barometer in the hall can be a prognosticator of more than simple weather change, for at times it can also predict variations in our mood, energy levels and proneness to accident.

★ *Temperature*   Man is by nature a sub-tropical animal, and it is no coincidence that all the major civilisations of the past have sprung up in maritime countries with an average temperature of about 70°, such as Egypt, Persia, East China, Babylon, Carthage, Mexico and Sumaria. This is the temperature at which we function best, feel more active and think most clearly. When the thermometer rises above this point we feel lethargic, and instinctively cut down our level of activity to minimise internal heat production and so reduce the strain on the body's mechanism of temperature regulation. This helps explain the slower pace of life in tropical climes.

Educationalists are also realising the importance of classroom temperatures on children's scholastic performance. Children work best, and are most alert and attentive, in temperatures of about 61°, according to Canadian lecturers Simon Kevan and John Howes. Writing in the *Educational Review*, they claim that the ideal classroom climate – temperature, humidity and air movement – is so crucial to a child's development that all teachers should become 'educational micro-climatology specialists'. Glenn Doman, founder and director of the Institute for the Achievement of Human Potential, would no doubt support this view. He believes that geniuses are made, not born. 'No genius is an accident,' he claims. 'Every child is born with a greater potential than Leonardo da Vinci.' To foster the vitality and intellectual development of the children enrolled at his Better Baby Institutes, Doman insists that classes are conducted in rooms held at a steady 62°, the maximum temperature he believes for optimum brain temperature.

Unfortunately many schools, offices and homes today are kept at temperatures considerably higher than the 62° recommended for concentrated mental work, or the 68° advocated for the comfortable enjoyment of sedentary leisure time activities like watching TV or reading. Many modern schools and office blocks are constructed like giant greenhouses, with vast expanses of sealed windows which make the accommodation expensive to heat in winter and extremely difficult to keep cool in summer. Every year in Britain there are thousands of breaches of government regulations concerning the optimum working temperatures in offices and factories. Public health inspectors claim that the temperature level and humidity in shops is sometimes worse than the conditions permitted in the engine rooms of naval ships operating in tropical waters. As one air conditioning engineer said: 'It is unreasonable to expect sales girls to work and housewives to shop under these conditions, which can be 108°F and 80 per cent relative humidity.'

By custom we're also heating our homes more now than ever before. This applies particularly in America, where living rooms in winter are often dryer and hotter than on a summer's day in the Sahara desert. This level of heating may be cosy, but it's not conducive to liveliness of either body or mind. In high temperatures we become lethargic and irritable. Statistics indicate that more murders are committed in July and August than at any other time of the year. They also reveal that crimes of sex and violence are twice as high in the south of Italy and France as in the cooler North.

Hot environments strain our tempers, deplete our stores of energy and place a heavy load upon our cardiovascular systems. Tests carried out one summer at an American hospital showed that the hearts of patients accommodated in warm, humid wards are forced to perform 57 per cent more work than those of patients housed in air-conditioned wards. This helps to explain the 15 per cent rise in deaths reported during many heatwaves, a rise accounted for largely by the increased fatalities among men aged fifty or above who are particularly prone to coronary disease.

If you want to work with maximum efficiency, and minimum fatigue and strain, lower the temperature in which you live and work. In the winter reduce the thermostat setting of your central heating, and keep cool in the summer by throwing open windows and doors. When temperatures soar, keep your body temperature low by wearing the lightest poss ible clothing and taking frequent cool showers. Even immersing your arms in cold water from time to time can prove immensely invigorating, and will ease the strain on your body's cooling system far more than fanning your face or swallowing cold drinks.

Children, in particular, must be prevented from getting overheated since they are especially prone to temperature change. Tests on nursing infants show that their sucking movements at the breast become less vigorous when the surface temperature of their bodies rises from 80 to 90 degrees. Similar studies on toddlers demonstrate that their activity in the summer is much reduced when they're clothed than when they're allowed to play in the nude.

Adults have less freedom to dispense with clothes when the temperature soars. Male office workers are particularly handicapped in this respect. It's possible to take heat photographs which demonstrate quite clearly the pathways thermal currents take as they circulate round the body. They reveal a concentration of flow from the crotch and armpits up through the neck opening. If garments are loose at these three points the dissipation of heat will be aided and the development of sweaty armpits and groins prevented. The ideal summer garment for a male executive is probably a loose Arab *djebella*. Since this is rarely considered *de rigueur*, a useful compromise in warm weather is to wear light trousers and a short-sleeved, open necked shirt. Removing the jacket of a male worker is equivalent to lowering the environmental temperature by three degrees. Dispensing with the customary tie saves another one degree.

Keep your cool in summer and winter, and you'll work better and be less likely to experience fatigue.

★ *Air movement* Stagnant atmospheres are exhausting. This age-old observation was at one time attributed to the build up of noxious toxins from plants and animal exhalations. One of the earliest medical textbooks on ventilation, *The Effects of Air on Human Bodies*, recommended that homes should be aired daily. The treatise, which was published in 1753, advised that: 'Private Houses ought to be perflated once a Day, by opening Doors and Windows, to blow off the Animal Steams.'

A century later British physicians were sending their patients to convalesce in resorts which were chosen according to their meteorological qualities. Some resorts were recognised to be bracing, others relaxing. If patients needed to rest they were sent to towns like Bournemouth or Bath, which were set in sheltered sites where there was little movement of air. If they needed an invigorating tonic, they were directed to bracing centres like Skegness or Brighton where the air was in constant motion.

In times past, ill-fitting windows, draughty doors and open fires ensured a rapid turnover of air in the dwellings of even the wealthiest citizens. Now we tend to live and work in a constant overheated fug. Rooms are hermetically sealed to conserve heat. Draught excluders, double-glazed windows and blocked-in fireplaces act as barriers to the loss of heat, but also prevent the normal circulation of air. In these stagnant conditions we grow lazy and soporific. A moving fan can set the air in motion and provide a useful stimulus. But if you're cooped up indoors and need a more substantial energy boost be brave enough from time to time to throw wide the windows. Better still, get out into the open whenever you can, climb the nearest hill and enjoy the stimulus of the good, country air. This will shake off your lethargy more effectively than any herbal tonic or pharmaceutical pick-me-up.

★ *Humidity*   Man is most comfortable when the relative humidity of the atmosphere lies between 45–55 per cent. When the humidity rises considerably above this level listlessness sets in, since it becomes increasingly difficult to keep cool, because if the atmosphere is already overladen with water vapour, it cannot readily take up the perspiration which evaporates from the body. Lacking this essential way of keeping cool, the body has no alternative but to lower its level of activity to reduce the rate of internal heat production. In climates plagued by high humidity, fatigue can be lessened by the installation of effective air conditioning or by the use of fans, and light, porous clothing which facilitate the evaporation of sweat.

Less well appreciated is the hazard of excessively *low* humidity. This is often encountered in the winter in centrally heated homes and offices, but rarely ever in the wild. Even in the most arid desert, the relative humidity scarcely ever drops below 20–30 per cent. In an overheated, enclosed room it's not uncommon for it to fall as low as 3–5 per cent! In these arid conditions furniture warps, indoor plants wilt and pianos go out of tune. Excessively low humidity also dries out the skin and mucous membranes of the eyes, nose and throat, increasing the risk of conjunctivitis, sinusitis and infections of the upper respiratory tract.

Behavioural studies of people working in banks, prisons and schools also reveal that excessively low humidity produces an increase in complaints of tiredness, insomnia, nervous tension and general 'restlessness of mind'. Museums protect their precious *objets d'art* by keeping a constant watch on the humidification of their galleries. We should be no less careful to safeguard our personal treasures, for are not our health and working efficiency more important than a Louis XV commode?

In the past when the atmosphere became excessively dry in the winter a favourite remedy was to place a bowl of water in front of the fire, or to drape wet towels over the radiators. This may have been an adequate response in the days when rooms were being constantly ventilated by an influx of moisture-bearing outside air. Such measures are unlikely to be sufficient today, when rooms are more effectively draught-proofed. In these circumstances, when the central heating is going full blast, the average home may require an additional 60 pints of moisture per day to maintain an adequate level of humidity. This can only be provided by purpose-built humidifier.

If you find your energy level falling during the winter in dry, over heated rooms, beg, borrow or buy a hygrometer. Instal it in the rooms you most commonly use, and if you find that the humidity level regularly falls below 40 per cent, invest in a humidifier. This will restore not only the moisture content of the air but also your possibly fraying temper and flagging reserves.

★ *Ionisation* Another climatic factor which has a considerable influence over our mood and level of vitality is the ionisation of the atmosphere.

The air is normally teeming with electrically charged particles, produced as a result of storms, the bombardment of cosmic rays, the steady release of radioactive substances in the soil, ultraviolet radiation from the sun and the constant frictional movement of water, wind and particles of sand and soil. Every time we breathe we draw these particles into our lungs, from where they are picked up in the bloodstream and transported throughout the body. Here they have an energising effect, stimulating metabolism and facilitating the activity of many of the body's most vital enzyme systems. This is particularly true of particles bearing a negative charge, which increase the uptake of oxygen to such an extent that a whiff of negative ions can be as exhilarating as a draught of pure oxygen. Positive ions, on the other hand, tend to reduce the tissue uptake of oxygen.

A short while ago Dr Igho Kornblueh, of the American Institute of Medical Climatology, arranged a telling demonstration of the body's responsiveness to variations in the ion content of the surrounding air. On a sweltering summer's day he placed a man before a machine designed to generate positive ions. Within minutes the man's eyes began to smart, and his head felt stuffy and started to ache. A short while after he started to complain of feeling vaguely tired and depressed. At this point Dr Kornblueh switched off the machine and turned on instead an identical-looking device arranged to release a stream of negative ions. Quickly the man overcame his lethargy and started to feel alive and alert.

Tests on university students show that the beneficial effects of negative ions are not purely subjective. When set the monotonous task of assembling nuts and bolts they quickly tired and showed a decline in productivity when they were subjected to high concentrations of positive ions. But when they were exposed to the stimulus of negative ions they worked both faster and more contentedly.

Normally there is a slight excess of positive ions in the atmosphere, which usually outnumber negative ions in the ratio of 12:10. On days when there is a marked preponderance of positive ions we tend to feel irritable and weary. This can happen before a storm, when the turbulent movement of masses of warm air leads to a build up of positive ions. It also arises when warm air sweeps across the earth over long distances, for the earth bears a negative charge and so repels all the negatively charged particles in the air. This explains the enervating effect of hot, dry winds such as the *mistral* in France, the *sirocco* in Italy, the *khamsin* in Egypt, the *fohn* in Austria and the *harmattan* of West Africa. These have been described as ill winds that do nobody good.

Surveys carried out in Israel reveal that when the *khamsin* winds blow, practically half the inhabitants of Jerusalem experience adverse symptoms, such as lethargy, tension, headaches and increased irritability. Similar symptoms can arise in enclosed offices and living rooms, since buildings act as a shield against ion penetration.

When the reverse conditions prevail, and there is an excess of negative ions, we tend to experience feelings of euphoria and increased vitality. This is encountered at the top of mountains and after storms, which release vast quantities of negative ions. Negative ions are also generated by moving water, which helps to explain the revitalising effect of seaside holidays, and the Japanese people's predilection for living by fountains and waterfalls.

Tests show that the preponderance of negative ions may vary from 10,000 per cc in high mountains, down to 2,000 per cc in hilly countryside and seaside towns, 200 per cc in city streets, and a meagre 20 per cc in homes and offices. Dr Albert Kreuger, Professor of Bacteriology at the University of California, has said: 'People travelling to work in polluted air, spending hours in urban dwellings, inescapably breathe ion-depleted air for substantial portions of their lives. There is increasing evidence that this ion-depletion leads to discomfort, enervation and lassitude, and loss of mental and physical efficiency.'

What is the answer to this contemporary malaise? We can't be forever trekking to Switzerland to bathe in the ion-rich Alpine air, or travelling to eastern California to inhale the heady atmosphere created by the waterfalls 'in the Yosemite National Park, which generate negative fields of several hundred volts per metre. But we can spend more time in the open air. At the weekends we can climb nearby hills and take strolls beside local rivers and streams. And during the working week we can perhaps open the windows of our stuffy, overheated homes and offices.

A two-week study of one office containing four people showed that the ion concentration of the air dropped steadily as each day went by until at the end of the afternoon it reached a stultifying level of only 34 positive ions per cc and 20 negative ions per cc. Throwing open the windows would bring in a breath of fresh, invigorating air, for it would introduce many more electrically-charged particles and help restore a more healthy balance of negative and positive ions.

Another solution is to instal a machine specifically designed to generate negative ions. These were developed nearly fifty years ago and since that time have proved their effectiveness in many different settings. In America they have been fitted into space capsules and atomic submarines to maintain the health and efficiency of the crews. In Russia they have been tested on athletes, who have shown an amazing 59 per cent increase in their dynamic work performance after operating for 25 days in an ion-enriched atmosphere.

Another particularly valuable application of negative ion generators is within cars. The metal body of a car acts something like a Faraday Cage shielding driver and passengers inside from the entry of ionised particles

As a result with the windows closed on long journeys the negative ion concentration in a car can fall to a fifth or less of optimum levels. The introduction of a negative ion generator can restore the ion balance within about ten minutes, and so alleviate fatigue and lessen the risk of accidents linked to tiredness, failing concentration and increased irritability.

★ *Pure air* A few years ago doctors discovered a hitherto undisclosed cause of tiredness among office workers. They called the syndrome 'copy paper sickness', because they found it was due to exposure to the modern ranges of carbonless copy papers. These are coated with chemicals which are released when the paper is hit by the typewriter keys. This releases a vapour into the atmosphere, which unless removed by proper ventilation can give rise to irritation of the eyes, nose and throat, headaches and drowsiness.

A more common pollutant of office air is carbon monoxide. This gas is released whenever cigarettes or pipes are smoked. It is highly poisonous and causes unnatural tiredness by reducing the oxygen carrying capacity of the blood. Toxic levels can be reached whenever smoking takes place in a confined space. Smoking ten cigarettes in an unventilated car, for example, can send the carbon monoxide content of the air soaring way above the levels permitted in industry. The answer to this energy-sapping menace is simple. 'No smoking' signs should be posted in offices, cars, theatres, restaurants and all other public places. And the prohibition should be rigidly adhered to. You can't expect to feel fresh and vibrant if you're breathing polluted air.

Vitality Programme – Step Seventeen Tiredness, together with smarting eyes, headaches and increased irritability, can be part of what Scandinavian doctors call the 'indoor climate syndrome'. This can be overcome by providing a wholesome, invigorating environment which affords: equable temperature (62°–68°F); adequate ventilation and air movement; comfortable humidity (45–55 per cent); optimum ionisation; and air free from noxious chemicals, gases and irritating dusts.

STAGE FOUR

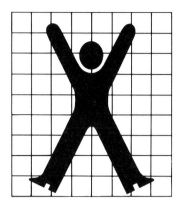

Eliminating Sources of Energy Wastage

STEP 18

Poised to Win

Fatigue is sometimes the price we pay for walking upright. In our evolutionary drive to raise ourselves head and shoulders above our primordial competitors, and free our hands to manipulate weapons and tools, we have assumed a posture that requires great control. For a large part of our waking lives we are forced to perform the gravity-defying feat of balancing an ungainly, top-heavy frame over a miniscule base. Few are masters of the art. Sit beside a public swimming pool and within minutes you'll see exhibited before you, like a military sick parade, the entire range of postural defects. You'll see craned necks, rounded shoulders, dowager's humps, sway backs, sagging bellies and prominent behinds. These defects are not just trivial anatomical aberrations, they are major functional catastrophes leading to tension, tiredness and premature joint decay. They're also ageing and unattractive.

A short while ago children were given lessons in deportment by both their teachers and their parents. Now they're allowed to slouch. Gangling schoolboys stoop to minimise their sudden spurt in height; teenage girls round their shoulders in an attempt to hide the embarrassment of their developing breasts. Often these unsightly slouches cause no obvious discomfort until much later in life, but they can have an insidious effect on a child's vitality and development. Two physical therapists at the Children's Hospital School, Baltimore, examined the posture of 12,000 people, both adults and children, in sickness and in health. Even in this large cross-section of the population they could find no one they considered to have a perfect carriage. Many were unaware of their postural defects, but were likely to be suffering unnecessary fatigue because of the faulty way in which they held and used their bodies. According to the researchers, the children with postural problems revealed, 'a slowing of weight gain, impairment of general appetite, fretfulness and lessened stamina'.

Poor posture wastes energy It's easy to appreciate the energy drain caused by poor posture. The head weighs about ten pounds, and is balanced above the shoulders largely by the contraction of the muscles running down the back of the neck. When the head is poised directly over the shoulders the neck muscles have precious little to do; when the head juts forwards they have to contract vigorously to prevent the chin sagging on to the chest. The same applies to all the other major masses of the body. The further the centre of gravity of the head, chest and pelvis strays from the midline, the more work the muscles have to do to hold them poised above the feet. Good posture is not just something that's attractive to look at, it's something that's comfortable to live with, and economical to maintain.

In a sedentary age, it's not surprising that the head and neck should provide the most common sites of postural defect. Whenever we're sitting – driving a car, watching television, reading a book or doing desk work – the head is inclined forward. The same applies to many standing chores at work and in the home. Machine minders and lathe operators work with their heads bent forward. So too do housewives when they're ironing clothes, vacuuming the carpets or preparing food. This constant forward flexion of the head places a permanent strain on the muscles of the neck and shoulders, leading initially to tension headaches and muscle aches and pains, and later to cervical spondylosis, a form of degenerative arthritis which is now so endemic in the Western world that it affects 87 per cent of people over 50. Doctors sometimes use the term 'desk neck' to cover the multitude of orthopaedic problems which plague office workers. These ailments are more common now than they were in the days when bank tellers and tally clerks stood at upright desks with sloping tops. Inclined working surfaces place the necks under far less strain, a benefit enjoyed today by draughtsmen and architects using angled drawing boards. How much longer before we lighten the occupational strain of office workers by introducing raised paper stands for copy typists, inclined book rests for proof readers, and sloping writing desks for executives?

Until that time, office workers should take care to correct the position of their heads, if not when they're working over their desks, at least when they've left their offices and are walking home, going shopping, or taking a stroll. It's all too easy for sales representatives to hold their heads thrust aggressively forward, even when they're not piloting their cars through heavy traffic. Equally, housewives and typists can maintain the forward bend of their necks through sheer habit, even when they're not stooping over a sink or typewriter.

Walk tall   When you're walking – whether you're chemist, clerk, or company director – walk tall. Imagine that your head is like a toffee apple on a stick. To balance the apple you'd have to align it directly over the end of the stick. So it is with the head. If you want to maintain an easy, graceful carriage, keep your head back and up over your spine. This is the essence of postural control for, as sportsmen know, where the head leads the rest of the body follows. Hurdlers appreciate that the lower they keep their heads as they cross the hurdles the quicker they'll run, for the sooner their feet will make contact with the ground on the opposite side. In the same way generations of golfers have been trained to keep their eyes firmly fixed on the ground when they complete their swing, for if they lift their head too soon the shoulders and trunk will follow suit with the result that their shot will be pulled out of line.

Similar considerations apply to postural control. If the head is allowed

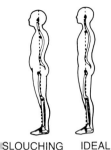

SLOUCHING IDEAL
STANCE POSTURE

to slump forward, a compensatory adjustment must be made in the remainder of the body. An easy posture is maintained when the centre of gravity of the major weights of the body – head, chest, and pelvis – lie in line one above the other, as shown in the diagram.

Problems arise when the head droops forward, for this throws the body into an unstable position, with its centre of gravity in front of the midline. To compensate, the shoulders and upper part of the chest are invariably rounded backwards, and the stomach and pelvis tipped forwards. This restores the balance, but produces a sway-back posture which provokes spinal strain, looks unattractive and is exhausting to maintain. The greater the malalignment, the harder the muscles have to work to maintain the uneasy balance. This produces an energy drain which is directly proportional to the postural imbalance.

At birth the human spine – like that of apes – is held in a single backward curve. A reverse curve appears in the neck the moment we learn to hold our heads erect, and another in the lower back once we discover how to walk upright. These curves enable us to hold our bodies erect, and also increase the strength and suppleness of the spine, a curved spine being reckoned to be sixteen times stronger than a rigidly straight one. Troubles arise only when these curves become excessive.

If you want to discover whether or not you're suffering from an increase in your postural curves, stand with your back to a wall and your feet four inches from the skirting board. In this position the head, shoulder blades and seat should all make easy contact with the wall, leaving a gap in the small of the back which is just deep enough to accommodate the flat of the hand. Any exaggeration of your back curves will leave the head thrust forward from the wall, and produce a hollow in the lower part of the back which may be enough to take the entire fist rather than just the flat of the hand.

Standing badly places an unfair strain on the spinal ligaments, and adds considerably to the work load imposed on the muscles. Slouching can also affect your mood, for there's nothing like an alert posture to induce an on-top-of-the-world feeling. Conversely, when you hold your head low you quickly develop a hang-dog feeling to match your pose. That's why soldiers wore peaked caps and busbies, and Victorian clerks were dressed in high, starched collars, to keep their heads and spirits jaunty and alert.

Poor posture also has a profound effect on the funcion of the body's internal organs. This is most obvious in the case of the lungs. When the body slumps, the rib cage is lowered and the diaphragm sinks, which makes breathing more difficult and reduces the capacity of the lungs. The actual effort of breathing is also increased. It's estimated that a weight of about 20 pounds is lifted during every respiration. If the ribs are initially low because of a slouch, this weight has to be lifted further with a consequent increase in energy expenditure. Since we breathe approximately 26,000 times a day, this represents a great deal of wasted energy.

People with poor posture are prone to fatigue for several reasons: because they work inefficiently, overload their muscles and hamper their breathing. They also run the risk of impaired circulation. Some years ago a research team from the Mayo Clinic in America, led by Dr J. E. Goldthwaite, carried out a remarkable study into the widespread effects of faulty body mechanics. This revealed that diseases as diverse as diabetes, heart failure and nervous exhaustion could have their origins in poor posture. When we are at rest approximately half of our total supply of blood is held in the abdominal organs. When the posture is poor the circulation through this vast reservoir is slowed. This may explain why conditions such as varicose veins, piles and severe period pains are more common in subjects with poor posture and sedentary occupations. The researchers examined the relationship between postural faults and the speed of circulation of the blood, injecting volunteers with a substance known as 'decholin', which causes an intensely bitter taste when it reaches the tongue. They were able to get an accurate measure of the time the chemical took to travel round the body from the arm vein into which it was injected, via the heart to the small capillaries in the tongue. In this way they demonstrated that many persons with poor posture suffer a marked reduction in their speed of circulation. In some cases it was possible to speed the blood flow a third or more by improving the posture. Such improvement must enhance the carriage of oxygen throughout the body and so lessen fatigue. Goldthwaite reported in *Body Mechanics*, the book based on this research: 'When the body is used rightly, all of the structures are in such adjustment that there is no particular strain in any part. The physical processes are at their best, the mental functions are performed most easily, and the personality or spirit of the individual possesses its greatest strength.'

The Alexander technique Other workers have confirmed the manifold problems caused by faulty body carriage, and demonstrated the benefits which can be derived from postural correction. F. Mathias Alexander was a pioneer of postural re-education, who numbered among his pupils such eminent men as Henry Irving, Bernard Shaw, Stafford Cripps and Aldous Huxley. Alexander started out in life as an actor, but achieved little success because he was plagued by a chronic throat complaint which defied all forms of medical treatment. He overcame his handicap only when he realised that it was associated with faulty positioning of his head, which tensed the muscles of his neck and throat. As soon as he adjusted the position of his head, his throat muscles relaxed and the timbre in his voice improved. This discovery impelled him to leave acting and devote the remainder of his life to promoting the Alexander method of postural re-education, a technique which has helped thousands of students all over the world to improve their well-being and energy levels.

One of Alexander's most ardent disciples is Professor Nikolas Tinbergen, the Dutch zoologist who was awarded a Nobel Prize in 1973 for his outstanding studies of animal behaviour. On that occasion he devoted the major part of his acceptance speech to paying tribute to the efficacy of Alexander's teaching. He told his distinguished audience that he himself had become a guinea pig to test the validity of Alexander's claims. His wife and daughter also visited different Alexander teachers. The results amazed him. All three, he said, noticed, 'striking improvements in such diverse things as blood pressure, breathing, depth of sleep, overall cheerfulness and mental alertness, resilience against outside pressures, and also in such a refined skill as playing a stringed instrument.'

The dangers of slouching Alexander's postural teaching stresses the importance of the proper carriage of the head. Goldthwaite's work on the other hand, underlines the vital role of a strong abdominal wall. These are among the most neglected muscles in the human body. Even youngsters today are developing pot bellies. When Dr Rachel Woods, a noted American pediatrician, carried out a postural examination of well over a thousand first year students at Yale University she discovered that 42 per cent had unduly prominent abdomens. Some no doubt were flabby through lack of exercise, others she believed drooped through idleness or fatigue. When she reported her findings at an annual convention of the American Osteopathic Convention, she urged her colleagues: 'Tell your youngsters before they have problems that if they are too tired to stand or sit up straight they should get more sleep – but never allow them to slouch.' Unless these defects are corrected at an early stage they can give rise to permanent deformity, and the youngster with a mild abdominal droop can become the adult with abdominal organs that permanently sag, a defect which can shorten lives. A recent study at the University of Gothenburg, Sweden, showed that men with a pot belly were more prone to heart disease than those whose excess weight was more evenly spread throughout the body.

Dr Goldthwaite showed that sagging bellies slowed the circulation and impaired the function of the body's internal organs – heart, lungs, stomach, pancreas, colon and womb. His recommendation was often to wear an abdominal belt. A more satisfactory solution, I believe, is to strengthen the muscles of the abdominal wall and so provide your own muscular corset. Build up the strength of your tummy muscles and you'll find you'll gain a better figure, improved posture, a stronger spine, better breathing, improved circulation *and* you'll lessen fatigue.

My favourite exercise for strengthening the abdominal muscles is the abdominal curl, which is depicted in the diagram.

To perform the exercise, lie on your back with knees bent and back flat against the floor. Then slowly curl up into the sitting position, bringing your head as close as possible to your knees. Repeat six times. Do this once a day and you'll quickly develop a strong, flat tummy.

If you find this exercise too difficult, content yourself with carrying out occasional abdominal retractions. Suck your tummy in and try and pin your navel to the front of your spine. You can perform this exercise whenever you've got a moment to spare: when you're taking your morning walk, when you're standing waiting for the kettle to boil, or when you're driving the car on the open road. Some exercises are tedious and unrewarding, but you'll never regret the time you devote to conditioning your abdomen. A few moments a day spent performing abdominal curls or abdominal retractions will pay rich dividends, improving your appearance, vitality and freedom from disease.

Whether you're sitting, standing or walking you'll function better and tire less if you maintain a good carriage, with tummy flat, trunk erect and head held high. You'll also save yourself needless energy throughout the day if you always adopt the most economical pose you can. Standing, for example, uses up 40 per cent more energy than sitting, so take the weight off your legs whenever you can, when you're answering the telephone, talking to colleagues at work or ironing. In the same way when you're taking a rest, lie down rather than sit if you get the opportunity, since this uses up 18 per cent less energy. Energy is far too precious to squander, so follow the Turkish proverb: 'Never stand up when you can sit down; never sit down when you can lie down.'

Vitality Programme– Step Eighteen Overcome postural fatigue by learning to sit and stand and walk tall. Improve the condition of your stomach muscles by doing appropriate exercises every day.

STEP 19

The Pain Drain

Pain is an essential part of the body's machinery for self preservation. A stab of searing pain as your fingers touch a lighted hotplate makes you withdraw your arm in double quick time and so protects your hand from further harm. The agony of a broken shin ensures that you take the weight off the injured leg and don't compound the damage to the shattered bone.

Some people are born without the ability to appreciate pain. They are to be pitied rather than envied, for they may die from straightforward conditions such as appendicitis which could have been cured at an early stage had it given rise to recognisable warning symptoms. Other individuals lose their pain sensitivity as a result of disease. Victims of leprosy lose their flesh not only from the direct action of the infection, but also because the disease attacks their nerves and destroys their defensive pain response. Cases have been reported of lepers who lost their fingers during the night, because they didn't notice that they were being gnawed away by rats.

Pain is vital to the survival of the body, but it can also be extremely debilitating. Skin rashes may be unsightly and alarming, but they're not as exhausting as aching feet. The person who suffers repeated attacks of migraine is generally exhausted by the unending struggle. No sooner have they recovered from one bout of excruciating head pain than they are plunged into another. The classical symptoms of migraine are said to be nausea, sickness, head pain and visual disturbance; but to these could be added a fifth – chronic fatigue. The same could be said of sufferers from sinusitis. This disease causes widespread weariness and misery, even though officially it is no more than a local inflammation of the sinuses.

Even minor aches can be wearisome if they persist unabated, for like the steady dripping of a tap, the constant irritation of nagging pain can wear away at the strongest constitution. Besides, minor pangs have an unhappy knack of developing into major discomforts once the attention is focused on them, and even more so when fatigue sets in and lowers the pain threshold.

Tests carried out at Texas University's medical school reveal that people burn up far more energy when they're sick or in pain. A patient who might consume 2,500 calories during a normal working week may need up to 10,000 calories when they're admitted to hospital suffering from multiple injuries. So don't tolerate even the slightest chronic pain. It may be no more than a trivial twinge – a throbbing tooth or chilblain – but it's still enough to drag you down and erode your store of nervous energy.

Pain relief Some people are fortunate in that they have a high tolerance to pain, like Lord Raglan, who had his arm cut off without anaesthetic after the battle of Waterloo. He was stung more by sentiment than by pain. 'Here, bring that arm back!' he called out to one of the nursing orderlies. 'There is a ring my wife gave me on the finger.' Others are less stoical and are bowled over by the tiniest gripe. They tend to be constantly at the bottle, resorting to painkillers at the slightest muscle twitch or nerve twinge. They would be better served using other, non-pharmacological, methods of pain relief.

Recent medical research has introduced many novel techniques for preventing pain. An Italian doctor has developed a tiny silicone rubber dome, about the size of half a ping-pong ball, which is filled with morphine and implanted beneath a patient's breast, releasing 5,000 or more shots of morphine at the touch of a finger. Other doctors are experimenting with a pocket-sized battery operated machine known as a transcutaneous nerve stimulator which fires a stream of electrical impulses through the skin to 'jam' the transmission of pain signals.

This research has also thrown light on certain natural ways of relieving pain, some of which are as old as time itself:

★ *Relaxation* Most of the agonies the body suffers arise as a result of muscle spasm. This includes the pain of childbirth, coronary disease, leg cramps and renal colic. Dr Grantly Dick Read and other protagonists of Natural Childbirth Training showed that if expectant mothers are taught to relax they can learn to lessen, if not completely eradicate, their labour pains. The same applies to other pangs. Tests show that the majority of subjects can decrease their pain by a third or more by acquiring the art of relaxation. If you're tense and anxious in the dentist's chair, for instance, you'll feel pain more intensely than if you remain relaxed and calm. And if you experience more pain, and maintain a high level of tension, you'll inevitably find the visit unnecessarily fatiguing.

★ *Distraction* Mothers of children suffering from wind or teething troubles will instinctively try to switch the youngsters' minds to other things. The more we focus on our pains, the more prominent they become. Rather than retiring to bed and wallowing in the misery of a painful period, many women find that they are happier if they busy themselves about the house. Work or play can switch our attention from life's agonies to its ecstasies.

★ *Reassurance* Fear always magnifies pain. If your heart skips a beat in the night you may be convinced that you're about to suffer a heart attack. If so, you'll soon experience cramp-like spasms in your chest and stabbing pains down your arm. Five minutes with your doctor will ease the anxiety. As children we may be terrified when a piece of grit enters our eye. A quick inspection from one or other parent, plus a reassurance that the offending particle of dirt has been removed, is all we need to restore our equanimity. As adults we should be equally willing to turn to our doctors when we have any fears about our health. Only in this way can we relieve our energy-sapping, nagging doubts.

★ *Imagination* Many real discomforts are more in the mind than in the body. Under hypnosis subjects can be made to feel pains which are *not* there, or be rendered totally unaware of pains which *are* there. If you're given an inert pill which you think will make you sick, the chances are it will make you nauseous, even though it contains nothing but sugar; in the same way 30 – 40 per cent of patients with pain will get relief from taking placebos. The subconscious mind is exceedingly powerful. If you think your pain is worsening, it will. If you imagine it's getting better, the chances are it will slowly start to ease.

★ *Counter* A pain in the stomach can sometimes be eased by biting the lip, and a *irritation* severe bout of lumbago soothed by applying a blistering·mustard plaster to the back. This principle of counter irritation has been in use for thousands of years. The Romans found relief from headaches by needling their scalps with the tiny shocks from electric ray fish. The Chinese eased a wide variety of pain by applying acupuncture needles at carefully designated spots.

Recent research has helped to explain the efficacy of this therapy. Studies show that the body is capable of producing its own pain-killing drugs, known as endorphins. These are released when the skin is stimulated by acupuncture needles or electric shocks, and probably also when it is irritated by rubbing or the application of some creams commonly used in the treatment of rheumatic aches and pains.

Tests on rabbits reveal that it's possible almost to double the animal's ability to withstand pain by subjecting it to a few moments deep finger pressure, a technique employed by the Chinese for over four thousand years, and known as acupressure. In recent years this method has been used in the West to provide a satisfactory degree of pain relief during gynaecological and abdominal surgery.

If you want to use acupressure to relieve your pains – toothache, lumbago, migraine or menstrual cramps – try applying firm pressure to the fleshy web between your thumb and index finger, a favourite acupuncture point called *Ho ku*. Alternately you can grasp your ear lobe, or the *quenlum*, the classical pressure point just above the achilles tendon. Rapid pinching of these sites, at a frequency of about two nips per second, has been shown to raise the pain threshold significantly and produce a substantial increase in the output of pain-relieving endorphins.

But these techniques are only palliatives. Pain is an indication that something is amiss with the body. It's a warning sign that shouldn't go unheeded, any more than one should ignore the knocking of a car engine. If you suffer persistent pain anywhere in your body you should seek medical advice, for it could be a symptom of serious disease that needs immediate treatment.

On the majority of occasions, however, your doctor will probably reassure you that there is nothing seriously wrong. Perhaps you're merely suffering from tension headaches, lumbago or indigestion for which he'll no doubt give you a prescription for some painkilling tablets, anti-inflammatory pills or antacids. But don't be too ready to settle for this easy solution. If you're suffering discomfort of any kind, try to discover the root cause and eliminate it, rather than be satisfied with endless palliation. Recurrent tension headaches may not kill you, but they *will* make you jaded, tired and irritable.

It's estimated that 80–90 per cent of head pain stems from tension in the muscles of the neck. This can often be eased in the following ways:

★ *Relaxation* When we're under tension the first muscles to bunch up are those of the forehead, neck and jaw. This can be eased by following the advice given on pages 79–86, and by regular use of the Norfolk Mandala. At other times it may be necessary to adopt a more relaxed approach to life. Dr Harold Wolff, professor of medicine at Cornell University and probably the world's leading authority on head pain, gives four tips to people who suffer recurrent headaches:

1. Try to be less fussy about trivial issues.
2. Accept that there are times when we all feel tired, irritable and less efficient. Refuse to push yourself on these days.
3. Learn, as far as possible, to avoid needless anxiety and non-productive worry.
4. Lower your standards if this is necessary to avoid disappointment and frustration. Adopt sensible goals and make sure you enjoy the things you have and can reasonably achieve.

★ *Postural strain* If you often wake in the morning with a splitting headache check on the height of the pillow. Perhaps you're sleeping in a tense, uncomfortable position. For maximum relaxation during the night the head, neck and spine should be kept in a straight line. This is generally best achieved by sleeping on one pillow rather than a pile of two or three. When sleeping on the side the ideal is to fill the gap between the shoulder and the side of the head, as shown in the diagram below.

GOOD SLEEPING POSTURE   BAD SLEEPING POSTURE – PILLOWS TOO HIGH

★ *Neck exercises* Maybe you can date the onset of your headaches to a definite accident to your head or neck, a plank of wood falling on your skull or a 'whiplash' injury in the car. This may have damaged the muscles, ligaments or joints of your neck and left you with permanent tension and stiffness. Dr Wolff once investigated a series of 63 patients suffering from headaches following such accidents, and discovered that in every case the pain was arising from sustained contraction of the neck muscles. This can generally be relieved by exercise, massage or skilled osteopathic treatment. Try to stretch out the tissues of your neck by putting the vertebral joints through their full range of movement. Bend the head to the left so the ear rests on the shoulder, then repeat to the opposite side. Follow this up by rotating the neck in each direction, looking as far as possible first over the left shoulder, then over the right. Now drop your chin and stretch the neck downwards to its full limit. Do this once a day and you'll gradually relieve your stiffness and tension.

★ *Massage* Massage will also help. If you haven't a masseur or Geisha girl handy don't despair. You can achieve a lot by self-administered kneading. Start by relaxing the muscles of the scalp. Do this by placing your thumbs behind the ears, with fingers spread out over the front of the scalp, down the midline. From this position start to make small circles with the fingertips so that the scalp is gently rotated on the skull. Then move the fingertips first outwards towards the temple, then backwards towards the ears, following a zig-zag pathway until the entire surface of the scalp has been covered. (Take care when doing this that the scalp is moved on the skull, rather than the fingers dragged across the scalp, which can damage the hair roots.)

A different approach is needed to massage the base of the neck and the upper part of the shoulders. To cover this area, place your right hand so the fingertips rest on the back of the neck fractionally to the *left* of the midline. From here slowly draw the fingers downwards and outwards until they are about two-and-a-half inches from the midline. Then relax the pressure and make a circle outwards and upwards until the fingers regain their starting position. Repeat this circular movement with the hands placed half-an-inch lower, and continue until the entire neck has been massaged. Now switch hands and do the same for the right hand side of the neck. With a little practice you'll find this massage very soothing and beneficial, not only for relieving tension headaches, but also for easing the tension of a long drive, or the strain of prolonged desk work.

Postural aches If your headache is provoked by sitting at a desk, you'll probably gain relief by switching to a more comfortable chair. Five thousand years ago there were no seats. Now we spend a large proportion of our lives in them. This is a cause of untold discomfort, spinal strain and postural fatigue. A survey of a group of office workers showed that the majority found desk work uncomfortable and tiring. One in eight suffered headaches, 57 per cent had backaches, 24 per cent fibrositis in their neck and shoulders, 29 per cent pain in their feet and legs, 19 per cent discomfort in their thighs and 16 per cent aching in their buttocks. Much of this malaise can be relieved by better seating.

Radiological studies reveal that in the slumped sitting position, the lower vertebrae are tipped forward as far as they can go. This means that a desk worker can suffer as much ligament strain from three hours' sitting in an unsupported position as a gardener gets at the end of a morning spent bent over the weeds in the garden. If the chair has an effective lower back support this strain is greatly lessened. The discomfort and fatigue of sitting can be reduced if chairs are selected according to the following criteria:

★ *Firm seat* It's a big mistake to equate comfort with softness when purchasing either beds or chairs. No position – standing, sitting or lying – is comfortable if it's maintained too long. Slight shifts of posture are always needed to lessen fatigue and prevent the prolonged compression of delicate tissues. These minor adjustive movements are best made from a firm base.

★ *Optimum seat height* Studies show that sitting is most comfortable when the weight of the body is taken primarily by the feet and the bony haunches at the base of the pelvis. This is achieved when the feet are firmly planted on the ground and the thighs run more or less parallel with it. To ensure this optimum positioning, select a chair with a seat height slightly less than the length of the lower leg from knee to foot.

★ *Firm back support* To prevent slumping, and rest the spinal muscles, the back of the chair should provide firm lower back support. This should cover a depth of four to eight inches and should be sited about five inches above the seat, to allow a hollow for the buttocks.

★ *Seat-tilt* A seat should have a slight backward slope, to ensure that the weight of the body does not slip forward but is constantly being eased backward into the support of the chair. Tests show that people are most comfortable in seats with a backward slope of 7 or 8 degrees.

★ *Correct seat depth* Most easy chairs are so deep that it's impossible to contact the back of the seat without slumping. To make proper use of the support provided by a chair, the depth of the seat should not exceed two-thirds the length of the thigh.

★ *Proper height of work surface* To avoid tension in the arms and shoulders when working at a table or desk, make sure that the working surface is at approximately the same height as the elbows. This enables the hands to be used in a relaxed fashion, with no hunching of the arms and shoulders.

With care you can avoid the exhaustion of constant headaches and postural back pains. In the same way you can overcome the tiring, nagging pains of chronic indigestion, by eating more slowly, cutting out smoking and excess drinking, and avoiding the foods which you know upset your stomach.

Vitality Programme – Step Nineteen Never be content to endure chronic pain. If your feet hurt consult a chiropodist. Seek the help of a gynaecologist for your period pains, and an ear, nose and throat specialist for your persistent earache. Don't rest until you've found complete relief. Pain is a warning signal to observe, not a martyr's cross to bear. Rid yourself of your nagging aches and pains and you'll be brisker, brighter and less prone to troublesome fatigue.

STEP 20

The Battlefield Within

Scientists are always anxious to find a rational explanation for the phenomena they observe. This is certainly true of doctors who find it difficult to live with diagnostic mysteries. Rather than admit to occasional bewilderment, they will often attribute diseases to nebulous benign influences, such as 'nerves', or 'a virus', 'old age' or 'the change of life'.

This happened 60 years ago when the medical profession welcomed the 'auto-intoxication' theory of disease as a convenient explanation for a rag-bag of vague, sub-health syndromes, ranging from depression and debility to pimples, fibrositis and chronic fatigue. The theory was simple, and had enormous appeal to a generation brought up to believe in the doctrine of original sin. Sickness was caused by self-poisoning. It arose from the spread of toxins from hidden pockets of infection within the body. How could anyone expect to feel lively and energetic when their bloodstream was laden with poisons poured out by pus-filled tonsils or decayed teeth?

The argument carried conviction and the treatment, which was aimed at cutting out the inherent rottenness in man, was pursued with almost messianic zeal. Patients queued up at the dentists, to have each and every one of their teeth extracted, in the belief that this would cure their fibrositis. Children had their tonsils and adenoids removed as a routine in the hope that this would ensure them a virile manhood or radiant womanhood. The chronically debilitated had their sinuses irrigated, their vaginas douched and their gall bladders excised. They took powders to purify their blood, pills to cleanse their livers and salts to flush out their kidneys. Some who were both wealthy and gullible submitted to operation to remove large sections of their colons, so they could be forever rid of these festering sewers. Others sought to overcome the risk of intestinal infection by taking hefty daily doses of purgatives. But few felt any better for their heroic struggle to attain the desired state of 'inner cleanliness'. So the theory of auto-intoxication slowly became discredited and sank into oblivion. This is unfortunate, for chronic infection is undoubtedly one of the causes of persistent and seemingly inexplicable exhaustion.

This simple fact would not have needed stating a generation ago, when thousands of people were suffering the ravages of tuberculosis, a chronic debilitating disease associated with wasting and extreme exhaustion. For some strange reason the 'white plague' appeared to show a predilection for men and women of genius – Charlotte and Emily Brontë, Edgar Allen Poe, Robert Louis Stevenson, Mozart, Chopin, Keats, D. H. Lawrence, Raphael, Watteau and Modigliani. For as long as they were afflicted these artists suffered excessive tiredness, a disability shared by many consumptive heroines of the period, such as Marguerite Gautier in Dumas' novel *La Dame aux Camélias* and Mimi in Puccini's *La Bohème*.

Civil War The body enters a state of civil war whenever it is invaded by harmful bacteria. The adrenal glands are immediately alerted to activate the body's defence mechanism. The circulation of blood to the infected area is increased. The manufacture of white blood cells is accelerated, and masses of these germ-destroying cells are dispatched to do battle with the invading germs. Normally the general body temperature is also raised, since heat accelerates most of the physiological changes which are takihg place. All this is tiring, as anyone knows who has had to cope with glandular fever, pneumonia, flu or even a heavy cold.

The human organism draws heavily on its stores of energy whenever it's engaged in a struggle for survival with the infidel hordes of invading bacteria. Hippocrates recognised this 2,000 years ago, when he pointed out that the fight against disease involved not only *pathos* ((suffering) but also *ponos* (toil). Survival is the body's principal objective, but sometimes this can only be achieved at considerable cost. Many people become battle-fatigued, exhausted by their constant struggle against disease, which leaves them weak and wan. Dr W. A. Jerrett, a general practitioner from South Wales, investigated a group of 300 patients who were all complaining of being tired, run down and 'one degree under'. He subjected them to a full examination which included analysis of their urine and blood tests. Nearly two-thirds were found to be suffering from functional fatigue, unassociated with any specific medical disorder. Of the remainder, the most common organic cause for tiredness proved to be infection, which troubled a third of those who had a recognisable ailment.

The more depleted these individuals became, the more liable they were to succumb to further illness. In this way we can be caught up in a vicious circle, in which a low state of health renders us more prone to infection, which makes us weak and tired, and therefore more liable to further infection. So we are locked in the morass of sickness; second-class citizens trapped in a life devoid of vitality and drained of the *joie de vivre* which is our birthright.

If you feel you may be a victim of this dilemma, take heart. One purpose of this book is to bring about an improvement of general health which will make you not only less prone to fatigue but also more resistant to infection. The goals in fact are synonymous. If your general health is improved, as it will be if you follow the **Vitality Programme**, you'll tire less readily, feel happier, work more creatively, be more successful, age less rapidly and suffer fewer bouts of infectious illness.

Treating the To make an improvement in human well-being it's necessary to treat the
whole person whole person, rather than one or two isolated symptoms. This is the basis of holistic medicine, which is often regarded as a contemporary doctrine, but which is in fact as old as medicine itself. Hippocrates said, 'to heal

even an eye one must heal the head and even the whole body,' and Plato stated, 'the part can never be well unless the whole is well.'

If you've followed the **Vitality Programme** so far, you will have already strengthened your resistance to infection. An improved diet alone can have this effect. It is no coincidence that breast-fed babies are more resistant to chest infections than bottle-fed infants, or that epidemics flourish in times of famine, for animal experiments show that latent infections can be activated by nutritional deficiencies. Guinea pigs fed with fresh spring greens, for instance, markedly increase their resistance to tuberculosis.

In the earlier sections of the book I advocated aerobic exercise, largely as a means of improving the function of the heart and lungs. But this can also assist you in your fight against disease. Every time you work up a sweat by jogging, or playing an energetic game of tennis, you help to rid your system of unwanted germs. Whenever the temperature of the body is raised, the white blood cells are stimulated to produce a protein known as endogenous pyrogen, which is released into the blood stream, where it attacks any circulating bacteria. This defensive response occurs naturally during a fever. The favourite country remedy for influenza – wrapping up warm and going to bed surrounded by hot water bottles and layers of extra blankets – is an obvious, if unwitting, attempt to stimulate the release of such proteins. Vigorous exercise can have the same effect, for every time sportsmen work up a sweat they increase the internal temperature of the body by about four degrees.

By improving your general health, you'll increase your resistance to infection and with it your liability to fatigue. But your anxiety to consider the body in its entirety should not blind you to the needs of its separate parts. If one or two infected teeth are sapping your reserves of energy, get them treated straight away. (A six-monthly dental check will often bring to light symptomless pockets of infection.) If your gall bladder is infected, and you're intolerant of fatty foods or have pain over the right side of your abdomen after tucking into a plate of eggs and bacon, consult a doctor.

Don't wait indefinitely for nature and time to heal you. Use the combined resources of the healing professions to restore you to full vibrant health as soon as possible. In this way you can convert a vicious circle into a virtuous spiral, for just as ill health is debilitating, so the relief of infection can be rehabilitating. In the last chapter I urged you to leave no stone unturned until you found the answer to chronic pain. Now I urge you to take no rest, and accept no temporising solutions, until you obtain relief from chronic infections.

Everyday infections It's easy today to be complacent and think that we've overcome the problem of infectious disease, but while we may have mastered the major scourges of malaria, cholera, typhoid and tuberculosis, we still have a long way to go to overcome the everyday infections which plague our lives and sap our vitality. These ailments may not be medical emergencies but they're physically and mentally depressing, and should be tackled as seriously as a bout of pneumonia or peritonitis. Often they can be overcome by simple self-help measures.

Take the case of cystitis, the inflammation of the bladder and its outlet. This is one of the commonest of all gynaecological ailments, which is reckoned to affect four out of every five women at some time in their lives. Many doctors regard it as a trivial complaint easily controlled by antibiotic drugs, and yet many women suffer its ravages for years. Victims know only too well that recurrent bouts of cystitis cause not only pain on passing water, but also depression, irritability and profound fatigue. Just over two-thirds of one group of sufferers complained that their home life or careers had been adversely affected by the disease, while nearly three-quarters confessed that it had also impaired their normal enjoyment of sex and led to conflict within their marriages. Some accept these privations as part of a woman's inescapable burden; others take regular courses of antibiotics or submit themselves for painful surgery, treatments which are sometimes almost as exhausting as the disorder itself. No woman should resign herself to such a load without first trying self-help measures, which have brought new life to many sufferers from recurrent cystitis, such as always urinating after intercourse, washing scrupulously to keep the crotch clear of infectious bacteria, wearing cotton rather than nylon underpants and drinking a good deal of fluid each day.

Women who endure regular episodes of thrush, a thick, irritating, white vaginal discharge caused by the yeast *candida albicans*, may keep the disease under control each time by using pessaries containing the antibiotic nystatin. But permanent relief can be achieved by such simple remedies as reducing the sugar content of their diet and inserting a little yoghurt into their vaginas, both of which measures discourage the growth of yeast organisms. In recent years an increasing number of women have been found to be suffering pelvic inflammatory disease from the *actinomycetes* organism, a fungus that normally inhabits the mouth and throat, but which often gains entry into the womb when women are wearing contraceptive coils or loops. A recent survey at a British birth control clinic revealed that over 30 per cent of women fitted with a plastic intra-uterine device (IUD) showed signs of pelvic actinomycosis, a disease that was not found in any of the women using the contraceptive pill. Initially the symptoms of pelvic inflammatory disease are mild, as they are with most other forms of smouldering low-grade infection – fatigue, general malaise, mild fever and night chills and sweats. Later an offensive vaginal discharge may appear, followed by tenderness and swelling at the pit of the abdomen as pelvic abscesses form. In the early stages of the disease, relief can be obtained, sometimes dramatically, by dispensing with the IUD and switching to another form of contraception.

Mercifully, the body is always striving to heal its own ailments, and will often do so readily if we remove the obstacles to recovery. Sufferers from sore throats and sinusitis may have benefited already by the advice given in Step Seventeen, for if they now maintain their rooms at a comfortable level of humidity they will run less risk of drying out their mucous membranes and so be less prone to nose and throat infections. Another simple tip may benefit other sinus victims. Germs entering the nose are normally wafted harmlessly into the stomach where they are killed by the strong gastric acid. The invention and use of the handkerchief as a socially acceptable alternative to spitting and sniffing can hamper this normal process. People who close *both* nostrils when they blow their noses run the risk of driving germ-laden secretions into their sinuses. The same can apply to stifled sneezes. According to New York physician Dr David Mezz, the over-enthusiastic suppression of sneezes can lead to nose bleeding, ringing in the ears and sinus trouble. The safe alternative is to sneeze openly into a handkerchief, and to close only one nostril at a time when blowing the nose. A simple modification of habits like these is sometimes enough to alter the balance between health and disease.

Dental disease This certainly applies to dental disease. The World Health Organisation believes that most of the adult population of the civilised world suffers from gum disease. In fact, after the age of 40 we're far more likely to lose our teeth from gum disease than from dental decay.

In normal health our teeth are surrounded by a tight collar of gum tissue. This ends in a sharp fringe, similar to the cuticle at the base of a nail, which seals the tooth and prevents food particles, bacteria and dirt from entering the tooth socket. If the gums are allowed to become diseased they change from being firm and hard to being soft, swollen and tender. This weakens the seal around the teeth and permits the formation of small pockets in the gums where food debris can lodge and germs multiply, which leads to a condition known as pyorrhoea, literally a 'flow of pus'. If left untreated the infected gum tissues recede and the teeth become loose.

As the years advance we become 'long in the tooth', not because our teeth grow, but because disease makes our gums recede. Losing teeth, having bleeding gums and foul breath may seem a trivial, localised disease, but there's evidence that persistent pyorrhoea can sap our energy and impair our general health. Alex Hailey, author of *Roots*, tells how plantation owners assessed the value of slaves not only by studying their muscular strength but also by examining their teeth and gums. This one can accept as a reasonable precaution, because gum disease can lower a worker's health and general efficiency. A speaker at a recent dental congress warned: 'The bacteria and toxins from gum infection may be absorbed into the bloodstream and even the gastro-intestinal tract, where they are thought to be a significant contributory factor in a wide variety of diseases.' The rot may start in the mouth, but it doesn't necessarily end there. So don't be a martyr to gum disease. Visit your dentist every six months to have your teeth cleaned. Use dental floss or wooden toothpicks to cleanse the spaces between your teeth. Eat more fibrous foods to clean the teeth and stimulate the flow of saliva. And revert to the old Elizabethan practice of using a dental cloth or face flannel, giving the gums a daily friction rub to enhance their circulation.

Be alert to infection   Without becoming hypochondriacal, try to rid your body of every vestige of lingering infection. Seek medical help if you notice any untoward symptoms, such as tender, swollen glands, a raised temperature, vaginal discharge, or a persistent, purulent cough. An itching anus, particularly at night, may be the only symptom of threadworm infection, an infestation which studies at a Berkshire general practice suggest may trouble one in three young children in Britain. An inflammation of the eyeball may be the only sign of an infection with toxocariasis, a worm disease carried by about one in eight of Britain's cats and dogs, and now believed to infest some two per cent of the human population. Pet owners who insist on kissing their animals, or 'sharing' their meals, may pick up the toxocariasis eggs in their mouths. From here they travel into the lower part of the intestine, where they may hatch out into larvae, enter the bloodstream and be deposited in the liver, chest, heart, brain and eyes. This can cause serious chest trouble, liver damage, blindness or brain disease. More often, however, the infection merely causes symptons of mild ill health no different from those produced by scores of other infections.

If you visit your doctor complaining of general malaise, he may take a blood sample and carry out an ESR test – an estimate of your erythrocyte sedimentation rate. This is a measure of the speed at which a column of whole blood becomes divided into two distinct layers, the denser, red blood cells sinking to the bottom, the lighter, practically colourless plasma remaining at the top. The rate of separation will be appreciably quicker if you have an acute or chronic infection, or are suffering from a disease which causes tissue destruction. But the ESR test is totally non-specific. It will alert your doctor to the fact that something is amiss within your body, but will provide no clues regarding its nature or location. To fill in these gaps and establish a more exact diagnosis he will have to carry out further questioning, clinical examinations and possibly laboratory tests. That is his or her duty, in cases of hidden disease, and a fascinating quest it can be. But you must first recognise that your unnatural tiredness and malaise could be the result of hidden infection or disease, and to seek appropriate medical help.

Vitality Programme – Step Twenty   Tiredness can be the result of chronic infection. This was found to be the case in one out of every ten patients who visited one general practitioner's surgery with the complaint of being perpetually exhausted. If you have reason to believe that you are suffering from a low-grade infection – consult your doctor. And take sensible precautionary measures to minimise the risk of chronic infections such as cystitis, gum disease and sinusitis.

STEP 21

One Man's Meat

Struggling with unremitting pain can exhaust the body's stores of energy. Battling with hidden infections can be equally fatiguing. So too can the fight against allergies. 50 years ago it was said that allergy, after infection, was the greatest cause of sickness in the Western world. Today many doctors believe that allergy has become Public Enemy Number One. Others reckon that the hazard is greatly exaggerated. The difference of opinion is easily explained. Some doctors reserve the term allergy to describe only those cases when a foreign substance triggers off an abnormal response within the body which can be measured in terms of an increase in circulating antibodies. This is a condition which it's generally agreed afflicts about 15 per cent of adults in Britain and 40 per cent of children. Others use the term in a more general sense, to cover hypersensitivity to a wide spectrum of substances, ranging from Chinese food to knicker elastic and even mothers-in-law! Estimates suggest that as many as 80 per cent of patients attending a doctor's surgery may be suffering from this non-immunological type of allergy.

Once again the problem is one of recognition. It's simple to suspect the role of allergies in clear-cut cases of asthma, hay fever or contact dermatitis, but far less straightforward to spot when the symptoms are diffuse and vague, and bear no obvious relationship to contact with a specific allergen. Many puzzling cases of persistent sub-health, which doctors might once have labelled psychosomatic are now believed to stem from these masked allergies.

Masked allergies The term 'masked' allergy was first used by Dr Herbert Rinkel of Kansas City. Rinkel was a powerfully-built, athletic man who played football as a full-back before he enlisted as a soldier in the First World War. But his great ambition was to be a doctor, and as soon as he was demobilised he enrolled at medical school. From that point on his health deteriorated inexplicably. He became a victim of chronic catarrh, fatigue and headaches, which made it difficult for him to concentrate on his work. Despite this handicap he struggled on with his studies, fortified by regular supplies of eggs from the family farm. At the end of the course he graduated top of his class. Once in practice he decided to observe the maxim, 'Physician heal thyself!' For some while he'd taken an interest in allergic disease, and he began to wonder whether his general malaise might not be due to his love of eggs, which he ate every day. So one day as a test he ate six eggs in quick succession, reasoning that if he was hypersensitive to them, this would provoke his symptoms. As he felt better rather than worse for the experience, he felt justified in dismissing the matter from his mind. But a lingering doubt must have remained, for four years later he decided to carry out the experiment of eliminating all trace of egg from his diet. After two or three days he started to feel decidedly better. Then on the fifth day he ate a piece of homemade birthday cake, which he didn't realise had been made with eggs. Ten minutes later he was on the floor in a faint. Once he recovered he asked his wife for the recipe. On learning that it contained three eggs, he deduced that this must have been the cause of his loss of consciousness. Five days without his favourite food had reduced his tolerance, and increased his level of sensitivity. So for the next five days he followed a strict, egg-free diet. During the time his health steadily improved. Then he sampled an egg. This again provoked an acute allergic response, a simple test which clinched the diagnosis. He was allergic to eggs, a food he'd eaten every day of his life since he was a child, a food he enjoyed, and which he ate with relish! It seemed paradoxical, and yet when Rinkel experimented with his patients he found that many of them were also suffering from unsuspected food intolerances. If they kept away from the offending foodstuffs for five days their health improved. If after a spell of abstinence they sampled the forbidden items, they suffered an acute sensitivity reaction. Rinkel called this masked allergy. He wrote: 'If one uses a food every day or so, one may be allergic to it but never suspect it as a cause of symptoms. It is common to feel better after the meal at which the food is used than before mealtime. This is called masked food allergy.'

This strange reaction is easily explained in terms of stress physiology. When we're exposed to any form of stress – shock, extreme cold, or excitement – the body increases its output of stress hormones to activate its defence mechanisms. The immediate effect is to stimulate and energise. But if the stress persists too long exhaustion sets in as the body's powers of adaptation are gradually drained. Recovery takes place once the stress is over, and the body regains its reserves of energy. In the case of masked food allergies, the sequence of events – alarm reaction, exhaustion, recovery – can span a variable number of hours, but rarely lasts longer than three days. Attacks can be of varying degrees of severity, but often follow a course similar to the one depicted overleaf:

The common symptoms of masked food allergies are:
a) Persistent fatigue not relieved by rest.
b) Abdominal discomfort, rumblings, excessive wind, colicky pain, diarrhoea.
c) Headache.
d) Palpitations, particularly after meals.
e) Runny nose and frequent sneezing.
f) Excessive sweating unrelated to exercise or environmental temperature.
g) Skin irritation, eczema or rash.

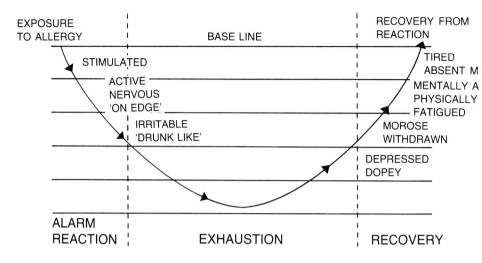

If you suffer a number of these symptoms for no obvious reason you may be suffering from a masked food allergy. This is particularly likely i the symptoms fluctuate, with occasional attacks being followed by period of complete remission. Milk products are the commonest foods to provoke an allergic response. The second most common offender is egg, closely followed by nuts and fish. An analysis of a series of cases of food allerg studied at two London hospitals revealed that 88 per cent stemmed from an abnormal sensitivity to either milk, eggs, nuts or fish. Other frequen dietary culprits are wheat flour, chocolate, artificial food colouring agents coffee, pork, bacon, chicken, tomatoes, soft fruit, cheese and yeast.

To confirm the diagnosis of food allergy you've got a choice of two courses of action. The most popular confirmatory test is the eliminatio diet. This can be a somewhat laborious process since it involves eliminatin suspect foods from the diet for four-day periods at a time. For example if you have reason to believe that you might be sensitive to eggs, like D Rinkel, you shun eggs and all egg-containing foods for four days. If you hunch is right, your health will improve towards the end of this period a you eliminate all traces of egg protein from your system. To clinch th diagnosis you then sit down and eat a hard-boiled egg. A sudden retur of symptoms will confirm your suspicions beyond all shadow of doubt. i you show no sensitivity to eggs, you must then go on to test your respons to the other common allergens, going without milk for four days, the nuts, fish, wheat flour, chocolate and coffee until you finally trace th source of your hypersensitivity. Serial testing like this is frequentl necessary, for many people are sensitive to more than one foodstuff.

The other confirmatory test is the five-day fast. This is a quicker wa of proving the existence of food allergies, but one which should not b undertaken without medical supervision, since it involves going witho all food and drinking only pure water, for five days. If you still feel tired and sick at the end of this time you can be sure your symptoms don't stem from food allergy. But if the fast proves invigorating you can reasonably suspect a specific food allergy. To identify the offending foodstuff, gradually re-introduce milk, eggs, nuts, fish, wheat, chocolate and coffee into your diet a day at a time. Any reaction will pin-point the source of your sensitivity.

Non-food **But** foods are not the only causes of sensitivity reactions. The world we
allergies inhabit is filled with gases, microbes, plants, synthetic textiles, cosmetic creams, drugs and strange new chemicals, any one of which can provoke an allergic response. Many people are sensitive to lipsticks, grass pollen or house dust, and recognise that this is the cause of their recurrent rash, hay fever or asthma. Less well appreciated is the role of these non-food allergies in provoking symptoms of general ill health, depression, irritability, tiredness, and headache. Every time the body's immune responses are brought into play, we suffer a reduction in our store of energy. This is every bit as tiring as exposure to persistent pain or chronic infection.

Some doctors are now specialising in this new field of 'bio-ecological' medicine. They have discovered, for instance, that a quarter of all adverse drug reactions are due to hypersensitivity, with one out of four asthmatics being sensitive to aspirin. In the world of nature they have found the most common allergen is grass pollen, followed by the house-dust mite, cat dander, plantain pollen, plane-tree pollen, mugwort pollen, horse dander and dog hair. In Chicago, bio-ecologist Dr Ted Randolph discovered that one-third of the patients attending his food allergy clinic showed a strong allergic response to new materials in the chemical environment. A common offender was house gas. In his book *Human Ecology and Susceptibility to the Chemical Environment* he cites the case of a 31-year-old housewife who suffered recurrent bouts of fatigue, headache, running nose, irritability, and muzzy headedness. These symptoms occurred largely during the winter when she was confined indoors, which naturally made Randolph suspect an allergen within the home. Tests showed that the patient was sensitive to house dust, but her major improvement in health came when she discarded her gas cooker, gas refrigerator and gas water-heater and installed electrical appliances in their place. Since that time Dr Randolph has identified over two thousand people in the Chicago area who are hypersensitive to gas fumes.

The more natural the life you lead the less you're likely to suffer allergic fatigue. The purer the air you breathe, the less adulterated the food you eat, the fewer the chemicals and drugs you pour into your stomach, the less demands you'll place on your body's defence mechanisms.

If despite this you find you're allergic to penicillin, pork or pets, take sensible steps to avoid the offending allergens. For it's surely better to part company with the family cat or give up your fondness for scrambled eggs than to suffer persistent tiredness, headaches, depression, colitis or catarrh.

Vitality Programme – Step Twenty-One   Fatigue may be caused by the body's constant exposure to substances to which it is allergic or hypersensitive. Try to identify those allergens and take steps wherever possible to eliminate them from your diet or environment.

STEP 22

The Great Stoned Age

We are living in an era which has been described as the Drugged Decade. From a twilight birth to a narcotised death, our lives are being subjected to increasing chemical control. We take pills to help us sleep and pills to wake us up. Law-abiding citizens visit their doctors to get their fix of 'uppers' or 'downers'; while others get their 'highs' from smoking, snorting or mainlining drugs which are illicitly obtained. Tiredness is one price we pay for this narcotic addiction. We recognise the numbed apathy of the heroin addict, but this is only the dramatic tip of the massive iceberg of drug-induced lethargy. For every comatose victim of drug overdosage carried into a casualty ward, there must be thousands of undisclosed sufferers from minor forms of drug intoxication; people who are dragging themselves about in a state of perpetual exhaustion because their nerve and muscle cells are constantly doped with marijuana, Valium, alcohol or nicotine.

Lack of vitality and *joie de vivre* is one of the earliest symptoms of drug abuse. When the parents of young heroin addicts in Britain were asked what tell-tale signs alerted them to their youngsters' plight, 90 per cent said they noted their lack of drive and inability to concentrate, and 80 per cent commented on their slumped posture and abnormal desire to lie down and sleep. The same no doubt could be said of businessmen after an alcoholic lunch, or pensioners struggling to rouse themselves in the morning after a sedated night's sleep. Any drug which is powerful enough to suppress one symptom is equally capable of suppressing other metabolic functions. Sir Derrick Dunlop said, when chairman of the British Safety of Drugs Committee: 'There is no such thing as a completely safe and effective medicine. Most drugs are given to modify or repress some biological process. Without this capability they will be useless in treatment; with it, they are bound to cause adverse effects from time to time.' One of the most common of these untoward effects is tiredness unrelieved by rest.

Medicinal drugs and tiredness Doctors now use the term iatrogenic fatigue to describe the run down feeling which comes as a by-product of taking medically prescribed drugs. When Dr Jerrett carried out his investigation of patients complaining of general fatigue at his practice in South Wales, he discovered that fatigue caused as a by-product of taking drugs was the third most common cause of chronic tiredness, being responsible for considerably more complaints than anaemia, diabetes, cancer or thyroid deficiency.

Some drugs are notorious offenders in this respect. The antihistamines used in the treatment of allergies and travel sickness so commonly cause weariness that they are issued with the official warning that they may cause drowsiness and so shouldn't be taken by people driving cars or in control of potentially dangerous machinery. The whole range of tranquillisers and antidepressant pills which are used to suppress symptoms of mental distress can also produce an unacceptable level of general fatigue. Likewise the barbiturates and other hypnotics. These are taken at night to induce sleep, but since they persist in the body for up to twenty-four hours they can cause sleepiness well into the following day. Many cough mixtures contain codeine phosphate, a drug which can suppress energy levels almost as well as it suppresses coughs. One of Dr Jerrett's patients was the driver of a high-speed train who complained that he was constantly tired at work and found it difficult to keep awake at the controls of his locomotive. He recovered the moment he stopped taking high doses of a proprietary, codeine-containing cough mixture.

Patients who take beta-blockers to control their blood pressure may suffer such fatigue. So may those using Stemetil to alleviate their giddiness or lithium salts to lessen their manic-depressive mood swings.

Some drugs cause tiredness by provoking anaemia, others by impairing the function of the liver. Recent tests show that cimetidine, the drug commonly used in the treatment of peptic ulcers, causes a one-third decrease in the blood flow through the liver. This must reduce the speed at which the liver inactivates toxins in the blood.

The only way to overcome the problem of drug-induced fatigue is to be far more discerning in your use of medicines. Assume that all drugs are harmful until proved innocent. Take them only when they're absolutely essential. You wouldn't fill the petrol tank of your car with a strange liquid, so why fill your body with chemicals of unknown composition? If your doctor prescribes a drug, insist on knowing its name, its intended action and possible side effects. The pharmaceutical companies produce hundreds of new drugs each year and your doctor can't possibly keep up to date with every one. So use him as an adviser, as you would an insurance broker or bank manager, rather than an infallible guru. Where drugs are concerned be a discriminating consumer, and always remember that the ultimate responsibility for your health is yours and not your doctor's.

Tobacco tiredness This responsibility should be exercised in many other spheres. You can't expect to be brim full of energy if you're hooked on cigarettes. Study after study has shown that smoking has a depressing effect on physical performance. Tests on British soldiers training to become physical training instructors have shown that non-smokers consistently outperform smokers in three-mile cross-country runs. Treadmill tests on policemen reveal that smokers tire more readily than non-smokers, and experience among American airmen proves that smokers derive less benefit from physical conditioning programmes than non-smokers.

The harm is done in several ways. In the first place smoking constricts the peripheral blood vessels, and so impedes the passage of blood around the body. It also reduces the capacity of the lungs which impairs the oxygenation of the blood, and quickens the pulse rate, making the heart work harder even when at rest. But the greatest damage of all stems from the inhalation of carbon monoxide, the toxic gas which forms about four per cent of tobacco smoke. Carbon monoxide is poisonous because it combines with the haemoglobin in the blood and so blocks the transport of oxygen around the body. Inhale a little and you'll feel mildly sick and drowsy; inhale too much and you'll sink into a fatal coma. Even working in a smoke-filled room can make you feel tired, for carbon monoxide molecules have an affinity for haemoglobin which is 250 times greater than that of oxygen. As a result 10 per cent or more of the haemoglobin in a heavy smoker's bloodstream can be permanently bound up in the form of carboxyhaemoglobin, and so made useless for its primary function of nourishing the tissues with oxygen. You can't function at peak efficiency if you smoke, nor can you expect to overcome the problem of chronic fatigue if you continue to inhale the toxic gases from your, or other people's, cigarettes.

Car exhaust gases The exhaust gases from cars provide another common cause of carbon monoxide poisoning. Every year in Britain cars belch out some 5,000,000 tons of carbon monoxide gas. This can reach toxic levels in confined spaces such as garages, tunnels and underground car parks, and also in heavy urban traffic. Surveys show that the carbon monoxide levels in crowded city streets sometimes exceed the maximum safety limit permitted in industry.

A few years ago a scientist provided startling evidence of this risk. Using himself as test subject, he set out to monitor the levels of carbon monoxide in his blood first in the country and then after he'd wandered around the streets of London. He discovered that after he'd inhaled the city fumes for a couple of hours his blood carbon monoxide level was twice as high as it had been in the country. By the end of the evening rush hour it had quadrupled. But the steepest rise of all came when on top of this he smoked three cigarettes in quick succession. This sent his carbon monoxide level soaring to *six* times its base rate. Anyone with this degree of blood pollution is bound to feel a trifle below par, if not decidedly dopey. This is why Tokyo policemen on traffic control duty are given occasional whiffs of oxygen to clear their heads and keep them alert.

Carbon monoxide levels within cars can also be unacceptably high, even when the occupants observe a sensible no-smoking precaution. One doctor who has made a special study of the subject claims: 'In any street most people in cars are in a partly drugged state.' This may not be enough to produce obvious symptoms of carbon monoxide poisoning, but can be sufficient to impair judgement, provoke fatigue and slow reaction times. This must be a contributory factor in many road accidents, for a survey in Paris showed that 38 per cent of drivers involved in car accidents had dangerously high levels of carbon monoxide in their blood. This risk can be reduced in five main ways:

★ Do not allow smoking in your car.

★ Keep your exhaust system in good repair and see that there are no leaks between the engine and passenger compartments. (Make an immediate inspection for defects at the first whiff of fumes or suggestion of headaches or drowsiness while driving.)

★ If the air intake of your car is in a low forward position, make sure that it is switched off in dense, slow moving traffic.

★ Turn your engine off quickly when stationary in underground car parks or prolonged traffic jams. This is vital, since an idling engine generates four times as much carbon monoxide as one driven at normal cruising speeds.

★ See that your car is properly serviced, for an over-rich petrol/air mixture caused by dirty spark plugs or a badly adjusted carburettor wastes money, and doubles the output of carbon monoxide.

Lead poisoning Cars are partly responsible for another insidious source of drug fatigue. Since 1923 compound lead salts have been added to petrol as a cheap way of increasing its octane rating and improving its anti-knock properties. This has increased the risk of lead poisoning. When the Californian Institute of Technology mounted a polar expedition in the mid-sixties they seized the opportunity of analysing the layers of snow and glacial ice, measuring the amount of airborne lead which had been deposited during the preceding centuries. They found little evidence of lead in the pre-1750 deposits. Then came the Industrial Revolution, which resulted in a gradual quadrupling of the lead fall-out during the next two centuries. From that point onwards the increase in lead pollution soared, the rate tripling in the brief period from 1940–65. This can only be attributed to the widescale use of leaded fuels.

Today it's estimated that a third to a half of airborne lead comes from car exhaust fumes. There can be no doubt that this has added to the amount of lead entering the body. One study showed that children living near a major New Jersey highway had twice as much lead in their bodies as those living in the town's back streets. Some authorities claim that this does not pose a significant health threat. But this is not the view of Dr Bryce Smith, one of Britain's foremost experts on heavy metal poisoning who says: 'To my best knowledge no other toxic chemical has accumulated in man to average levels so close to the threshold for overt clinical poisoning.'

Unfortunately the early signs of lead poisoning are vague and easily overlooked. Even when the initial tiredness, weakness, muscle aches and general malaise give way to vomiting and severe abdominal pain, the disease may go undetected by all but the most alert physician. Even these low levels of lead poisoning have been found to cause anaemia, by impairing the formation of haemoglobin.

Reducing the lead content of petrol will improve the health of the environment, but it will not remove the risk of lead pollution. According to calculations made by the Medical Research Council's Air Pollution Unit, four times as much lead is introduced into the body in the food we eat and the water we drink as through the air we breathe.

This has been a problem for at least two thousand years. Some historians even attribute the fall of the Roman Empire to the steady decline in the people's vitality, brought about by their heavy consumption of wine stored in lead-glazed jars and water carried in lead-lined conduits.

It's estimated that the average Briton today eats about 0.4 mg of lead per day, but this intake is subject to considerable variation. Some soils have a particularly high lead content due to the composition of their parent rocks, and this may increase the lead content of vegetables grown on them a hundredfold. Crops grown close to a busy road will also carry an abnormally high dose of lead, for about half of the lead particles emitted from car exhaust fumes fall within thirty yards of the highway. For this reason city dwellers may find it safer to buy produce from the market than eat vegetables grown in their own polluted backyards. But the greatest precaution you can take is to cut down your intake of tinned foods, which often have an unacceptably high lead content. This stems mainly from the solder which is a mixture of lead and tin. The statutory limit for the lead content of food is two parts per million, but a check of canned foods carried out by a Worcestershire public health department revealed that all samples contained above the recommended dosage, the levels of contamination ranging from 2–10 parts per million. One tin of sardines was even found to contain 20 times the legal limit of lead!

Drinking water provides another common source of lead pollution. Tests carried out by the Department of the Environment in 1976 suggest that about one in ten British homes have water supplies carrying a proportion of lead which exceeds the EEC safety regulations. This applies particularly to older homes in Scotland, Wales and Northern England, where soft, slightly acidic water acts on the domestic lead plumbing, or on old fashioned, lead-lined storage tanks. If you live in one of these high-risk areas there is one simple measure you should take which, if regularly observed, can reduce your blood lead levels by about one-fifth. The precaution is always run the taps for a brief while before drawing off supplies for drinking or cooking. This gets rid of water which has stood long enough to absorb a high level of lead pollution, a safety measure which is particularly important with the first drawn water of the day.

Alcohol and fatigue   But however serious the hazards of lead and carbon monoxide pollution, they are statistically insignificant compared with the risk of alcohol poisoning. If the fall of Rome was due to chronic lead poisoning, the decline in vitality of the Western world today could with equal justification be attributed to chronic alcoholism. Alcohol is undoubtedly the world's favourite drug. When stress levels rise Mexicans rush to their tequila bottles, Japanese swallow a generous tot of sake and Russians sedate themselves with slivovitz. But while modest occasional drinking is relaxing and convivial, steady drinking is enervating and debilitating.

Pharmacologists classify alcohol as a non-specific central nervous system depressant. This means that in small measures it acts as a gentle sedative. In larger doses it paralyses the neuromuscular system, causing muscle weakness, unco-ordination, slowed reaction times, sleepiness and impaired brain function.

A sound night's sleep may be enough to relieve the exhaustion caused by a single drinking spree, but it won't be sufficient to overcome the persistent drinkers' chronic fatigue. They are tired before they start the day. Some of this lethargy may stem from malnutrition, and particularly from a deficiency of riboflavin (Vitamin B$_2$) which is used up rapidly in the metabolism of alcohol. Some may derive from damage to the liver, the early symptoms of which are weakness, fatigue and general malaise. Alcoholic tiredness can also stem from the accumulation of lactic acid in the system, this being one of the by-products of alcohol metabolism, or from a low blood-sugar level, since hypoglycaemia is one of the body's responses to alcohol ingestion. Persistent drinking also leads to chronic sleep disturbance, since it impairs that part of sleep known as REM or dream sleep. You can't be lively and alert if your nerve cells are constantly poisoned with alcohol. This doesn't mean you've got to sign the pledge and lead a life of total abstinence. You can enjoy all the pleasures of alcohol, with none of the attendant enervating risks, if you observe the four rules of sensible social drinking:

★ *Drink in moderation*   Just over a century ago a Scottish doctor, Dr Francis Anstie, laid down the 'safety limit' for drinkers as one-and-a-half ounces of fluid alcohol per day. This is the equivalent of half a bottle of wine, two pints of beer or three-and-a-half measures of spirit. Subsequent research has confirmed the soundness of this advice. Keep within this limit and you won't find your energy sapped or your thinking slowed. These figures apply to person of average build.

★ *Drink slowly*   If your liver is in good condition it should be able to detoxify up to 1 mg of alcohol per hour, which is the equivalent of a single measure of spirits, a glass of wine or a half-pint of beer. Keep your consumption within this limit and you can drink steadily through the evening without becoming intoxicated. Conversely it can take you hours to sober up if you drink too rapidly and build up a high concentration of alcohol in the bloodstream. Drink four schooners of sherry in quick succession and eight hours later you'll probably still fail the breathalyser test even though you've had a good night's sleep in between.

★ *Never drink on an empty stomach* The risk of developing symptoms of alcohol poisoning are greatly reduced if drinks are consumed with food, since this delays the rate of alcohol absorption. For instance, the man who goes out to a business meal and takes a double Scotch before dinner, a couple of glasses of claret with his main course, a port with the cheese and biscuits and a leisurely tot of brandy to help him through the after-dinner speeches, will remain cheerful but not inebriated. Throughout the evening his blood alcohol level is unlikely to rise above 60 mg per 100 ml, which is comfortably within the legal driving limits. But if the same man goes to a cocktail party on an empty stomach and drinks the identical amount of alcohol as four double gins, his blood alcohol level will probably soar to 140 mg per 100 ml. This will make him tipsy, tired and tottery, and legally unfit to drive for possibly six or seven hours.

★ *Take occasional temperance breaks* The liver has vast reserves and remarkable powers of recovery. Remove three-quarters of an animal's liver and the remaining cells will multiply rapidly until the organ is completely restored within about eight weeks. The liver suffers permanent damage from the toxic effects of alcohol and other chemicals only when it's subjected to long continued poisoning. The popular dry-cleaning fluid, carbon tetra-chloride, is a potent liver poison, but tests show that the liver recovers rapidly from even large doses of it providing the exposure is intermittent. The danger lies in continuous exposure, which even in small dosage can cause permanent scarring of the liver.

The same applies to alcohol. Give the liver cells a brief respite and they will recover from an occasional night on the tiles. Paralyse them with a heavy daily dose of alcohol and they'll give up the struggle for survival and die.

Tests show that the liver cells require about three or four days to get back to normal after being exposed to alcohol poisoning. So if you should succumb to a night of intemperate drinking, give your liver a chance to recover by going on the wagon for three or four days. One study in Scotland has shown that two-thirds of continuous heavy drinkers suffer liver disease, compared with only a third of those who indulge in heavy binges followed by periods of relative abstinence.

Vitality Programme – Step Twenty-Two The cells of your body will function best when they're in a pure, wholesome environment, not when they're poisoned with alcohol, cigarette smoke, car exhaust fumes or unnecessary medicinal drugs. The watchword is moderation. Don't take pills unless they are absolutely necessary. Stop smoking, avoid fume-filled atmospheres and let your drinking be governed by sensible rules.

Step 23

The Bombardment of the Senses

'Fight or flight'

Every animal has a complex set of protective reflexes which enable it to react promptly to environmental threats. When a primitive tribesman spotted a tell-tale stirring in the bushes, heard the roaring of a lion, or felt the first clammy touch of a snake's embrace, a whole host of changes took place within his body which prepared him for instant action. With muscles tensed, he was automatically ready for 'fight or flight'. Once the danger was over his body quickly returned to its resting state.

These inbuilt responses are common to every species and every age, for even the most primitive blob of protoplasm will react to light and touch. But the reactions which ensured the survival of primeval man now threaten the lives of contemporary man, by their deafening and unrelenting pressure. We still respond in an atavistic way to unexpected noise, but the reaction is now invariably inappropriate. When sirens blare, telephones ring, whistles sound, or cars backfire, we continue to react as though our lives were at stake, even though the incidents themselves present no threat. From the moment we wake up in the morning to the time we go to bed at night our bodies are subject to a constant bombardment of sensory stimulation, raucous noise, flashing lights, jostling crowds and jarring vibrations. The young secretary travels to work every day in an overpacked commuter train. Stations and hoardings flash by. The train stops, starts, rolls and lurches. Then she jostles her way through the rush-hour crowds to the office, where she works to the accompaniment of a cacophony of typewriters, duplicators and adding machines. On the way home she faces another struggle through traffic-snarled streets, where the bray of horns and the muffled explosion of internal combustion engines assault the ears, and a conflict of ever-changing neon signs, traffic lights and flashing beacons insult the eyes. At the end of the day she is exhausted, not from overwork but from over-stimulation. So numbed is she by this sensory bombardment, that if she opts for a little extra excitement in the evening she will go to a discothèque where the decibel levels of the amplified music are louder still, and the flashing of the lights yet more intense. Even if she is too tired for gallivanting, she will stay home and watch a flickering television screen, or listen to the full-throated roar of a hi-fi set. For her whole day she, and thousands like her, will have borne the burden of sensory overload. This is one of the common contemporary causes of fatigue.

The dangers of City workers may grow accustomed to working in noisy environments,
noise just as they accept the privations caused by traffic jams, artificial lighting,
polluted air and long commuting journeys. But familiarity with the
clamour does not necessarily produce an increased level of noise tolerance.
Experiments reveal that noise is an insidious hazard that can damage our
health and impair our efficiency even though we are blissfully unaware of
its impact. Tests show that prolonged exposure to everyday city noise
increases muscular tension, raises blood pressure, impairs digestion,
decreases concentration, lowers working efficiency and provokes more
rapid fatigue. One American study revealed that typists working in a noisy
room use up to 19 per cent more energy than those working in a quiet
environment. As a result they tire more readily and are more prone to
make mistakes.

Some simple measures can be introduced to protect against sensory
overload. Ear plugs and muffs can be introduced to protect the ears from
excessive sound, and dark glasses worn to shield the eyes from excessive
glare, but it's far more difficult to protect the body from other forms of
noxious stimulation, such as putrid smells, overcrowding and unpleasant
vibrations.

With the increased use of industrial machinery, there is a risk that many
factory workers may be suffering the effects of vibration-induced sickness.
If a glass can be shattered by a soprano hitting a high C from the other
side of the room, think what effect the constant pounding of a die-casting
press has on the machine operator who stands beside it. And if Joshua's
men could topple the walls of Jericho with a few blasts on their horns,
imagine what damage can be done to the framework of the human body
by the perpetual bone-shaking rattles of buses, trains and cars. Reports
from Russia suggest that many long distance lorry drivers suffer vibration
sickness, a disease characterized by nausea, indigestion, headaches and
rapid fatigue. And in America it's reliably estimated that over 8,000,000
workers are exposed to levels of occupational vibration sufficient to
damage their health, reduce their energy levels and impair their working
efficiency.

Brainwashing Pavlov, the great Russian physiologist, in his classical study of conditioned
reflexes showed that every animal is liable to a 'rupture of higher nervous
activity' if subjected to excessive sensory stimulation. This discovery has
since been put to sinister use in the brainwashing of political prisoners.
In this process the morale, resistance and vitality of prisoners is destroyed
by a calculated process of nervous over-stimulation. Here is a typical
account of this steady process of detrition, published in the *Times*:

'The torture consisted of a treatment which prevented him from sleeping
for ten days. Sleep was forbidden during the day. At night, lying under a
bright electric light in his cell, he was awakened every fifteen minutes.
Fifteen minutes after "lights out" he would be awakened by pounding on
his cell door, fifteen minutes later there would be shrill whistling, and next

the electric light would be connected to an automatic device alternating a dim red light with a fierce white light from a powerful bulb . . . . This was repeated night after night for ten nights until he collapsed with shivering fits and hallucinations.'

The same 'rupture of higher nervous activity' is seen in front-line soldiers who become shell-shocked by sleepless nights and exposure to the deafening roar of guns and the ceaseless flashing of flares, fires and exploding mines. City workers may also become battle fatigued, even though they're not exposed to the same level of sensory overload.

City working A short while ago a survey was made of a large group of white-collar workers in the London area, including bank employees, journalists, teachers, local government officers, managers and university administrators. Nearly a third admitted that they felt the strain of working in London. The most frequent complaints concerned the fatigue of commuting long distances to work, the constant noise, the overcrowding, the lack of identity, and the rapid pace of city life. It seems that we are not yet adjusted to the noise, pace and congestion of city living. Urbanisation has arisen at a pace which has far outstripped our powers of adaptation.

Sensory overload is sapping our strength, spoiling our pleasures, souring our tempers and shortening our lives. Gerontologists have come up with some surprising findings when they've studied the lifestyles of communities with an abnormally high proportion of centenarians. They've found that the old stagers in the Caucasian mountains are frequently heavy smokers, while Siberian centenarians appear to break the dietary rules of health by consuming large quantities of reindeer meat and other animal fats. And in Ecuador the inhabitants of the Vilcabama valley often reach the age of a hundred despite drinking two to four cups of rum a day and smoking two or three packs of cigarettes. Only two common factors recur in these longevity studies: that people who live to a ripe and vigorous old age tend to take plenty of outdoor exercise, and invariably live in villages rather than in cities.

Death rates have always been higher in urban communities than in the country. At one time this was attributed to the harmful effect of inhaling polluted air. Now it's accepted that the increased mortality is due in part at least to sensory overload, which increases the prevalence rates of crime, divorce, mental breakdown, suicide and psychosomatic illness. Overcrowding is another potent hazard.

Personal Animals in their natural environment rarely suffer from psychosomatic
territory illness: they do not murder, develop stomach ulcers, mutilate themselves, suffer high blood pressure or form homosexual bonds. In captivity they do all these things. This is thought to be due to the strain of living in close proximity to other animals, which makes it impossible to escape the tensions of territorial conflicts and hierarchical struggles. Every animal

likes to create a buffer zone around itself, which ethologists call the individual distance. Within this personal zone animals feel at home and inviolate. Here they can retreat when danger threatens and feel secure.

Workers in large cities, like animals in a cage, have forfeited their right to an inviolate individual territory. They have lost their privacy and have no personal foxhole into which they can retreat when the outside battle grows too fierce. They grow exhausted from the constant need to respond to the demands of others and cope with a ceaseless round of interpersonal conflicts, status struggles, aggressive displays and appeals for emotional sympathy and support.

There is a simple answer to this problem. If the battle grows too fierce it's time to sound the retreat. When animals are sick they instinctively hide themselves away in a quiet, dark corner until they have restored their equilibrium. When troops are found to be suffering from battle fatigue they are taken to a base camp far from the fighting zone to recuperate. The same recovery technique should be used from time to time by city dwellers.

A generation ago doctors made great use of the Weir-Mitchell treatment for nervous exhaustion. This recognised the fact that most debilitated nervous systems will recover if given adequate rest. Like a battery drained flat by constant use they can be recharged, providing they're switched off for a while to check the constant energy loss. To this end patients were placed in a quiet, darkened room. Visitors were barred, and food made light and easy to digest. Sometimes straw was placed outside their homes to deaden the sound of passing traffic; and they were even encouraged to wear clothing that was loose and light to reduce the stimulation of the fine nerve endings in the skin. With this careful sensory shielding they gradually overcame their exhaustion and were able to return to the daily fray.

Vitality Programme – Step Twenty-Three

If you're tired of the hurly-burly of modern life, make sure you provide yourself with ample refreshing breaks. Give yourself regular periods of solitude when you can be truly on your own away from the demands of family, friends and business associates. And schedule quiet times when you can escape the bright lights, noise and bustle – in the bath, lying under a tree in the garden with eyes closed, or sitting with lights turned out at the closing of the day watching the dying embers of the fire. You'll find these precious moments of solitude and quiet reflection will do more to restore your depleted resources of nervous energy than an entire pharmacopeia of tonics, tranquillisers and pick-me-ups.

STEP 24

The Hormonal Power House

Chronic fatigue is often attributed to the stress and strain of modern life. Business executives complain of being drained by the constant struggle to hold their place in the industrial rat race. University students resort to alcohol or sedatives to help them cope with heavy work loads and keen competitive pressures; while dual career housewives, forced to struggle with tensions and responsibilities both at work and at home, find themselves too tired in the evening to read a book, make love or enjoy a reasonable social life. It's easy to make the contemporary hurly-burly the cause of all our ills and woes. There is good reason to believe that many of the ailments we suffer – peptic ulcers, headaches, nervous breakdowns, hypertension and heart attacks – are provoked by stress. But the fault lies less in the nature of the stress itself, than in our response to it. We are not yet well adapted to twentieth-century living.

Stress is a powerful drug. When mishandled it can lead to untold unhappiness, irritability, tiredness, psychosomatic disease and even premature death. When carefully used it enhances both the quality and quantity of life. When we are its master rather than its slave, we can use stress to tap the hormonal well springs of vitality and excitement.

Many people are tired, not because they are overworked but because they are bored. With insufficient to arouse them, they sink into a state of lacklustre apathy. This happened to a colony of mice reared in the laboratories of the National Institute of Mental Health. They were brought up in conditions of great luxury, where they had no need to struggle for either food, comfort or security. In this rodent paradise they quickly lost their vitality and zest for life. The youngsters became listless, the mice of reproductive age became disinterested in sex and the older stagers began to show signs of psychosomatic distress.

Animal groups rapidly lose their vitality when they are deprived of the stimulus of the struggle to survive. The same applies to human communities. It's no coincidence that some of the major cultural and technical advances of the past have been made during periods of great social upheaval. Orson Welles recognised this historical fact, and commented on it in *The Third Man*, in words that he added to the original Carol Reed script. As he said: 'In Italy for thirty years under the Borgias they had warfare, terror, murder, bloodshed, but they produced Michaelangelo, Leonardo da Vinci, and the Renaissance. In Switzerland they had brotherly love, they had five hundred years of democracy and peace. And what did that produce? The cuckoo-clock.'

Too cosy for comfort We can be too cosy for our comfort, and too secure for our sanity. We need challenge and excitement to keep our brains agile and alert. When conditions become too easy, we sink into a state of physical and mental torpor. This has been the experience in Britain during recent years. Reports show that depression has become increasingly common in the socially placid areas of the United Kingdom, but has shown a significant decline in those parts of Northern Ireland most heavily troubled by outbreaks of civil violence and unrest. This is because exposure to danger activates the body's defence mechanisms and stimulates the release of energising hormones.

Nature is very economical in its use of energy. When we're secure and well fed the body's metabolic fires are turned down to conserve fuel. When danger threatens the alarm call goes out and every organ, gland, nerve cell and muscle fibre is called into action. The response is rapid, automatic and never changing. Under the stimulus of stress, messages are flashed from the hypothalamus to the pituitary gland to increase its output of master hormones such as ACTH, thyrotrophin, and gonadotrophin. These are despatched in the bloodstream to the adrenal glands, sitting astride the kidneys, where they increase the output of the stress hormones cortisol, adrenalin and noradrenalin; also to the thyroid gland to stimulate the production of thyroxine, and to the sex glands to increase the output of androgen and other sex hormones. At the same time the brain increases the tension in the voluntary muscles and whips up the activity of the sympathetic nervous system. The net result of these neurological changes is that the body is prepared for immediate action. The pupils dilate, the nostrils flare, the respiration and pulse rate quicken, blood pressure soars, the muscles tense, and fats and glucose are poured into the blood stream as fuels for muscular activity. One other effect of increasing the output of adrenaline and stimulating the sympathetic nervous system is to delay the onset of fatigue.

As a result of these changes we feel aroused and invigorated. Under their stimulus we are able to work at optimum efficiency. Concert pianists are not alarmed by the butterflies they feel before they go on stage because they know that a modicum of anxiety helps them to give a peak performance. In the same way athletes welcome the feeling of anxiety before a major competition, because they know that this signifies the full arousal of their bodily reserves. The time for them to worry is when they enter a race without feeling worried!

Stress can improve performance When wisely handled, stress helps to banish fatigue and improve performance. Most of the world's work is done by people who would feel tired if they did not know how to stimulate themselves to carry on rather than knuckle under. Stress also makes life more colourful and rich. When w step up the production of our hormonal power house we think more clearly and work more creatively. We're also happier and enjoy a more vigorous sex life. Experiments show that students laugh more at clips of comedy films if they are given a prior injection of adrenalin to increase their level of arousal. This explains the humour which flourishes naturally and seemingly paradoxically in times of adversity, among soldiers in the trenches or displaced people in ghettoes. It also accounts for the levity of generals on the eve of battle, an oddity sometimes erroneously attributed to the *joie de combattre*. Oliver Cromwell, that most sober and god-fearing of all military leaders, was often given to fits of giggling when under tension. This happened before the Battle of Naseby, when according to one contemporary reporter: 'He did laugh so excessively as if he had been drunk, and his eyes sparkled with spirits.'

Parents of young children know that they can generally make their offspring laugh by involving them in anxiety-creating games of peek-a-boo. In the same way generations of artful swains have discovered that they can often melt the resistance of their girl friends by sitting them in the darkened back row of a cinema during the showing of a horror movie. Once one emotion is quickened, all feelings are heightened. Thus there is a narrow gap between laughter and tears, and only a small bridge to be crossed between arousing anxiety and stirring passion. This has been proved by several fascinating psychological studies.

In one series of experiments research workers from the University of Columbia asked male students to cross one of two bridges which had been erected across the Capilano River for the purpose of the test. One of these bridges was a rickety construction of boards, perilously suspended by wires 230 feet above the river. The other was a solid structure built only ten feet above the water level. As they crossed the bridges the students were approached by a male or female interviewer and asked to complete a questionnaire and perform a brief psychological test. They were then given the interviewer's phone number and told they could use it if they wanted to get further details of the experiment. Analysis of the responses showed that men who confronted a female interviewer as they crossed the dangerous bridge were nearly 60 per cent more likely to provide sexual expressions and imagery in their responses than those who met her on the stable bridge. Even more revealing was the discovery that whereas half the men phoned the girls they met while making the hazardous crossing, this was done by only one in eight of the men who made their encounters on the lower, safer bridge. This suggests that stress arousal can add zest to all aspects of life, in the bedroom as well as the battlefield and boardroom.

Excitement in life   Many people appreciate this and try to inject a little excitement into their routine lives. Some spend their evenings playing bingo or operating fruit machines, monotonous activities which are exhilarating only because they introduce an element of chance. Bored housewives may embark upon an illicit love affair, less for sexual satisfaction than to raise their level of arousal and cure their crushing ennui. Other stress-seekers climb mountains, drive fast cars, start risky business ventures, wage crusades against the government or fight legal battles with their neighbours over rights of way. Aldous Huxley wrote in *The Devils of Loudun*: 'There are many people for whom hate and rage pay a higher dividend of immediate satisfaction than love. Congenitally aggressive, they soon become adrenalin addicts, deliberately indulging their highest passions for the sake of the "kick" they derive from their physically-stimulated endocrines.'

Executive burnout Others give up the ghost and, like pampered mice, retire into the security of their well-stocked cages to live a life stripped of vitality and drained of colour. This fate overtakes many men in their middle years, when they relinquish all ambition and give up all hope of excitement and change. When this occurs among hitherto successful managers, the condition is often referred to as 'executive burnout'. Men who gained whizz-kid reputations when the noradrenalin was surging through their bloodstreams now become stolid and hypercautious. Their early enthusiasm is replaced by a world-weary cynicism. Where they were once cheerful and gregarious, they are now increasingly irritable and withdrawn. If they were honest they would admit that they are merely marking time on the corporate treadmill, sitting at their desks with their brains switched on to automatic pilot until the day for their retirement comes. Generally at this stage these men do not need an escape from responsibility and stress, but a switch to a job which offers them more variety, challenge and excitement.

In life we badly need to balance the *yin* of stability with the *yang* of change. Medical studies have shown that people are particularly prone to suffer stress-related disease if their lives are fraught with too much upheaval. Resistance suffers if we have to face a succession of upsetting events, such as bereavements, marriage, births, divorce, changes of job, or house moves. Some while ago Dr Thomas Holmes, Professor of Psychiatry at the University of Washington, made a detailed study of the impact of change on human health. He found that 'four out of every five people who have experienced many dramatic changes in their lives over the past year can expect a major illness within the next two years'.

Stress management Variety is the spice of life, but equally well it can be the kiss of death. The art lies in steering a narrow course between the boredom of too little change and the exhaustion of too much. Moderation is the secret of stress management. The right amount of work load, excitement, challenge responsibility, and change will arouse our neurohormonal system, push back the limits of fatigue, improve performance, and enhance our enjoyment of life. With too much stress we exceed the body's powers of adaptation and become irritable, tired and prone to psychosomatic illness.

Numerous psychological experiments have shown that task performance can be improved by injecting a modicum of stress, by setting deadlines, offering incentives or introducing an element of competition. Naturally the improvements cannot continue *ad infinitum*. There comes a time when the stress level rises too high and performance falls. The consistent results of these experiments has led to the formulation of a principle – the Yerkes-Dodson law – which is probably the only example of a truly scientific psychological law. This states that anxiety improves performance until a certain optimum level of arousal has been reached. Beyond this point performance deteriorates as higher levels of anxiety are attained.

The changes in performance can be plotted on a graph, which is sometimes referred to as the Human Function Curve.

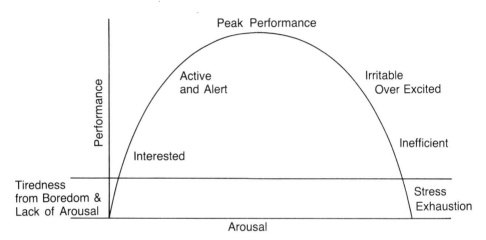

Human Function Curve

On the left side of the curve it will be seen that performance improves as levels of arousal rise. Throughout this phase stress acts as a useful spur to greater endeavour. Here it is the shark behind the swimmer, the fear which makes a hiker run that little bit faster to escape the attentions of a pursuing bull. Many sufferers from chronic fatigue spend their lives at the very bottom of this curve. They are weary and morose because there is nothing to waken them from their slumbers, nothing to tap their energy stores or arouse their latent powers. If they are to overcome their lethargy they must live more adventurously, be more competitive, take on extra responsibility, pursue new hobbies, and tackle fresh challenges.

On the other hand there are those people who have passed their peak and are on the downward limb of the function curve. They need a temporary relief from stress to help them regain their normal vigour.

Viewed in this way it's easy to see how a relatively trivial increase in responsibility or work load can bring about a rapid decline in health and work performance. When you're working flat out, at the maximum of the function curve, any additional stress can be the final straw breaking the camel's back. In the same way it's easy to understand why workaholic sometimes drive themselves to an early grave. They know from experienc that at times they can overcome their depression and fatigue by loadin themselves with extra stress, which activates their neurohormonal power house and taps their energy reserves. But they do not realise that thi only applies when they're on the left hand, rising limb of their functio curve. If they take on additional burdens once they've passed their func tional peak their health and performance will deteriorate. They frequentl notice the decline, but instead of taking a well-deserved break at thi point, they often overcompensate and try a little harder in the hope tha this will overcome their incompetence. But the harder they try the mor inefficient they become and the greater the depth of their fatigue. A di of the spurs may speed a lazy horse, but it's counter-productive to use th same technique to urge a tired horse.

The body's limits The question is how can you recognise when you're working at the limit of your capacity? Pain will tell you when you're straining the ligaments c your back, and hunger pangs will tell you when you've gone too lon without food, but how do you know when you're over-stressed?

The symptoms vary from individual to individual, but fall into seve main categories:

★ *Tiredness* Tiredness not easily relieved by rest or stimulation.

★ *Psychoso-* Most individuals have one organ which is particularly susceptible to stres *matic ailments* fatigue. As a result when over-pressurised they begin to suffer the tell-tal symptoms of tension headaches, palpitations, asthma, fibrositis, nervou dyspepsia, colitis or vertigo.

★ *Sleep* Insomnia, restlessness and troubled dreams are early symptoms of stres *disturbance* fatigue. Once established they aggravate the tiredness and speed th decline in health.

★ *Habit change* People on the downward path of their function curve generally smok more, drink more and resort increasingly to nervous tics and obsessiona behaviour.

★ *Alteration in* Over-stressed individuals laugh less and become increasingly irritable an *mood* impatient.

★ *Decline in* Memory and concentration are two of the early victims of stress fatigue *performance* Mistakes are made more readily, and even the simplest problems take o the magnitude of insurmountable catastrophes.

★ *Other signs* In the early stages of stress fatigue posture becomes tense, gait an gestures jerky, and speech rapid and slightly higher pitched. As the leve of tiredness deepens, posture becomes slack and dejected and movement and speech ponderous and slow.

Warnings No two people succumb to stress fatigue in exactly the same way, but th individual response is invariably consistent. Learn your personal warnin signs – maybe heavier drinking, increased irritability, clumsiness, teet grinding and migraine headaches – and you'll know when you've over-stepped the limits of useful stress arousal. The moment you reach this point ease up. Don't battle on in the hope that you'll sail through the storm into calmer waters. All you'll do if you struggle on is further deplete your energy reserves and drive yourself into a state of more profound collapse.

People who make a success of their lives, who are cheerful, productive and energetic, are able to control the level of stress in their lives. They appreciate how and when to increase their vitality by stepping up their level of arousal, and equally well how and when to decrease their arousal level the moment it oversteps the optimum and threatens their happiness, health and working efficiency. They are not born with these gifts, these are skills they acquire as they go through life.

If you want to live life to the full you must learn to harness the energising force of stress. This is an art that can be developed by anyone, by observing the following coping techniques:

★ *The survival of the fittest* If you've followed the first few points of the **Vitality Programme** you will have already increased your capacity for handling stress, for both clinical experience and laboratory experiments reveal that healthy people are better able to cope with stress than those who are unfit.

At the start of his pioneering research work in Montreal, Dr Hans Selye took ten under-exercised rats and subjected them repeatedly to the sort of stress that many city workers face every day of their lives – shrill noises, pain, shocks and blinding flashes of light. At the end of a month every one of these sedentary rats had died from the incessant strain. Then he took a similar batch, accurately matched for age and breed, and trained them with regular treadmill exercises until they were in peak physical condition. They were then subjected to exactly the same stresses and strains as the first group, but by the end of the month none had died. Their far greater tolerance provided convincing evidence that fit animals can withstand far higher levels of stress than those whose health is poor.

★ *Know thyself* There is a great individual variation in the capacity for handling stress. Scientists at the Walter Reed Army Institute of Research developed a stressing technique which invariably produced peptic ulcers in monkeys, but they were unable to predict their time of onset. Some of the monkeys developed ulcers after only eighteen days exposure, others could withstand the stress for six weeks before they showed signs of ulcer formation. The same applies to humans. Just as we vary in height, nose shape and colour of hair, so we differ in our tolerance to stress.

We also differ in the way we respond to particular forms of stress. In this respect one man's fear can be another man's fillip. One man may be terrified by the prospect of giving an after-dinner speech, another may revel in the experience.

For some the human function curve is flat. They are phlegmatic types who take a lot to get them roused. In others the curve rises and falls as sharply as a hair pin. They are the highly-strung, excitable individuals who can take very little stress before they are thrown into a state of nervous collapse.

Everyone should study their own stress responses and handle them accordingly.

★ *Experience*   The ability to cope with stress increases with experience. People who lead sheltered, stable lives are less able to tolerate stress than those who have had experience in dealing with unexpected challenges, threats and upheavals. Tame rats find it difficult to survive if they are released into the wild, because their neurohormonal systems are not geared up for coping with stress. Thirty years ago workers at the Johns Hopkins University, Baltimore, studied the effects of safe, sedentary living on the endocrine system of laboratory rats. They found that strains of rats reared in captivity for over seventy years became enfeebled. Their adrenal glands were much smaller than wild rats', which reduced their capacity for coping with life in the raw. This was demonstrated in dramatic fashion when a pair of rats escaped, and quickly established a colony in a nearby rubbish tip. Some time later a couple of new, wild arrivals turned up and in a single night killed four hundred of the colony.

Just as vaccination stimulates the immune system and increases our resistance to disease, so the innoculation of adversity strengthens our defence mechanisms and increases our resistance to stress. During the Second World War it was found that nervous breakdown in the Navy was twice as common among inexperienced enlisted men as among hardened, professional sailors.

Instead of running away from threats and challenges, we should welcome them as a way of strengthening our nerve. Like steel we become hardened by exposure to the fire. Before paratroopers make their first descent from a plane they carry out a number of practice jumps from a thirty-foot training tower. When asked to assess on a ten-point scale the amount of fear they experienced, they reported a gradual decline of anxiety from an average of six points on the first jump to three points on the seventh jump.

Face up to your fears and you'll find they lose their potency.

★ *Take action*   The physiological changes which occur in the body during times of stress are all preparations for physical activity. But the stresses we commonly experience today – driving through heavy traffic, anxiety over wayward children, financial problems, personal conflicts – rarely call for violent physical action. So the biological changes persist – muscles remain tense, pulse rate and blood pressure stay raised and the circulation continues to be flooded with unneeded fats and glucose. The persistence of these primitive responses is uncomfortable, tiring and in many instances life threatening.

When caught in this dilemma animals automatically indulge in some form of displacement activity. Herring gulls let off steam by pulling up tussocks of grass, stags clash their antlers against a tree and stickleback fish turn themselves upside down and bury their snouts in the river bed. In this way they dissipate their pent-up tensions.

Humans also find it easier to cope with stress if they take some form of vigorous activity, digging the garden, playing squash, or taking a brisk walk.

When two American psychologists studied the different stress responses of pilots and radar operators in two-seater fighter planes they found that the crew members with the less active role – the radar operators – were most anxious and suffered more psychosomatic complaints than the pilots. As they concluded: 'being engaged in activity – rather than remaining passive – is preferable for most individuals in stressful situations.'

It's better to exercise briskly to burn up the stress changes in the body, than allow them to linger on as a constant drain of nervous energy.

★ *Stress evaluation* Even though we cannot always escape the impact of stressful situations, we can always modify the manner in which we regard them. Psychologist Carl Anderson studied the way in which a group of nearly a hundred small businessmen responded to the tragedy of having their businesses damaged by floods and hurricanes. He found that the extent of their financial loss was not the crucial factor in determining how successfully they coped with the disaster. The key determinant was how they chose to *perceive* the event. Those who regarded it as a challenge, a spur to greater endeavour, recovered far better than those who saw it as a threat, an overwhelming catastrophe which it was futile to contest. The stress was roughly the same in every case, only the response differed. Some chose to fight back, others decided to throw in the towel. Those who accepted defeat ended up feeling tired and dejected. Those who overcame the setback enjoyed the victor's elation and triumphant surge of energy.

★ *Avoiding anxiety* We now live in a global community, in which we are made constantly aware of the calamities happening in the farthest corners of the world. We open the papers or switch on the television and learn of race riots in India, earthquakes in Turkey, droughts in Ethiopia, floods in Holland and guerrilla warfare in Angola. We get the impression that the world around us is in a state of constant turmoil, with communities everywhere torn by industrial unrest, political upheaval, sickness, drug trafficking and violent crime. In this *milieu* our bodies are held permanently in a state of high arousal, which produces an unnecessary and futile activation of our hormonal defences. If we are not going to take action to stem the riots in India or dam back the floods in Holland it's pointless holding our muscles tense and our blood pressure raised. This useless response when long maintained can be exceedingly tiring, and does nothing to solve the world's problems.

Many people today are exhausted, not from the strain of tackling the day to day problems of their personal lives, but from absorbing and carrying with them the collective anxieties of the world. Even Atlas was bowed down by the strain of carrying the burden of the world upon his shoulders. Anyone can cope with their own share of trouble, at least until nightfall. But few are not made weary by coping with the problems of the past, the anticipated dilemmas of the future, plus the collected cares and responsibilities of the world.

To avoid this drain of nervous energy, make a point of living in the 'here and now'. Do not dwell on newspaper reports of crimes at home or wars abroad. Think instead of the peace and security of your own life. And every time you wake up in the morning and go to sleep at night make a point of counting your blessings. Sound the 'all clear', and lower your level of arousal by reminding your subconscious mind that all is well in your personal world. You are safe and secure, you are well fed, you are adequately provided for financially, and you are surrounded by a supportive circle of family and friends. You have everything you need to make you happy, and nothing to threaten your long-term security. This reassurance will be strengthened if you have a religious faith and are part of a close, caring community.

★ *Recuperative breaks*
Stress is an inescapable – and delightful – part of life's rich tapestry. We may think of it as a peculiarly twentieth-century phenomenon, and yet it has been around since time began. But stress for primitive man was shortlived, and rapidly dissipated in the struggle for survival. Stress today is long drawn out, and rarely terminated by purposeful activity. In contemporary society we are not facing the occasional threats of the jungle, but the constant strain of exacting jobs, rapid technological change, uncongenial city environments, marital friction and the never ceasing struggle to keep up with the Joneses. Under this non-stop bombardment we become prey to tiredness, irritability and a whole host of psychosomatic ailments – ulcers, high blood pressure and coronary disease – which make our lives poorer and often briefer than they need be.

Experiments show that animals live longer when they are exposed to stress, provided the stress is intermittent rather than prolonged. Exactly the same is true of humans. Battle fatigue among soldiers was less common a century ago because military campaigns then were short-lived. Now troops are worn down by the constant exposure to stress. This is especially true of soldiers who penetrate deep into the enemy lines and remain for weeks or months on end in a constantly threatening environment. They often develop a paralysing lethargy, which army doctors refer to as Long Range Penetration Strain. The solution is to limit the period of time on active service. This was done systematically in the Royal Air Force during the Second World War, when bomber crews were given a six-month respite after every 30 sorties over enemy occupied territory.

Civilians too should cultivate the habit of interspersing long drawn out periods of stress with regular spells of rest. Musicians playing with symphony orchestras are under continual strain, meeting the exacting standards of regular public performance, coming under constant critical scrutiny at rehearsals and recording sessions, squeezing in teaching and freelance engagements, and often motoring long distances between performances. They have a death rate which is significantly higher than the national average. Conductors, on the other hand, are under only intermittent stress. As a result they have a mortality rate which according to the Metropolitan Life Insurance Company of New York is 38 per cent lower than average.

We need to plunge ourselves into the battle of life, but equally well we need to know when to step back from the firing line. If you master this art you can enjoy an existence which is colourful, productive and exhilarating, with little risk of suffering from nervous fatigue or stress-related sickness.

It's noticeable that many of the giants of the past have mastered this invaluable skill. The Duke of Wellington was able to switch off during the height of the Battle of Waterloo and take a snooze; and when Jesus Christ was drained after healing the sick and preaching to the multitude on the shores of the Sea of Galilee he was able to restore his vitality by sleeping in a small fishing boat, even when it was pitching perilously on a storm-tossed sea.

Vitality Programme – Step Twenty-Four

When you're bored you need to raise your level of arousal by injecting a little more variety and challenge into your life. When you're tired from overstress you need to **retreat** for a brief while to a quieter pace of life. In this way you can harness the energising power of stress and become its master rather than its slave.

STEP 25

Emotional Conflict

Persistent pain can cause an energy drain; so too can the struggle against infectious disease, food allergies, noise, and other forms of hyper-arousal. The impact of those common biological adversaries is generally easy to detect and simple to comprehend. Less obvious is the fatigue stemming from conflicts which take place within our minds rather than within our bodies.

Tiredness can be the sign of a sick psyche rather than a troubled body. It can be as exhausting to bear an invisible burden of guilt as to carry a sack of cement; as fatiguing to do battle with internal demons and doubts as to struggle with an unruly child or drug-crazed teenager. Our subconscious minds never rest. So long as we harbour anxiety, fear, resentment, frustration and pent-up anger we suffer a constant drain of nervous energy. If our minds are not at peace we will grow tired even while we sleep, for nightfall does not bring about an armistice in the civil war taking place within our souls.

Mental exhaustion In one study, a group of a hundred victims of chronic exhaustion were subjected to a detailed medical examination and psychiatric interview. Every one complained of feeling depressed and tired without reason. They were 'all-in' whether they worked or rested. Tests showed that none was physically sick, but all had severe anxieties about some aspect of their private lives. They were trapped in wearying conflict situations from which they could find no escape. Mental exhaustion was the outcome of their dilemma, and a convenient scapegoat which gained them sympathy and provided them with an excuse for not trying to remedy their plight. In these situations tiredness can become, in the words of the researchers, 'the body's defence against a difficult situation'.

Mental and moral conflicts are inescapable in closely-knit, civilised communities. Once man ceased to be a nomadic hunter and settled in permanent communities he needed to develop a high measure of conscious control over his emotions and instinctive reactions. But though we may push our emotions underground, they still retain their innate driving force. We hold them in check only as we do the steam in a pressure cooker, by applying an equal and opposite restraining force.

The constant effort of this repression can lead to metabolic changes within the body which can be just as profound and debilitating as those caused by external stress. In his book *A Doctor's Case Book*, Dr Paul Tournier tells the story of a young girl who was plagued by persistent fatigue. Her tiredness was attributed to anaemia, a diagnosis confirmed by repeated blood tests. But after several months treatment with iron tonics her condition was no better. She was still exhausted by the slightest exertion. In desperation the young girl was sent to a mountain sanatorium to convalesce. By the time she got there her health and blood picture had shown a remarkable improvement, a recovery which appeared to be totally unrelated to her treatment. 'Has anything out of the ordinary happened in your life since your last visit?' her doctor queried. 'Yes,' she replied, 'something has happened. I have suddenly been able to forgive someone against whom I bore a nasty grudge; and all at once I felt I could at last say yes, to life!' Bitterness had been souring her life and sapping her vitality. The energy which she had once dissipated on festering resentment now became available for more productive use, and life once more became a joy instead of an ordeal.

Sickness and sin The ancients believed that sickness was always and invariably the result of sin. Rabbi Ami wrote: 'There is no death without sin, and no pains without some form of transgression'. When this idea held sway it was natural to believe that health would only be restored when patients did something to expiate their sins. So it was that healing came to be associated with prayer, fasting and self-negation. Even today we hold to the strange notion that we've got to suffer to get well. To overcome our aches and pains we've got to be purged and pummelled. Acupuncture needles must be prodded into our skin, enemas thrust into our rectums and evil tasting nostrums poured down our mouths. The more we suffer the more we feel we're making restitution for our sins.

Fortunately such therapeutic penance is rarely necessary, even if it is occasionally useful in assuaging a guilty conscience! Mental sickness is undoubtedly the cause of much ill health, tiredness, and depression, but it's not to be cured by asceticism or Stoical self abuse, but by rational treatment.

Psychological medicine has a long and fascinating history. The Greek and Roman philosophers preached a doctrine of healthy-mindedness. These principles were again reiterated in the nineteenth century when a profusion of mind-cure cults – such as Menticulture, New Thought, and Mental Healing – revived the idea that a healthy body can only be sustained by and through a healthy mind. One of the foremost practitioners of this belief was Phineas Quimby, a clockmaker who started out as a mesmerist and finished up practising the Science of Health or Christ Science, which brought about cures by cultivating habits of right-thinking. One of Quimby's early patients was Mary Baker Eddy, who developed Quimby's therapy into the faith known to millions throughout the world as Christian Science. Many cures have been ascribed to this faith. The essence of their beliefs is simple. We are to a large extent the product of our thoughts. Just as wrong thoughts make us sick, so right-thinking can make us well. The philosophy is simple and inspiring, for if wrong patterns of thought are learnt, they can equally well be unlearnt. The possibility of cure, from mental exhaustion or psychological sickness, lies within our own hands. By directing our thought processes aright we can make ourselves healthy or make ourselves ill.

Sigmund Freud preached a similar message. He showed that illness can stem from the subconscious struggle between the powerful animal instincts represented by something he called the id and the controlling forces of our personal value system, the ego. The whole of civilisation and modern culture, he said, was based on the suppression by the ego of the id. When successful this mechanism turns animals into artists and aesthetes. When the control is oppressive, it kills all passion and vitality, and transforms vibrant men and women into drab, neurotic invalids.

Freud was a religious non-believer, but he recognised that over and above our own individual moral standards was a force, an amalgam of ethical beliefs set by society, which he termed the super ego. Problems arise not only when there is a battle between the ego and the id, but also when there is a conflict between the ego and the super ego. We experience guilt when our ego drives us to amass a personal fortune, and our super ego tells us to give all we have to the poor. Some may see this as a struggle between man's inherent selfishness and his moral conscience or the still, small voice of God. Whatever the viewpoint, the outcome is the same. Whenever our minds exist in a state of civil war we become tired, depressed and dispirited. Health can only be achieved when there is harmony between body, mind and spirit.

This is a traditional belief of American Indians, as was pointed out recently by Dr Frank Clarke, Service Unit Director of the Indian Health Center in Fort Hall. Western medicine, says Dr Clarke, tries to separate the body from the mind and spirit. 'The body is taken care of by a physician. If it gets sick, it is sent to a hospital. If the mind is sick, the patient goes to a psychiatrist, and to a mental hospital or jail for care. The spirit is associated mainly with religion and goes to church on Sundays.' This leads to a disjointed approach to health care. We heal not a whole person but a painful back, an upset stomach or a depressed mind. But these are mere symptoms of what might well be a state of mental disease. In these cases painkillers may ease the backache, antacids soothe the stomach and Largactil lift the depression, but they cannot cure the underlying sickness of the soul. The Indians have a more wholesome approach. 'Indians believe that the body, mind and spirit are interrelated and function together,' says Dr Clarke. 'Health to an Indian is the power to exist and to function harmoniously.'

Many doctors now appreciate the need for this harmonious, tripartite approach. Dr Louise Sands practises in Sutton, Surrey. She started her career as a traditional psychotherapist, but now uses what she describes as Soul-directed therapy, an approach which she finds is quicker and more effective than conventional psychotherapy. Her aim is to help her patients attain a state of mental and spiritual peace. She says: 'You can't be well if you are full of anger and guilt.'

Soul-sickness Other physicians direct their soul-sick patients to their local ministers and priests, who are becoming increasingly accepted as vital members of the holistic health team. One such patient was a sales executive with a large American company. He had at one time been a man of outstanding drive and creative ability; now he was a spent force, an exhausted shadow of his former ebullient self. The company president, anxious to see his key man restored to his previous potency, sent him to the firm's doctor for a check-up, then paid for him to have convalescing vacations first in Atlantic City, then in Florida. But these trips did nothing to restore his flagging spirits. As a last resort he was recommended to visit the religio-psychiatric clinic at the Marble Collegiate Church of New York City, founded and directed by the Reverend Norman Vincent Peale. The man went with considerable reluctance, but knowing that if this final approach failed he was due to be fired from his job. The result is related in the Reverend Peale's best-selling book *The Power of Positive Thinking*.

The executive was at first sullen and unco-operative. He didn't understand why he was being sent to a preacher when he was so obviously sick of body. He mellowed a little when the minister explained to him the mechanism of soul fatigue. 'Often a person gets into the state in which you find yourself because the mind is filled with fear, anxiety, tension, resentment, guilt or a combination of all of them. When these emotional impediments accumulate to a certain weight, the personality can no longer sustain them and gives way.' Gradually his confidence was won. At this point he was invited to unburden himself of whatever fears, resentments or guilt he might be harbouring, with the assurance that everything he said would be held in strictest confidence. Given this guarantee he started to lay bare his soul. He had committed a number of sins, which he'd managed to conceal behind a framework of lies, but his mind was in a state of perpetual turmoil, and he lived in constant fear of exposure. Once the confession was complete he felt an immediate sense of relief. 'I shall never forget the manner in which he reacted,' Peale recalls. 'Standing on his feet he began to stretch. He stood on tiptoes, reaching his fingers towards the ceiling, and then took a deep breath. "My," he said "I feel good." ' A moment before he had been bowed down with worry, now at once he could stand tall. Previously he had caught his breath with fear, now he could heave a sigh of relief.

With the minister's encouragement he gave a brief prayer of repentance and asked that God would give him peace. Then he returned to his office. Nothing was said, but his colleagues instantly realised that he had regained his old liveliness and efficiency. As the president said when he next met Peale: 'I don't know what you did to Bill, but he certainly is a ball of fire.'

There was no mystery in Bill's cure. We have only a limited supply of nervous energy. If a large proportion of this is spent on sustaining internal doubts and fears and mental conflicts there will be that much less to devote to the real business of living.

Some people are fortunate, in that they have acquired the habits of mental hygiene in childhood. Others have to make a conscious effort to adopt the practice of right-thinking. They have to go through the painful process of unlearning and relearning. The procedure is tedious, but richly rewarding. Those who pass through it gain in health, happiness and vitality.

Here are seven ways in which you can overcome mental exhaustion and soul fatigue:

★ *Catharsis* Just as it's valuable to have a regular spring clean of your wardrobe, so it's helpful to purge the cupboards of your mind of all their unwanted refuse and junk. Hidden pockets of infection in your body can lower your level of vitality, so too can the sores which fester in your psyche. Try to free your mind of all pent-up emotion and long-harboured negative feelings. If you're at loggerheads with your neighbour, attempt at once to make peace. If you've cheated your friend in a business deal, assuage your guilt by making suitable restitution. If you think you've been badly treated at work don't be resentful or bear a grudge. Compose a letter explaining your grievance and send it to your boss. If nothing else this will help to clear the air and get the problem off your mind. Forgiving your enemies is not just a pious ethical principle, it's sound psychology and excellent energy husbandry.

Often you'll find it useful to put your emotional hang-ups in concise, written form, for the very act of setting them down on paper lessens their sting and helps to clear them from your mind. One writer has a neat way of dealing with abusive letters and hypercritical reviews. He composes a stinging reply, which gives him the immediate pleasure of retribution. The next morning he reads the missive again, and gets another glow of satisfaction. Then he screws it up and throws it away in the wastepaper basket, knowing that its job is done and his anger dissipated. It's a wise policy every night to rid your mind of all self-destructive emotions – anger, bitterness, and resentment – before you go to sleep. The Bible sensibly advises: 'Let not the sun go down on your wrath.'

And if you're mentally exhausted by carrying a long-standing burden of guilt and sin, seek the help of a wise friend or professional counsellor – doctor, minister or psychotherapist. Confession, you'll find, is good for the weary body as well as the tormented soul.

★ *Face up to* Large numbers of people are beset by fears and phobias. They dread
your fears spiders, the dark, open spaces, closed spaces, flying, speaking in public, or the sight of blood. These deep seated anxieties are a never-ending drain of nervous energy. Often they are no more than chimeras, figments of our imagination rather than solid entities. We are conditioned to respond anxiously when we catch sight of a mouse, so we come to believe that a mouse is a genuine object of fear. If we had the courage to face up to a mouse it would quickly lose its power to terrify. There is a piece of ancient

Irish folk lore which says that if you run from a ghost it continues to chase you, but if you run towards it, it quickly vanishes into the night. The same is true of our numerous phobias and anxieties. Ralph Waldo Emerson said: 'Do the thing you fear and the death of fear is certain.'

★ *Take positive action* There are few things more tiring than indecision. A patient came to me a short while ago complaining of backache and numbing fatigue. She was so tired at times, she told me, that she couldn't even compose a letter to a friend. Often she had to retire to bed as soon as dinner was cleared away. Even then, after nearly twelve hours sleep, she woke feeling no fresher than when she went to bed. I found her body to be a mass of muscular tensions. These were simply and quickly eased, which gave her immediate relief. But the fibrositic aches and pains quickly returned, and the numbing exhaustion persisted unabated. The explanation was soon revealed. On the outside she appeared calm and composed, but inside her brain was in a turmoil. She was leading a double life. For over twenty years she had been locked in a long-standing, but loveless marriage, in a small-town community where she was a respected and much-loved member of society. More recently she had fallen in love with a foreigner who met her life-long yearnings for a warm, intimate relationship. She was in a dilemma. Should she maintain her façade of respectability with her husband? Should she stay with the friends she knew and loved, in the familiar surroundings where she had been born and bred? Or should she, for the sake of love, sacrifice her material comforts, the security of her home town and risk the censure of her friends? She was paralysed by uncertainty and crippled by guilt and fears of the unknown. Eventually she took the plunge and left home. From that moment onwards her health began to improve. No longer wasting energy on an endless shall I, shan't I debate, she quickly regained her lost vitality.

Many people are trapped in a similar plight. In contemporary society we have an embarrassment of choice, with often very little to choose between the merits of rival options. Should we send our children away to school, and if so what establishment should we select? Should a mother of young children go out to work? Should a good Jewish girl marry out of the faith, or a well brought up Catholic girl resort to methods of birth control? Moral dilemmas like these abound, and the only way to resolve them is to take some form of positive action. It's better to make the wrong choice occasionally than to make no choice at all, for mistakes are rarely irrevocable, whereas the time and energy wasted on endless shilly-shallying is always irredeemable.

★ *Let off steam* In the past, communities were always provided with socially acceptable ways of giving vent to their feelings, occasions when they could lift the lid off the emotional pressure cooker. The most popular of these methods was the carnival. This provided a psychic safety valve, a carefully circum-scribed period of permissive licence, when convention was turned upside down, minor laws broken and etiquette thrown to the wind. During this time strangers embraced, men dressed up as women, and the inhibited let down their hair and danced through the streets. Nowadays it seems that only the young – with their rock festivals and disco parties – have organised opportunities for Dionysian revelry. But adults have an equal need to give vent to their pent-up animal energies. From childhood onwards we are taught to hide our emotions, to choke back the tears and conceal our feelings behind a rigid, poker face. But the constant effort to suppress the dark forces of the id is energy consuming. We need to channel them rather than suppress them. We need at times to bellow with rage, weep with sorrow, dance with excitement and laugh with joy – not always easy to do in a way which is culturally acceptable. As a general rule we should only give free reign to those emotions which are not antagonistic. Happiness, grief and joy can be safely shared, but wild displays of aggression should be curbed, since they generally beget a violent response which heightens rather than lessens the general level of tension. Anger is best dissipated in displacement activities, such as competitive games or vigorous tree felling, rather than in direct confrontations. The other emotions can be vented in conventionally acceptable ways, such as parties, fetes, public dances and mourning ceremonies, which is generally far less tiring than trying to hold them in check.

★ *Think positively* Negative thoughts poison the mind as surely as tainted food poisons the body: so try to banish from your conversation and thoughts all expressions of anxiety, fear, resentment, bitterness, hatred, pessimism, doubt, distrust and criticism. You'll feel under a cloud if you're always complaining about the weather, and you'll become dejected if you constantly dwell on your misfortunes and ill health.

The best way to avoid this sick-thinking is to fill your mind with positive, uplifting thoughts. Focus your attention on those things that are pure and holy and of good report and you will have no time for those that are depressing and enervating.

★ *Be cheerful* Moods come and go, like ripples on a pond, but temperament is the permanent finger print of the personality. Psychologists often use the term 'emotional set' to describe this underlying quality. Several people I know will always come back smiling even if they lose every penny they possess. Some are permanent pessimists, looking at the world through a veil of gloom, seeing despondency everywhere they turn. Others are never content. If a distant cousin dies and unexpectedly leaves them a country mansion they immediately complain that the windows are dirty and the lawns overgrown. For a while they may be happy, but soon they return to their discontented state, for this is their set attitude. This conditions the way they feel, look and act. It also determines to a large extent their measure of happiness, health and vitality. Anxious people will be paralysed by fear; those with a gloomy temperament will be for ever bowed down with sorrow.

To that extent we are like lead-weighted wobbly dolls. Our emotional equilibrium may be disturbed for a while, but we quickly rock back to our resting state. In Britain in the eighteenth century, young gentlemen were trained to be resolute and calm in the face of adversity. Those who succeeded were said to have 'bottom', a much admired temperament at the time, associated with courage, coolness and solidity. We need to cultivate a similar mental set of cheerful equanimity if we are to face the turmoils of contemporary life with minimum fatigue and strain. If we do, we carry with us a more effective pick-me-up than can be found on the chemist's shelves, for as the Bible says: 'A merry heart doeth good like a medicine.' Doctors have found this in their fight against stress-related sickness. According to Dr Irvine Page, a well-known heart specialist, the best way to escape heart attacks is through the 'achievement of equanimity'. Some people attain this with the aid of a religious faith, or by adopting a positive philosophy of life. 'Others,' he says, 'achieve equanimity emotionally, through a belief in beauty, in ideals, in unselfishness. They let the annoyances of life pass in one side and out the other.'

Just as a pointillist painter builds up a picture from a series of tiny dots, so we build up our characters from a series of individually insignificant acts. How we react to the events of the day determines not only our present mood, but also our long-term emotional set. In this way we are the *creators* as well as the *creatures* of our temperaments.

★ *Spiritual retreats* Everyone has some degree of cosmic consciousness, even if we do not all hold to a specific religious belief. We realise that our lives are inextricably bound up with the natural world around us. We appreciate our need for rain to quench our thirst, air to oxygenate our lungs, and sun to sustain the plants on which all animal life depends.

One of the great tragedies of the Industrial Revolution is that it has torn so many urban people from contact with their grass roots. Cardinal Newman wrote: 'The human race is implicated in some terrible aboriginal calamity. It is out of joint with the purpose of its Creator.' This has created a spiritual schizophrenia, a state of global insecurity and alienation which is often referred to as *Weltschmerz* or 'world ache', which cannot be cured by psychotherapy or drugs. It is a form of soul fatigue which can only be remedied by recapturing what Freud described as the 'oceanic feeling'. In an age of rush and bustle we need to recapture the timelessness which comes from contemplating the natural kingdom where there is a time and season for all things, and nothing can be hurried. In a period of insecurity and rapid flux, we need to experience the constancy of the rising sun, the permanence of the tides, and the solid security of standing on *terra firma*. If we are at loggerheads with our neighbours we need at least to feel at one with the world around us. We gain strength from observing the beauty of the mountains; derive comfort from witnessing the unity and harmony of the world of insects, birds and flowers; and experience a feeling of great freedom from observing the vastness of the oceans and sky.

From time to time we need to step back from the hurly-burly and take time to enjoy this revitalising transcendental experience. Some may achieve this by prayer and religious contemplation, others by spending a weekend at a spiritual retreat, gardening, holidaying in the country or meditating on the beauty of a rose.

Some while ago a traveller in Papua reported that his bearers and guides would often sit down at the roadside to rest and meditate. It was not just that they were physically fatigued they explained. 'We must give our souls time to catch up with our bodies.' If we are to avoid psychic fatigue, we too must arrange regular periods for mental repose and spiritual refreshment 'to give our souls a chance to keep up with our bodies'.

Vitality
Programme –
Step Twenty-Five
Tiredness is not just a product of the body, but also of the mind and spirit. Don't let emotional conflicts fester or allow doubts to lie unresolved. Take action. Face up to your fears, resolve your doubts, banish your hang-ups, conquer your inadequacies and make peace with your conscience. Learn to give vent to your emotions – frustration, laughter and tears – in socially acceptable, purposeful ways. Setting your mind at rest, you'll find, is an essential part of putting your body to rest.

STAGE FIVE

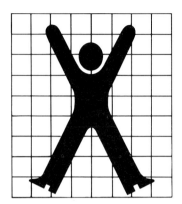

Releasing the Life Force

STEP 26

The Motivational Key

If you've faithfully followed the earlier stages of the **Vitality Programme** you will by now be in possession of a power house of stored energy. Maybe you still don't realise what you have achieved. You probably recognise that you're slimmer, livelier, fitter and more youthful looking, but maybe you're not yet bubbling over with vitality, like Ethel Merman, Tommy Steele, President Kennedy or any of the other dynamic personalities you've always envied. This is easily understood. So far you've been engaged in the painstaking, unspectacular work of converting your body into a slick, efficient power house. Now you can reap your reward. Now you've come to the exciting moment when you can throw the master switch which sets the metabolic wheels in motion.

With the energy you now possess you have the opportunity to achieve your heart's desire. It's said that there's enough stored energy in a single matchstick to move a mountain. Your body holds much more. With it you can travel the world, start a new career, build a successful business empire, go back to college and get a degree, or simply push back the limits of fatigue and enjoy a richer, fuller life than you've ever known before.

The master switch All you've got to do to release the pent-up power is flick the master switch. It sounds so simple, yet this is where thousands of people fail. They suffer from what is known as motivational fatigue. They wake up in the morning, dreading the prospects lying in front of them. They have no heart for the monotonous office routine or the humdrum household chores, so their brains refuse to operate the power switch. They drag themselves through the day, not because they lack energy, but because they're not connected to their power supply.

Many young girls working in London offices have told me of the exhaustion of their jobs. They complain that by the end of the day they are all-in. After they have commuted home and cooked themselves a simple supper they are fit for nothing but a warm, relaxing bath and an early bed. So great is their fatigue, they say, that they generally cannot even summon up the strength to read a few pages of a novel before they fall asleep. My response to these sad recitations is by now fairly standard. If I suspect that the underlying problem is boredom rather than true physical fatigue, I ask a simple question. 'If in the evening you had an unexpected phone call from an attractive fellow you've always admired, asking you out to a dance or party, how would you feel?' Their responses are normally identical. With a pert grin they usually admit: 'That would be different. I'd soon find the energy for something special like that.' Obviously these girls do not lack vitality. All they need is something or someone to turn them on.

Many great artists have suffered from motivational fatigue. Most writers suffer a total power failure when they slip a sheet of blank paper into their typewriters and set out to write a book or feature article. According to James Boswell: 'When faced with work, Samuel Johnson was sometimes so tired, languid and inefficient that he could not distinguish the hour upon the clock.' Schumann was another eminent victim of motivational fatigue. According to his doctor, whenever he started to compose a new work he 'was seized with fits of trembling, fatigue and coldness of the feet.'

When there are things we don't want to tackle, the mind calls the body out on strike. This vetoes unpalatable action in a way which generally gains us sympathy rather than reproof. A leading neuropsychiatrist has said, 'Fatigue has become the socially acceptable excuse for not doing things.' Charles Darwin loathed social gatherings, and got out of most of them by falling into a state of nervous prostration. This made an ordeal of even family weddings. His son reported: 'At the wedding of his daughter, my father could hardly bear the fatigue of being present during the short service.'

The motors of the human body have the same potential as those of a jet airliner. If the pilot gives the appropriate signal the engines rev up and the plane surges down the runway and powers its way into the sky. Alternatively he can switch the engines onto reverse thrust and bring the plane to a sudden, grinding halt. We have a similar choice. We can use our energy to drive ourselves forward or hold ourselves back. We can be motivationally energised or motivationally fatigued.

The stronger our driving force, the more energy we release. This same is equally true of caged animals. Pet hamsters, rats and mice are often given a wheel to increase their opportunities for exercise. In the past it was believed that the animals used these wheels simply to let off steam and express their innate *joie de vivre*. Now it's realised that they use them in a frustrated urge to attain some hidden goal. This was revealed by two-year study carried out by Manchester zoologist Janice Mather. She studied the animals' 'wheel-running response' and found that the rats ran faster when they were hungry than when they were full. The same happened when they were thirsty. When female rats were on heat they travelled three times further than when they were out of season. And Janice Mather concluded: 'The wheel is used by a caged animal when the individual is motivated to reach an unattainable resource.'

We are quiescent when there is nothing to arouse our interest or urge us on. We spring into life only when we are spurred on by some burning desire. Like the caged rats, if we are to unleash the full power of our pent-up energies we need to have fire in our bellies and passion in our hearts.

This is the great secret of every high-activity man or woman I have studied. They are highly motivated, and this provides the key which unlocks their energy stores. This is a priceless gift which anyone can cultivate. The art can be mastered in three simple steps:

★ *Establish clear-cut goals*   Motivation comes from appointing a definite target to which you can direct your flow of energy. Suppose you select the venal yet most popular aim of amassing material wealth. That, if you wish, is within your grasp. Some while ago I made a detailed study of self-made millionaires, which showed that it's not difficult to make a fortune, provided this is your over-riding goal in life. If you'd trade in the chance of making a few thousand pounds for a fortnight in the Bahamas you might as well give up all hope of becoming a second John D. Rockefeller. To accumulate riches you've got to share King Midas' love of money, just as Mr Bernstein said in *Citizen Kane*: 'It's no trick to make a lot of money, if all you want is lots of money.' Problems arise only when you can think of other ways in which you'd rather spend your time, like playing golf, relaxing with the family or idling in the sun. The promoters of get-rich-quick schemes demonstrate their shrewd knowledge of human nature when they ask their would-be customers the fundamental question, 'Do you sincerely want to be rich?' If the answer to this question is an unqualified 'yes', you're already halfway toward making a fortune, because the quest for wealth will be like the caged rat's search for food or sex, a powerful driving force which taps your reserves of energy and keeps you travelling on the treadmill of life. But if your motivation is weak, and you value pleasure, leisure and comfort before the quest for riches, your chances of becoming a millionaire are few.

The same is true of all other pursuits. If you sincerely want to create a magnificent garden, become the world's leading authority on butterflies or compile a seven-volume history of your family you have the energy to do so, provided you are truly hungry for these ends.

★ *Enthusiasm*   It's not difficult to find energy to make love to the mate you adore and haven't seen for several months. Nor are you likely to feel too tired to travel thirty miles to collect the new three-litre car that you've just won in a charity raffle. Enthusiasm is the great motivator. In fact Ralph Waldo Emerson once said: 'Nothing great was ever achieved without enthusiasm.' Joan of Arc, the simple maid of Orleans, would surely have left little mark on history had she not been fired with religious zeal. She had the fire of God within her, *en-theos*, which is the derivation of the word enthusiasm. In the same way it's difficult to imagine Christopher Columbus having the courage and tenacity to continue his voyages of discovery unless he'd been driven by a fervent desire to find a western passage to China and India.

All high-activity people, and every charismatic leader, have been driven by some passionate interest or desire which has enabled them to summon up their last ounce of energy to overcome tiredness, frustration, ridicule, failure, poverty and sickness in the relentless pursuit of their goal.

Foster this enthusiasm, and you'll experience no difficulty finding the energy to achieve your aims. Amanamayee Mee, one of the most influential of contemporary Hindu sages has said: 'Whatever you seek can be obtained, provided the thirst for the object of your desires is strong enough.'

★ *Concentration* Even the frail and elderly can generate remarkable force if they concentrate all their efforts on a single task. The sun's rays may seem weak on some days, and yet we can use them to burn a hole in a piece of paper if we focus them with a magnifying glass. This is one of the arts of energy conservation which is applied, consciously or unconsciously, by most high achievers. Inventors and research scientists have a reputation for being absent-minded. But they're not so much absent-minded as other-minded. They do not notice that they are wearing non-matching socks, or are pouring salt instead of sugar on their breakfast cereals, because their attention is focused exclusively on their work. They are blinkered because they do not want to dissipate their vitality on trivial tasks.

Napoleon's enormous capacity for work has been attributed to this capacity for single-minded effort. He is quoted as saying: 'When I have done with one subject, I close the compartment drawer, and open another, so that my various jobs never overlap one another, and there is neither confusion nor fatigue. And when I feel sleepy I shut up all the drawers and fall asleep immediately.'

What applies to the focusing of mental effort applies equally well to the marshalling of physical force. Students of karate quickly discover that their reserves of energy and strength are far greater than they previously imagined. In the West we are taught to work at a steady, constant pace. In the East the custom is to keep the body completely relaxed for as long as possible, and to apply effort only when needed in sudden, dynamic bursts. Karate novitiates are trained to concentrate their life force, or *ki*, on a single, explosive act, like lifting a heavy load, or breaking a pile of bricks. With this co-ordinated action a nine-stone man can generate the power of a heavyweight boxer. Sometimes they accompany their effort with a sharp, piercing cry, or *kiai*, which means a 'spirit-unifying shout'. This is another aid to focused endeavour. It's easy to explain the mechanical advantage of carefully pin-pointed physical effort. Most British schoolboys are trained to punch with the closed fist, a kindly technique which dissipates the force of the blow over a relatively wide area, for the fist's surface measures about eight square inches, and it's easy to calculate that if a youngster packs an 80 lb punch his resulting blow will land with a force of 10 lb per square inch. But if he lands the same blow with a karate chop, using a small portion of the outside of his hand, probably measuring no more than one square inch, the force delivered will measure 80 lb per square inch or eight times greater. The superiority of the concentrated mental effort of the karate expert is no doubt equally great, although it cannot be so easily demonstrated or exactly calculated.

If you set your sights on a clear goal, and approach it with enthusiasm and concentrated effort, there is little that is beyond your reach. That was the firm conviction of William James, that most practical of all psychologists. These were his words, which you would do well to recite to yourself again and again if you're short of confidence or lacking in resolution: 'In almost any subject your passion for the subject will save you. If you only care enough for a result, you will most certainly attain it. If you wish to be rich, you will be rich; if you wish to be learned, you will be learned; if you wish to be good, you will be good. Only you must, then, *really* wish these things and wish them with exclusiveness, and not wish at the same time a hundred other incompatible things just as strongly.'

Vitality Programme – Step Twenty-Six You'll overcome your tiredness and generate the vitality and driving force of leaders like Napoleon and Joan of Arc if you concentrate your life force on goals which are clearly delineated and passionately desired.

STEP 27

The Hidden Power

High-energy individuals are generally liberal with their emotions. They are warm, passionate beings who live life to the full. They laugh when they are happy, and cry when they are sad. They plunge headlong into ventures which would frighten those with lesser nerve; they make mistakes, but don't allow themselves to dwell on the errors of the past or be deterred by the possibility of failure in the future. They are romantics, and yet they do not live in a world of fantasy for they are also the world's great doers – explorers, crusaders, fighters, creators, lovers.

They have the ability to harness their emotive driving force for positive ends. The link between their passion and their power is close and causal for feelings are preludes to action. When we feel intensely about renaissance music, or the preservation of endangered plant life in Madagascar our bodies are prepared for some kind of physical activity. Our level of arousal is increased, fats and sugars are released into the circulation to give us energy, and hormones released to delay the onset of fatigue. In this way emotion is but a nerve twitch away from motion. And the delightful thing is that these changes are non-specific and pervasive. We may start out by being moved by a particularly fine rendering of Beethoven's Choral Symphony, but we end up being more alert to the beauty of the countryside and everything else around us.

In this way energy and love are somewhat similar. The more love we have for one person, the more we have for everyone else who come within our orbit. The more affection we transmit, the more we find we have to give. So it is with vitality, the more energy we pour out, the deeper our stores become.

Knowing this, one might reasonably ask why we do not all express the stamina and high-vitality of Titian or Ninos de Lenclos. The answer is simple. Many of us have become slaves of convention. Just as drugs carry unfortunate side effects, so modern culture has brought us both blessings and banes. One great drawback is that it has created social taboos and inhibitions which dam back the free flow of life force. For generations we have been encouraged to hold a tight rein on our emotions, a repression which embraces not just the socially disruptive feelings of anger, bitterness and resentment, but also the uplifting, life-enhancing emotions of elation, joy, playfulness and sexual love.

Laughter For many years society frowned on the free expression of laughter, considering it vulgar. The Puritans went one stage further and tried to stop people giving vent to all forms of animal high spirits, even when it was channelled in the form of an organised game. John Bunyan, for instance, considered that to dance, or play hockey on the village green, was 'an ungodly practice'. We are still trammelled by some of these puritanical strictures. We still find it difficult to indulge in rollicking laughter or uninhibited, childlike play. As a result our lives are drained of colour and verve, for we cannot starve one emotion without impoverishing all the others. We cannot hold back the tears without stifling the laughter. Nor can we curb our sexual passions without diminishing our love for our neighbours, friends and family.

If we are to achieve our energy potential we must open up the emotional sluice gates, break down the pointless social taboos, free the neurotic inhibitions, and let the life force come flooding through. Passion and energy are inseparable partners, like the genie and the lamp. Possess one, and you'll never lack the other. Rub the lamp of passion, and you'll release the mysterious powerful spirit locked within.

What then holds us back? Why do we not all enjoy the rich, vibrant life which is our birthright? Some are imprisoned by repressions which only a psychiatrist can cure. A few are trapped behind a schizophrenic mask which cuts them off from the responsibilities and terrors of the world and prevents them from feeling both pleasure and pain. But for most the emotional dams are shallow and easily lifted. Here are the three blocks I encounter most commonly in my neurotically tired patients:

★ *Suppressed grief* It is natural to feel dejected and tired after the loss of a loved one. Konrad Lorenz, one of the world's most distinguished experts on animal behaviour and director of the Max-Planck Institute in Bavaria, has made a close study of the bereavement responses of the greylag goose. He finds that the death of a mate provokes a brief period of agitated activity, as the bird searches frantically for its missing partner. Once the loss is accepted, the bird settles into a period of mourning, during which it withdraws from purposeful activity and becomes silent and morose. It emerges from this, and regains its normal vitality, only when it has had a chance to adjust to the loss. Bereaved humans show a similar reaction, except that they sometimes refuse to accept the reality of their situation. When this happens they remain in a state of prolonged mourning, maintaining an apathy and exhaustion which long outlives its usefulness.

This happened to R. Buckminster Fuller, the great American architect, a man of boundless vitality who liked to describe himself as 'an engineer, inventor, mathematician, architect, cartographer, philosopher, poet, cosmologist, comprehensive designer and choreographer.' He entered an alcoholic depression after the death of his four-year-old-daughter. For five years afterwards he remained apathetic, dejected and tired. Then suddenly, he decided to end his period of mourning. Standing on the shore of Lake Michigan he told himself: 'You do not have the right to eliminate yourself. You belong to the universe.' From that moment onward his vitality returned and he entered the most productive period of his life designing buildings, cars, mobile homes and geodesic domes.

There is 'a time to weep' the Bible says. Those who are able to do so at the appropriate time, when they are disappointed, frustrated, grief-stricken or sad, find that their mood quickly lifts. Grief repressed is accompanied by mental and physical enervation, grief expressed is followed by tension release and elevation.

★ *Fear of failure* We live in an achievement orientated society, in which success is the spur and fear of failure the snaffle bit which reins in many an otherwise able workhorse.

A study was made at one hospital of a group of middle-aged managers suffering from the 'burnt-out executive syndrome'. All the men had started out full of talent, vigour and ambition, but somewhere along the line they seemed to have lost their enthusiasm and drive. Their main symptoms were dejection and oppressive fatigue. One of the doctors commented: 'It seemed that their mainsprings were broken.' But the men were not physically sick. Most of them, it was found, were suffering from antici-patory dread. Instead of being driven on by pride in their past achieve-ments, they were paralysed by the fear of failure in the future. This is a common cause of under-achievement and suppressed vitality.

We are hierarchical animals, and retain more than a vestige of the atavistic emotional response which helps to maintain the stability of all animal pecking orders. When two equally matched gorillas are in conten-tion for the leadership of the troop, only one can win. To put an end to the rivalry, and ensure the long-term peace of the community, nature automatically promotes the potential of the one, and depresses the potency of the other. Success makes the victor stand a foot taller, full of confidence, elation and vigour, while the vanquished rival shrivels in stature and becomes depressed and apathetic, a shadow of his former self. Given this disparity a re-match is unthinkable.

Humans respond to success and failure in an identical way. It's not difficult to spot the members of a winning football team. They're the ones who, even at the end of a strenuously contested match, can find the energy to go on a triumphant lap of honour. Their defeated opponents are the ones who, while struggling just as vigorously until the final whistle blew, suddenly find themselves bowed down with despondency and fatigue.

Everyone must at times suffer fatiguing setbacks and disappointments. The important thing is to relegate them quickly to their chronological place in the past, rather than carry them forward into the future. Just as over-extended periods of mourning perpetuate tiredness, so too do long spells dwelling on past failures and defeats.

★ *Repressed* Youngsters are prepared for their entry into adult society by being trained
sexuality to conceal all expression of emotion. 'Big boys don't cry', they are told. 'Pull yourself together!'; 'Don't let yourself go!'; 'It's bad to lose your temper'; 'Don't show that you're afraid'.

Laughter and tears and expressions of joy are all right for infants, but they have no place in the world of conventional adults. Grown-ups have to show self-control. And the way they achieve this is by holding their bodies in a tight muscular straitjacket. To attain this rigid control, children are taught to keep a stiff upper lip when they want to cry; grit their teeth when they want to groan with pain; and hold their chin up high when they want to bow down and accept defeat.

Wilhelm Reich, one of Freud's favourite pupils, was the first doctor to give a detailed description of this defensive mechanism, which he described as 'body armouring'. He noted that his neurotic patients were damming back their experience of fear, anger, anguish or sexual passion by holding their bodies rigidly tense. They contracted their diaphragms to choke back the tears, and tensed their pelvic muscles for fear that they might be sexually aroused or give way to a full, convulsive, orgasmic response. But by shielding themselves from emotions that were painful or socially taboo, they were also building a barrier which prevented them experiencing pleasurable feelings. Their body armouring also acted as a barrier against the free flow of life force. Reich wrote in *The Function of the Orgasm*, in italics which are of his choosing rather than mine: '*Sexual energy can be bound by chronic muscular tensions. The same is true of anger and anxiety.*'

Reich found that by encouraging his patients to break down their body armouring he helped them overcome their repressions, physical tensions and chronic fatigue. Once the emotional dams were lifted, the life force surged through them unimpeded and they felt revitalised, enthused and free. The techniques he used were unconventional. He taught his patients breathing exercises to get rid of the tensions checking the experience of pleasurable sensations. '*Deep expiration brings about spontaneously the attitude of sexual surrender*', he wrote, again using italics to emphasise the importance of his words. He also relaxed the abdominal and pelvic muscular armouring by manipulating the bellies of his patients, a hitherto unheard of thing for a psychiatrist to do. These techniques have since been refined, particularly by his pupil Alexander Lowen, who founded the body therapy known as Bioenergetics. Lowen's work confirms that the release of body armouring leads to a great increase in energy flow.

Reich placed major stress on the oppressive effects of sexual repression, an emphasis which may seem quaintly outdated today, when there are on open sale so many manuals of sexual technique to dispel the crippling legacy of Victorian ignorance and prudery. But the mores and moral strictures of the past die hard. Sex manuals may have liberated our minds, but they have not always freed our bodies. The complaint that doctors hear from so many patients today is not that they do not have enough sex, but that they do not derive enough enjoyment from the sex they have. The new era of sexual freedom has brought us to the stage when we have sex with all the motions, but none of the emotions.

When Victorian women of refinement carried out their wifely duties they were taught to lie back rigidly and think of England. Those days are past and yet many men and women today have still not discovered the joy of total sexual surrender. They are still too inhibited during the sexual act to groan with pleasure or writhe with ecstasy. For them Wilhelm Reich's message is still of vital importance. If they lift the emotional sluice gates and open their bodies to the experience of sexual passion – or grief, excitement, triumph and joy – their lives will be enriched and invigorated. For then they will have released the life force, the powerful emotive genie which lies within each one of us.

Vitality Programme – Step Twenty-Seven Learn to live life to the full. Harness the emotional driving force within you by being an enthusiastic, totally committed participant in everything you do. Don't dwell on past failures, or be anxious about the possible problems of the future. Instead be content to concentrate your energies on living joyously in the here-and-now.

STEP 28

A Picture of Health

This is the last stage in the **Vitality Programme**, and probably the most difficult to master. Everything that has gone before has involved a straightforward effort of the conscious mind. If you've had sufficient determination you've got yourself in better shape. You've lost weight with the W.O.W. diet, strengthened your legs with the Limb Trim exercises and improved your stamina by taking a daily constitutional walk. If you've had the will power, you've also made whatever modifications have been necessary in your breathing, diet, posture and habits of rest, work and sleep. You deserve a pat on the back for what you've achieved. You've gained stamina and vitality by your sheer hard work and dedication. Now you have only one small step to take before you reap the just rewards for all this dedicated effort. But unlike the stages that have gone before, this final step, happily, requires neither will power, self discipline, nor dogged labour.

We're so deeply imbued with the Protestant work ethic, that we believe nothing worthwhile can be gained without hard graft. This is not always so. Sometimes it's better to *let* things happen, than try to *force* them to happen. This is particularly true when the subconscious mind is involved.

Breaking barriers Many barriers to human performance are figments of the imagination rather than true physical limitations. For decades athletes were unable to run a mile in less than four minutes. This was regarded as an insuperable obstacle, just as the sound barrier was believed to impose an impenetrable upper limit on air travel. Then on the 6 May 1954 Roger Bannister made running history when he covered the mile in 3 min. 59.4 sec. Immediately the psychological barrier had been broken, the feat was repeated by other athletes, and soon the sub-four-minute-mile became commonplace.

Similarly, for many years it was believed that only a few, exceptionally well-endowed athletes could run non-stop for 26 miles, the distance Pheidippides ran when he carried the news of the Greek victory at Marathon to his fellow citizens in Athens. Now every week tens of thousands of ordinary men and women throughout the world are showing their ability to run the marathon. These stumbling blocks were purely illusory. In both cases they were the products of a limited imagination rather than an inadequate physique.

All too often we hedge ourselves round with these mental barriers. We *think* ourselves tired, *imagine* ourselves weak, and *believe* ourselves to lack endurance.

Pushing back The recognition of these self-imposed constrictions was another one of
fatigue William James's major contributions to the field of practical psychology.
He pointed out that people are generally as tired as they expect to be.
'Some of us are really tired,' he admitted, 'but far more of us would not
be tired at all unless we had got into the wretched trick of feeling tired.'
We come home from the office after a tedious journey and expect to feel
jaded. Inevitably as a result each night we suffer anticipatory fatigue, for
the body is only the slave of the mind. We think tired, stand and talk in
a weary fashion, and slump exhausted into a chair. But the lassitude is
invariably of our own making. If we chose we could just as easily imagine
ourselves fresh and lively as picture ourselves frayed and weak.

In his early days William James himself had to battle with ill health and
overwhelming fatigue, which was sometimes so severe that the mere effort
of writing a letter was enough to confine him to bed for the remainder of
the day. He conquered this disability by practising the art of positive
thinking. He found that he could push back his fatigue point, and work
well into the night, providing he didn't at any time countenance the
concept of feeling tired. In this way he did not block the flow of vitality
from the body's vast stores of energy. Anyone can achieve similar results,
for as James said: 'As a rule, men habitually use only a small part of the
powers which they actually possess.'

During my student years I used to feel worn out and unable to think
clearly whenever I'd had a disturbed night's sleep or been to a late-night
party. This, I was quite convinced, was the inevitable outcome of true,
physiological fatigue. I continued in this habit of thinking until one
December day when I had to play an important game of football and
complete a complicated essay after a night completely bereft of sleep. I
was holding down a vacation job at the time, doing a twelve-hour night
shift as a porter at one of London's main railway stations. The job was
energetic and I had every reason to feel tired when the stint of work
ended, but on this occasion, such was the excitement of the match and
the importance of the essay, that I felt exhilarated throughout the entire
day which followed. I realised then that the symptoms of sleeplessness are
often largely subjective. The tiredness we experience after an impoverished night's sleep is conditioned as much by our expectations as by any
physical changes in our bodies. From that moment on I have ceased to
worry about going short of sleep for one or two nights. If I could go
without a wink of sleep and still play a vigorous game of football and
compose a complex essay, I've certainly no need to fear that I'll be too
tired to work after three or four hours' sleep.

Fatigue research confirms this belief. We grow weary when we allow
thoughts of tiredness to enter our subconscious minds. In one series of
sleep deprivation experiments soldiers were asked to stay awake for
varying periods of time. When their symptoms were monitored, it was
found they grew tired at the end of each stint irrespective of its actual
length. When they were given the task of staying awake for 96 hours, they

claimed to be full of energy after 80 hours, but started to feel 'all-in' after 94 hours. At this point, towards the end of their ordeal, they expected to feel whacked. But the same applied when they stayed awake for only 72 hours, they still complained of feeling 'beat' at the end of the experiment, only this time at the 70-hour point. Their sensation of fatigue was obviously linked to their expectations and imaginings rather than to the exact length of time they'd stayed awake.

Picturing What applies to the experience of tiredness, applies equally well to the
ourselves experience of stamina and strength. We're said to be as old as we feel. In the same way we're as powerful and vigorous as we picture ourselves to be. Each one of us builds up a body image, which as the word suggests is often more a creation of our imagination than of factual self-analysis. Some people see themselves as tough, fit, resilient, tireless individuals. Others, in their mind's eye, regard themselves as sickly, frail and wan, even though they may in fact be equally well endowed. Once we have built up these body images they become powerful conditioners of the way we feel and act.

Television journalist Sheila MacLeod always thought of herself as being passive, weak and physically vulnerable, a mental self-portrait which was confirmed when she became the victim of a rapist's attack. Her attitude changed when she enrolled in a course of self-defence. During her second visit she was asked to perform an exercise called the unbendable arm. She placed one hand palm uppermost on a classmate's shoulder and tried to hold it firmly in position against her opponent's resistance. She failed the test ignominiously, as she had expected. With her puny arms she was an easy pushover. Then she was asked to repeat the exercise, this time imagining that she was a powerful tree, her feet firmly rooted in the ground, her arms reaching solidly upwards into the sky towards the universal source of light and strength. This time her arm proved immovable. In the few moments between the two trials she had discovered her hidden strength. Her muscles were no more powerful than before, but with the aid of mental imagery she had suddenly changed her body concept. This proved something of an existential shock, as she revealed in an article in the *Sunday Times*. In later classes the teacher insisted that she must give up the luxury of being weak, an indulgence which she later realised was 'as perverse and crippling as the bound feet of those ancient Chinese ladies'. Originally she had seen herself as a gentle blue stocking, a well-developed mind precariously housed within a frail and feeble body. Now she was forced to amend her view, and recognise her latent physical powers. The experience proved immensely liberating and invigorating. She wrote: 'Walking through Regent's Park after one of the more physically strenuous of the classes I found that, instead of feeling exhausted, I was actually in a state of euphoria: intensely aware of myself and everything around me . . . I had the oddest sensation of inhabiting my own body and finding it a perfect fit.'

Like Sheila MacLeod, many people are trapped inside a false self image.

They picture themselves as frail, and so go through life sickly, weak and tired. They are locked inside a mental straitjacket of their own construction and generally have no conception whatsoever of their secret inner strength.

The power of the mind Some while ago a mother was involved in an appalling accident which trapped her daughter under the rear wheels of a car. There were no strong men present to come to her aid, and rescue teams with lifting gear would probably arrive on the scene too late to save her daughter's life. So she reached down, and summoning all her strength, lifted the chassis of the car and freed her daughter. Afterwards she couldn't credit what she had done. Once the emergency was over she resumed her old self-image, and reverted to being a weak and helpless woman, incapable of lifting sacks of potatoes let alone the weight of a car. But the potential was still there, waiting only to be released.

This has been demonstrated by experiments carried out under hypnosis. Put a person in a hypnotic trance and give them suggestions which revise their body image and you can make them sick or well, depressed or happy, tired or lively, weak or strong. Under hypnosis men with a natural grip strength of 101 lb have managed to exert a grip of 142 lb when told they were strong, but have been reduced to weaklings able to exert a pressure of only 29 lb when told they were feeble. Such is the incredible power of the imagination.

Sixty years ago the European medical world was electrified by the reports of miracle cures wrought by Dr Emile Coué, the father of autosuggestion. At his clinic at Nancy he taught patients to heal themselves of a wide range of ailments – asthma, sinusitis, lassitude, headaches – by harnessing the powers of the subconscious mind. The trick lay in controlling the force of the imagination. Coué preached: 'When the Imagination and the Will are in conflict the imagination invariably gains the day.' The example he liked to cite was the case of the man who wanted to walk across a narrow plank. When the plank was on the ground he had no difficulty in holding his balance, but when the plank was placed at the height of a cathedral the task became impossible. In essence there was no difference between the two tasks, but there was an enormous gap in the mental concept. As Coué said, 'In the first case you *imagine* that it is easy to go to the end of the plank, while in the second you *imagine* that you cannot do so.' Trapeze artists can walk at these heights along tight-ropes but only when they've rid their minds of the fear of falling.

The same applies to everyday events. If a tennis player reaches a crucial point in a game and starts to think of the risk of serving a double fault the likelihood is that he'll drive the next two balls into the net or out of court. In the same way if a child is learning to ride a bicycle and spots a stone in front of him that he's desperately anxious to miss, the mere thought of hitting it and being thrown is enough to draw him to it like a magnet. In these cases our actions follow our imagination rather than our will.

Emil Coué cured many people suffering from nervous exhaustion simply by teaching them to change their body image and fill their mind with positive energising thoughts. He also advised them to apply the principle of minimum effort. 'Always think that what you have to do is easy,' he wrote. 'In this state of mind you will not spend more of your strength than just what is necessary; if you consider it difficult, you will spend ten, twenty times more strength than you need; in other words you will waste it.'

One of his many grateful patients was a young woman suffering from lassitude and despondency. She went away claiming to have discovered a freedom, peace and self-confidence she had never known before. In a letter of thanks she described her transformation. 'I can without fatigue do twice as much work as before. During the vacation I have been able to get through two quite extensive tasks, such as a year ago I should never have attempted . . . Nothing could stop me, nothing could prevent me from doing what I had planned to do; you might almost have said that things were done by themselves, without the slightest effort on my part.'

Countless other patients found that they could take out a new, more vigorous lease of life by changing their negative thought pattern. Doctors nowadays may regard Emil Coué's work with slight suspicion, and yet in recent years numerous medical experiments have reaffirmed the power of the imagination. Athletes are using conscious thought control to improve their sporting skills. To test the efficacy of this approach a psychologist took three groups of basketball players who were anxious to improve their ability to score from free throws. The first group spent twenty minutes a day practising this particular technique on court, the second had no coaching at all, while the third spent twenty minutes a day sitting still and *imagining* that they were aiming the ball at the basket and steering it successfully through the net. When the men were tested at the end of the three-week trial it was found that the first group had improved their average scores by 24 per cent, the second showed no improvement at all, while the third, who'd carried out their practice only in their imagination, notched up average gains of 26 per cent.

Experiments have also shown that mental imagery can lead to a direct increase in muscle strength. The abdominal muscles, for instance, can be strengthened not only by carrying out actual abdominal exercises, but also by performing *imaginary* sit-ups. Mental imagery can also be used to enhance the resistance of cancer patients. Two well-known American cancer specialists, Carl and Stephanie Simonton, have pioneered the use of visualisation in the fight against cancer. They train their patients to imagine that their cancer cells are being devoured by sharks, or regiments of soldiers, and claim that this aids their recovery by helping them make full use of their natural defences.

An even more remarkable example of the power of the imagination is provided by the research work carried out by Dr Richard Willard at the Institute of Behavior and Mind Sciences in Indiana. He took 22 female volunteers who wanted to enlarge their breasts, and gave them nine sessions of self-hypnosis and visual imagery spread over a period of three months. During these sessions the women were asked to imagine that their breasts were bathed in warmth, either from a heat lamp or from being covered with damp, warm towels. As they felt the heat perfusing their skin, they were encouraged also to sense the increased flow of blood through their breasts. These exercises they were asked to perform at home each day. At the end of the trial, as at the beginning, their breasts were measured by a totally independent doctor, and the figures compared. The results were startling. Nearly half the women reported that they had had to buy a bigger bra and 85 per cent showed a significant increase in breast size, the average increase in circumference being 1.37 inches.

Mental imagery is a powerful therapeutic tool. It can combat fatigue, build muscle strength, sharpen sporting skills and even fill and firm sagging breasts. In Napoleon's words: 'Imagination rules the world'.

However faithfully you've followed the instructions in the earlier stages of this book, you won't be able to unleash your full latent powers until you've harnessed the power of your subconscious mind. Perhaps you may need to change your body image, and give up the luxury of being weak. Few people appreciate how much they are conditioned by the past. Our bodies are like barrel organs. The tune we play is preset in our mind, and appears every time we turn the handle. If you visualise yourself as frail and easily fatigued, that's the way you'll be. Think of yourself as being tireless, lively and energetic and that's how you'll behave. No man or woman is energetic unless they think themselves so.

Vitality Programme – Step Twenty-Eight   This is the all-important final step in your **Vitality Programme**: to make full use of your latent powers, each night as you go to bed, and each morning as you wake, lie back with your eyes closed and in a state of maximum relaxation whisper these three messages to your subconscious mind: 'Each day I'm getting stronger. My stores of energy are growing. I have the power to conquer fatigue.'

In this way you can transform your life.

APPENDIX I

A Guide to Self Diagnosis

Chronic fatigue can be a symptom of a large number of medical conditions. The most common of these are anaemia, malignant growths, myxoedema, thyrotoxicosis, diabetes, worm infections, and chronic diseases of the kidneys, liver, chest and heart.

If you have any reason to believe that your persistent tiredness stems from a disease such as these, consult your doctor. Only he can make a proper evaluation of the signs and symptoms you display, and he may need a variety of special tests (urinalysis, sputum tests and haemoglobin estimations) before he is able to make an accurate diagnosis.

You may however throw some light on your problem by carrying out the following examinations:

Urine Cloudy or flecked with blood?

Pulse Faster or slower than normal? (Average pulse rate 72 beats per minute)

Feet and legs Swelling of ankles, feet and legs? Any septic spots or ulcers on the feet?

Hands Blue and cold? Finger nails pale? Enlargement of the ends of the fingers? Any signs of tremor?

Face Any paleness of lips or inside linings of eyelids? Is the face puffy, eyes bulging, skin and hair dry, face and lips blue? Are the whites of the eyes yellow?

Body Is the skin yellow? Is the surface of the body hot and sweaty? Are there any unexplained lumps in the breast, neck, armpit or elsewhere? Are there any chronic sores or ulcers that will not heal?

Temperature Is it normal or regularly raised? (Average body temperature is 37°C or 98·4°F)

Once you have carried out these investigations, sit down and answer the following questions:

1 Are you breathless on exertion?
   a) Is your breathlessness worse when you lie down at night?
   b) Do you find it more difficult to breath in than out?

2 Have you a persistent cough?
   a) Is your cough non-productive (brings up no sputum)?

b) Is your cough worse on getting up in the morning?

c) Is your sputum white or flecked with blood?

3   Do you suffer palpitations?

4   Have you suffered an unexplained loss of weight?

5   Have you put on weight for no apparent reason?

6   Are you hoarse?

7   Have you noticed any abnormal bleeding or discharge?

8   Has your appetite increased without reason?

9   Has you appetite decreased without reason?

10   Has there been an unexplained change in your regular bowel or bladder habit?

11   Are you suffering from chronic indigestion?

12   Are you finding it difficult to swallow?

13   Do you feel abnormally hot?

14   Do you feel abnormally cold?

15   Do you feel nervous and agitated?

16   Are you passing water more frequently?

17   Are you abnormally thirsty?

18   Do you suffer itching over your genital area?

19   Do you suffer itching around your anus, especially at night?

20   Is your vision blurred?

21   Do you suffer cramps and nerve pains in your legs?

22   Do you have a dull ache in your loins and lower back?

23   Do you suffer nausea?

24   Do you feel faint?

25   Do your muscles feel weak?

On the basis of your response to these tests and questions you may get an early warning of the presence of some underlying disease process, by studying the symptom guide which follows. But be aware of the dangers of do-it-yourself medicine. It's never wise to become too introspective about your health. Everyone has a few odd symptoms – the occasional headache, dizziness or bloodshot eyes – and these are rarely harbingers of serious disease, unless the disease is hypochondria! If you have any serious doubts about your health consult your doctor. He alone is qualified to diagnose your problem and assess your needs.

The Common Pathological Causes of Chronic Fatigue	DISEASE	SIGNS AND SYMPTOMS
	Anaemia	Swelling of ankles Breathlessness on exertion Palpitations Paleness of lips, fingernails and inside linings of eyelids
	Malignant growths	Unexplained loss of weight Persistent cough or hoarseness Chronic sore or ulcer which will not heal Unusual bleeding or discharge Any unexplained change in regular bowel or bladder habit Chronic indigestion or difficulty in swallowing A lump in the breast, neck, armpit or anywhere else in the body
	Myxoedema	Increase in weight, but not in appetite Skin and hair dry Puffiness of legs and face Slow pulse Feeling of coldness
	Thyrotoxicosis	Weight loss but appetite increased Rapid pulse Bulging eyes Palpitations Sweating Feeling of heat Nervousness and tremor
	Diabetes	Increased frequency of urination Increased thirst Itching of genital area Septic spots and ulcers on the feet Blurred vision Cramps and nerve pains in legs
	Worm infection	Itching around anus at night Loss of weight Appetite increase
	Kidney disease	Cloudy urine Puffiness of legs and face Pallor of skin Mild fever Dull ache in the back and loins Increased frequency of urination Headache Nausea Loss of appetite

DISEASE	SIGNS AND SYMPTOMS
Liver disease	Jaundice of skin and especially of whites of eyes Skin itching Muscular weakness Indigestion
Heart failure and valvular disease	Breathlessness especially at night, worse when lying down Cough (non-productive) Palpitations Faintness Muscle weakness Swelling of feet and ankles (forms pits on pressure) Hands and face blue
Chronic chest disease Chronic bronchitis Emphysema Bronchiectasis	Cough (worse on getting up in morning) Breathlessness (especially inspiration) Blue lips and face Thickening (clubbing) of ends of fingers

APPENDIX II

It would be needlessly cumbersome to give references to all the sources I have quoted, but I would like to draw your attention to the following general reviews:

Broadbent, D. E. 'Is a Fatigue Test Now Possible?' *Ergonomics*, 1979, Vol. 22, no. 12, 1277–1290.
Cameron, C. 'A Theory of Fatigue' *Ergonomics*, 1973, Vol. 16, no. 5, 633–648.
Grandjean, E. 'Fatigue in Industry' *Brit. J. Indust. Med.*, 1979, no. 36, 175–186.
Hargreaves, M. 'The Fatigue Syndrome' *Practitioner*, 1977, Vol. 218, 841–843.
Jerrett, M. A. 'Lethargy in General Practice' *Practitioner*, 1981, Vol. 225, 731–737.
Kaye, P. L. 'Fatigue: Pervasive Problem' *N.Y. State J. Med.*, 1980, July, 1225–1229.
Rose, E. A. and King, T. C. 'Understanding Postoperative Fatigue' *Surg. Gyn. & Obst.*, 1978, Vol. 147, 97–101.

INDEX

A

abdominal muscles 139
abreaction 187–8
ageing, changes in sleep pattern 72, 76
   and city living 169
   and cold exposure 26
   and disuse atrophy 12
   premature, xi
   role of fatigue x, 91
   and soured milk products 59
   vigorous old stagers xii
air traffic controllers 99
alcohol and calcium absorption 51
   and fatigue 164
   guide to safe drinking 164–5
   and iron absorption 40
   and mineral absorption 54
   and Vit B metabolism 58
Alderman's nerve 75
Alexander method 138
allergies as cause of sickness 154–7
Ami, Rabbi 183
anaemia 38–40
Anderson, Professor Carl 179
Anstie, Dr Francis 164
aspirin, adverse effects of 38
Atkins, Dr Robert 43
atmospheric pressure 124–5
autogenic training 83
auto-intoxication 148
autosuggestion 75, 83, 203–8

B

Ball, David 21
Bannister, Roger 203
Benny, Jack 77
Benson, Dr Herbert 82
bio-ecological medicine 157
bioenergetics 201
biometeorology 123–31
biorhythms 95–6
Bliss, Edwin 116
blood doping 37–8
blood pressure, reduced by exercise 11

body armouring 201–2
body image 205
boredom, as a cause of fatigue 171–5
Bortz, Dr Walter 11
bread, as a source of minerals 51, 52, 54
breakfasts, importance of 45
breast development by imagery 207–8
breathing,
   eastern method of control, 29, 34
   effect of poor posture 137
   emotional modification 30
   E.P.I.C. exercises 33–5
   hyperventilation syndrome 31
   and relaxation 82
   shallow 31
British Heart Foundation ix
Brown, Professor Frank 124
Bruner, Professor Jerome 79
Bunyan, John 199

C

calcium metabolism 50–2
carbon monoxide poisoning 161–2
carrying, without strain 119
catharsis 186
change, coping with 101–2
   as a cause of stress 174
Chest diseases and physical activity 30
Chiari, Professor Karl 119
Christian Science 183–4
Churchill, Sir Winston 16, 46, 71, 113
Christie, Dr David 30
circadian rhythm 93
circulation and cold bathing 26
   and poor posture 138
city living and fatigue 167–8
Clarke, Dr Frank 184
Clarke, William B. 115
climate and human health 123–31
coffee drinking, effects of 40, 69
cold baths as a circulatory stimulus 24
concentration 114–15, 196–7
confession 186
Constable, John 115
Conti, Tom 16

Coolidge, President Calvin 88
copy paper sickness 131
Coué, Emil 83, 206–7
counter irritation 143
Creasey, John 116
creativity, enhanced by activity 17
Cromwell, Oliver 173
cystitis, self help treatment 151

D

dairy foods, nutritional value 51–2
Dali, Salvadore 71
Darwin, Charles 102, 194
Delbarre, Professor Pierre 105
dental infection and fatigue 150
Dickens, Charles 18
Disraeli, Benjamin 24
diuretics, side effects of 53
Doman, Glenn 126
Dubois, Paul 84
Dunlop, Sir Derrick 159
Dyer, Christopher 118

E

Eddy, Mary Baker 183
Edison, Thomas 67–8, 70
Ekblom, Dr Björn 37
elimination diet in allergy testing 156
Elizabeth I, Queen 11
Emerson, Ralph Waldo 114, 195
emotional set 188–9
Energy Quotient Questionnaire xvi
enthusiasm as a motivating force 195
ergonomics 117–21
Erythrocyte Sedimentation Rate (ESR) 153
Eskimos 21
executive burnout 174
exercise
    as an aid to sleep 69–70
    and brain function 17
    effects of unaccustomed 37
    and resistance to infection 150

F

failure, coping with 200
fatigue,
    and alcohol 164
    and allergies 154–7
    in athletes 37, 90
    and boredom 171
    and drug abuse 159–60
    and excess noise 168
    folk cures 39, 49
    and inadequate motivation 193–7
    and infection 149–53
    and pain 141–6
    and postural strain 135–40
    of psychological origin xii
    role of obesity 3–5
    subjective xii
    as a symptom of disease xii, 209–12
fears, coping with 186–7
fertilization of land 49
Floyer, Sir John 25
folk cures for fatigue, 39, 49, 56, 59
Ford, Henry 79
Foster, Brendan 90
fresh fruit, nutritional importance 61
Freud, Sigmund 184, 189
Fuller, R. Buckminster 199

G

gas fumes and allergic reactions 157
gingivitis, self help treatment 152–3
ginseng x
Gladstone, William 115
glucose metabolism 41
goal setting 110–11, 195
Goldthwaite, Dr J.E. 138
Goodhew, Duncan 90
Googe, Barnabe 106
Guéniat, Dr 32
gum disease, self help treatment 152–3

H

haemoglobin 36–8, 60, 161, 163
Hailey, Alex 174
Hargreaves, Dr Michael 101
headaches, self help treatment 144–5
heat,
    debilitating effect of 22
    effect of high temperature 97–8, 124
Hersey, Rex 96
Hilliard, Dr Marion x
Hippocrates 149
holidays 105–7
holistic medicine xi, 149, 184
Holmes, Dr Thomas 174
homeostasis 87
honey 57
honeymoon fatigue x
housework and ergonomic planning 121
Howes, John 125
human function curve 175
humidity 128–9
Huxley, Aldous 174
hydrotherapy 25

hyperventilation syndrome 31–2
hypoglycaemia 43–7
  and high salt intake 53
hypokinetic disease 18

I

iatrogenic disease 159–65
indecision and its effects 113–14, 187
indigestion, self help treatment 146
indoor climate syndrome 131
infection, as a cause of tiredness 148–53
infradian rhythms 96
insomnia, natural remedies for 72–8
Institute of Breathing 33
iodine intake and metabolism 53–4
ionisation of the air 129–31
iron and its role in blood formation 38–40
IUDs and infection 151

J

James, William 102, 197, 204
Jarvis, Dr D. C. 49
Jerrett, Dr W. A. 149, 159
jet lag 94–5
job rotation 102–3
jogging as a conditioning exercise 18
Johnson, Samuel 194
Jong, Erica x

K

kelp as a source of minerals 50, 54
Kennedy, President John xii, 71
Kevan, Simon 125
Khalune springs 25
Kneipp, Father Sebastian 25
Knowles, William 32–3
Korda, Michael, xii, 111
Kornblueh, Dr Igho 129
Kreuger, Professor Albert 130
kumyss 59

L

Lao Tze 79
Lapp sickness 21
laughter as a therapy 198–9
Lowen, Alexander 201
Leiber, Dr Arnold 97
leisure time, planned use of 107
liver
  and alcohol poisoning 165
  as a source of nourishment 39, 58
lobe stroking as an aid to sleep 75

long range penetration strain 180
Lorenz, Konrad 199
lunar cycles 97

M

MacLeod, Sheila 205
magnesium intake and metabolism 54–5
mandalas 84–6
Mann, Dr George 19
mantra, use in relaxation 84
Masai tribesmen 19
Mather, Janice 194
Mayer, Dr Jean 3
Mee, Amanamayee 196
menstruation 39, 93
mental fatigue and emotional conflict 193–7
  and hyperventilation syndrome 31–2
  and hypoglycaemia 43
  and oxygen supply to brain 31
mental imagery 207
menticulture 183
Metchnikoff, Professor Elie 59
Mezz, Dr David 152
Mill, John Stuart 84
Mills, Professor Clarence 123
mineral requirements 48–55
moon, influence of 97
motivational fatigue 193–7
motoring, and carbon monoxide hazard 161
musicians and stress 181

N

Napoleon 196, 208
natural childbirth training 142
negative ion generators 130–1
Newman, Cardinal 196, 208
New Thought 183
Nicholas, Cindy 76
nightcaps 72–3
night starvation 72
Norfolk Mandala 85–6
Nureyev, Rudolf 16

O

Onassis, Aristotle 70
oranges as an aid to slimming 7
  as a source of Vit C 61
Oswald, Professor Ian 69
overcrowding as a source of stress 170
overweight as a cause of fatigue 3
  caused by inactivity 4, 6
  failure of usual diets 6
  and the Nibbler's diet 47

and the pinch test 5
as a status symbol 4
and sugar intake 45
and the W.O.W. regimen 6

P

Page, Dr Irvine 189
Pai, Dr Mangalore 46
pain relief 142–3
Pavlov, Ivan 73, 168
Peale, Rev Norman Vincent 185
perseverance 115
pets, diseases transmitted by 152
pilots and fatigue vii
pinch tests as a measure of obesity 5
Plato 150
play, the value of 107
politicians and fatigue ix
positive thinking 188
postural fatigue 135–40
potassium, intake and metabolism 52–3
potatoes as a source of Vit C 61
    as a source of energy 45
procrastination 112–14
pyorrhoea, self help treatment 152

Q

Quimby, Phineas 183

R

Raglan, Lord 142
Randolph, Dr Ted 157
Reagan, President Ronald 115
red blood cells 36–7, 97
Reich, Wilhelm 201–2
Reid, Dr Grantly Dick 142
Reiter, Dr 98
rest pauses 87–92
rejuvenation cures x
    and breathing exercises 32
    and cold baths 25
relaxation training 79–86
respiration, effect of poor posture 137
Rinkel, Dr Herbert 154
Roberts, Dr Sam 43
royal jelly 56
Ruskin, John 111
Russell, Bertrand 19

S

Salads, nutritional value 61
Salt, the dangers of excess 52–3

iodised 54
Sands, Dr Louise 184
Saxena, Dr S. R. 75
Schultz, Dr J. H. 83
Schlz, Nicholas 98
Schweitzer, Dr Albert xi
sea bathing, as a rejuvenant 25
self image 205–6
Seneca 112
sensory overload 167–70
sexual function and fatigue x, xii, 200
Shakespeare, William, 100
Sheenan, Dr George 18
shift work, 94, 99
siestas 71–2
Simonton, Carl and Stephanie 207
sinusitis, self help treatment 152
sitting, postural strain of 145–6
skin, physiological importance 20
sleep deprivation 204–5
    needs 65–78
    pillow height 144
sleeping pills 69
sleep therapy 66
Sleye, Professor Hans, 103, 177
Smith, Dr Boyce 162
smoking and air pollution 131
    and endurance 161
    and sleep pattern 69
solar activity and effect on health 98–9
solar conservatories 20
solitude as an antidote to stress 170
soul sickness 184–6
spiritual retreats 189–90
Spivak, Dr Jerry 40
spring fever 97
Steincrohn, Dr Peter ix
Steinhaus, Professor Arthur 82
stress and circadian rhythms 99
    and its effects 171–6
    management 177–181
success, role of vitality xii
sugar, harmful effects of 44, 45, 55
sunbathing, the benefits of 20
    and childhood growth 21
    effect on behaviour 98
    effect on mood 21
    effect on sexual behaviour 20
Swoba, Herman 95–6
Sydenham, Dr Thomas 104

T

Taoist breathing practices 29, 13
Tchijevsky, Professor A. L. 98
tea drinking, effects of 40, 69

temperature control 23
temperature and human function 97–8, 124–6
testosterone, cyclical output 96–8
Thoreau, Henry, 88, 97
thrush infections, self help treatment 151
Thurber, James 77
thyroid gland 53–4
time management 109–16
time zone fatigue 94–5
Tinbergen, Professor Nikolas 138
Titian xi
tonics x
Tournier, Dr Paul 182
traffic accidents and air pressure 125
    and biorhythms 95–6
    and ionisation 131
transcendental meditation 82
transcutaneous nerve stimulation 142
Trollope, Anthony 111
tryptophan 73
Twain, Mark 113

V

vegetables as source of nutrition 51, 52, 61
ventilation 127–8
vibration and its effect on health 168
visualisation 207
Vitamin B 57–9
    C 40, 59–61
    E 56
    therapy 56

W

walking, as a cure for obesity 7
    decline in use 11
    as an effective exercise 18, 19
    effect on circulation 7, 19
    mental effects of 18
    without effort and strain 117
water supplies and lead pollution 163
    and mineral content 51, 54
Weir-Mitchell treatment 170
Welles, Orson 171
Wellington, Duke of 24, 71, 181
Wesley, John 39, 109
white flour, mineral content 49
Willard, Dr Richard 207–8
Williams, Leonard 123
Wilson, Lord (Harold) 77
Wolff, Dr Harold 144
Woolworth, F. W. 112
women and fatigue ix
Wood, Sir Henry 24
Woods, Dr Rachel 139
words as emotive symbols 84
Wordsworth, William 18
workaholics 175–6
W.O.W. regime for slimming 6
Wright, Dr Beric 105

Y

Yerkes–Dodson law 175
yoga, breathing exercises 34, 82–3
yoghurt, nutritional value 59
Yudkin, Professor John 57